NO QUESTIONS
ASKED

Chapter One

Lexi

There's been a long-running debate in Geekdom as to the geekiest president of the United States. Is it Abraham Lincoln, known for his tall, gangly appearance and awkward social skills, yet possessing a brilliant mind and the ability to sway people to his point of view? Or perhaps John Quincy Adams, whose legal theories and philosophical musings are so complex that scholars today are still trying to figure them out. Others say it should be Woodrow Wilson, the only president to have ever earned a doctorate. My fiancé, Slash, however, insists the significance of Thomas Jefferson's scientific and agricultural discoveries make him the geekiest.

In my opinion, it's definitely Lincoln. I mean, the guy had an eidetic memory, giving him instant recall on a huge number of facts, and he also managed to keep the country together during a civil war. Plus, we tall, gangly people with photographic memories and awkward social skills have to stick together. So, it's unfortunate that Slash refuses to be brought around to my point of view. It's turned out to be such an intense debate between us—two geeks arguing about presidential geeks—that it's already resulted in a twenty-four-hour cooling-off period where we barely spoke to each other.

It may seem like a strange argument, but we can be stubborn, and perhaps a bit obsessive, when it comes to our beliefs. It's a geek thing.

My name is Lexi Carmichael and I'm a twenty-six-year-old woman working in the largely male-dominated field of information technology. I'm a former employee of the National Security Agency, but now work for a private, cutting-edge cyber-intelligence firm called X-Corp in the suburbs of Washington, D.C. I double-majored in mathematics and computer science at Georgetown University with a specialty in cybersecurity. I'm a hacker, gamer, coder, book nerd and fangirl. I'm in love with a man who's a seriously good-looking Italian-American, a hacking wizard, and all-around good guy despite his misguided belief that Thomas Jefferson is the geekiest president. It's something I'm willing to overlook because other than that, he's been a great boyfriend, and his Italian grandmother, Nonna, is the best cook I've ever met. That combination ensures I'll be both happy and well fed for the rest of my life. How could anyone pass that up?

I had the memory of our fight over U.S. presidents on my mind because at that moment I was sitting in the back of an official government limousine with Slash, heading for the White House and a private meeting with the current U.S. president. We'd been summoned unexpectedly, and I had no idea why. It wasn't unusual for Slash, who's the current Director of the Information Assurance Directorate at the NSA, to be summoned. But why had the president specifically asked for me to be included?

"I just don't get it," I muttered to Slash. "Why do I have to be there?" He glanced down, to where my fingers tapped on an imaginary keyboard. It was a nervous, reflexive gesture. I hated surprises almost as much as I hated meeting people, even if they were the president of the United States.

"I've already told you, *cara,*" Slash said patiently. "I don't know why he asked specifically for you. We'll find out soon enough."

I stared at him, wondering if he knew but wasn't telling me because we weren't in a secure location. He seemed calm while he looked out the window, but I knew he was expertly scanning the traffic and environment.

When it comes to us, there are always ever-present threats.

I used to be an ordinary geek girl who worked at the NSA, liked crossword puzzles, chocolate eclairs, *Doctor Who,* and living my life online. But a series of events and people over the past year had changed all that. I made friends, found a new life outside my virtual one, got a boyfriend and then got engaged, saved the world a couple of times, and became tight with a little black cloud of trouble that wouldn't seem to leave me alone. A summons from the president seemed ominous. Frankly, Slash and I needed a break from ominous.

After going through several security checkpoints, and having our IDs and retinas scanned and fingerprints logged, we were ushered inside to an internal security area where a guard checked our identification yet again and asked us to sign in on an electronic pad. A Secret Service agent led us through the halls of the White House, past more static agents, and through a couple of biometrically guarded entrances until we were ushered into the Oval Office.

It was pretty cool to walk into America's center of

power. I took a minute to marvel at the furniture, the heavy velvet curtains, the presidential rug, and the detailed, historic paintings, making sure I could recount every detail to my friends, Basia, Elvis, Xavier and Finn when they asked me about it later.

President Jack Paulson rose from behind his desk and came to greet us. General Norton, who was sitting in a visitor chair, also stood. Both men were smiling and seemed completely at ease. In fact, everyone looked so happy, it immediately made me suspicious. I'd never been to the Oval Office before, but somehow I'd expected it to be a somber occasion if I were ever invited— exactly the opposite of the vibe I was getting. Not that I was good at getting vibes, but even Slash seemed puzzled by their upbeat demeanor.

"Slash, Miss Carmichael, thank you both for coming." The president shook our hands firmly, making eye contact and ensuring we felt as if we were the most important people in the world.

The president was obviously good at making people feel at ease in his presence—not surprising since he was a politician—but today his blue eyes were sparkling with good humor. While I wasn't a people person by any stretch of the imagination, his favorable mood seemed genuine, which baffled me even more.

"I appreciate you taking time out of your busy schedules to meet with me," he said.

Right. Like we were busy in comparison to the president of the United States. However, I appreciated he was trying to put us at ease. He ushered us to a set of chairs near General Norton, who also shook hands with us. Slash and I sat and waited to see what would unfold.

President Paulson pulled a chair over, joining us. He

sat back, crossing his legs and putting his hands on the armrests. I'd never been this close to him. I could see the gray streaks running through his hair, something that was hard to distinguish on television. But no question, he was just as handsome in person as he was on television.

"I'm sure you're both wondering why I've asked you here," he said, spreading his hands. "I recently had a conversation with the pope and your names came up."

I exchanged a glance with Slash. What had happened in Rome a few months ago had been a mostly personal matter involving Slash, me, the pope, and the future of the Vatican. But President Paulson was a devout Catholic, and whatever the pope had said about us had obviously made a deep impression and piqued his curiosity.

"The Holy Father said you helped him with an important personal matter," the president continued when we didn't offer a ready explanation. "While he was unable to reveal the nature of the matter, he said he was deeply appreciative for your assistance. Although it was not official U.S. business, he said it served to further strengthen ties between the U.S. and the Vatican. As a result, I summoned General Norton to learn more about our star NSA employee and his fiancée, both of whom are trotting around the globe strengthening national ties while on personal leave."

A hint of color touched Slash's cheeks, but his expression remained neutral. "Sir, the personal matter involved my younger brother who's getting married at Christmas. There was a minor complication getting his marriage approved by the church, and since I used to work at the Vatican, I went to Rome to intercede on his behalf. While there, I was able to assist the Holy Father with a matter close to his heart. I'm glad he was so pleased with the outcome he saw fit to further fortify U.S. and Vatican relations."

Only I knew what a broad and noncommittal explanation he'd just given, but I was impressed he'd come up with it on such short notice. Slash was good like that, whereas I sucked at that kind of on-the-spot conversational flexibility.

The president leaned forward in his chair, his elbows on his knees. "Well, whatever you did and however you did it, your country thanks you, as do I. Well done, both of you. I'll be meeting personally with the pope next year to discuss a number of important initiatives. That timetable was moved up, thanks to you, and comes at a good time for me personally and professionally."

He didn't offer details and we didn't ask.

"I may be reaching out to you closer to that time with some thoughts and ideas I'd like to run by you, if that's acceptable to you," he continued.

Slash dipped his head in agreement. "Of course."

"Excellent." The president turned his laser-blue eyes on me. "Now, Miss Carmichael, I hear you're planning a wedding."

Thwunk! There went that spear of anxiety right into my gut, which I always got when someone asked me about wedding plans. Jeez! Why had the topic of conversation changed so rapidly, and why did that question have to be addressed to me? I took a few precious seconds to get my thoughts together before I answered.

"Ah, yes. *We're* working on it." I put a heavy emphasis on *we're*, which didn't go unnoticed by either the president or Slash.

"Of course, you are. Congratulations to you both. Did you know my daughter just got married?"

Was he serious? Who *didn't* know? It had been all over the news for the past month, with endless updates across every media platform regarding her dress, the wedding party, the venue—which happened to be the White House—and the ceaseless stream of celebrity guests. Ugh. I couldn't get away from it, even when I tried.

"I saw it on the news," I said carefully. "Looked like a great time was had by all." I hoped that was an appropriate thing to say because I couldn't have cared less. Even though I was engaged to be married, weddings and wedding planning were not my thing. I looked to Slash for help, but he avoided my gaze, even less inclined to talk about the White House wedding than I was.

"It was a magical event," the president said. "Have you sorted out the details yet?"

Truthfully, we'd barely even started, mostly because we didn't know what we wanted for a wedding. In the meantime, my mom had kind of hijacked the process just to get things moving. Slash told me there was no way he wanted to get in the middle of that, so he'd jumped ship, leaving me alone to figure things out with my mom. Not that I blamed him. If I could have jumped ship with him, I would have. Unfortunately, being left alone to the machinations of my mother meant things had gone exactly nowhere because I was in a resistance mode and couldn't make up my mind about anything.

"Um, no," I said. "We haven't had time to do any planning yet. We're really busy. Really, *really* busy, and I just said that. But as Slash mentioned, his younger brother is getting married at Christmas in Italy, so everyone on his side of the family is preoccupied on getting past that event first." Thank God for that. At least that left me with only one side of the family to deal with—mine—and my mom was more than just a handful. "Our wedding will likely be sometime after that."

In truth, Slash and I would have already eloped if not for our families, especially my mother, who expected a big wedding and my extensive involvement in said planning.

"Weddings can be a stressful time," the president said, sympathy crossing his face. "I don't know what we would have done if not for the assistance we received from my daughter's wedding planner. She was absolutely spectacular, a real go-getter. I can't recommend her highly enough. If you're worried about things, she'll help you out."

He walked over to his desk, pulled open a drawer and rummaged around. "Ah, here it is." He pulled out a business card and held it up between two fingers. "Amanda McCormick, Event Planner to the Stars. Kind of a pretentious title, but I assure you, she knows her business. If you need someone to do everything for you, she'll get the job done."

He jotted something down on the back of the card, then presented me with it. The raised letters of her company name on the card, along with fancy logo of thin gold and silver entwined hearts, made my stomach churn uncomfortably.

"Amanda may have an exclusive clientele, but tell her I sent you, and she'll give you the friends and family rate."

"Um, thanks." I quickly stuck the card in my sweater pocket where it felt as if it were burning a hole in the material. "That's really nice of you, Mr. President. We, ah, appreciate the suggestion, don't we, Slash?"

"Absolutely."

The president leaned forward in his chair. "Although it's quite an important event, your wedding is not the only reason I brought you here today. I'm well aware of the things you both have done in the past year to support our country, including moving up my timeline for meeting the pope. General Norton has apprised me of all of the activities and the significant risks you've undertaken on behalf of our nation's national security. I wanted you to know that your actions have been noted, and I'm personally grateful for your commitment and dedication to the protection of our nation."

"As am I," General Norton added. "Your work at the NSA, Slash, has been beyond exemplary, and we are fortunate to have you. Miss Carmichael, your assistance has been invaluable, as well. I'm really sorry we lost you to the private sector. You're welcome to return to the NSA any time you'd like."

That was *not* going to happen anytime soon, but I appreciated the sentiment.

"It's an honor to serve my country, sir," Slash said.

"Me, too," I added, wishing I'd said it first.

"We're fortunate to have you both." The president clapped a hand on Slash's shoulder and sent one of his famous beaming smiles my way. "Now, young man, hopefully you won't argue with your president when I insist that you take off the next three weeks to do whatever you'd like, courtesy of Uncle Sam. I'd offer the same to you, Miss Carmichael, but unfortunately you no longer work for the government."

The surprise on Slash's face was priceless. "But… I couldn't possibly," he protested. "There's so much work to be done. I don't dare be away for that long."

"I'm sure General Norton will hold down the fort in your absence. There's always work to be done, but you've earned this break. This past year has been exceptionally busy for both you and Miss Carmichael. Stopping the terrorists in Sweden, putting an end to industrial spying in the nanotechnology market, helping to take down those terrorists at the high school, eliminating the worst cyber mercenary this world has ever seen, masterminding the cyber standoff with the Chinese, and now strengthening U.S.-Vatican relations. Trust me, son, you deserve it. You *both* do."

General Norton nodded vigorously. "Listen to him, Slash. That's an order from your boss, not a suggestion. Take a well-deserved break. Three weeks should do it. That means I don't want to see you at all during that time. Come back to us after Thanksgiving, nice and relaxed. Trust me when I say the work will be waiting for you."

Slash glanced at me as if hoping I had a good excuse to say why he couldn't take the vacation. I didn't. But even if I did, I certainly wasn't going to argue with the president of the United States and the director of the NSA. Not that I thought they'd listen to me anyway.

Apparently at a loss as to how to successfully decline, Slash accepted the inevitable. "Well, then, I guess it's decided. I thank you both for your generosity."

"I figure you can spend some of that time working on those wedding plans," the president said. "Take the pressure off your fiancée."

Slash smiled, but appeared slightly alarmed. It occurred to me that since I'd known him, he'd never just taken time off for himself. It had always been to help me or his family, to save the world, or manage an international crisis. Now he was going to take time off to plan our wedding?

For a moment, I panicked, wondering if my mother had been talking to the president. I wouldn't put it past her to petition all the way up to him if she thought it would light a fire under Slash and me to get the wedding planning underway. But she hadn't mentioned mingling with the president before, and I was pretty sure she would've said something if she had. But still, when it came to wedding planning, I wouldn't put *anything* past my mom.

Apparently the meeting was over, so the four of us stood, politely shook hands, and Slash and I were escorted out of the White House. We were taken back to the security checkpoint where we retrieved our phones and personal effects. After we climbed back into the limousine and were sitting side by side, I turned to him.

"Three weeks off?" I said. "What are you going to do for all that time?"

He stared at me, looking dazed. "Slash?" I prodded when he didn't answer. "What are you going to do?"

As the car began to move, he looked out the window. "*Cara*, I have no idea."

Chapter Two

Lexi

"This is not surrender, Basia, it's a compromise." I scowled fiercely when I said it, as if my frown would make the statement truer.

It didn't.

My best friend, Basia Kowalski, rolled her eyes and filled my wineglass a little fuller. I'd already downed half of the glass in one gulp. I needed to slow down or I'd face plant on my kitchen counter in the next ten minutes. Was it wrong I considered face planting an acceptable alternative to what I was about to do?

"Of course it's a compromise, Lexi." Basia slid onto the barstool next to me and frowned back at me. "Stop being so grumpy. We haven't even started yet."

We sat at the breakfast bar in my kitchen, staring at my laptop and a page full of wedding gowns. I'd set up the virtual viewing to placate my mother, who, if she'd had her way, would have already dragged me to thirty-five boutiques looking for the right wedding dress. Basia had agreed to be my wing woman for the virtual viewing, and had tried to make the situation as smooth as possible by adding wine, cheese and crackers to the agenda. It wouldn't eliminate the pain, but I was glad to have her by my side. Regardless, I still wished I were anywhere else but here.

"I can't believe I took a half a day off of work to do this." I tried to dial back the crankiness, but it was hard. "I can't believe *you* agreed to take a half day off to do this with me. That's true friendship."

Basia took a sip of her wine. "It was the only time all three of us were available to do it. Your mom is wicked busy."

My mom was involved in numerous charities and active on the Washington, DC social circuit. Wicked busy was probably an understatement. Still, I wasn't sure why I'd agreed to this. In some odd way, I supposed the president had nudged me in the direction of getting the wedding planning underway. I wasn't happy about it, but I reasoned that the sooner I made some progress, the faster the entire thing would be over.

Slash popped into the kitchen. He stole a piece of cheese from Basia's spread and dropped a quick kiss on my head.

"Hello, Basia. C*iao, cara.*"

"Hey, wait," I said. "Where are you going?"

"To run some errands."

That was clearly code for *I'm not going to be here to get between you and your mother in regards to wedding planning.* Just the same, I wished he'd take me with him. But since it wasn't *his* mother coming over, he was able to disappear.

Lucky.

After he left, Basia ran her fingers through her bob-length dark hair. "Lexi, while I'm proud of you for agreeing to look at some dresses, I still don't see how you're going to get out of an actual fitting once you pick one. You do know that, right?"

I blew out an unhappy breath. "Of course, I know." I pulled my sweater tighter around my body, as if it might somehow protect me. "And you know what happened the last time I was at a wedding gown fitting. Yours! I don't want a repeat of what happened there."

I'd almost burned down the bridal store, sent the bridal assistant to the hospital, and ruined Basia's first dress. None of it had been done on purpose, of course, but still, it didn't bode well for me trying on my own wedding gown.

Basia giggled at the memory. Thank goodness she was able to look back at it and laugh. I hadn't quite got there yet.

"Oh, God, no, we definitely *don't* want a repeat of my fitting." She reached over and picked up a piece of cheddar from the plate and delicately nibbled on one corner. "Don't worry, we'll figure that part out later. You were clever to think of this compromise, and even smarter to talk your mom into it."

"It wasn't easy."

"I'm sure it wasn't. But here we are, so let's make the best of it. You know, this is pretty sweet, living so close to you. I can pop in at any time to be a buffer between you and your mom."

"I agree, that's one plus to living in the same neighborhood."

She lifted her wineglass, clinking against mine. "Cheers."

"Cheers." I took a drink and hoped it would help the butterflies in my stomach. It didn't. Nothing short of a nuclear bomb would help.

My front doorbell chimed. I did a quick check on my phone app and confirmed it was my mother. She stood on my porch looking gorgeous in a green coat and matching hat, holding a bottle of red wine and a bouquet of colorful flowers. I crossed into the foyer and opened the door. Mom immediately stepped inside, gathered me into her arms and hugged me, smelling as pretty as she looked.

"Oh, Lexi," she said. "I'm so excited to look for your dress today. Even if we have to do it online."

I loved my mother. I really did. She'd always been there for me when I needed her. I knew she wanted the best for her only daughter. The problem was we had two completely opposing views on where my life should head. She saw me and my potential through the prism of *her* experiences. While her experiences had worked out great for her, I was never going to be the beautiful, fun-loving, friendly, social butterfly that she was. Not that I wanted to be. My life was happily filled with computers, technology, hacking, and math.

Regardless, I was grateful to have a supportive family, including my dad and brothers, a few close friends I trusted with my life, and a soon-to-be husband and soulmate who'd pulled me out of my shell and taught me more about life than anyone I'd ever met. But my wedding had become really, *really* important to my mom. I had no idea how to reconcile that with what I wanted— which was to elope and skip the entire ceremony thing. In fact, the only thing standing in my way of starting that happy life as a married woman was a fancy wedding that neither Slash nor I wanted but were destined to have in order to make the people we loved happy. So here I was, sucking it up and preparing to look at wedding dress after wedding dress online, hoping I could find one that would satisfy me, as well as my mother.

But mostly my mother.

"Hey, Mom. Come on in." I forced a smile and took the flowers and wine from her. "Thanks for coming. Hang up your coat in the closet and join us in the kitchen. I've already bookmarked the sites you suggested so we can look through the dresses."

"Excellent!" Her pretty face lit up. "This will be so much fun, Lexi."

I couldn't remember when I'd seen her so happy, except for when I told her I was engaged, which only made me feel worse about my inner struggle.

I set the wine on the kitchen counter. While I put the flowers into a vase with water, Basia poured my mom a glass of wine. Then the two of them started looking through the photos without me, which was fine by me.

"Hey, this one would look great on you, honey," Mom said, turning the laptop toward me while I dried my hands on a dishtowel.

Tight, clingy, with a daring dip down the front. Oh, heck no. My boobs, what little I had, would be barely covered. Hell would freeze over before I put that on.

"Let's keep looking," I suggested.

Eventually, I climbed on one of the barstools, drank wine and offered mostly noncommittal comments like *hmmm* or *mmm* to all the photos they showed me. One hour passed, then two. Mom bookmarked several dresses that I didn't reject outright.

At some point, I stood up to go to the bathroom. I stumbled, a bit tipsy, then steadied myself with a hand on the counter. A rectangular card fell from my sweater pocket and fluttered to the ground.

Mom leaned over and picked it up. "You dropped this. Are you okay, Lexi?"

"I'm great." My voice sounded slurred. Jeez, I was definitely tipsy. They were looking and I was drinking.

She held up the card between two fingers. "What's this?"

"A business card, I think." I squinted at it.

Mom read the card. "Amanda McCormick? You have a business card from Amanda McCormick?"

I frowned and took the card from Mom, trying to figure why the name sounded familiar. My eyes settled on the silver and gold entwined hearts. *Crap, crap, crap!* I'd forgotten to throw out the business card for the wedding planner.

Basia hopped off her stool and came to look at the card, too. "Amanda McCormick is the most sought-after wedding planner in the U.S. Is there something you aren't telling us, Lexi?"

My brain, unfortunately impaired by one glass of wine too many, sorted through a variety of plausible explanations, none of which would make this issue go away. I decided honesty was the best policy.

"I didn't forget to tell you anything...because there's nothing to tell," I said. "The president gave me her card as a courtesy. I forgot about it. End of story."

"The president?" Mom pressed her hand to her breast. "As in Jack Paulson, *the* president of the United States?"

Uh-oh. I had to tread carefully. "Um, Slash and I met with him a week ago, and—"

My mom held up a hand, stopping me midsentence, a look of horror on her face. "Wait. You *met* with the president of the United States and you didn't think to mention it to your father or me?"

Ugh! This was getting worse and worse. Why had I agreed to this virtual viewing? Why had I drunk alcohol?

"Um...sorry?"

My mom shook her head in disbelief or perhaps disappointment. "The president gave you Amanda's card and jotted down on the back that you should get the family and friends rate on his suggestion. And you didn't think it was worth mentioning to me?"

"You make it sound like a lot bigger deal than it was."

"We're talking about the president of the United States personally giving you an in with wedding planner extraordinaire Amanda McCormick," she said with a frown of disapproval. Definitely disappointed with my failure to communicate. "Amanda just put on the wedding of the year. How can that not be a big deal?"

Obviously, I had no answer to that question. Even Basia looked at me as if I'd committed a major faux pas. Mom gave me her steely disapproving look when I remained silent—a look she gave me when she thought I was being unreasonably obstinate, like when I'd refused to wear a pink frothy tutu to the ballet recital in which I'd never wanted to perform. In the end, I played a tree in the recital—seemingly a safe bet for someone as awkward as me—except I fell off the stage, taking two dandelion dancers with me. I'm pretty sure it was the highlight of the show, even though no one in the audience said so outright.

"You do know that Amanda McCormick was the wedding planner for his daughter, right?" Mom continued, her voice rising. "It was broadcast around the world, and was the most beautiful wedding I've ever seen, and that includes the British royal weddings. *Your Wedding Day* is devoting an entire issue next month to her wedding. Lexi, do you realize what this means?"

"That her vendors will get a lot of free advertising?" I offered.

Mom gave me an exasperated stare. "No. It means you have an in with Amanda McCormick. And not just *any* in. The president-of-the-United-States in. Do you have any idea how exciting this is?"

Of course, I had no idea. Did she have to ask? "Mom, I just don't think Slash and I are going to need anything so elaborate it would require a planner."

"Every wedding needs a planner." Mom threw her arms around me, suddenly happy. I was baffled by the quick change in emotion, so I cautiously watched her for clues, wondering what had changed. "Oh, Lexi, don't look so worried. This is a stroke of luck! I can't wait to tell your dad. Have you discussed using Amanda's services with Slash?"

"I have not."

"Well, put that at the top of your planning agenda." She turned back to the computer with a new kind of energy and enthusiasm—one that frankly scared me. "Okay, now that it's settled, let's not lose our focus here. Today it's all about the dress. Lexi, what do you think of this one? I like the off-the-shoulder look."

I wanted more wine, but was afraid I'd agree to something while under the influence. The one she showed me was too lacy, had too many pearls, and I'd never wear it. Ugh.

"Um…well…" Before I could find an appropriate answer, my cell rang. I was grateful for the interruption, so I snatched the phone out of my pocket and checked the number.

Slash, thank God. The guy had impeccable timing.

"It's Slash. Sorry, I've got to take this." I swiped the phone open as I walked into the living room, pressing it to my ear. "What's up?"

"Not much. How is it going?"

Like he needed to ask. "I'm sure you can imagine." I lowered my voice to a whisper. "Now imagine it ten times worse."

"That's...unfortunate." He paused. "How many glasses of wine have you had?"

"How can you tell that I've had any?"

"A bottle was already open before I left, your mom and Basia are there solely to discuss the wedding, you're barely pronouncing your words, and I presume you're still looking at dresses. Need I say more?"

Dang, he totally had me pegged. "Fine. For your information, I've only had three glasses, but I'm contemplating four more before I'm done. When are you coming home, and please tell me soon. You have to save me."

"Soon." I heard a beep in the background and figured he was driving. "I need gas, so I'll pop into the Quick Mart on the way. I noticed we're out of skim milk, so I'll pick up a carton while I'm there. Do we need anything else?"

"Yes. I need a box of tampons. Regular. Can you pick those up at the Quick Mart?"

There was dead silence.

I waited for him to respond and then checked to see if the call had dropped. "Slash, are you there?"

"I'm here. I, ah, don't know what you mean."

"I need a box of regular-size tampons. How much clearer do I need to be? Don't worry, it will say regular right on the box. Thanks and see you soon. Just hurry, okay?"

I hung up and slipped the phone into my back pocket as I returned to the kitchen. "That was Slash. I'm sorry, but we're going to have to wrap this up. He's on the way home. Apparently there's a matter of national security that we have to discuss as soon as he gets here."

"I thought Slash was on vacation," Basia said.

"And it's eight o'clock at night," my mom added, narrowing her eyes.

"You're both right," I answered, trying to keep the guilty look off my face. "But national security doesn't take a vacation or a weekend off."

Basia rolled her eyes at me from behind my mother's back, but since she was my best friend, she didn't call me on it. To my relief, she stood and started putting food away. Seeing no other option, Mom rinsed our wineglasses and retrieved her coat from the closet.

"You'll look at the dresses I bookmarked, right?" Mom asked as she fastened a button.

"Of course I'll *look*." I was careful not to promise more.

"Good." She gave me a peck on the cheek. "See that you do. Just remember, if you decide on a summer or fall wedding, you've given yourself less than a year to prepare. But if you have Amanda McCormick working for you, she'll have everything organized in no time at all. That really was a stroke of brilliance to ask the president for her number."

I hadn't asked, but no sense in pointing that out now. My mom was apparently thrilled with the possibility of having Amanda as my wedding planner. Even Basia seemed kind of excited about it. "Well, thanks for coming over, Mom."

She gave me a hug before leaving. Basia joined me in the foyer and began putting on her coat, as well.

"A matter of national security?" she said. "That's the best you could come up with?"

"Do you have a better idea?" I asked. "Because I'm all about collecting excuses to add to a spreadsheet for memorization and future use."

Basia laughed and then shook her head. "Look, Lexi, I know you don't want a big wedding, but you have to have *something*. I guarantee you Amanda McCormick will get you what you want and need. Even if it's small, she'll do it your way."

"But I don't *know* what my way is," I protested. "Slash doesn't either."

"Then let her help you get your head in the right place. That alone would be worth it. Why don't you consider giving her a call?"

I didn't agree or disagree with her, but the thought of calling a wedding planner filled me with about as much dread as getting fitted for a dress. I'd been stressed to my limit planning a bachelorette party for Basia, and that had landed us all at the police station, so I had no idea how I was going to pull off my own wedding.

Once Basia left, I returned to the kitchen thinking about what she had said. I looked on the counter for Amanda's card, but I couldn't find it. I checked my sweater, the floor, the trash, and for good measure, the refrigerator.

Nothing.

That meant only one thing. Someone else had Amanda McCormick's business card.

My bet was on my mother.

Chapter Three

Slash

It had taken him under a minute to locate the tampons at the Quick Mart, but he hadn't expected the sheer product volume and variety. Boxes of all sizes in blue, red, pink and green. A half dozen labels and different companies. And this was a Quick Mart. He shuddered to think of the options that might be present in a supermarket or retail store.

He shifted the gallon of milk to his other hand and thought back on their conversation. Had Lexi mentioned a specific company or box color? No, she'd said only regular, as in size. Was company or brand important? He tried to remember the color of the box that usually resided under their sink. Blue. No, it was pink.

Damn, he had no idea.

He bent down, taking a closer look at the boxes. Super plus, overnight, slim, pearl, plastic, cardboard applicator...what the hell? How was he supposed to make a decision based on one variable—regular size? Speaking of which, where was the box—*any* box—that said regular?

He heard a snort behind him. The cashier, a skinny kid with stringy hair, tattoos and a cigarette dangling from his mouth, smirked at him. They were the only two people in the store at the moment. If the kid made some snarky comment when he brought the tampons to the register, he'd have to hurt him, and that wouldn't look good for a director at the NSA.

He ignored the kid, finally finding a box that said regular size. He had no idea if these were the right brand, but hopefully they'd do. He spent an additional four seconds trying to decide whether to buy a box of twenty-four or forty-eight. He decided on forty-eight as a precaution, because there was no way in hell he wanted to do this again anytime soon. Grabbing the box, he tucked it under his arm and headed to the cashier.

He'd just put everything on the counter when the bell on the door tinkled. He glanced over his shoulder just as a man with a ski mask and gun entered the store.

Gwen Sinclair

It was hard to act like a normal scientist when she felt like she was going to burst with excitement. But she gave it her best effort. Smiling a little, she pulled her cell out of her lab coat and quickly tapped out a text. When she was finished, she sat at an empty table in the company café and took a deep breath.

Life was amazing. She had the best boyfriend in the world, a supportive family, including a cool little sister, a few really good friends, and a job she absolutely loved. Things didn't get much better than that...except they just had, and she could barely contain herself.

Less than a minute later, her significant other, Elvis Zimmerman, slipped into the chair across from her. His glasses were a bit crooked on his nose and his thick dark hair was mussed, like he'd been running his fingers through it, which he sometimes did when he was deep in thought. Her heart did a little pitter-patter when he focused his gaze on her.

"So, what's so urgent you had to see me now?" Elvis asked. Curiosity was alight in his intense blue eyes. His insatiable intelligence was one of the things she loved about him. When she leaned forward, he reached across the table and almost took her hand. He stopped himself, most likely remembering they were at work.

"I stopped by your office, but you weren't there," she said quietly. "I wanted to tell you right away."

The interest in his eyes flared brighter. "Is this about the meeting you just had with Director Cutler?"

"It is." She loved that he remembered that she had an important meeting this morning, even though she'd forgotten to remind him about it at breakfast. He remembered everything important—her birthday, their first kiss, the first time she told him she loved him, and the fact she liked gelato more than ice cream. He was thoughtful in the way he thought about her, and she not only appreciated it, she tried to reciprocate it.

"You know that project I've been working on?" she said, keeping her voice low.

"The malaria vaccine?"

"Exactly." She leaned forward, excited to share the news. "The client, Vaccitex, is over the moon with our research. Apparently they intend to implement our contribution right away and want to bring a microbiologist on board temporarily to integrate it. Cutler personally thanked me for my contribution and…" She paused, taking a breath. "Elvis, I'm among the scientists being considered for the project. Can you believe it?"

Elvis's eyes widened, and she was grateful to see the flash of pride that crossed his face. "Gwen, that's fantastic. You deserve it. You worked so hard on that project."

"I know, but I'm still in shock." She didn't care who saw. She put her hand over his and squeezed. "Just knowing my work might help to save millions of lives is so gratifying. But being recognized for that hard work and having the chance to be part of the implementation is really exciting."

"It's more than exciting. It's prime. Freaking awesome. We're definitely celebrating tonight."

His support meant everything to her. "Well, we can't celebrate just yet. I have to go to an interview with the client at three o'clock. After that, Vaccitex will make the final decision on which one of us to take. But just the fact that I'm among the scientists being considered is thrilling. I'm still trying to wrap my head around it."

"I'm not surprised at all. You're a brilliant woman and your work on the project was both innovative and smart. You'll kill it in the interview."

"You know I love you, right?" she whispered.

He grinned at her and made a little heart with his hands. It was a cheesy, adorable thing to do, and it made her fall just a bit harder for him.

"So, who else from ComQuest was selected to interview tomorrow?" he asked.

"Well, obviously, John—he's the director, after all—but I don't think he'll go for it in light of his recent illness. It would be too hard for him to travel. So that leaves Em Cook, Tom Kobayashi, and me."

"Travel?" Elvis's grin faded. "Travel where?"

"Brazil! Elvis, I could be going to the rainforest. Whoever is selected will get to be part of the field team and ensure the integrity of the formula while in the field. That kind of opportunity has always been a dream of mine."

"Brazil? The rainforest?"

"Yes, to several remote villages. I don't know all the details yet. So, what do you think?"

"I think…wow. Just wow."

"I know, right? It's so incredibly cool. I just hope it doesn't fall through. Cutler told me Vaccitex is in serious trouble in terms of information protection. Someone has been hacking into their systems, trying either to steal or corrupt their data."

"Why would anyone want to corrupt or steal data on vaccines?"

"Seriously, Elvis? Vaccitex is a nonprofit organization. They're supported by charities and governments around the world. But if a commercial company can make the vaccine first, think of the killing they could make. Cutler told me Vaccitex is looking for help to protect their critical systems."

"That happens to be right up my alley."

"Believe me, your name was the first thing out of my mouth when Cutler said that, not like he didn't already know. But he said he can't spare you or Xavier right now. He needs your focus on the Astro 10 project." Elvis and his twin brother, Xavier, had been working hard on a network security issue for NASA, so while it had been disappointing, it hadn't surprised her when Cutler nixed her idea of adding Elvis to the team.

"Oh." Elvis looked seriously disappointed. "I presume you recommended Lexi, then?"

"Of course I recommended Lexi. But Cutler was already ahead of me. He said he'd already passed Lexi's name and information about X-Corp to Vaccitex."

"That's great, but her time won't be cheap. It will be hard for a nongovernmental organization like Vaccitex to afford."

"That's the thing, Elvis. Cutler said ComQuest is willing to subsidize Lexi's time and whichever one of us the client chooses to be on the project. It's part of a larger strategy to rebuild the company's reputation after the recent disaster in the British Virgin Islands."

"That's smart." Elvis rubbed his chin and looked at her thoughtfully. "Really smart. There's a lot to like about this situation in terms of saving lives. But the threat is real. If commercial companies get the breakthrough first, or steal the vaccine data, they would control the pricing. That means people who really need it aren't going to get it."

"I know. Hopefully I'll find out more at the interview. I don't want to be a downer about my possibilities, but both Em and Tom are more senior than I am, so the odds I'll be selected over them are not in my favor. But I did make some significant contributions to the project, so I'm going to give it my best shot."

"You'll be amazing."

"Thank, Elvis." His confidence in her was infectious and she appreciated it more than she could say. She wanted to kiss him, but remembering they were still at work, leaned toward him until their heads were almost touching. "Let's celebrate later no matter what happens at the interview. Just the two of us at home…alone."

"Deal," he agreed. "Now, go slay that interview."

Chapter Four

Slash

The gunman stepped into the store and aimed his weapon at the cashier while glancing at Slash, presumably trying to determine if he was a threat.

Oh, great. The first day of my vacation is turning into a nightmare.

Slash plastered a scared look on his face, raising his hands and taking several steps backward. It was just his luck that the Secret Service detail that normally followed him around had recently been cut for budgetary reasons. Not that they couldn't track him down or stop his heart before he could spill any state secrets, thanks to a specialized chip in his left wrist. But still, the timing sucked.

"You're in charge," he said, keeping his gaze slightly downward so he didn't present a challenge. "Not my store. Not my fight."

"Good. Keep your hands up and don't do anything stupid." Without looking away from either Slash or the cashier, the gunman turned the dead bolt behind him, locking people out, but also effectively locking himself in.

Idiot.

It took Slash about ten seconds to assess the situation. No matter how he looked at it, this was not going to play out well. The gunman's hand was shaking uncontrollably. That meant he was either scared, inexperienced or on drugs. Possibly all three. Any one of those things was dangerous, but a combination of any of them heightened the risk significantly. The odds were high he'd start shooting if he felt cornered; that's if he didn't pull the trigger by accident.

As expected, the gunman turned his attention to the kid behind the counter, who'd lost his cigarette and smirk. The color had drained from his face, leaving him looking like a scared teenager, which he probably was.

"Give me all the money in the cash register," the gunman said. His voice was slurred, which signaled to Slash that drugs or alcohol were definitely a factor. "If you reach for something else, I'm going to blow your head off. Are we clear?"

The kid swallowed hard. "C-can I push the buttons to open the register?"

The gunman waved the gun. "Nice and slow."

Slash took an imperceptible step sideways to place himself at a more advantageous angle. A half dozen scenarios played in his head as to which way would be the best to take the gunman down with the least amount of risk to the kid behind the counter, himself, or the perpetrator. Before he could decide, the gunman abruptly fired twice above the head of the cashier.

Idiot times ten.

The first shot took out a row of cigarettes behind a glass case, while the second miraculously hit the camera, which was presumably the intended target. Glass, metal and plastic exploded onto the counter. The cashier screamed in terror and dropped to the floor. That's when the gunman made a big mistake. He completely turned his back on the only person in the store who could take him out.

"Get up and get my money," the gunman screamed, ran toward the counter, then leaned over it waving the gun at the kid. "I'll kill you!"

Slash lunged forward, grabbing the man in a bear hug from behind. He trapped the gunman's arms at his side, squeezing the man's wrist with the gun and twisting it away from the cashier. The weapon discharged, shattering a storefront window this time. The kid shrieked repeatedly while the gunman tried to free himself of Slash's hold, snarling and fighting like a wild animal. He was definitely juiced.

They staggered for a bit before Slash managed to bring him to the ground using the weight of his body. As they went down, the gun discharged again, taking out the glass on a cooler door. Slash kept his focus on the gun, relying on his training and muscle memory to fight the rest of the battle.

But the gunman wasn't letting go, so he continued to apply pressure points to the guy's wrist to get him to release the weapon. They rolled into the snack aisle, bags of chips, Cheetos and pretzels raining down on them, popping and crunching beneath their bodies as they grunted and fought for control of the weapon. Deciding he had no other choice, Slash crushed the wrist at its most vulnerable point, feeling the bones snap beneath his fingers. Pain made its way through the haze of drugs because the man howled, releasing the gun.

Slash knocked it away with the back of his hand and it slid under a display of apple and cherry pies. He managed to wrestle the guy to his back, using his weight to keep him still. Wedging his forearm against the guy's throat and windpipe, he took the position of power. He could hear the sirens in the background and was thankful the kid behind the counter had the foresight to call the police while Slash was fighting with the wannabe robber.

The gunman started to squirm again, so he put some additional pressure on the man's windpipe. Not being able to breathe immediately got his attention.

"I'd advise you not to move because not only will it hurt a lot, you'll stop breathing if I press harder," Slash said. The guy stopped moving, but he still couldn't focus on anything. His eyes were still glassy and wheeling. "We're just going to stay here quietly and no one will get hurt unless you try to move."

He had only to apply pressure one more time to convince the guy it was in his best interest to stay still. He gave up the fight with a half gasp, lying remarkably motionless until the police arrived and the cashier opened the door for them.

The police secured the gunman, cuffing him, and removing him from the scene. Slash directed the officers to the guy's weapon before dusting off his pants and giving his statement. Within minutes, the place was swarming with additional officers and a crime scene investigator. The cashier was in another corner of the store, loudly reciting his version of the events to the police. Slash made his statement, keeping his answers brief and pointed.

At some point, the owner of the Quick Mart arrived. He identified himself as Mr. Shemar Revani and pumped Slash's hand, slapping him on the back several times, thanking him profusely.

When the police finally said he could leave, Slash

went to the counter to pay for the items he'd collected. He felt his phone vibrate in his pocket and saw Lexi had texted him twice. He tapped back that he'd be home soon, before sweeping the debris off the milk carton and box of tampons. As he reached for his wallet, Mr. Revani came to the counter.

"No, no, no! Absolutely not. You will not pay. You've done a good deed for me today. I insist that the milk and—" he picked up and examined the tampon box "—womanly product is on the house. Hooray to the hero!"

Everyone in the store cheered, although he was certain he heard some snickers from the police.

No good deed ever goes unpunished.

Revani handed Slash his items and slapped him once more on the shoulder. "I'm sorry, my friend, but we're out of plastic bags. You're welcome back here anytime."

"Thanks." Slash just wanted to get the hell out of the store—the sooner the better. It'd been a heck of a day, and, damn it, he was supposed to be on vacation.

He'd just taken two steps out of the store when he heard the shouting and saw a half dozen television cameras pointed at him. He tried to slip the box of tampons under his jacket, but it was too late.

In seconds he was swarmed by reporters.

Chapter Five

Gwen

I'm a scientist and will remain calm and logical during the interview.

It sounded easy, except it wasn't when you were interviewing for the opportunity of a lifetime and the competition was two other amazing scientists you happened to know well and who were more experienced than you.

Regardless, I made important contributions to the project. I may be younger, but I'm every bit as qualified to go as they are.

She gripped the steering wheel a little tighter as her GPS signaled her destination was one minute away. Breathing deeply to calm herself, she took a left and pulled into the parking lot of a modest red brick building. A large crowd of people assembled on the front entranceway, holding signs and shouting.

What the heck?

She found an open parking spot and pulled into it, killing the ignition and getting out of the car, her purse over her shoulder, her briefcase in hand. For a moment, she just stood watching the crowd, trying to figure out what was going on and how in the world she was going to get through it to make her interview on time. Clearly, they were protesting something. But what? What could they have against a nonprofit organization trying to protect people against malaria?

Squaring her shoulders, she began to wind her way through the crowd. She stopped beside a young woman waving a sign and screaming, "No experimentation on people!"

Gwen glanced up at the sign and saw a crude drawing of a woman jabbing a needle into a child's arm. "What's going on?" she asked the woman.

"Vaccitex is experimenting on children," she shouted even though Gwen was standing right next to her. "They're going to kill them with their experiments."

Gwen frowned and wanted to tell her that this wasn't the case because she knew firsthand what was going into the vaccine and it was going to help, not hurt, children. But from the look in the woman's eyes, she had a feeling the woman wouldn't listen. Gwen continued moving through the crowd because—demonstration or not— there was *no* way she was going to miss this interview.

She was nearing the building entrance when a dark-haired guy with a beanie and a red bandana tied across his face suddenly tossed a brick through one of the glass doors at the front of the building. The glass shattered and the crowd cheered wildly.

Gwen froze. Things had taken a violent turn. Where were the police?

It was one thing to be in the middle of a peaceful protest, but a violent protest was something entirely different. People could get hurt. People could get *killed*.

A figure appeared in the shattered doorway and appeared to be about to exit, perhaps to talk or confront the angry crowd. Given the current mood, Gwen thought that would be an exceptionally bad idea. Just as she slipped a hand in her purse to grab her cell and dial 911, she heard sirens in the distance.

About time.

Now she was having second thoughts about the interview. As important as it was to her, she couldn't imagine the people inside would be receptive to having one with all the screaming and shouting going on outside. The protest would be a perfectly acceptable reason as to why she wasn't able to make the appointment. Not that she even believed it would happen at this point.

Her gaze sought out the dark-haired man with the bandana who had thrown the brick. She saw him among several young men huddling near the open door of a car near the front line of the protest. He was crouched on the ground working on something while the others closed ranks around him in a circle. She didn't know what he was doing, but she didn't have a good feeling about it.

Against her better judgment, she pushed closer to get a better look. Before she'd gone far, a dark-haired woman from inside the building stepped through the shattered glass door, and stood in front of the building, her arms crossed against her chest, staring calmly at the crowd.

For a moment, the crowd went silent. Gwen thought her impossibly brave or incredibly stupid. She stood there alone and unafraid, and that made her an imposing sight.

The moment passed and the crowd went wild screaming hate-filled obscenities. The woman started speaking, but Gwen couldn't hear anything she said.

The mood turned even uglier.

Maybe it's time after all to retreat until the police calm things down.

As she started to return to her car, the young man who'd been kneeling in the middle of the circle stood. He held a bottle with a flaming rag coming out of it. As he turned, the rag fell out. His friends laughed and scooped up the rag, but they couldn't get it back inside without burning their fingers. They stomped it out while another guy ripped off a piece of an old T-shirt and stuffed it in the bottle.

OMG. They were planning arson or worse. If the bottle hit the woman, it could hurt or even kill her. Moreover, whoever else was in the building would be in danger from fire and the police would be too late to stop things.

But I could stop it.

Before she talked herself out of it, she pushed quickly toward the men. The new rag had been lit and now the guy was creeping closer to the front door to throw it.

He'd pulled his arm back, preparing to throw, when Gwen swung her briefcase at his arm. She mostly missed, but a corner of the briefcase glanced off his arm. It was enough to disrupt his swing. The bottle only went a few feet before falling to the pavement and shattering, spreading an oily liquid that quickly ignited.

The guy turned to her, his lips curling in a snarl, and she took a step back in alarm.

Oops! Guess I should have thought through to this part.

She prepared to run when the flames caught hold of his pants. He yelped and started swatting at his clothes, extinguishing the fire on his legs. Others, seeing the fire spreading, backed up as flames began to take purchase and roar. A couple of the guys who'd started the fire tried to jump in their cars, but the flames had already spread under the back of their vehicles, so they wisely abandoned the idea and started running.

At last, police cars roared into the parking lot and officers spilled out. The crowd began screaming and pushing to get away.

Gwen moved off to the side as the crowd dispersed and the police stomped on the fire trying to put it out. After a moment, she dusted off her briefcase, adjusted her purse over her arm, and walked toward the dark-haired woman who was still standing in the shattered doorway.

Gwen carefully stepped over the broken glass. "Hello. My name is Gwen Sinclair and I have a three o'clock appointment with Lilith Burbridge. I'm one of the microbiologists from ComQuest."

The woman looked at her for a long moment before snapping her mouth shut. Then she smoothed down her hair and held out a hand. "Hello, Gwen. I'm Lilith. I just saw what you did. I'm a little rattled at the moment, and not exactly certain which position you're interviewing for, but I'm sure of one thing. Whatever position it is, you're hired."

Chapter Six

Lexi

As soon as I heard the front door open, I rushed into the foyer.

"Slash, where have you been? My mom and Basia left nearly three hours ago. You weren't answering my texts. What happened?"

He kissed me on the cheek and handed me a gallon of milk and the tampons, then walked into the kitchen. I looked down at the items. Everything seemed covered in a fine coat of dust.

"What the heck?" I said as I followed him. "Slash? Are you okay?"

He grabbed a bottle of water from the refrigerator and gulped it down. "Sorry I'm late. I stopped a robbery at the Quick Mart. Good news, no one got hurt and we got the stuff for free. Bad news, photos of me holding a box of tampons are going to be all over the news tonight."

"*What*?" I set the things on the counter before pulling on his arm and turning him toward me. "Are you kidding me?"

He glanced at me, a pained expression on his face.

"I'd never kid about me being on the news with a box of tampons."

"Oh my God. A robbery? Are you hurt?"

He opened the cabinet with the recycling bin and tossed in the empty bottle. "I'm fine. The guy was high on something, which means he was harder to take down than I expected, but his lack of judgment—on many levels—played to my advantage. Other than a shattered display case, a broken window and several destroyed bags of potato chips, the store, the cashier, the perpetrator and I came out mostly unscathed."

I cupped his cheeks in my hands, looking at him intently and trying to gauge if he was really okay or covering up for my sake. "Are you sure you're not hurt?"

He kissed my nose. "I'm not hurt. Really." He gave me a brief accounting of what had happened, and I listened without interrupting.

When he finished, I shook my head. "And I thought *I* had a black cloud of trouble following me around. Thank goodness nothing happened."

"All is well, except for one thing." He slid one arm around my waist and dipped his head at the counter toward the items he'd purchased. "Did I get the right box?"

Was. He. Kidding. Me? "You just took down a guy who might have killed you, and you're worried about a box of tampons?"

"Of course I'm worried." He lifted a hand, brushing my hair away from my ear, and whispered, "Did I pass the test?"

I frowned, searching his expression for clues. "Test?"

"The I'll-do-anything-for-my-girl test."

"Oh." I raised an eyebrow and wrapped my arms around his neck. "There's a test for that?"

He gave me such a pointed look, I laughed. "Okay, okay. Since I'm apparently the one grading your performance, I'm giving you an A-plus. You passed with flying colors, even though it wasn't really a test. I really did need a box."

"I know." He looked around the kitchen, noting the wine and cheese were gone, the dishes had been done and the counters were wiped. "So, how did *your* afternoon go? Looks like you're alone."

I dropped my hands and stepped back, sighing. "It was hell of another sort, although not nearly as dangerous as your afternoon. I looked at a lot of wedding dresses I'm never going to wear, drank too much wine, and wished with all my heart I was facing down terrorists or dealing with a matter of national security."

"Welcome to my life." A smile crossed his face. "We're a pair, aren't we?"

"I guess we are."

He trapped me between himself and the counter, sliding a hand behind the base of my neck and pressing a kiss against my mouth. "Best pair in the world."

"Absolutely," I murmured against his lips. "Now about that matter of national security…"

"Ah, *cara*, I think the fate of the world can wait another day. Let's salvage what's left of this one by spending it with our feet up, drinking beer, eating chocolate, and doing a little gaming."

I leaned back, not sure I heard him correctly. "Whoa. Did you just say beer, chocolate and gaming in the same sentence?"

"I did."

"Wow. You realize you receive extra credit points for that, right?"

He tapped me on the chin with his fingertip, sliding it up and across my lips. His eyes darkened. "Trust me, professor. I'm keeping score."

Gwen

"I got the assignment!"

Gwen launched herself into Elvis's arms the second she walked through the door, nearly knocking him over. She wrapped her arms around his neck, and he held on tight, spinning her around a couple of times before setting her down.

"I knew it!" he said, giving her a kiss. "What happened?"

She gave him a brief rundown of the events. He listened quietly, taking it all in. She'd never met a better listener in her entire life."

"Wait. You took on protestors with a Molotov cocktail, all by yourself?"

"Well, I'm not one hundred percent it was a Molotov, but definitely incendiary. Flash fire and all."

"So, you saved the CEO, and it was she who was planning to do the interview. Then she hired you on the spot?"

"Pretty much."

He shook his head, but not in disagreement or surprise, as if he were trying to get it all straight in his head. "I'm beyond impressed. When did you become such a badass?"

She couldn't help it, she was proud of herself. "I have no idea. I just saw it unfolding and decided to stop it. I guess, maybe the way Lexi is so brave all the time encouraged me."

"But…you had no backup." She heard it in his voice—he didn't like what she'd done. She appreciated his concern, but had no doubt she'd done the right thing.

"Look, Elvis, there wasn't time to do anything differently. She could have been seriously injured or worse. It was not a good situation. So, I made the decision to do something. I'm happy it worked out for the best and no one got hurt, including me."

"Thank God." He sighed and leaned his forehead against hers, his breath warm on her nose. "I learn something new about you every day, Gwen Sinclair. So, did the CEO even interview you?"

"She did. Even though I think I got the job before we had the interview, she still wanted to talk to me. She asked me a lot of questions about my experience doing fieldwork and was really interested when I told her I'd interned at the Center for Disease Control in Atlanta and had done some research in the field while I was there. I also told her about working with you in Egypt, even though that matter was a personal one. I only gave her a sanitized version of that, but she thought it was so cool. It wasn't an easy interview, though. She drilled me hard about my research. Then, finally, when we were done, she told me the job offer still stood. We shook hands and that was that. She's going to tell Cutler I'm on board effective immediately. OMG, Elvis! I'm still in shock."

"You deserve this. The introduction of yeast into the vaccine process was brilliant, Gwen. You have such an incredibly important career in front of you. Think of all the people you can help and save."

"I don't think I could love you more for supporting me, Elvis. I'm so excited, and yet completely terrified I'll mess something up."

"You won't." His belief in her was unwavering, and it meant a lot to her. "So, what happens next?"

She ran a hand through her hair, still feeling a bit dazed by all that had happened over the past twenty-four hours. "I've scheduled for some shots tomorrow. Then I'll have three days of orientation and we head out."

"For the Brazilian rainforest."

"Yes, for the rainforest. We've been given permission by the Brazilian government to access remote villages to test the vaccine. Vaccitex is on an accelerated timeline, so we aren't wasting any time getting there."

"Why the accelerated timeline?"

She didn't want to worry him, but she didn't want to hide the truth either. "The attacks on the infrastructure are getting worse and more vicious. Not to mention the ugly turn the demonstration outside their office took today."

Elvis's face clouded in concern again, and she hated that she kept putting that worried look there. "Define *vicious* for me."

"Well, physical offices being attacked, like what I interrupted today. It appears someone or some company is spreading false information about the vaccine in order to incite orchestrated media assaults on Vaccitex and their research. Also, the cyberattacks have become more frequent and concentrated."

"Did they contact X-Corp and Lexi yet?"

"Yes, and I added my voice in strong recommendation of Lexi. They have a meeting with Finn and Lexi tomorrow morning."

"Good, then at least they can rest assured that part is in capable hands."

"As am I." She rested one hand against the side of

his cheek. "I know you're worried about me, but don't be. What could possibly happen in the middle of a rain-forest?"

"I wish you hadn't said that."

She kissed the tip of his nose. "I'll be back before you know it with tons of really interesting photos and stories to tell. Then one day, we'll go back together on vacation. Okay?"

She was pretty sure she hadn't erased his concern, but at least he didn't say anything. Instead he pulled her in closer and nuzzled her neck. "That had better be a promise."

She closed her eyes in relief. At least he wasn't going to try to stop her from going, not that she had expected him to do that. But the fact that he hadn't meant every-thing to her. It meant her instincts were right about the kind of guy he was, and she loved him even more for it.

"That's a promise," she confirmed. She wrapped her arms around his neck. "So let's celebrate."

Chapter Seven

Lexi

There are many truths in life. One of *my* truths is I'm not a morning person.

By nature, I'm a night owl. I do my best thinking when the world is dark and I have few distractions. I'd recently read a report that scientists now believed night owl tendencies are hardwired in our genes. A study of several families of night owls supposedly found there's a gene mutation, CRY1, that's common in families of night owls, which causes our circadian clocks to run behind. I'm pretty sure my brothers and I get the gene from my dad, because my mom is the only one in our family who is a morning person, which annoys the heck out of the rest of us.

Unfortunately, my current job as Director of Information Security at X-Corp in Crystal City, Virginia, requires me to be at work by eight. Slash, however, seems able to work on less sleep than a normal human and is both a night owl and a morning person, which you'd think is scientifically impossible, but somehow he does it. He goes to sleep when I do, which is late, and almost always wakes up before me, spending at least thirty to forty minutes in our home gym—running on the tread-mill, lifting weights or doing tai chi. Personally, I'm lucky if I can make it down the stairs in the morning without breaking my neck before coffee.

This morning when I awoke, his side of the bed was empty. I brushed my teeth and pulled on a dark pair of pants and a white blouse, adding a black pullover sweater. After sweeping my hair back into my signature ponytail, I stuck my head in the upstairs room that serves as our gym and saw Slash on his back on the bench, lift-ing hand weights.

He saw me and smiled. *"Buongiorno, cara."*

"Good morning, Slash." I strolled across the mat and bent down to give him a kiss. "What do you want for breakfast?"

I used to skip breakfast, or consider coffee an accept-able substitute, but Slash makes me eat healthy. I ap-preciate it, but sometimes when he's traveling, I sneak Pop Tarts and a bowl of Frosted Cheerios. I try to be better about it because my health is important, but I'm still learning.

"I already made breakfast," he said. "Let me finish these reps and I'll join you."

When I got to the kitchen, I could smell the coffee that's always set to brew automatically. Slash had al-ready cut a honeydew melon into chunks and added a few raspberries. He'd also toasted a whole grain bagel and smeared it with almond butter. A glass of orange juice sat near my plate on the counter.

Yep. He's a keeper.

I poured myself a cup of coffee, added a generous dol-lop of milk, and sat on a barstool. I nibbled on the bagel and started reading the newspaper on my phone before

Slash joined me ten minutes later. Dressed in a light blue dress shirt and dark slacks, his long black hair slicked back, he took my breath away. I've known him for over a year, and had been dating him for several months, so logically I should be used to the way he looks, but somehow I'm not. Maybe I won't ever be.

"Why are you dressed for work when you're supposed to be on vacation?" I asked.

As he leaned over and gave me a kiss on the cheek, I caught a faint trace of shaving cologne. He smelled heavenly.

"I'm going to New York for the day," he explained. "I want to run some tests on the new simulation software I've been working on."

Besides working at the NSA, Slash owns a company in New York called Frisson International, LLC. The company works on data integration, tactical computing, sensor management, simulation-based training, and fusion analysis. He'd hired scientists and engineers to run the company while he worked at the NSA, but the vision is his, especially the new cryptologic simulation and training system he's developing for the U.S. government.

"You'll be there overnight?"

"Of course not. Any day away from you that's unnecessary will be avoided at all costs. My flight lands at 6:15 this evening, and I should be home by 7:00. Will you hold dinner for me?"

"Sure."

He was pouring some coffee into a travel mug when his cell rang. He pulled it out of his pocket, reviewed the number and answered it.

"Good morning, sir, what can I do for you?"

I caught his eye with a question and he put the call on speaker so I could hear.

"It's been brought to my attention that you were involved in an armed robbery situation yesterday." I recognized the voice. General Norton, Slash's boss.

Uh-oh.

"Yes, sir. I was in the Quick Mart when the perpetrator entered with his weapon drawn. Luckily there was no one else in the store at the time other than the cashier, and I was able to bring him down without anyone getting hurt."

"You do understand you're supposed to be on vacation, not fighting crime."

"It was a chance encounter."

"Well, good job. I saw you on the news last night talking to reporters and juggling…items."

There was a long, uncomfortable stretch of silence before General Norton cleared his throat. "Anyway, as your boss, I'm ordering you to relax, avoid dangerous situations, and be ready to get back to work after Thanksgiving. No more incidents like the Quick Mart or I'm personally reinstating your Secret Service detail."

"No need for that. I'm working on relaxing, sir."

"That's what I want to hear."

Norton hung up and Slash turned toward me, slipping his phone back into his pocket. He looked strangely relieved.

I studied him for a moment. "What is it?"

"What is what?"

"You seemed relieved about something. What?"

He took a sip of his coffee from the travel mug before popping the top on. "I'm grateful he had the courtesy not to mention the box of tampons I was holding front and center."

I turned my phone around to show him the article I was reading in the *Washington Post*. The headline read *Man Buying Tampons for Girlfriend Ends Robbery/Hostage Situation*.

He slowly lifted his gaze to mine. "The *Washington Post*?"

"Don't worry. It's buried in the back of the local news. No one will read it."

"So, she says." Sighing, he joined me at the counter, sliding on a barstool. "How's the bagel?"

"Delicious. Who knew I'd actually like almond butter?"

"It's a much healthier option than a Pop Tart."

"Healthier, yes. And it tastes good—it's just not better than a Pop Tart."

"My work with you is never done." He took a bite of his bagel. "So, what's on your agenda for today?"

I finished swallowing and wiped my mouth with the napkin. "I've got a nine o'clock meeting with Finn and a new client. This will be our third new client this week."

"X-Corp is growing by leaps and bounds."

"I know. It's been crazy busy these past few months. We've hired two new cyber analysts and three new admins—two in accounting and one in human resources. My own department is becoming so large, I'm considering hiring an administrative assistant to help me keep it all straight."

"Sounds like a good idea to me." He slid his hand into mine so our fingers were threaded. "Even though you're completely capable of handling whatever Finn throws at you."

His words, as well as his faith in my abilities, meant a lot to me. I squeezed his hand. "Thanks. It's not easy and I'm still learning how to manage people. But it's getting easier. Finn has an enormous amount of patience and faith in me."

"As he should. You're the company's star asset and Finn knows it."

I appreciated his sentiment, even if I wasn't certain I believed it. After a parting kiss, we went our separate ways, Slash driving toward the airport, and me swinging by Basia's house to pick her up before heading toward X-Corp's headquarters in Crystal City, Virginia. Despite my initial misgivings about carpooling, it had its advantages. Basia did most of the talking, we could stagger the driving, and we were able to split the parking costs. Win-win.

Because I'd taken a half day off yesterday, I expected our workload to be heavier than usual. It was. I barely had time to do a cursory first pass through my unread emails and respond to a few before I had to grab my laptop and head to the conference room to meet Finn and the client.

As I entered the conference room, Finn rose from his chair—the consummate gentleman. Dressed in a white button-down shirt rolled up to his elbows and blue tie, he pulled out my chair as I set my laptop on the table and dropped into the chair. We'd once been quasi-dating until we figured out we were better off as friends and colleagues. I'd helped him launch X-Corp and, in Finn's eyes, that made me an integral part of the company, even though he'd put up all the capital for it. To my surprise, not dating had made our relationship thrive and strengthen. I counted him as one of my closest friends, which was a miracle in itself.

"Good morning, Lexi. You're right on time. Glinda is bringing the client here momentarily." He spoke in a soft Irish lilt that sounded musical to me. I was grateful for our comfortable friendship, as well as our professional rapport.

"How did the afternoon of wedding dress viewing go?" he asked. I could hear the amusement in his voice. He knew I'd rather endure forty-six root canals than have to look at wedding dresses.

"Awful. But at least it was a virtual viewing. I didn't have to take my clothes off once to try anything on, so there's that."

"Och, you're always looking at the bright side of things." He patted my shoulder and tried to look sympathetic. Unfortunately, it wasn't working. His lips were twitching into a smile. "I take it to mean you didn't find the perfect dress."

"There's no such thing as the perfect dress. It's a myth perpetuated by clothes retailers to get you to spend a ridiculous amount of money on a dress you will only wear one time."

Now he laughed, apparently unable to contain himself. "Chin up. I'm sure it will all work itself out. As we say in Ireland, 'Your feet will bring you to where your heart is.'"

"Well, my feet and heart are determined to stay as far away as possible from a wedding dress fitting. Intellectually, I know I have to pick out *something* to wear. If only I could wave a magic wand and be dressed in a way that everyone likes."

The smile faded from his face and his green eyes narrowed. "Everyone else can bugger off. What's important is what *you* like, Lexi. You should wear whatever the hell you want."

"Wow. That makes a lot of sense when you put it like that. Can I quote you on that?"

"Yes, you can. If anyone has anything to say about it, send them to me. I'll threaten them with litigation."

"You really are a good friend, Finn, not to mention a good boss. You know that, right?"

"I certainly do."

Just as he said that, Glinda, Finn's administrative assistant, appeared in the doorway with a man and a woman.

"Hello and welcome to X-Corp," Finn said, stepping forward and holding out a hand to the woman first. She looked to be in her fifties with thick brown hair wound into a bun at her neck and dressed in a tan suit with a deep-rose-colored blouse. Small earrings accented with a pink stone and diamond chip winked as she turned her head.

"I'm glad you're here. I'm Finn Shaughnessy, CEO."

"Lilith Burbridge." The woman took Finn's hand and shook it. "CEO of Vaccitex."

"Hayden Pogue, founder of Vaccitex." A man with steel-gray hair and a mustache held out his hand next. "Thanks for agreeing to meet with us on such short notice."

"We are happy to be of assistance." Finn shook his hand, then turned to me, ushering me forward. "This is our Director of Information Security, Lexi Carmichael."

Lilith took my hand and shook it with a firm, no-nonsense grip, looking intently at me with light blue eyes, as if judging my character and integrity on the spot.

"I've heard a lot about you," she said. "You come highly recommended, especially from the executives at ComQuest."

"We've done some work with ComQuest and are pleased they recommend us," I answered, hoping that was an appropriate response. "I'm looking forward to working with you."

The lines on her face eased slightly. "We appreciate you seeing us without a lot of lead time."

"That's what we're here for," Finn said. "Most emergencies, especially those of a cyber nature, don't provide a lot of advance warning."

After Hayden shook my hand, and Finn closed the door, we all sat down at the rectangular conference table. I opened up my laptop and logged on, ready to take notes. Finn liked to jot down notes the old-fashioned way with pen and paper, but he hadn't picked up his pen yet. It didn't surprise me, as I was familiar with his approach. He liked to let the client talk for a while to get a feeling for what they wanted and what we could do to help them.

"So, how can X-Corp help you?" Finn asked.

Lilith and Hayden exchanged glances, but it was Lilith who spoke first. "Maybe it would be helpful if we told you a little about our company first. Vaccitex is a non-profit, NGO or nongovernmental organization. We've been working exclusively for the past several years on a revolutionary malaria vaccine. We've made some exciting breakthroughs in recent years with promising results, especially in regards to use with small children and infants."

"Wait. Isn't there a shot or something you can get to prevent malaria?" I asked.

"There is, but it's expensive and isn't safe for children

and infants. The shots can reduce a person's chances of getting the disease by about ninety percent. But there's another ten percent of the population to account for, not to mention the medication will not protect the most vulnerable of the population—children. Moreover, four shots are required for maximum efficiency, and studies have shown that about forty-six percent of the populations studied only ever receive one shot, which means significantly reduced or ineffective protection after a period of a few years. Our vaccine will change all of that. Two doses over a lifetime is all that's needed. Phase I and II of our field trials have indicated the vaccine is safe for children under two years of age, with any adverse reactions being similar to those of other childhood vaccines. After an in-depth review, it was decided the benefits of the vaccine would far outweigh any risk. So, three months ago, Vaccitex received a nod from the World Health Organization to move to Phase III of the trials, which means widespread introduction of the vaccine in targeted areas as part of a precursor to a large-scale pilot implementation program. It will be the first malaria vaccine provided to young children through a routine immunization program. We entertained requests from thirteen countries with populations at high risk and eventually selected Brazil—helping a few of the indigenous tribes of the rainforest."

Finn jotted down some notes and I tapped out a few of my own on the computer. "Why Brazil?" he asked. "What made that area more attractive over other areas of the world?"

"There were a lot of factors considered," Hayden replied. "Primarily, we received the assurance of the Brazilian Ministry of Health that they would fully cooperate and help with the implementation of the vaccine. In addition, the country already has a good vaccine program in place and has dedicated significant funds and resources to protecting its population, even the indigenous ones."

Lilith folded her hands on the table. Her fingers were long, elegant and devoid of jewelry, the nails painted a soft pink. "Not to mention, from a biological point of view, the rainforest is located fairly close to the equator, which means the conditions for the mosquitos are more standardized, as opposed to various locations in Africa and Southeast Asia." She glanced at Hayden, who nodded. "For clinical trials, the standardization is an important factor. There are many more reasons we could give you, but those are the big ones."

"Fair enough," Finn said.

Lilith leaned forward, her voice taking on a sense of urgency. "But we are now at a critical stage in our testing and implementation. We're experiencing an enormous amount of concentrated effort to break into our company's database to either steal or alter data. A malaria vaccine is like the Holy Grail to pharmaceutical companies. The money it could bring in would be in the billions. Vaccitex has no desire to make a profit from this. We will want only to have our operating costs covered, and all additional funds will be recycled to pursue research that will further refine the vaccine or aid in developing new ones."

Her statement was admirable, even saintly. But the danger was real. Years of hard work could be stolen or the data corrupted to a point where it could take the organization years to rebuild or repair, giving other drug companies time to come up with a vaccine of their own.

The cost would be incalculable. But now we were in my zone. It was time to dig down to the details.

"How do you know you're being attacked online? Who's in charge of your cybersecurity?"

"We've been protected by a variety of sources, most often government cybersecurity agencies or individuals, and occasionally private companies," Hayden explained. "We have an excellent IT guy heading up what little staff we have. They've all done a good job, considering the sheer volume of attacks we've been under, but we've come to a critical juncture in the research and we need a higher and more consistent level of protection to finish things off."

I wasn't sure how to take that. Different governments had different levels of ability in terms of cybersecurity. Not knowing who had built the security architecture, I couldn't know how impenetrable it might actually be.

"We've been given a grant by the WHO and several charitable organizations and companies around the world are helping to subsidize the costs of hiring a cyber-intelligence company full time to protect our information," Lilith added. "You—" she looked directly at me "—and X-Corp come highly recommended."

I exchanged a glance with Finn, who lifted his eyebrow slightly. "Okay, what exactly are you thinking?"

"We need a team of experts to review our database and security setup at our New York office and ensure it's fully protected," she responded without hesitation. It was clear she and others at Vaccitex had given a strategy some thought, which I appreciated. "That means, at minimum, a one-year contract with X-Corp, possibly longer. We also want one team member to accompany us periodically in the field to ensure any transmission and data collection remains secure and safely encrypted." She paused, as if to give the next statement more emphasis. "We want that field team member to be you, Lexi."

Chapter Eight

Lexi

"You want *me* to go to the rainforest to ensure data protection?"

"Yes." Lilith kept her gaze steady on mine. "We'd like you to set up a team at our headquarters in New York first and then accompany our scientists to our portable lab in Brazil on our next trip, which happens to be in five days."

"Five days?" I'm pretty sure I sounded like a parrot repeating everything she said, but it was a lot to take in.

Lilith nodded, an apology flashing in her eyes. "I know it's an extremely accelerated timeline, but as you can imagine, time is of the essence. We want the best with our field team in Brazil. The rest of your team would be working out of our headquarters in New York. I know it's a lot to ask of you personally, and not a lot of time to bring you up to speed, but here we are. We'd like to have you and your team on a plane to New York first thing in the morning. Do you think you can assemble a team that quickly?"

I sat there stunned before Finn stood up and motioned

for me to do the same. "If you'd excuse us for a minute, I'd like to speak privately with Lexi."

"Of course," Hayden said.

I followed Finn out into the hall. He closed the door behind me, leaning against the opposite wall, looking concerned. "This sounds a little crazy. What do you think?"

"What do I think? I *think* it's insane. Five days for me to assemble a cyber team, examine Vaccitex's current security setup, plug any holes, and then pack and fly to the rainforest to review yet another security architecture I'm going to have to troubleshoot with spotty, if any, wifi? Technically, that's passing insane and moving into lunacy territory. Plus, they're asking me to take a trip to the rainforest. Me. The girl who hates to fly, loathes heat, humidity, bugs and spiders, can't swim, and gets seasick just standing on a beach. Not to mention, I'm still not recovered from the *last* time we were in the jungle."

Finn grimaced. I presumed he was remembering our adventure in the jungle. It hadn't been a good one and we were lucky to have survived.

"I'll tell them we can't do it," he said.

I blew out a breath, pinching the bridge of my nose with my fingers. "It's not that simple, Finn. I wish it were, but it's not. We can't just say no. Look at what's at stake. A vaccine that could save millions, maybe billions, of lives, most of them children."

He pushed his fingers through his brown hair, his eyes clouding with concern. "I know. But if we can't do it in five days, we have to say no. Not to mention, I'm not going to send you back into the jungle if you don't want to do it."

"I can do it in five days," I said glumly. "That's not

the problem. *I'm* the problem. I just have to suck it up and deal. Let's examine the pros and cons."

I started to pace the hallway. Was there any other way around this that didn't involve me going to the rainforest? "First the pros. It's at least a year's commitment for our team in New York, which means a decent financial investment for X-Corp. Just so you know, I'm fine with setting up an X-Corp team in New York, but I'm not moving there."

"I wouldn't expect you to. But it's not the New York jungle I'm worried about."

"I know. The rainforest scares me…a lot. It's not that I can't go, I'm just not crazy about the idea. I know intellectually it would be different this time around. No plane crash—hopefully—and no bad guys with guns chasing me around. I'd just be sitting in the lab, keeping tabs on a small computer setup and chatting with scientists. It doesn't seem so bad when I envision it like that."

"Things are never that simple with you, Lexi, and you know it."

"I know. But, dang it, Finn. I'm also intrigued. Rainforest humidity, giant spiders, and long plane rides aside, it's an amazing opportunity. Plus, what an incredible challenge. How, in good conscience, could I turn this down?"

"You're going to want to discuss it with Slash."

"That goes without saying." I looked down at my engagement ring, pressing my thumb against the band. "But I already know what he'll think. If it means helping people, especially children, he won't be against it. That's just the way he is."

"Think again. It won't be that simple. He'll put you before everything else, as he should."

He was right again, but I also knew if I decided to do it, Slash would support me. We'd recently learned our lesson on that matter.

Finn leaned against the wall and pushed his fingers through his hair. "So, what's next? Do you want to move forward on this? Offer a partial solution minus the rainforest? Or tell them we need twenty-four hours to discuss further."

I appreciated that Finn had given me several opportunities to consider. He valued my input and expertise, and it meant a lot that he treated me as a valued employee, as well as a friend. "Let's move forward. If after talking to Slash, I decide not to go to the rainforest, Ken can go in my place. He'll do a good job. But I want to help as much as I can, and I know you do, too. You've got a softer heart than me. Plus, it's a good thing for X-Corp all around—a win-win situation for the company in terms of money, jobs and public relations. Virtually overseeing a team in New York will be the easy part. Although it may be way out of my comfort zone, I can survive in the rainforest if I play it safe at the camp. The Brazilian government, the World Health Organization and other important charities are funding this effort, so other than snakes, bugs and potential cyberattacks, I don't anticipate any real danger. Simple, right?"

Finn snorted. "Nothing is *ever* easy with you, but if you're on board, let's see what we can do. Are you sure about this?"

"How can we not be sure? I still want to clear it with Slash, but let's do it. You okay with that?"

He patted me on the shoulder and the gesture reassured me. "I'm better than okay, lass. I'm lucky to have you on the team and as a friend." He got a faraway look on his face, almost as if he were rehearsing what he was going to say to Lilith and Hayden. "All right then, Lexi. Let's go back in and see what they think of our plan."

Chapter Nine

Lexi

"I've been asked to go on assignment to the rainforest in Brazil."

I winced as soon as the words came out my mouth. That hadn't come out the way I'd planned. I'd wanted to ease Slash into the news, let it pop up naturally in conversation about our days. But unfortunately, I suck at conversation, even with my fiancé, which means things rarely go the way I plan. Besides, when I get nervous, I have a tendency to blurt things out. So, instead of letting Slash relax after his busy day of work and travel—not to mention, try the brand new shrimp and broccoli stir fry recipe I'd fixed—I blurted out the announcement before he'd even eaten a single bite.

He carefully lowered his fork, balancing it on the side of the plate. "Rainforest?"

Sighing, I picked up my wineglass and took a sip, looking at him in the flickering candlelight. "Yes. X-Corp caught a case today. ComQuest has been working with an NGO company named Vaccitex on the development of an anti-malaria vaccine. Vaccitex is in the final stages of clinical trials, but their data is in danger. Not surprisingly, they're being virtually attacked by agents unknown who want to steal or corrupt their data. Com-Quest suggested they get in touch with us to protect their critical information. The CEO says she wants me to be the one overseeing a team in their New York headquarters, but also travel with a team to Brazil to ensure the security of the field data."

He seemed to mentally digest that before he spoke. "The last part, about wanting you in particular, doesn't surprise me. Your reputation precedes you. But I have a lot of questions. If Vaccitex is an NGO, how are they funding their research?"

"They've received a grant from the WHO and are apparently being supported by various governments and charitable organizations around the world."

"The name Vaccitex is familiar." Slash reached for his wine, his brow furrowed slightly. "I've heard it before, but I'm not sure where. Tell me what else you know about the organization."

"Well, they're one hundred percent charitable, covering only their operating costs. Any excess funds that are donated to the project will be recycled to further research into the vaccine and distribution."

He took a sip of his wine and then picked up his fork, trying the shrimp. I held my breath as he ate. After he swallowed, he tipped the fork in my direction. "It tastes good. I'm impressed."

That meant a lot, because I was deeply insecure about my cooking abilities. Especially since he was an excellent cook himself and came from a family of Italian cooking geniuses. That gave me a lot to live up to.

He took another bite and set his fork on the plate. "So, tell me more about this assignment in the rainforest."

I gave him a brief rundown of the meeting. When I finished, he sat back in his chair and lifted the wineglass to his lips, watching me thoughtfully.

"So, you'd be in the portable lab in the rainforest ensuring the infrastructure and data are protected? That's it?"

"I assume that's correct. I can't see why I'd have to actually go to the villages or anything. I'm not a doctor or a microbiologist."

"Hmmm. And how often would you have to be in New York overseeing the team? Is a permanent living arrangement required?"

"Absolutely not. I already told Finn I'm not moving to New York. That's nonnegotiable. The client agreed and instead proposed a once-a-month trip to New York for a couple of days to oversee the operation. My staff should be able to run the project virtually without any problem."

He paused for a moment, looking at me thoughtfully. "So, they insisted on having you."

"Yes." I looked down and fiddled with my fork. "ComQuest recommended me."

"I bet they did. Tell me more about the rainforest trip."

"Well, the next field team is leaving for Brazil in five days. They want me on that flight. But first, I'd have to head to New York to assemble a team to be based out of there. It's all crazy fast, and I don't have all the information at my fingers, but they're under an accelerated timeline."

"So, you've decided, then?"

Now it was my turn to reach across the table and take his hand. The blue diamond in my engagement ring winked and sparkled in the candlelight. "Actually, no. I told them I needed to talk with you about it first. To consider your input and thoughts. That's what we do now. Make decisions together as a couple."

He nodded, perhaps remembering a recent decision he'd made that excluded me, and the consequences that had entailed. I felt confident we wouldn't be going down that path again.

"Then my question to you is…do you want to do it?" he asked.

I hesitated, trying to get my thoughts in order. "Honestly, Slash, I'm conflicted. I'm not crazy about going back into the jungle again unless I can stay in a nice hotel with wifi. I could easily handle the New York part of the assignment, but it's the rainforest part that has me worried. I don't like spiders, snakes, or bugs of any kind, and I'm easily overheated. I hate flying, boating, and riding long distances in the car, and this is a long trip. But having said that, I could suck it up for a worthwhile cause. Think about it. This appears to be the first-ever malaria vaccine that's safe and effective for infants and children under two years of age. Only two doses of the vaccine are required for an entire lifetime. It could save millions, no, billions, of lives around the world. The doctors, scientists and microbiologists at Vaccitex have been working hard—not even for profit—but for sheer passion and dedication, to bring this to the people who need it most. How could I not want to be a part of something that important?"

I knew he'd understand and sympathize with that statement. He squeezed my hand, his expression turning thoughtful. "How are they paying for you, your team, and X-Corp in general? I know it's not going to be cheap."

"As far as I know, ComQuest is partially subsidizing

Vaccitex and will be sending one of their microbiologists as part of the field team, *pro bono*. Finn thinks it's intended as a public relations maneuver to repair their reputation after the British Virgin Islands debacle. If that's true, I agree it's a good plan. I suspect there are other charitable foundations chipping in to help the company out. Finn might yet offer them a discount—he's still running the numbers. What's clear to everyone is how important information security has become at this stage of the game. They need all the help they can get, and they want me."

He released my hand and rubbed his unshaven chin, his gaze drifting off just above my left shoulder. I wondered what he was thinking. His mind worked on so many different levels, it was hard to anticipate.

He finally spoke. "What if I, or in particular, my company Frisson, made a sizable donation to the organization? In addition, I would offer my cyber services, *pro bono*, to X-Corp, and by extension, to Vaccitex, for at least the next few weeks while I'm on vacation? I could accompany you to New York and Brazil, helping out with whatever was needed. But let me be clear, this is your show. If everyone agrees, I would be an extra set of cyber hands and eyes only."

I stared at him in surprise. I hadn't expected that, but given his generosity, maybe I should have. "Wow. You'd do all that? On your time off?"

"Of course I would. I honestly don't think I can stand one more day of vacation that doesn't involve you and me together. This is torture. Not to mention, I sure as hell don't want to have idle hands and be roped into any wedding planning. It's a win-win situation for everyone, especially me. So, what do you think?"

I couldn't help it, I laughed. How could I not when I totally sympathized, especially about the wedding planning? Sometimes we were more alike than I'd ever imagined. "Don't you have more work to do with Frisson?"

"My company is doing exceptionally well running itself without me. I've realized when I pop in there to 'oversee things,' I'm basically sticking my nose into a well-oiled machine. I have good people in place who would prefer I didn't muck things up, and they're right. I put up the capital, formed the company, and gave my very capable and well-paid engineers, scientists and program managers some ideas to run with. They're doing really good work, bringing in numerous contracts, and making me a lot of money, so I believe it's in my best interest to mostly sit back and watch."

"A hacker, an inventor, a manager and an astute businessman." I shook my head in wonder. "How do you keep it all straight in your head?"

"Very carefully. So, what do you think of my offer, *cara*?"

What did I think? I thought he was the most incredible man I'd ever met and I was the luckiest person in the universe that he loved me.

"I think it's an incredibly generous offer, Slash. That being said, I should run it past Finn and the executives at Vaccitex and see what they think. I suspect Finn will be on board, mostly because it means you can keep an eye on me. But if I were the CEO of Vaccitex, I'd be ecstatic to have more money, as well as a valuable asset on the team for free."

"I guess we'll find out."

I took his hand and lifted it to my lips, kissing his amazing hacker fingers. "I guess we will."

Chapter Ten

Arjun Singh

Bangalore, India

Arjun Singh sat in an expensive leather chair, looking out of the floor-to-ceiling window that provided an expansive view of Bangalore, better known as the Silicon Valley of India. His fingers tapped absently on the arm of the chair as he considered how to handle a problem that wouldn't go away. It mystified him how this little problem had grown until it now threatened his empire. He hadn't worked all his life to let a bunch of do-gooders ruin all that he'd built. Not that he was worried it would happen, but the problem had to be dealt with immediately.

The intercom on his desk chimed and Arjun reluctantly tore his gaze away from the bustling city and turned back to his desk. Being the CEO of one of the largest tech companies in India was an honor, but he hadn't built it by being reactive or passive. Stealing, industrial spying, and hacking were a critical part of the game, and he was an expert at turning the fruits of that labor into exceptional global and financial success.

He leaned across some papers and pressed the button once.

"What is it?"

"I'm sorry to bother you, sir," his executive assistant said. "But your brother and Mr. Anand are here to see you."

"Good. Send them in."

"Yes, sir. Right away."

Moments later, two men stepped into his office. His brother, Vihaan, was the younger of the two and had thick black hair that curled around his ears. He looked about eighteen years old even though he was nearly twenty-three. Arjun had made him his Director of Security because in the business world, absolute loyalty was a precious commodity. Vihaan adored his older brother and Arjun leveraged it in a way that suited him and his empire.

Vihaan smiled at his brother, but kept it formal, shaking hands and sitting down in one of the visitor chairs. The man accompanying him was only a year older than Vihaan, but tall and thin with a bit of scraggly facial hair on his chin. Arjun preferred clean-cut employees, but he made an exception for Krish Anand due to his brilliance and talent with computers.

He shook hands with Krish and they sat in the chairs on the other side of Vihaan. Arjun wanted an update, so he was pleased he didn't have to wait to get one.

"Sir, we wanted to let you know our progress on gaining access to Vaccitex's files," Krish said, leaning forward, his hands dangling between his knees. "We aren't there yet, but we're close. Very close."

Arjun had designated Krish as the special projects information technology guru in charge of gaining access to their competitor's research. In other words, Krish was a master hacker.

"Close isn't good enough," Arjun said, slightly disappointed. He had faith in Krish, but he needed him to try harder and work faster. Star Pharma needed the details being used for the vaccine so they could replicate it for production and fast. They'd created the production capability, but they needed the process...and soon.

"Sir, it's only a matter of time. We've successfully penetrated their mail server and have full access to all their emails and the test results database, but the process and research information is behind a second firewall that we have not yet breached. I'm certain we can breach it soon, but a speedy approach may not be the best." He paused, clearly considering how best to explain it to his boss.

Alarm skittered up Arjun's spine. "Why not?"

Krish leaned back and pressed his long fingers together. "Well, there's a real possibility that by breaching the second firewall in such a manner, we'll inadvertently reveal our presence and run the risk of being interrupted while collecting the critical information. Or we could be aggressively tracked. I'm careful, and I'm sure they can't find us, but I think the best approach at this point is to try repeated subtle attempts to breach the firewall at a level below the threshold they would detect, while also monitoring the emails for a mistake or a way to compromise one of the Vaccitex administrators."

That was not what Arjun wanted to hear, but he needed all the information before he decided on a definitive course of action. "How much longer will that take?"

"It's hard to tell, but hopefully within days, but perhaps two weeks at the outside," Krish said. "This is delicate work."

Frustration and impatience swept through him, but he kept a calm exterior. He couldn't afford to rush things at this stage of the game, but time was running out for himself and his investors, and his team needed to know that.

"You have exactly ten days to break through," Arjun said. "If not, I want the team prepared for a brute force assault on the system. Do I make myself clear?"

Krish swallowed, but to his credit, didn't flinch. "Yes, sir."

Arjun turned to his brother. "Vihaan, how are things going with preparations to disrupt the vaccine trials in Brazil? I understand the organized protests have been successful in rattling the executives in the United States and calling their reputation into question."

"It's been better than we expected." His brother sat back in his chair, a satisfied look on his face. "They have spent an inordinate amount of time dealing with the media fallout of the protests and defending their reputation."

"Good. I want them in disarray. Keep them distracted from the research. Unfortunately, it hasn't delayed the trials."

"True, but the penetration of their email has been quite helpful as it has given us key details of their planning and timing. I've been working through an intermediary in Brazil to find us some inside assistance in the Amazon region where the trials are expected to occur. I'm happy to report I've been successful."

"You've got us someone on the inside?" That would be a critical part of his plan.

"I do," Vihaan said. "Their instructions are to monitor and disrupt the trials, as well as report back to us. It worked out better than I expected."

Arjun considered his brother. Despite his youth and occasional brashness, Vihaan was clever and committed—useful commodities in the cutthroat business world. "How much is this going to cost me?"

Vihaan shrugged. "A lot, but given what's at risk, how can we not afford to do this?"

Arjun stood and walked over to the floor-to-ceiling glass window, looking out over his beloved city. "I'll not provide a big cash payment up front. See if our new associate is willing to take a smaller initial amount with a promise of profit sharing once Vaccitex is out of the way and our vaccine is the only game in town."

"But why?" Vihaan protested. "What if he backs out? Why would you risk our connection with the associate at this point?"

Arjun turned and gave his brother a hard, cool look. "Do not *ever* question how I run the company. *My* company."

Vihaan had the grace to look down at the floor. Good, it was important he understood his place. "Of course. I apologize, brother."

Arjun let the uncomfortable moment linger before he spoke again. "I will not provide a big payout before the work is done. I need to be convinced of how committed our associate is. This arrangement will allow enough money to make it worthwhile, and the promise and lure of additional money should provide sufficient motivation to make sure Vaccitex does not succeed. If Vaccitex can be made to fail spectacularly, and in a way that makes other countries reluctant to support future local trials against different malaria strains, then it would be most advantageous to us in the long run."

Vihaan's cheeks were red, but he nodded. "I'll communicate the information to our Brazilian associate."

"Good." Arjun sat behind his desk, resting his elbows on top of the papers scattered there. "Mr. Anand, inform me the moment you crack the firewall and have the data. Understood?"

"Yes, sir," Krish said and both men stood, realizing the meeting was coming to a close.

After they left, Arjun sat down at his laptop to draft an email asking his major investors for just a little more time.

They were close. Really close. He could feel it.

Chapter Eleven

Lexi

"Ouch. My arm hurts."

I glared at Slash, cranky and stressed. In the span of four and a half hours, I'd had to pack a bag for a few days in New York, organize my stuff at the office, make last-minute arrangements with my team, skip lunch, and swing by the doctor to receive a couple of shots. From the doctor's office, it was straight to the airport for the short hop to New York. Short or not, it still meant flying, which I absolutely hated, so that didn't help my mood. Added to that, I didn't do well with change—especially not on an accelerated timeline—so I was maxed out and looking for a fight.

The most convenient target at the moment—Slash. He'd met me at the airport and immediately assessed my mood as dangerous. My eyes narrowed as we walked toward the airport exit, pulling our carry-on suitcases behind us. "It's not fair you've already had all your shots."

"One of the perks of the job." He tried not to smile, but I saw a small one anyway, which made me crankier. "Now, let me carry your laptop bag for a bit until your arm is feeling better."

I tried to temper my crankiness. I'd been relieved Finn had been on board with the plan to bring on Slash, and so had Hayden and Lilith. Not surprisingly, they were more than happy to accept Slash's generous donation to the organization, and even more thrilled that a man of Slash's qualifications and experience was volunteering his vacation time to help them out. Even though Hayden and Lilith knew Slash only as the CEO of Frisson, and not as a director at the NSA, his qualifications and work at his New York company were enough to sway them. Lilith had requested only that she could clear it with their head scientist and lab director, who was already in Brazil in the field. Apparently, the scientist was highly protective of the work and not inclined to collaborate with people she didn't know, especially at this stage of the vaccine development. However, when she was informed of Slash's donation and assured he would be working on information security only, she agreed, and Slash was officially brought on board.

That was *really* good news for me. First, having Slash with me in the rainforest would go a long way to making me feel comfortable in that environment. If I was comfortable, and not too freaked out about the spiders, snakes, heat, and the little black cloud of trouble that always followed me around, I could focus my full attention on my job. It didn't hurt that he was also one of the most accomplished hackers and keyboard wizards in the world, which was a huge bonus for the entire operation. Finally, as evidenced by my crappy attitude, I hated flying, so having him next to me on any plane would be of enormous personal comfort.

So, it was a win-win for me.

I tried to remember that as I handed him my laptop

bag. That left me with just my purse and the carry-on suitcase that I rolled behind me. "Thanks. Sorry I'm out of sorts."

Slash shifted my laptop bag from his right shoulder to his left and leaned over to kiss my forehead before murmuring, "You've got this."

We exited the airport and waited in line for a taxi to our hotel near Vaccitex's headquarters. The two of us were coming early to scope out the situation with the organization's security setup and information infrastructure, while Finn began to assemble a long-term team for the project. The plan was to have at least two more people from X-Corp in place in New York before Slash and I left on Wednesday. While Slash had an apartment in New York, it wasn't close to Vaccitex's headquarters, so for convenience's sake, we'd opted for a hotel a block away.

We arrived at the hotel, dumped our suitcases in the room, and headed out on foot with our laptop bags. The office was on the sixth floor of a shabby building, which reminded me that we were working for a nonprofit and not a high-tech company. That made me wonder what kind of antiquated equipment I'd have to deal with. A security guard inside the building stopped us, and after reviewing our identification, waved us to the elevator. We had to push a button on an intercom and state our names before we were buzzed into the office. A young woman, who was apparently expecting us, led us to the cramped office of Tim Wilson, who was currently in charge of information security for the organization.

Tim looked up from behind the monitor where he was typing madly on his keyboard when we were ushered in. He was completely bald with full, ruddy cheeks and dark eyebrows. He rose from behind his desk and walked around it, carefully avoiding toppling the stacks of books and files piled on the floor.

"Lexi Carmichael," he said in a booming voice, vigorously pumping my hand and making the arm that had just received the shots hurt more. "I've heard a lot about you. That article you wrote on cyber proxy wars for *Cybersecurity Today* was brilliant. It's an honor to meet you in person. You can't imagine my surprise and delight to hear you'd be helping us out here."

I wasn't sure what to say to all that, so I fell back on my failsafe, which was to say nothing.

Tim didn't seem bothered by my lack of response, thank goodness, and he immediately turned to Slash. "I haven't heard anything about you, sir, but I understand you know your way around a keyboard. I'm Tim Wilson. Glad to make your acquaintance and look forward to your help. We could really use it around here."

Tim's exuberance was kind of catching, and to my surprise, I found myself liking him without even knowing him, which was a pretty unusual thing for me. He looked around his office, ruefully shaking his head. "I'd ask you to sit, but I don't have a free chair in here and it's too small for the three of us anyway. Let's head to the Server Room and I'll show you around. We can talk there."

We walked down a hall and Tim stopped in front of a door, using a key to unlock it. Single file, we headed into a dim, cool room filled with a decent array of computers, routers, wires and monitors. The servers, mounted on a table, had been stacked into a tower and several empty workstations held a variety of laptops and desktop computers, most of them running various programs. It was a small setup, but looked efficient.

"Why don't you start by telling us what problems you've had," I said to Tim, trying to figure the best way to get a handle on things. Slash continued to walk about the room inspecting the equipment.

"It's pretty straightforward. We've been fighting off systemic and a series of well-executed attacks. One of them has been recently successful."

Tim's blatant admission surprised both Slash and me, as we both turned to face him. "How recent?" I asked.

"A few days ago," Tim said. "Possibly the day you signed on to help us out. I haven't been able to tell how long they've been inside, but they penetrated our email system. As soon as I discovered it, I let the staff know. I advised them to be careful about anything they transmitted for the time being. But I couldn't afford to shut them out until I knew where they'd been and what they were looking at. In other words, I don't want them to know we know they're in…yet. After some discussion, we made a collective decision to proceed as if nothing had happened."

"That's smart," I said quietly and I meant it. A rookie might have panicked and shut everything down. Tim had thoughtfully considered his options and taken one that had given us the best chance to trace the hackers, while still alerting staff to the compromise and to be careful with what they said in electronic communication.

"Luckily we have a separate firewall protecting the scientific data and research material," he continued. "I'm reasonably confident they haven't breached that one yet, but obviously everyone is concerned about protecting the integrity of the data as we head into field testing of the vaccine. I just don't know how long we can hold them off, which is why we're bringing you guys on board."

I liked this guy even more because he'd been absolutely straight with us from the start. My initial assessment was that he would be an asset to us as we figured this out. "So, what approach do you think we should take from here?"

Tim looked surprised by the question. "Wow. That's nice that you've asked me. I wasn't sure what to expect when I heard they had got a couple of heavy hitters in here to help out with things. I guess I envisioned a *Men in Black* scenario where you storm in, take over and freeze me out. Which would have been fine with me as long as you helped the organization. Vaccitex has a bunch of really good people with big hearts and brains who are dedicated to making the world a better place. It's not hard to step aside and put that above my ego."

His confession impressed me yet again. "Well, you're not going to get a *Men in Black* scenario from us, Tim. We need your help. This is your system, your baby. So far, you've done what I would have done, given the circumstances. Your setup looks solid. Obviously we'll want to take a closer look, but my question still stands. What are your thoughts on a forward plan of action?"

"Well, I think the most important first step is verifying the research and vaccine formula haven't been compromised. Second, we need to strengthen the hell out of the firewall to keep them out for good."

"Excellent first steps," I agreed. "But we can't ignore the intruders in the email, either. We need to know who they are and exactly what they want, all of which will help us as we strengthen our defense. We need to set a trap so we can backtrack them."

Interest sparked in Tim's eyes. "What kind of trap did you have in mind?"

"The kind that makes them *think* they've successfully broken through the firewall. It could hold a repository of research files that look like the real thing, but are riddled with errors and loaded with a special malware of our own."

"A honeypot?" he asked.

"A honeypot," I confirmed. "Once they download the files, I'll be able to create a backdoor into their system and it will be our turn to take a look around in their system."

"If they download," Tim cautioned. "That's a big if."

"They will," I said, completely confident. "At some point those files will go all the way to the top of whoever is orchestrating these attacks. And when they do... we'll have them."

Chapter Twelve

Lexi

Slash and I spent a couple of hours getting familiar with the system, asking Tim a lot of questions and getting a feel for the rhythm and flow of the operation. The three of us took a quick break for lunch at a local deli and then returned for the more interesting part of the day—taking a look at the hacker's penetration and learning what we could from it.

It didn't take Slash or me long to determine the hackers were very skilled. Vaccitex was lucky the firewall held up as long as it did.

"Have you considered disconnecting the research database entirely from the Internet?" I said, tearing my eyes away from the code scrolling across the screen. "If it's that critical, does it have to be online?"

"I wish it were that simple," Tim replied. "But things are changed and tweaked in the formula on a daily basis. The company has researchers and scientists all over the world. Unfortunately, being disconnected isn't an option at this point."

"Who are your competitors for the vaccine?" Slash

asked. He was methodically taking notes on a small note-pad as the data moved rapidly across the monitor.

"We have plenty," Tim said. "But for that, you'd have to talk to Lilith or Hayden. They'd know better than me."

"Think we could talk to one of them?" I asked.

Tim stood, stretched his arms over his head. "Sure. Let me see who's here and available."

He disappeared out the door and I shifted in my chair toward Slash. "What are you thinking?"

"I'm thinking Vaccitex is lucky to have Tim. For a largely solo effort, he's done a damn good job. But they were right to bring us in. That firewall won't last much longer."

"My thinking exactly."

I rolled my neck and shoulders when Tim walked back in the room.

"Hayden is available now if you want to stop by," he said.

"Great. Let's go." I grabbed my laptop and Slash took the notepad.

We followed Tim to Hayden's office. It wasn't much bigger than Tim's, minus all the books and paper piles stacked on the floor. Hayden rose from behind his desk and shook hands with us. We were ushered to a small round conference table in another part of the office and Tim took his leave.

"Thanks for coming." Hayden looked at Slash. "Nice to finally meet you. We're happy to have you on board and greatly appreciate your generous contribution to the effort."

"My pleasure. It's a worthy cause."

"It is, indeed. Please have a seat. We consider our-selves quite fortunate to have you both on the team."

I thought it better to wait until we actually did something before they considered themselves fortunate, but whatever. "We've got some questions for you after speaking with Tim," I said.

"I'm sure you do. Ask away."

I put my thoughts in order to make sure I asked the right questions. Given the timeline we were on, I didn't want to be misinformed or make presumptions about anything.

"I realize I'm here to resolve the issue of information security, but I like to know the big picture because it helps me to put myself in the mind of a potential adversary. So, a couple of general questions first." I opened my laptop and pulled up the document containing questions I'd compiled while on the airplane. "First, why are you field-testing the malaria vaccine in the rainforest of Brazil instead of Africa, where the mortality rate from malaria-related deaths is so much higher?"

"That's an excellent question," Hayden answered. "We've already tested the vaccine in various regions of Africa during Phase II, but in a much more limited capacity. That's where we compiled the data results and it was shown to be dramatically effective. However, for large-scale testing, we wanted a different variation, and one where any potential consequences to the untested population serving as the control group would be less risky."

"How would that be less risky?"

"Despite the fact that Brazil accounts for around half of the cases of malaria in the Western hemisphere, only about a hundred people actually die from the disease annually. That's mostly due to improved treatments and a significant effort and investment by the Brazilian government. Most of those hundred, however, are children or the most vulnerable among the population. In addition, hundreds of thousands are affected by the flulike symptoms that accompany malaria, such as a high fever, chills, diarrhea, vomiting, dehydration and extreme fatigue. That creates a significant social and economic burden on the area, especially as many of those populations are rural famers and workers who, when affected by malaria, are unable to perform their jobs."

I could see the sense in this. "So, by testing a larger segment of the population, it made sense to run the trials on another location."

"Exactly. We chose the area for the research site carefully, and partially because there are seasonal differentiations of malaria and the transmission peaks are highest in this area for the next several months. Right now, the drugs we have to treat malaria are largely taken after the fact. But we are developing a vaccine against the bacteria, not just the viruses. Several companies want to be first, but none have had the success we have. We think that's what has been driving someone to try to steal or corrupt what we've developed."

"Can you provide a list of your potential competitors?"

"Of course. We've got competitors from Japan, Russia, India, China, Canada and the U.S. No surprise there, really. And those are just the ones we know about. I'll have my assistant provide you with a compiled list. For the record, we are the only nonprofit organization in the bunch."

"And the first to develop a vaccine," Slash murmured. "Interesting."

"Our scientists and staff are passionate about helping

people," Hayden explained. "I assure you, sometimes it makes all the difference."

"Is there any one competitor that sticks out to you for one reason or another?" I asked.

"Actually there's a couple. Star Pharma in India, and Acadia Solutions of Canada are the first two that leap to mind. But there are others."

"Why these two in particular?" I asked.

"Both Lilith and I know the CEOs personally. Let's just say we don't share the same set of moral values with either of them. Not that I'm not accusing them, mind you, but I wouldn't put it past them either."

I jotted the names down. It gave me a place to start. "Tim said you were informed the email system had been penetrated."

"Yes, it was quite a shock, but we've been careful not to overshare via emails. Regardless, we didn't waste any time bringing you on board."

"Tim made the right decision not to shut them out at this point," I said. "It will allow us to backtrack them."

"You can do that?" Hayden asked, his eyes widening.

"We can."

"Well, that's the best news I've heard today."

I asked several more questions and then wrapped things up. Slash took a few notes of his own, but did not ask any questions. I hoped that meant I'd asked all the right ones.

We stood and shook hands again. "Thanks again for your time," I said. "This gives us a good start at understanding the project."

"Anytime, and I sincerely mean that. Please don't hesitate to ask either Lilith or me any questions you might have while you're here," he said. "We're grateful to be

in your capable hands and are anxious to get both of you
to Brazil so we can get the trials underway. In fact, the
team is already in place except for you and one additional
microbiologist we are sending from ComQuest. We're
looking forward to having you all there next week."

"We'll have a handle on this before we go," I promised, hoping I was right. There was a lot at stake with this
job—millions of lives—and I didn't want to mess it up.

Slash and I headed back to the Server Room in silence. Before we went back inside, he stopped me in the
hallway with a hand on my arm. "What's your plan?"

My mind was racing in a million different directions.
I appreciated he asked because it gave me a minute to
get my head together before I went back to talk to Tim.
I considered, leaned back against the wall, and put my
options in order.

"It really comes down to one thing," I said. "Connectivity is critical. The best option is going dark or offline,
but that's not an option. That means it's up to us to ensure the safety, security and integrity of the data. That
being said, I also think it's important for us to determine
whether the hackers want to steal or corrupt the data."

"Who's to say one is mutually exclusive from the
other?"

"They aren't." I rolled my neck a couple of times to
release the tension. "But from what I've seen and heard
so far, my gut is telling me that this is a hack for information versus a destruction attack. That's the prize. Someone wants the procedure for that vaccine. Although, if
they aren't able to get it, I would certainly keep sabotage
and destruction on the table."

"Agreed."

"Good. So, first up for us is getting a tag on those

hackers. Who are they? How many groups are we talking about? Where are they from? Is it a country hack or private company or individual? Answers to any of these questions will help us get a handle on our adversaries and how best to defend against them."

He reached out, lightly trailing a finger from my cheek down to my jawline, his eyes warming. "Have I mentioned it really turns me on when you talk like that?"

"Jeez. Keep focused." Despite saying that, I looked up and down the hallway. When I confirmed it was empty, I leaned over to give him a quick kiss. "I'm glad you're here, Slash."

"I'm glad, too, although you don't need me. You've got excellent instincts that are getting better all the time."

His words meant a lot to me, especially coming from such a wizard behind the keyboard. "Instincts or not, I'm grateful for the assist. We've got a lot to sort out and not much time to do it."

"*Si*, we do." Slash stepped back from me. "Complex situation, a lot at stake, an accelerated timeline…that seems to be the story of our lives."

"No kidding," I said. "And you know what that means. We'd better get to work, and fast."

Chapter Thirteen

Lexi

We had the full list of competitors within the hour, so Slash and I got to work.

Hunting hackers was one of the best parts of my job. A puzzle wrapped in a mystery with a bit of a thriller edge. It was exhilarating. After about an hour of chasing, Slash and I decided to compare notes.

"What did you find?" I asked.

"It's looking like South Asia to me. Bangladesh, Pakistan, Nepal, India, Bhutan—that area. How about you?"

"I'm definitely ruling out Canada, U.S., Europe, and Russia. Doesn't feel like any of those to me. India seems the most likely candidate, although we have to keep China in the mix because they could be orchestrating this."

"Agree. If we cross-reference with the list Hayden just gave me, that narrows down the competitors to two— Changsha BioChain from China and the Indian pharmaceutical company Pharma Star. Pharma Star was one of the competitors Hayden mentioned."

"It was," I agreed. "Now, let's get a better feel for what damage they've done and/or attempted to do."

We changed tactics and did a thorough analysis of Vaccitex's system. I jotted down some notes and after another hour and a half, we'd completed a first-pass look.

"Okay, my take is they've had some success hacking, but they haven't penetrated the most current data involving the vaccine itself."

Slash tapped his screen. "Looks like penetration happened during the nightly backup. It's possible some data could be compromised and we just don't know."

"Yes, but the system in the rainforest appears to be untouched, so I think they're safe for the time being. I didn't find any evidence of a back door anywhere. How about you?"

"None." He scrolled through some data. "And there's no evidence of deep internal compromise. However, just like you mentioned, there's been low-level entrance in some areas. This means while they may not have access to the most important data, they might be aware of logistics, including the location of the final phase. They may also know of the discussion with the Brazilian government regarding approvals, timelines and final deployment."

"We've got to let Hayden, Lilith and Tim know. I've also discovered this." Slash moved his chair closer to me so he could see my screen better. "Some data fields in an older file were compromised, and some data altered."

"Altered?" He looked puzzled. "Why?"

"I'm leaning toward the theory that they want Vaccitex to fail. Screw up their research just enough to make things fall apart without being overly obvious about it."

"Again, I ask why?"

I shrugged. "I don't know. Maybe because they're close to developing their own cure?"

He mulled over my theory. "Which means huge money to whomever discovers the vaccine first and can execute successful trials."

"Exactly. Unless you're a small nonprofit organization not looking for profit, but to changing the world for the better."

We considered that for a moment and then turned back to our screens. Protecting Vaccitex had just become even more important.

Chapter Fourteen

Lexi

"Do you feel confident your team and Tim can handle the operation in New York while you're in Brazil?"

Slash asked the question while sitting on the corner of our bed as he took off his shoes. I stood next to him, unpacking my suitcase that lay open on the bed, dumping dirty clothes into the laundry basket. "Not a doubt in my mind." It was the truth. Tim was more than capable, and I trusted my staff. I'd personally trained them, and felt one hundred percent confident in their abilities.

Slash tossed his socks in the basket and leaned back on the bed, resting on his elbows. "It was a lot for them to digest in such a short time. However, I was impressed with how quickly they managed. You've trained them well."

Our trip to New York had passed in a blur. We'd spent long hours patching holes, setting traps, beefing up security and installing safeguards—basically laying the groundwork so my team could easily step into a protection role as soon as they arrived. We had only a twelve-hour crossover with my team, so I had to bring them up to speed quickly, efficiently and sometimes brutally.

They'd absorbed every task and challenge I'd thrown at them, which was why I was certain they could handle the job.

"Thanks, I appreciate that." I'd worked hard to nurture and encourage their talent, and was proud of it. The fact Slash acknowledged it meant a lot to me.

"Then on to the rainforest we go."

I threw the last dirty shirt into the basket. "So, what exactly do I have to pack for the rainforest?"

The last time I was in the jungle I hadn't exactly packed for it. Although I'd survived my time there—barely—I had no intention of traveling through the jungle unprepared like that ever again.

"You can wear your earrings, but be aware that as soon as we're in the rainforest, the GPS feature won't work. I'm working on a new prototype to change that, but it's not ready yet. You can take your watch. It's waterproof, right?"

"Yes, but I have no intention of swimming."

He laughed. "*Rain* forest, remember?"

"Good point." My cheeks heated. I needed to get seriously focused on travel. If I forgot something important, I'd be miserable. "What about my phone?"

"Take your cell for calls, texts and photos when we are in the towns of Manaus and Coari, but it will be useless in the rainforest, except for photos."

"Good to know," I said. "What else?"

"We have to be prepared for the heat and humidity, as well as an aggressive array of insects, animals, reptiles and a lot of rain," Slash replied. "That being said, we need to pack as light as possible as the chartered plane Vaccitex is flying us on will certainly have weight restrictions and will already be transporting equipment and supplies for the lab."

I put a hand on my hip. "That's too vague for me to handle. What *exactly* does that mean in terms of what I put in my suitcase?"

He grinned, reading both my anxiety and frustration accurately. "Don't worry, I've got us covered. I ordered some items online for us before we left for New York. Long-sleeve, lightweight, moisture-wicking shirts, and breathable, tightly knit fabrics for our pants. No thin materials or short sleeves. The mosquitoes and insects will be relentless, trust me."

"I do trust you, because I know you're right. It also reminds me how much I *didn't* enjoy my last jungle trek," I grumbled.

"That was not a trek, *cara*, it was survival, and it was brutal. This time will be much different. You might even enjoy yourself a little."

I sincerely hoped he was right. Finn, Basia and I had almost died in the jungle, so the thought of returning was causing me a lot of anxiety even though I *knew* it would be totally different. Slash sensed my nervousness and was doing his best to remind me that not only were we going to be prepared, he'd be going with me, which made everything much more doable this time around. It helped more than he knew.

"I also ordered special mosquito and insect spray," he added. "Just a heads-up, we won't be sleeping in the nude or in comfortable pajamas. We'll cover up fully at night, including socks, and sleep under special netting I purchased."

I knew he was right, but his practicality still wasn't

helping my mood. "You do remember it's hot in the rain-forest, right?"

He sat up, regarded me with amusement. "I remember. We're going to have to make a shopping run for hiking boots and extra socks this afternoon, but otherwise, we've got everything else we'll need, including sunscreen, wide-brimmed hats, and extra-large water bottles. I've already got notice that the boxes should be delivered in the next few hours."

He was very organized, my guy, and I had to give him points for that. So, I pushed my anxiety aside, sat next to him on the bed. "It's pretty handy having you around."

"Good to know." He put his arm around me, pulling me closer. "I just may use that to my advantage."

"You already do," I protested, resting my head against his shoulder. "You're such an overachiever."

He chuckled and then turned his head so his face rested against the crown of my head. "There's always room for improvement. Want to test that theory?"

"Right now?"

"Right now."

I lifted my head abruptly, bumping into his jaw. "Oops. Sorry. But what about the laundry and the packing?"

He winced, rubbing his chin. "What about it?"

I considered my options. If we managed our time well, which we usually did, we had time for a little distraction. Already I could feel the tight knot of anxiety in the pit of my stomach lessening. "Fine. Who am I to argue against improvement?"

He didn't answer because he'd already pulled me down on the bed and started kissing me. My anxiety disappeared as I wound my arms around his neck. As usual, he was right. The laundry and packing could wait.

We had far more important matters to tend to.

Lexi

Our flight didn't leave until late morning, so we had plenty of time to finish packing, eat and make it to the airport with time to spare. It felt weird to dress in long pants, long sleeves and hiking boots—for the plane. But it was both practical and logical, so I went with it. Hats, insect repellent and sunglasses were in our carry-on bags, along with our laptops and accompanying equipment.

The plan was to catch a flight to Miami from Dulles International airport, where we would change planes and then head for the city of Manaus, Brazil. From Manaus we'd take a chartered plane to the town of Coari that would also be transporting additional supplies and equipment for the lab. After reviewing the distance online and combining it with our flight data, I determined it would take us just shy of three hours from DC to Miami and then another five hours to Manaus. From there, it'd be another hour and a half on the chartered flight to Coari. After reaching Coari, we'd travel by jeep to the research site. Although I wasn't certain exactly how long that would take, I felt confident in calculating the entire travel time would take somewhere between ten and eleven hours.

Ugh. I hated flying.

I tried to temper my anxiety when we got to the airport about two hours before our flight and breezed through security. Slash suggested we get some coffee, so we grabbed a couple of cups and headed to the gate to wait. I'd just sat down on one of the hard plastic chairs and took my first sip of coffee when I spotted Gwen walking toward the gate carrying a large, orange duffel over her shoulder. Her eyes widened when she spotted us.

"Lexi? Slash? What are you guys doing here?"

"We're going to Brazil," I said. "What about you?"

"The same place. Didn't Elvis tell you I was selected as the microbiologist from ComQuest?"

"What?" I looked at her in total surprise. While Gwen was wicked smart, how in the world had she been chosen over the other senior scientists? "I haven't talked to Elvis for several days. I had no idea you were the ComQuest microbiologist that had been selected. Wow, Gwen, that's great. Congratulations."

"Thanks." She dropped the heavy duffel at her feet with a sigh of relief. Since the gate area was crowded, Slash stood, insisting she sit in his seat. After a moment, she agreed and perched on the edge of the chair, her knees turned toward me. "I've been working on this project for several months. It's a long story how I was selected to go to the rainforest, but I can fill you in on the flight. You guys are going down there, too?"

"Yep." I balanced the coffee cup on my knee, steadying it with one hand. "They wanted hands-on information security. Slash is technically on vacation so he offered to go with me and work *pro bono*."

"That's so cool. I'd heard X-Corp, and specifically you, had got the job, but I didn't know you'd actually be traveling to the field lab. Why do they need you there?"

"They're concerned with the integrity of the data that has to be transmitted from the lab. They want a hands-on person there to ensure protection at every level. I've got a team set up in New York, but here we are heading into the rainforest."

"Fantastic." She beamed. "Wow. I'm so glad to have you both coming along. It will definitely make Elvis feel better." She cheerfully tucked her red hair behind her ears. "So, off we go on another adventure together."

This wasn't the first time Slash and I had flown abroad with Gwen. The last time the three of us had been on a plane together, we'd been headed toward Egypt with Elvis, trying to track down his estranged father. I hoped this trip would be a lot less stressful than that one had been.

"This flight should go smoothly," Gwen said, as if reading my mind. "As should the work. It's going to be great having you both there, experiencing the rainforest with me. I'm so excited to be doing such important work."

I felt the same about the work, but I wasn't as confident about the flight as she was—and I had personal past experience to prove just how wrong one could go. But I had to believe this time luck would be on my side with Slash around.

As it turned out, I was right. Sort of.

Chapter Fifteen

Lexi

The flights from DC to Miami and then to the Manaus airport were largely uneventful, and I was deeply grateful for that. I snoozed, read an online coding magazine, and played several hands of gin rummy and poker with Slash. At some point, Gwen was able to switch places with an amenable passenger in our row so she could chat with us. She told us how she got the job from Vaccitex—stopping a protester from committing arson—and what she was told in regards to the work she'd be doing at the field lab. I was especially interested to know about her work as a microbiologist on the project, so she helpfully provided details, which was fascinating even though I knew little about the science behind vaccine development. I appreciated her smarts even more when she explained her contribution using yeast—a special technique she'd been developing and applying to microchips for some time at ComQuest.

It hadn't always been a bed of roses between Gwen and me. She'd helped her younger sister, Angel, form a club of people inspired by my career trajectory in the IT field. Our first meeting had been an awkward exchange of telling me about a fan club she'd formed for me called the Lexicons and me looking at her in horror. Then she'd made a romantic connection with Elvis Zimmerman, one of my best friends. At first, I'd been skeptical of their relationship, especially because Elvis was involved with someone else at the time. But the more I got to know Gwen and saw her and Elvis together, the more I realized what a good match they made. She was highly intelligent, loyal, and had a bubbly and outgoing personality—and while she was sometimes annoying, she'd brought Elvis out of his shell in a big way. I guessed that's what love was all about—finding that someone who could take you out of your comfort zone and help you grow and stretch as a person, while making you feel safe and comfortable.

When the captain alerted us we'd be landing in Manaus shortly, I looked out the window so I could view the landscape below. The lush expanse of the rainforest rushed past below us, broken only by low-lying areas of brush, river ways, and occasional villages. Manaus apparently was in a fairly remote location, because I didn't see many roads or railways leading into the city.

"Look at that gorgeous scenery," Gwen said in a hushed voice. "Did you know the rainforest hosts the largest concentration of uncontacted indigenous peoples in the world?"

I hadn't known. But I'd already made contact with previously uncontacted tribes while in Papua New Guinea. If it hadn't been for Sari—the courageous indigenous woman who had helped me—Finn, Basia and I would have died in the jungle. "That's fascinating, Gwen."

"I know." Gwen leaned forward in her chair. "Unfortunately, those indigenous populations also have scary health statistics. For example, most of the indigenous tribes have high incidences of viral hepatitis, including A, B, C, and D, as well as malaria, tuberculosis, and other contagious diseases. We didn't know until recently how bad the situation was with the uncontacted tribes due to their fierce desire to remain isolated. As a result, the Brazilian government excluded those tribes from any form of concentrated public health policy."

Hayden and Lilith hadn't mentioned that, but I supposed it made sense. "That's sad, but if that's what the uncontacted tribes want, why would the government force medicine upon them with the vaccine?"

"Because that's not what they want anymore," Gwen explained. "Their people are dying, Lexi. Malaria has wiped out two thirds of their infants and children, and they can't stop it. Additional diseases are razing their populations despite their efforts to remain uncontacted. So, they asked for help...and here we are. Brazil has made a national commitment to help as part of a larger effort to help preserve the tribes' culture and existence. The malaria vaccine is a first step toward preserving their way of life. If it works, the next step is Africa, then Asia, and then anywhere else that malaria remains a problem. So many millions of lives could be saved."

"The world is becoming more interconnected all the time," Slash murmured. "Walls, physical barriers, blockades are no longer effective. Isolation is nearly impossible. We are becoming more connected as a human species every day."

"It means we have to take care of each other," Gwen answered. "It's that simple."

I absorbed their words and their implication. It was a lot to think about, and I felt increasing pressure to make sure Vaccitex got the support it needed to ensure the vaccine would be distributed at cost to all people who needed it—especially to those who couldn't afford it. I had a small part to play, but I certainly didn't want to be the hole that caused the dam to break.

Houses, roads and more signs of civilization appeared beneath the aircraft, indicating we were entering the city limits of Manaus. I held my breath as we landed, my hands clutching the hand rests. Slash kept a hand lightly on my knee, just heavy enough to remind me he was there, without heightening my anxiety or drawing attention to the fact that I was petrified and having flashbacks of a plane crash in the jungle.

When the wheels finally touched the runway and the plane began to slow, I exhaled a huge sigh of relief. We were on the ground safe and sound and in one piece. I refrained from clapping and instead exchanged a glance with Slash, who understood my relief and patted me on the knee.

After we exited the aircraft, Slash, Gwen and I stood in line to go through customs. While we were waiting our turn, a tall man with a thick mustache and dark hair walked along the line, scanning faces. When his gaze fell on me, he quickened his step and approached us.

"Good evening," he said to me. "Are you Lexi Carmichael?"

"I am."

"It's nice to make your acquaintance. I am Joao Diaz, the Assistant Protocol Minister for Brazil. On behalf of our government, we welcome you to our country. I presume you're Miss Sinclair and Mr. Fortuna."

Slash and Gwen nodded, and we all shook hands. "I was instructed to meet you and smooth the way through customs," Mr. Diaz explained. "I understand one of you has the satellite phones."

"I do," Gwen said patting the orange duffel that had been thrown over her shoulder. "They're in here."

I looked in surprise at Gwen. "Why do we need satellite phones?"

"Apparently, they're required at the research site, as there's almost no cell phone coverage outside of Coari," she explained. "I was instructed to carry them in for the team. They're the only way to communicate, as well as use GPS, when we're at the lab and in the field."

I considered that interesting piece of information. Protecting sensitive data in such a primitive setting was going to be a real challenge for Slash and me.

"I have the forms from the Brazilian government to permit you to bring them into the country for research purposes," Joao said, pulling out some folded papers from beneath his jacket. "Come with me, please. I'll assist you as you go through customs."

With that, he maneuvered us to one side, where we went through a special line and were expedited through the customs procedure. Once we were cleared, Joao ushered us down a hallway and back out onto the tarmac to another awaiting plane, a small one with propellers. To say it'd seen better days would be an overstatement. It looked rickety and badly needed a paint job. And that was on the outside. I didn't even want to think of the condition on the inside.

I leaned against my suitcase and stood staring at the plane in shock, not quite believing he actually wanted us to fly in it. I shot a glance at Slash, but his face was expressionless.

It was Gwen who finally spoke. "Are you sure *this* is

the plane to Coari?" Her voice squeaked and her eyes looked positively terrified, probably a reflection of mine. I wasn't even able to speak yet.

"I'm sure." Joao must have noticed the looks on our faces because he sought to reassure us. "I know it looks rather small, but it's a quite dependable plane. It flies back and forth between Manaus and Coari every other day and has never had an incident…that I'm aware of."

That wasn't the most enthusiastic of endorsements. I gulped and looked at Slash again. He still hadn't said anything.

"Are you sure it's safe?" I managed to ask. "I think it's a good time to mention I get air, car, boat and train sick when things get bumpy."

"I'm certain it's perfectly safe, Miss Carmichael," Joao replied.

Easy for him to say. *He* wasn't going to fly in it.

"It's an Embraer," Slash said quietly.

I turned to him. "Excuse me?"

"It's an Embraer, a Brazilian-produced version of the Piper Cherokee," he replied. "It seats six. The wheels don't retract and the aircraft is limited to about twelve thousand feet in altitude because the cabin isn't pressurized."

"That's absolutely correct," Joao said to Slash. "You certainly know your airplanes, sir."

Slash dipped his head, but said nothing further. I wasn't sure if the Embraer was a good or bad plane because Slash didn't offer any further clarification, probably not to terrify us anymore.

"Are you sure there aren't any other options for getting us to Coari?" I gave myself points for asking the question on everyone's mind.

Joao nodded. "Of course. There are three options for traveling from Manaus to Coari. The easiest and most convenient is this airplane. Or you could take a boat up the Amazon. That trip would take about eighteen hours as the river is running high and fast right now, and there are a couple of small rapids that the boat would have to negotiate carefully. That's if I could manage to secure a large enough boat and a guide willing to take you on such short notice."

My stomach squeezed uncomfortably. A day on a boat on a jungle river with rapids sounded as bad, if not worse, than a plane ride.

"You could also take an SUV, but the trip is almost six hours and two hundred and twenty-five miles," Joao continued. "Unfortunately, there's only a paved road for about two thirds of the distance."

I considered that a viable alternative until Gwen spoke.

"I don't think we want to do that, Lexi. I heard that Vaccitex's research director took the road trip and was bounced around inside the jeep so badly, she had a headache for days. She also bit her tongue and it hurt like crazy for days afterward."

Exasperated, I threw up my hands. "That's it? There are no other options?"

A smile touched Slash's lips. "Hoping for a camel, perhaps?"

Gah! Did he have to remind of the time I almost killed myself riding a runaway camel? It hadn't been pretty—a geek girl trying to tame an overexcited animal. It didn't go well. I glared at him and then let out a sigh. "Fine. The plane it is."

As we walked toward the plane stairs, the pilot came

out at the top. He shouted something in Portuguese that Joao translated for us.

"Your pilot welcomes you and wants you to know he's flown this flight nearly every day for the past ten years with almost no problems, so don't be worried."

I didn't like the "almost" part, but seeing as how it wouldn't help matters if I freaked out, I kept my reservations to myself. Gwen boldly climbed the stairs first. I followed her and Slash came behind me. The plane was small with three rows of two seats and a seat next to the pilot. Gwen chose a seat in the front row, while I headed to the back of the plane. Slash strapped into the seat next to me. While we were settling in, Joao and the pilot stored our luggage and carry-ons.

Finally, Joao bid us farewell. After he deplaned, the pilot did a quick walk around and check of the airplane. Apparently satisfied with how everything looked, he pulled up the stairs and climbed into the cockpit.

My cell suddenly rang, so I fumbled in my purse to pull it out. "Hello?"

"Hi, Lexi, it's Mom, do you have a minute?"

"Mom? Ah, no, not really. I'm on an airplane that's supposed to take off momentarily."

"I just have a quick question. Do you have a preference regarding live band or a DJ at the reception?"

I glanced at Slash, who knew I was talking to my mom, but couldn't hear the conversation. He raised an eyebrow at what was likely the panic on my face. "Uh, I don't think so. Are we dancing at the reception?"

"Of course. Do you plan to have a father-daughter dance?"

The engine and propellers roared to life with just a few sputters. "Mom, I have to go," I said, raising my voice over the noise. "We're about to take off. Don't forget, I won't be able to get texts or calls once we are in the rainforest, so if it's an emergency, email me. Otherwise, I'll call when I get back, okay?" I hung up and stuck the cell in my purse with a sigh.

"What was that all about?" Slash asked.

"Don't ask," I said and he wisely didn't press further.

While the engine was warming up, a car suddenly zoomed up alongside the aircraft and a woman hopped out carrying something. I craned my neck to see what she was holding, but I didn't have a clear view. She ran over to the pilot's window and started gesturing and shouting. The pilot opened his window and the two of them hollered at each other over the noise of the engine.

Finally our pilot opened the plane door, and lowered the steps, taking whatever she was carrying. He returned to the plane and put it on the floor in the second row behind Gwen. For the first time I was able to see what she'd been carrying. It was a cage containing three chickens.

The pilot yelled something at Gwen, Slash and I, but I had no idea what he'd said.

"Did you understand any of that?" I shouted over the engines at Slash. He spoke fluent Italian, Spanish, French and German, so I figured out of the three of us, he had the best chance of knowing what was going on.

Slash shrugged. "I think he said he's doing this as a favor to his wife, who's giving the chickens as a present to her cousin or friend who lives in Coari. But don't quote me on that."

The pilot gestured for us to make sure our seat belts were fastened—they already were—before he gave us a thumbs-up. I guess that was the only in-flight safety training we were going to get.

I squeezed my eyes shut for the entire takeoff. I was hyperventilating a bit, but Slash's hand in mine anchored me to what little sanity I still had, if only by a thread.

The flight started normally as we rose above the jungle. After several moments, I dared to open my eyes. The engine noise was so loud it nearly deafened me. As Slash had mentioned, we weren't flying too high, as the plane wasn't pressurized. Once we moved away from Manaus, all I could see below us was green in every direction. Despite my abject terror, I had to admit it was breathtaking. I found it interesting that the Amazon River looked black from above. When I asked Slash about it, he told me it was from all the silt being washed downstream.

As we flew, I relaxed a little bit. I discovered the pilot was navigating by following the main branch of the Amazon River upstream to Coari. When we came to a large divide in the river, he veered left. I saw dark clouds on the horizon, probably rain, but so far, the flight had been fairly smooth, so I didn't panic.

Unfortunately, as we got closer to the dark clouds, the ride started to get a little bumpier. Thunder boomed, followed by a jagged rip of lightning flashing off to my right.

"Holy crap." I started breathing faster. "Maybe we should turn back. We could get hit by lightning."

"There's a small statistical chance of that," Slash said soothingly, holding my hand. "We have to trust that he's an experienced pilot, *cara*. Certainly rainstorms are the norm in the Amazon."

Despite the calmness of his voice, he didn't look as confident as he sounded. I gripped his hand as we started to descend slightly. Once in the clouds, it was difficult to see the river. I sincerely hoped the pilot relied on an instrumental GPS and not simply a visual charting of the river as his main source of navigation. The plane started bouncing around quite a bit, leaving my stomach at least five hundred feet above.

"I'm going to add terrifying airplane rides to my little black cloud spreadsheet," I said as my shoulder slammed against the side of the plane.

"I thought you already had that on the spreadsheet."

"No, I have plane *crash*." The plane was vibrating so hard, I could feel my tonsils shaking. "That one would also qualify as a terrifying plane ride, of course, so now that I think about it, I'll have two things to add to the spreadsheet, dependent on whether or not I survive this incident."

"You will," he said, bracing his legs against the seat in front of him. "Positive thinking and all."

"I appreciate you're focusing on a positive outcome when we may be moments from plummeting out of the sky. But in regards to the spreadsheet, do you think I should add it in a row or a column? If there are going to be a lot of different locales, such as jungles, mountains or oceans, maybe they would fit better in a row. But since this incident, and the previous one, involves jungles only, maybe it would be best to limit the data to a single column."

"Make it a row."

I stared at him. "You do realize that implies I'm going to be involved in more incidents involving scary plane rides."

"*Si*, I do. It also means you'll survive this one since you'll be alive to take the other ones. Positive thinking, remember?"

"Good point."

We hit another patch of turbulence, this one worse than the one before. The plane violently pitched up, then nosed down. This negative G movement caused everything in the airplane to float momentarily, defying gravity. In a slow-motion moment, I realized I was floating, held down only by my seat belt. In front of me, Gwen's hair flew straight up over her head, as if she were hanging upside down. The chicken cage floated directly in front of me.

With a violent slap, our downward movement was halted by another gust of air. We were all slammed back into our seats. The chicken cage bounced off some seats and hit the floor hard. The door popped open.

Three frightened chickens lunged out of the cage and screeched wildly, clearly looking for a safe haven.

Chapter Sixteen

Lexi

I was so terrified, I couldn't breathe. Floating chicken feathers distorted my view and I swiped at them, trying to fill my lungs with air. At last the plane leveled, and I could breathe again.

Our pilot shouted something at us, either telling us to say our prayers before our imminent death or instructing us to round up the chickens. I didn't know how either one would be possible. Despite the plane leveling off, we were all bouncing in our seats like freaking bobble-heads, watching as three scared chickens squawked in terror and flew around, shedding their feathers.

To my surprise, Gwen was the first to act. She un-buckled her seat belt and surged into the aisle, hold-ing on to the seats as the plane pitched back and forth. "We've got to get them," she shouted as if we hadn't already realized that. "Pick them up by pinning their wings from above and lifting them up. That way you won't hurt them."

I had to process two important things at once. First, how did Gwen know how to pick up chickens? Secondly, did she *really* think I was going to unbuckle my seat belt during severe turbulence to dash about a plane trying to catch a live chicken?

No. Freaking. Chance.

Everyone who knows me understands that animals and I do not mix. It's not that I don't like them, but they're unpredictable, which makes me anxious. Somehow, they sense my anxiety and try to dominate me. It's a statistical fact that something unfortunate *always* seems to happen when we're together. Therefore, it was logical to assume it would not be a sensible step for me to try to capture the chickens, especially since they likely did not want to be put back into the cage. Not that I begrudged them that. But having me involved in any way in this situation was *not* a good plan for anyone, especially the chickens.

Unfortunately, one of the fowl took the opportunity to fly into the cockpit just as we were hit by another batch of turbulence. The pilot, momentarily distracted, sent the plane descending again. I screamed, causing the chickens, and most likely Slash (since he was sitting closest to me) further trauma.

Despite the scary spiral, Gwen somehow managed to shoo the chicken from the cockpit and remain on her feet, allowing the pilot to recover again. The plane leveled off, leaving whatever was left of my stomach another several hundred feet above us.

In the meantime, Slash had unbuckled his seat belt in an attempt to help Gwen. He was larger than Gwen in a more confined space, so that hampered him. He lunged at a chicken, but his movement was stymied by the small aisle. The fowl eluded his efforts and flew directly toward me. I shrieked and held up my hands, mostly to protect my face. It landed on my arm, its claws becoming tangled in my sweater. It screeched and flapped its wings, but was effectively secured to my body.

"Help!" I shouted. "It's got me!"

"Great job, Lexi!" Gwen shouted back. "Two more to go."

"No, no, no!" Clearly she didn't understand what was going on. "You need to get it off me. *NOW!*"

No one paid any attention to me. Either they couldn't hear me over the squawking, shouting and whine of the engine, or they deliberately chose to ignore me. That left me alone with the chicken, locked in a fierce battle of wills. My goal was to get it OFF me.

While I struggled with the chicken, Slash and Gwen lurched around the plane like two drunks. The birds were somehow deftly eluding capture, screeching, pecking and filling the cabin with even more feathers and terrified shrieks. Another chicken flew toward the cockpit, but Gwen managed to keep it from entering.

"Get that one," she shouted as it veered off and headed toward Slash.

He darted out a hand and somehow caught the bird by its feet, swinging it upside down. Amazingly, just as Gwen had said it would, the bird hung there and stopped squawking. I was so surprised, I momentarily gave up the struggle with my chicken and stared in amazement.

That left only one chicken. Gwen jumped toward it just as the rear of the plane dropped a bit, propelling Gwen and the chicken directly toward me.

"*Aaaagh!*" I shouted as they both landed against me with a thump. I now had two chickens and a woman pinned to my chest.

Holy crap. I was the bottom slice of bread in a chicken sandwich.

"Sorry, Lexi," Gwen said in a muffled voice against my shoulder.

The chickens, dazed, but still alive, started squirming and squawking. I went into full panic mode until Gwen rose to her feet, triumphantly holding her chicken upside down by the legs. A moment later, Slash managed to remove the chicken stuck to my arm.

"We did it!" Gwen gave a whoop and then planted a kiss on Slash's cheek and then mine. I pulled a chicken feather out of my mouth, gagged, and tried not to empty the contents of my stomach on the floor.

One by one, Gwen and Slash managed to get the chickens back into the cage and close the door. The pilot shouted at us over his shoulder—maybe a thanks—as Slash wired the cage door closed with a twist tie he took from a piece of electronic gear he had in his carry-on bag.

Finally they stumbled back to their seats. I didn't move an iota, staring straight ahead, my sweater ripped, my hair and pants covered in chicken feathers. I tried to think positively like Slash had suggested earlier. One good thing, I'd been so thoroughly traumatized by my close-up with the chickens, I'd totally forgotten the plane could crash any minute.

Slash buckled his seat belt, looked over at me. "You okay, *cara*?"

"Do I look okay?"

He leaned over and plucked a feather from my hair. "You did a good job catching the first chicken considering you don't like animals much."

"I didn't catch anything!" I protested. "It flew at me like a bat out of hell and latched on to my sweater."

He had the nerve to crack a smile. "You do attract

them. It must be that soft heart of yours." He looked over my shoulder and pointed out the window. "Look. We've got blue skies again. I think we're past the worst of the storm."

I followed his gaze and saw he was correct. Now that the Great Chicken Recapture had passed, I realized we'd descended quite low and must be near our destination. Sure enough, signs of a town soon appeared. I could even see the runway in the distance. By runway, I meant a tiny strip of road in the middle of a forest.

The landing was bumpier than I liked, but at least we hadn't crashed, which was a miracle in itself. When the plane finally stopped and the door opened, the pilot saluted us cheerfully, as if nothing had happened. He took the chickens and disappeared down the stairs, and started walking down the runway toward a small building in the distance.

"Where's he going?" I asked.

"His job is done," Slash said, shrugging. "We're here in one piece after all."

"Barely," I said in a huff.

Somehow, I managed to unbuckle my seat belt, get my carry-on and wobble off the plane. Once I was safely on the ground, I sank to my knees and kissed the runway— literally pressing my lips against the road. I sat there for another minute, letting my stomach settle and hoping no other plane wanted to land soon. I was still shaky, but so grateful we'd made it in one piece, I could live with the discomfort. In the meantime, Slash had collected the rest of our luggage and the equipment we'd carted on Vaccitex's behalf and set it on the runway next to the plane.

We hadn't been there for much more than ten minutes when I heard the rattle of an engine in the distance. A guy in an old faded red pickup truck drove toward us, honking and waving a hand out the window.

"That must be our ride," Slash said, regarding the truck with arms crossed against his chest, dark sunglasses hiding his eyes.

The guy in the truck pulled up in front of Slash, cut the engine and hopped out. "Are you the scientists from Vaccitex?" he asked.

"We are." Gwen stepped forward to stand next to Slash. "And you are?"

The man stuck out his hand. "Salvador Reis, at your service. I'm the resident guide. You're right on time. Welcome to Coari." His dark hair was plastered to his head from the humidity and despite the heat, he wore scuffed boots and a long-sleeve shirt. He had a neatly trimmed mustache and a wide smile.

Slash and Gwen introduced themselves first and he shook their hands. He waited for me to approach and I did, dragging my carry-on behind me.

"I'm Lexi Carmichael from X-Corp."

"Lexi, yes. I've heard all about you…about all of you. Come, let's load your luggage and equipment into the truck and I'll get you to the research station."

It took us about fifteen minutes to load everything. I worried that the old truck wouldn't make it with the weight of four adults, our luggage and the boxes of equipment, but somehow the truck moved along. Since we were smaller than Slash, Gwen and I wedged into tiny jumper seats behind the driver and passenger seats. At five feet eleven, it was an uncomfortable position for me. At least my height permitted me to look out the window. Gwen, on the other hand, was shoehorned into the seat and trapped on either side by my long legs. Every minute of this trip would be too many.

Salvador sniffed the air. "Why do you guys smell like chickens?"

Slash glanced at me over his shoulder, his lips twitching. "It's a long story. We had a close encounter with a few on the plane. Luckily, all ended well."

As we tooled along, Slash made light conversation with Salvador, whose English was pretty good. We learned he was an official guide for this region of the country and was being paid by the Brazilian government to assist Vaccitex, leading them to the villages in remote areas. I had a lot of questions, but Salvador wouldn't have been able to hear me over the roar of the engine. Besides, I had to clench my teeth to keep them from knocking together as we hit every bump in Brazil. So, onward we went.

To say the road was bumpy would be an understatement.

To call the road a road was an understatement.

There were long stretches of time where the road abruptly ended and we continued forward over grass and fields. The humidity was torture—I was sweating, rivulets dripping down my temples and neck and sliding down my back. There was no air conditioning in the car, just the open windows. I tried, mostly unsuccessfully, to angle my head to get a bit of the breeze.

It took us about an hour to reach the research station. The station was protected with barbed wire and armed guards standing in front of a handmade wooden barrier. Inside were roughhewn structures and one modern-looking white building. Antennas and communication devices sat atop the white structure. A large bonfire was roaring on one side of the camp and was being tended to by a couple of people.

"We are currently located at a central location of the rainforest, near to Coari, but also a good landing site for us to travel to the various villages," Salvador announced. "Welcome to Vaccitex's scientific research center."

Chapter Seventeen

Lexi

The barrier was pulled aside and our truck drove inside and parked. We hopped out and started to help pull out the boxes and supplies as well as our suitcases. A bunch of people dressed in camouflage outfits and boots came to help us, chattering in Portuguese.

"Soldiers?" I whispered to Slash.

"Probably," he answered. "I suspect they're on loan from the government. This area is rampant with pirates and thieves, thus the barbed wire and guards out front and inside. The team needs them for protection here and in order to safely traverse to the villages."

"Well, that doesn't make me nervous at all," I said.

He dipped his head at one of the soldiers as he passed by. "Just glancing at the firepower on display, I don't think we'll have too much to worry about."

"I hope you're right."

Gwen was looking around excitedly. She'd caught the attention of several of the guards as she stood out with her bright red hair, blue eyes and glowing skin, but was oblivious to it. We collected our luggage and Salvador led the three of us toward a couple of huts.

"The lab is the white building. The dining area is next to the lab. To the right is the women's barracks, and the men's is directly across to the left."

My eyes met Slash's and he shrugged. Guess that meant that we wouldn't be sleeping in the same place. I tried not to be too disappointed. Gwen had headed toward the women's barracks, dragging her suitcase, so I reluctantly followed.

The sleeping area was more than I expected. While simple, it was sufficient. There was one large room with several bunk beds pushed against the wall and draped with malaria netting. A couple of open wooden shelves held assorted clothes, shoes and toiletries.

Electric lanterns hung from the ceiling and a small table with four chairs was positioned in the middle of the room. No rugs, nothing on the walls—including windows—and no bathroom. It wouldn't qualify as the Hilton, but it would do.

Even though no one was in the barracks, several of the bunk beds were already taken, so Gwen and I chose empty ones. She took the top bunk, which was good because I was afraid of heights. I pulled aside the mosquito netting and put my suitcase on the bottom bunk. It already had sheets, a pillow and a blanket.

"Let's go look around," I suggested. "We can unpack later."

"I'm good with that. I just want to put on bug spray first." She unlocked her suitcase and rummaged around. She withdrew a can triumphantly. "Found it. Want some?"

It was a good idea as I had no intention of getting eaten alive. "Sure. Hit me up."

I held my breath as she sprayed me and then herself

before capping the can. When I finally deemed it safe to breathe, I almost gagged on the scent. On the upside, it dried quickly despite the oppressive humidity. So, now I smelled like chickens and bug spray. I was sure everyone would be so happy to meet me.

Before we left, Gwen grabbed the satellite phones. They looked more like walkie-talkies than phones and had cords so you could wear them around your neck. I wanted to examine them, but she dashed out the door before I could ask. Slash was patiently waiting for us, but Salvador was nowhere to be seen.

Slash crinkled his nose when I got close. "Bug spray?"

"It was Gwen's idea." I waved my arms around to hopefully air out the smell a bit. "How are your accommodations?"

"Probably the same as yours." He pulled a small bottle out of a cargo pocket on his pants and sprayed himself with what I assumed was insect repellent. His spray didn't have the same strong scent as Gwen's, and I wished I had waited to put on his instead. On the upside, if I were a mosquito, I wouldn't come anywhere near me. Unfortunately, no one else would either.

"Salvador said to head toward the main lab when we're ready." Slash pointed at another structure, white and modern looking. "Most of the crew is in there now."

"Can we visit the bathroom first?" I asked.

"Good thinking, Lexi," Gwen said. "I wouldn't mind stopping there either."

Slash pointed to the left of the lab. "Over there. I'll hold the phones for you."

There were two outhouses, one for women, the other for men. Surprisingly, it wasn't a typically disgusting outhouse. There were three stalls, a sink, and two simple, built-in showers in a separate part of the structure. When we were done, we headed over to the lab, running into an armed guard who stood protecting it. Without a word, he stepped aside to let us enter, even though we hadn't asked him. Guess he'd been told we were coming.

"They're taking security very seriously," Gwen whispered as we entered.

"Good," Slash said.

The second we walked in, I was surprised at how sophisticated the lab appeared to be. Long rectangular tables held computers and scientific equipment, refrigerators, and small burners with test tubes. I could hear the hum of electricity and generators. A few scientists were working at a table, dressed in lab coats and safety goggles. We stayed where we were so as not to contaminate anything.

I whistled under my breath as I scanned the setup. "Wow. Impressive."

I spotted Salvador, who was talking to a pretty, middle age, dark-haired woman dressed in a white lab coat over jeans and hiking boots. Safety goggles hung around her neck, her hair pulled back into a bun at the back of her neck. Salvador said something to her and she came right over to meet us.

She greeted me first, holding out her hand and shaking mine warmly. "You must be Lexi Carmichael. It's so nice to meet you. I'm Natelli Sherwood, Vaccitex's lead field scientist. I'm glad you're here."

"I'm glad, too."

She let go of my hand and greeted Gwen next, saying something complimentary about her research. Finally, she greeted Slash. Was it just me or did she stare a bit longer at him than I thought was necessary? At some point, she must have realized she'd been looking at him for too long, because her cheeks flushed and she cleared her throat. Slash didn't seem to notice, or if he did, he was too polite to say anything.

"Anyway, we're grateful you made it safely. Welcome to our humble abode."

I looked around. "Looks far from humble to me. This setup is pretty impressive."

Her face lit up. "It's impressive, isn't it? The building itself is a mobile lab structure. It self-deploys at the touch of a button. It requires no manual labor, machinery or foundation. It needs just a battery-powered drill and the structure sets itself up in about ten minutes."

"Seriously?" Gwen said. "That's amazing."

Slash inspected the wall nearest to us. I could practically see the wheels turning in his head. As a shrewd businessman and innovator, he was definitely intrigued.

"How does it come down?" he asked.

"It folds back in on itself, the same way we transport it," she replied. "When it opens up, it expands to three times its size. The entire lab can be transported on the bed of a truck. It's revolutionary."

"It is," Slash said, patting the wall in admiration. "I look forward to learning more about it."

"I'll be happy to fill you in. It's really good to have you both here. I'm thankful you'll be able to help us protect our data. We need to ensure that it remains safe, encrypted and completely unhackable."

"Unfortunately, anything online can be hacked," I said. "But don't worry, we'll keep it safe."

"Thank you, Lexi. I'm counting on you." She turned to include Slash in the comment, her smile widening. "On *both* of you."

I looked away awkwardly before she put a hand on Gwen's shoulder. "I have to admit I was really intrigued by your contribution to the vaccine research, Gwen. I would have never thought to incorporate yeast."

"Well, I was using a similar technique in the design of ComQuest's microchips, so it wasn't that great of a leap," she replied. "I can't take all the credit. Mr. Peterson has been an excellent mentor and he gave me the courage to pursue that line of thinking. He's the one that should be here."

"Nonsense, you earned your spot on the team. However, I was distressed to hear of his illness and wish him a speedy recovery."

"We all do. He's a good man."

"Yes, he is. In the meantime, I'm glad you're here. Did you know I started out as a microbiologist as well?"

Gwen brightened. "You did? Where did you study?"

"Johns Hopkins University for both my undergraduate and doctorate degrees, with one year spent at Sapienza University in Rome, studying under famed Italian microbiologist, Francesco Arcuri."

Well, wasn't that an unusual coincidence? "Wait. You studied in Rome?" I asked.

"I did."

"*Parli italiano?*" Slash interjected.

"*Un po. Per lo più colloquiale.*"

"Um, well, that's…interesting," I said, looking between Slash and Natelli. "Did you know Slash is Italian-American and he studied at Sapienza University, too?"

"You studied at Sapienza?" Natelli's eyes widened. "Fascinating."

"*Si*, fascinating, indeed," Slash agreed.

"Well, I'm sure I was there a long time before you."

She laughed. "Still, we'll have to talk more about it later. Now, come and let me show you around the rest of the lab."

We followed Natelli as she described the array of equipment in the lab, rows of rechargeable batteries, generators, ice packs, vials, syringes and high-tech coolers, as well as solar-powered refrigerators and freezers. Seriously cool.

I rested one of my hands on top of the coolers. "Do you use these to take the vaccines to the villages?"

"We do." Natelli reached over and flipped open the top of the cooler. Inside were special vial holders and spots for ice packs. "We require a reliable system to keep the vaccines cold during the trek. These coolers contain temperature-sensitive vial monitors that will ensure the integrity of the vaccines. It's pretty high-tech stuff."

"Looks like it." We wandered around some more until I stopped when I saw a drone on one of the tables.

"Why do you have a drone in the lab?" I asked, inspecting, but not touching it.

"Research," Natelli replied. "We will likely use drones to drop vaccines for future use. We'll have to train some of the natives on how to inject or administer the vaccine. That way, the indigenous people aren't forced to interact with us more than necessary. We consider it our duty and responsibility to interfere as little as possible with the culture and way of life of these populations. You know, kind of like *Star Trek*'s prime directive—we shouldn't interfere or use our technology and knowledge to impose our own values or ideals on them."

"That's really admirable," I said. "Not to mention the coolness points you just racked up for using a *Star Trek* reference in a real-life scientific situation."

She laughed. "I'm a nerd. Scientist, remember?"

Yep, she definitely got points for that. Anyone who knew Star Trek intimately *and* could apply it to everyday life deserved my respect.

Natelli headed toward the corner of the lab, motioning at us to follow. "Come on, I'll show you the computer setup. But I warn you, you only have a short time to inspect it. We have to head to dinner shortly. You can come back after that if you have any energy after your long day of travel."

Natelli led us to the small computer setup they had running in the corner of the room. It was simple, with just a few laptops, one desktop and a mobile printer. Tim had already briefed us on the setup, so none of it was a surprise. Just the same, Slash and I had brought additional equipment and software to beef things up.

"Did you set this up?" I asked.

"I did, but it's totally basic and Tim had to walk me through it remotely. Trust me when I say I feel one hundred percent better turning this operation over to you. Computers, other than for word processing, research and calculating, are not my thing."

"You did a good job. We're looking forward to helping," I said. "And we brought a lot better equipment to work with."

After a minute, she left Slash and me alone and went off to speak with Gwen. Slash and I quickly familiarized ourselves with the arrangement, immediately seeing things we needed to do. The technology that had been sent by Vaccitex was sitting in boxes near the workstation. We decided to set up the company equipment first before we brought in our own stuff, which was now in our respective sleeping quarters, so while I focused on upgrading the software and operating system, Slash began unpacking the new company hardware and networking everything together.

Natelli asked me to set up a satellite-supported network, piggybacking on a Brazilian government satellite to better establish the Internet and network access. We were given the appropriate passwords and sites to access the needed information to get started. While I worked on that, everyone else began to pitch in and help label the vaccine samples and print out and stack the physical forms required for the distribution. Gwen was assigned to work the blood analysis equipment and would also help feed information and databases to us containing the information they were using to reflect the different tribal populations. There were several other people working in the lab, but everyone else was busy, and we didn't want to interrupt, so we saved our hellos for later.

We only had time to work for a half hour before Natelli insisted we go to dinner in the dining area. It was basically a large rough-hewn hut next door to the lab with three long rectangular card tables and several chairs. Security staff was already at one of the tables eating what looked like a scrumptious beef stew with thick slabs of dark bread.

Natelli saw me looking at it. "It's *feijoada*, a rich, hearty stew made with different cuts of pork and black beans. It's delicious."

I was suddenly famished, but we weren't ready to sit down yet. A man sitting at the table with the guards rose when he saw Natelli and us and she waved him over. He had thick dark hair and the bushiest eyebrows I'd ever seen. A gun was clipped to a holster on his right hip and a huge knife and sheath rested against the other. He didn't look happy to see us, his expression just one step away from a glower.

"Lexi, Gwen and Slash, I'd like you to meet the camp head of security, Gabriel Costa," Natelli said calmly. "He's responsible for the physical security of the lab, the research, and the staff."

We greeted him before he nodded curtly and returned to his seat without a single word to any of us. When we walked away, Natelli lowered her voice. "Don't take his gruffness personally. He's got a lot on his plate keeping us all safe."

"Does he speak English?" I asked.

"He does, but he's a man of few words."

"So I see."

"Is he a company hire or a government loan?" Slash asked.

"Company hire, but recommended by the Brazilian government. He's quite competent. Come on, I want you to meet Vicente."

She led us to another man who was eating, his back to us. When she tapped him on the shoulder, he turned around in his chair. Unlike Gabriel, he seemed happy to see us.

He thrust out a hand, shaking each of ours warmly. "Welcome to camp. I'm Vicente Lopes, the team translator."

We introduced ourselves and sat down in the empty seats next to him to eat our dinner. Natelli was pulled away by a lab-coated woman with a question, but she promised to check in on us later.

The serving staff brought us bowls of stew and pieces of bread. I didn't waste any time digging in. The stew was delicious and I dipped my bread in it like the others, realizing how useful it was to soften the bread. While we ate, we quizzed Vicente on his job as team translator.

"How many languages do you speak in addition to English and Portuguese?" I asked.

"Nine." He shrugged. "This area of the rainforest has many different local dialects. I grew up not far from here, so I know most of them."

"I presume that makes you one of the most valuable team members. Your translation skills will be crucial to gaining the trust of the village population."

"I'll certainly do my best."

"How receptive are the villagers in this area to receiving the vaccinations?" Slash asked him.

"So far, they've been open to it." Vicente finished the last bite of his stew and pushed the bowl away from him. He leaned forward on the table, picked up what I presumed was a mug filled with coffee and took a sip. "In fact, they initiated it. Their children are dying from malaria, and their population is dwindling. Most of the elders have come to see the light, especially if there's a way to preserve their way of life and end the suffering of their people. We will try to be as respectful as we can, and have as little contact as possible, so as not to interfere with their culture and way of life. But they're bound to be curious about us, just as we are about them."

I almost wished I could go on the visits to the villages with them before I remembered how much I hated the heat, snakes, water and spiders. "I'm sure it will be a fascinating experience."

"Oh, no doubt," he said. "But more importantly, we'll be saving lives. Well, at least those of you administering the vaccine will be doing that. I'm just a small part of the effort."

"Hardly." Gwen laid her spoon across her bowl and dabbed her mouth with a napkin. "How did you learn to speak English so well?"

"I went to the Federal University of Amazonas," he replied. "It's Brazil's oldest university. After a year, I transferred to the Humaitá campus, where I studied English and other subjects. Eventually I moved to Brasilia, our capital city, and took on a variety of jobs. I was offered this job due to my skills with the native languages of this area."

"Your English is excellent," I offered.

He smiled, clearly pleased by my compliment. "Thank you. That's kind of you to say."

We had just finished up dinner when Natelli joined us again, a mug similar to Vicente's in her hand, except I could see the string of a teabag dangling from the side. "I wanted to give you a quick update while we're all together here," she said, taking a seat next to Slash. "There's no rest for the weary. We're going to hit the ground running tomorrow, going to our first village to administer the inoculations. Gwen, I'd like you to come along to help preserve the cold chain preservation of the vaccine, as well as oversee the waste management."

"Of course." Gwen straightened in her chair, not able to keep the look of excitement off her face. "I'm looking forward to it."

"Great." Natelli looked at me. "Lexi, would you be willing to accompany us, as well?"

I choked on a mouthful of water. Slash had to smack me on the back twice before I could catch my breath. "Me? You want me to go to the village with you…in person?"

"Yes, I'm sorry if you're surprised by that. I thought

Tim might have mentioned it. I'd like you to enter the data right into the laptop as we go along. I know it sounds crazy, but I'd feel better if you were in charge of the laptop at all times, ensuring the data remains safe and uncorrupted, even if we won't be connected to the Internet. We can't afford to have anything go wrong with the computer while we are in the field. We're bringing a small team and I want everyone with just one focus."

I glanced at Slash. His face remained expressionless, but his body had tensed. I knew him well enough to presume he was going through a list of all the things that could go wrong with that scenario.

Regardless, I considered the request. My job was keeping the data safe, and they needed me along to ensure that happened. As much as I didn't like water, snakes, spiders and the heat, I felt like it was my job. Moreover, if I were honest with myself, I was greatly intrigued by the process. In spite of all my fears, I really did want to see how the vaccine administration and distribution played out. My curiosity was getting the better of me.

"Okay," I said. "I'll go."

Slash raised an eyebrow, but somehow didn't seem that surprised. "I'm willing to go, too," he added. "If you have room."

"We'll make room. Truthfully, Slash, we could use an extra set of hands to help us lug the equipment. Most of the security force has to keep their hands free, so it would be really helpful to have you along."

"I'm your guy, then."

We chatted a bit more about various logistics before heading back to the lab. Slash and I made a detour to our respective cabins first to grab our laptops and equipment.

"Are you feeling okay about heading into the jungle tomorrow?" he asked.

"Okay might be too strong a word. I feel a strong sense of responsibility and, if I'm honest, curiosity. However, I'm also feeling abject fear that I'll step on a snake or a spider will trap me in its sticky web and cart me off to a hidden lair for a slow feeding. But since you're coming along, I feel much better about that part. I'm only worried that you won't have a weapon to shoot anything."

"I can use my hands, and you could have said no."

"Do you think I should have?" I stopped, studied him. "Would *you* have said no?"

He reached out and touched my cheek. "No, I wouldn't have, and I don't blame you for being curious. But what I say doesn't matter. This is your show. If you're going, so am I. I admit to being as intrigued as you."

"How can we not be?" I asked.

"Exactly. Just promise me you'll do your best not to get into trouble or start a native revolution against the government."

"Ha. Trust me, regardless of the statistics on my Little Black Cloud spreadsheet, I do *not* intend to cause or invite any trouble."

He raised an eyebrow, but said nothing. We walked the rest of the way in silence until we arrived at our sleeping quarters.

"It's too bad we won't be sharing the same room," I said glumly, standing in front of the women's barracks.

"Or the same bed."

"We'll manage, I guess." I had a hard time sleeping away from him, and he knew that, but knowing that he was close would have to suffice. I yawned, swiping at the sweat pooling at the back of my neck. The humidity was killing me and the meal, combined with the travel, had made me lethargic.

Slash noticed. "Are you feeling all right, *cara*?"

"I'm okay, just tired. But I've got enough juice in me to prepare the laptop for tomorrow's journey. Natelli wants to bring me up to speed on the software as well. I think I can handle that before I pass out."

"Good. While you're doing that, I'll add a few enhancements to their setup. You fine with that?"

"I'm more than fine with that." I paused for a moment. "What do you think of Natelli?"

"Hard to say after such a brief introduction. She's obviously capable and bright or she wouldn't be lead scientist on this project." He leaned over and kissed me on the nose. "Now, go get your stuff and let's make sure *our* part of the project goes as planned."

Before I opened the door to the women's cabin, I looked over my shoulder at him. "It's all going to go smoothly, right?"

"As smooth as we can make it."

Chapter Eighteen

Lexi

I'd seen them in the dining room and lab, but it wasn't until we were getting ready for bed that I officially met the rest of the women at the camp. Greta Henrikson, a researcher and malaria expert, Melinda Michelson, a medical doctor and immunologist, and Sara Petrosian, a lab technician, rounded out our group.

After brief introductions, Sara excused herself to go lie down, and Gwen joined Greta and Melinda at the small table where they immediately began discussing topics related to malaria and microbiology. I was too tired and peopled-out to partake in the conversation, so I sat on my bunk beneath the netting, trying to change into my pajamas without anyone noticing. It wasn't easy. I'd just slipped my hands beneath my shirt to unfasten my bra when Natelli pushed aside the netting.

"Hey, Lexi. Do you have a minute?"

Technically I didn't have a minute to spare because I was exhausted and wanted to go to bed, but I didn't want to be rude, so I nodded. "Sure, Natelli. Sit down."

She perched next to me on the bed, so I slipped my

hands out from beneath my shirt, leaving my bra still fastened.

"What's up?" I asked, hoping whatever was on her mind would be fast and short. My ability to pretend to pay attention and engage in conversation wasn't as effective when I was tired.

"So, you and Slash are engaged?"

"Yes. We're engaged."

"That's wonderful. Congratulations. How did you meet?"

Now *that* was not a simple or short story. But if I ever wanted to get to bed, I had to tell her something, so I racked my brains for how to wrap it up in one sentence. "Well…we were introduced by mutual friends…sort of."

The truth was a lot more complicated than that. We were brought together by the Zimmerman twins, who, at the time, Slash had never met. And we hadn't exactly been introduced when Slash showed up in my bedroom unannounced. But those details were for another time, if ever.

"Oh. How long ago did you meet?"

"About a year ago." It seemed like a lot longer, especially since we'd been through so much together, but that's what it was.

"That's wonderful that you found each other." Natelli played with the netting, winding her finger around the gauzy material. "I understand he made a sizable donation to Vaccitex to help with our research, and he also volunteered to help out here even though he's on vacation. That's quite generous of him."

"Yep, that's Slash. He's a generous guy."

"Clearly. I found it interesting that he attended Sapienza University in Italy. Do you know what he studied?"

I shifted on the bed and stared at her. "Why are you asking all these questions about Slash?"

Color flooded her cheeks. "Oh, I'm so sorry if I'm being nosy. I'm just curious about you two. I like to know the people I'm working with, especially since this project is so important to me. I apologize. This wasn't the right time to do this. You must be exhausted and we have an early start tomorrow, so I'll leave you to get some sleep."

With that, she stood and headed off to her bunk. Mystified by the strange encounter, I got undressed and put my pajamas on, mostly under the covers. Gwen, Melinda and Greta were still at the table chatting softly about microbes. I didn't know how Gwen could keep her eyes open. I was so tired I began to drift off as soon as I put my folded clothes neatly at the foot of my bed.

My last thought was that although Natelli had said she was curious about Slash and me, she hadn't asked a single question about me.

Chapter Nineteen

Lexi

Morning seemed to come earlier than usual since I was roused by somebody's alarm going off. I rolled over and looked at my watch. Six fifteen. Ugh.

People in the cabin were already stirring, so I yawned, stretched and sat up. I'd slept more soundly than expected, especially since the small air conditioning unit and fan hadn't helped much in cooling down the room. Not to mention I'd been without Slash and with a bunch of strange women, except for Gwen. I must have been more tired than I thought.

I managed to get dressed in long pants, hiking boots, and a long-sleeve shirt while sitting on my bunk under the mosquito netting. I was already sweating. I slathered some suntan lotion on the exposed parts of my skin before emerging from the netting and grabbing my backpack and hat. Gwen was sitting at the table and putting suntan lotion on her face. She'd dressed similar to me, except she'd fixed her bright red hair into double braids. A brown wide-brimmed hat sat on the table next to her. I looked around. Natelli was nowhere in sight, and the other women were in various stages of dressing except for Sara who was still in bed.

"How'd you sleep, Lexi?" Gwen asked, her blue eyes alight with excitement. She had a glob of white suntan lotion on the tip of her nose. She snapped the tube closed and put it in her backpack.

"Okay, I guess. Are you ready for today?"

"I'm beyond ready and ridiculously excited. I hope it's permitted for me to snap a few pictures of the rainforest, although Natelli said we aren't allowed to take photos of the village or the villagers. I want to show Elvis what it looks like here."

He'd appreciate it. "That's nice of you. Come on, let's get some coffee."

Gwen rose from the table, slung her backpack over her shoulder and we headed out. The camp seemed busy with a lot of security guys milling around and people loading two jeeps with equipment and coolers. Despite my reservations about going on this trek, my heart gave a little leap of excitement.

We walked into the dining room where Slash already sat drinking coffee and talking with Natelli, Salvador and Vicente. Another man with dark hair and a thick mustache sat to the right of Salvador and was saying something loudly in Portuguese, gesturing with his hands. I hadn't met him yet.

Slash waved us over, so we joined them at the table. "Good morning, ladies," Vicente said, pushing a carafe of coffee and two empty mugs toward us. "How did you sleep?"

"Great," Gwen answered. "For what little sleep I got. Greta, Melinda and I talked late into the night. They're so interesting."

"They are," Natelli agreed. "Lexi, how about you? Did you sleep okay?"

"Better than I expected," I said.

Slash patted an empty seat next to him. As I sat down, our fingers brushed and my heart did a little flip. I wondered if it would always be like that between us—a special connection. I'd never had anything like this with anyone before, and for me, it went deeper than just a physical connection. It was an emotional bond where we didn't need to speak to know what each other was thinking. I never thought it possible scientifically, but here it was, irrefutable proof.

Natelli set her mug on the table and motioned toward the man with the mustache. "Lexi, Gwen, I'd like you to meet the newest member of our team, Mr. Martim Alves. Martim works in Brasilia for the *Fundação Nacional do Índio* or, as we call it, FUNAI. FUNAI is an official Brazilian governmental protection agency for the native Indian interests and their culture."

Martim held out a hand across the table to shake hands with Gwen and me. "Pleased to make your acquaintance."

"What role does FUNAI have in all of this?" Gwen asked pouring coffee into her mug.

"I'll accompany the team to the villages on behalf of the Brazilian government to ensure that the interests of the villagers are well protected," he replied.

"Oh, that makes sense," Gwen said. "It's a really important thing to do."

"It is, indeed. We are quite protective of our assets in Brazil. However, I'm of the opinion that this entire project is a waste of government time and money."

For a moment, we all just stared at him, digesting the

bomb he'd just dropped. Gwen spoke first. "What's that supposed to mean?"

Martim waved his hand dismissively, as if it wasn't even worth his time to answer. "These people want to be left alone. Forcing medicine on them defies natural selection."

Natelli bristled, the color high in her cheeks. "They came to the government for help. Their people are dying from malaria. We have medicine that can help them."

"I respectfully disagree. If they want to continue to live in the jungle like animals despite the advances of the modern world, then they should be left to do it...without interference. They can't have it both ways. However, my job here is to ensure that they indeed want this and their rights and protections as granted to them by the government of Brazil are duly served. Now, if you'll excuse me." He stood up and walked out of the building, leaving us all looking at each other in shock.

"What the heck was that all about?" Gwen said.

Natelli shook her head, looking depressed, but Salvador leaned forward, lowering his voice.

"He's a bureaucrat. He knows nothing about vaccines or disease eradication. And despite what he may claim to the contrary, FUNAI is not always favorably looked upon by the natives."

"Why not?" I asked.

Salvador shrugged. "Years of mistrust. The government says one thing and does another, or does nothing at all. Desperation, more than a desire to work with the government, is what's driving the villagers now. At least the government had a decent guy in here before he was abruptly pulled. Martim arrived just this morning. I spoke with him shortly after he arrived. He knows next to nothing about the tribes we are going to visit or the vaccine program. He also told me that he doesn't have much faith in the vaccine trials, seeing as how it's being run by a woman." He looked apologetically at Natelli. "Sorry."

"What a sexist idiot," Gwen said indignantly. "Natelli is brilliant. She's been the driving force behind the development of the vaccine."

"You don't have to convince me." Salavador held up his hands. "He's the problem, not me."

Natelli patted her hand. "Thanks, Gwen, but I don't need protection from Martim or his sexist attitude. It isn't the first time I've encountered these views in my career. His opinion changes nothing. We proceed as planned and try to marginalize Martim as much as we can."

I agreed with her, but I didn't know how easy that would be. At this point, there wasn't much we could do about it.

"Why would the government do that?" Slash mused. "Pull a team member who was already briefed, familiarized and entrenched with the team and replace him on the eve of the first expedition?"

"Who knows?" Vicente answered. "But I'm sure the government had their reasons and now we just have to deal with it."

Slash didn't look convinced, but said nothing more. I drank my coffee and tried not to worry about it.

After we finished breakfast, we filled up our water bottles and headed out to where the team was assembling. It was still early morning and the air was already impossibly humid and oppressive. While standing in the shade, I reached into my backpack and pulled out a bandana made from microfiber that Slash had bought for me. I tied it around my neck to help absorb the sweat.

While we were waiting for the last supplies and coolers to be loaded, Slash sprayed Gwen and me with insect repellent. I pulled my hair up into a ponytail and jammed a hat on my head before applying extra sunblock to my face and the back of my neck. Finally I perched my sunglasses on my nose where they kept sliding down due to the suntan lotion.

Natelli returned and we stood together in a group. I counted ten people. Natelli, Slash, Gwen, me, Salvador, Vicente, Melinda, Martim and two security guards who would apparently also act as drivers. Natalie divided us up into two groups of five. I was in a jeep with Slash, Melinda, Vicente and a security guard. Gwen, Natelli, Martim, Salvador and their security man were in the first jeep, with Salvador providing guidance to the group.

I sure hoped he knew where we were going, because I didn't want to get lost in this heat and humidity. I was pretty sure I wouldn't last an hour. Natelli seemed to read my mind, because she began to reassure us.

"Salvador will ensure we get where we are going," she said as we climbed in the jeeps. "The indigenous communities we will visit are scattered throughout this area, with many of them located in hard-to-find pockets of the jungle. Those on the banks of the Amazon are the easiest to find, but those areas are also the most dangerous for us since they're also the locations most often frequented by pirates."

I exchanged a worried glance with Slash and then looked back at Natelli. "Define pirates. We aren't talking pirates like Long Beard, right?"

"Well, in a way we are," she answered. "They're

thieves, pure and simple. But extremely dangerous thieves, who wouldn't think twice about slicing our necks for financial gain."

I swallowed hard. I appreciated she was keeping it real, I was even more thankful Slash was here with me, although I sincerely wished he were armed. Would two security guards be enough to protect us from danger?

Apparently Natelli thought they would, because the jeeps started and off we went. I was sitting in the back in the middle between Slash and Melinda, the computer bag and my backpack on my lap. Vicente sat up front with the guard, chatting with him in Portuguese.

I leaned forward, resting my hand on the back of the seat. "So, Vicente, what kind of animals can we expect to see in the rainforest?"

"A wide variety, of course. This area is one of the most biodiverse in the world. If you're lucky, you might see a jaguar, some cougars, caiman, anacondas, bats and a wide variety of snakes, spiders and insects. We also have some of the most colorful and beautiful birds in the world. Keep an eye out for them."

I'd stopped listening after he said cougars and scooted a little closer to Slash, who was viewing the area with interest. He didn't seem the least bit scared, which was both annoying and comforting.

"Many of the villages we will visit are on the waterways, so we typically take the jeep to the river's edge and maneuver our way in this manner," Vicente said. "But our first village is landlocked, so we'll take the jeep as far as we can and hike the rest of the way. I've been there before as well, and it's not too far a walk from where the jeeps will stop."

"What are we to expect at the village today?" Slash asked. "How advanced is their civilization?"

"This particular group has adopted some modern conveniences such as tools and guns and have used them to survive." Vicente braced himself with a hand against the dashboard as we hit several bumps. "But keep in mind, many of the tribes have lived in the rainforest for more than a thousand years. They've adapted to the climate and the environment, as well as learned to coexist with nature and live off the land. It's fascinating."

"How much contact have they had with the outside world?" Melinda asked.

"Some. Tourism has both helped and hurt the rainforest. Helped in the sense that it provides income and discourages the slaughter, sale and smuggling of threatened and endangered animals. Hurt because the rainforest is being deforested at a scary rate to accommodate all the tourists."

"A double-edged sword," Slash said.

"Indeed. Most of the tribes remain highly superstitious and suspicious of foreigners, however, so we have to get in, create some rapport and trust, administer the vaccines, and get the heck out."

"How long do you anticipate it will take us to get to the village?" I asked. The sun was blazing hot, and it appeared the road was following the river, so we were getting a lot more sun than we would have if we were traveling beneath the trees. Plus, it had started drizzling on and off which might have been helpful in cooling us off, except even the drizzle was hot and steamy.

"About two hours," Vicente replied. "Hang in there."

I pulled the brim of my hat lower across my face and mostly watched the jeep in front of us as it bumped and grinded along. I could see Gwen's red hair peeking out from beneath her hat and watched as she snapped photos with her phone. I didn't know how any of them would come out as we were bouncing around so much. Insects buzzed past my ears as we drove. I feared one would splat on my face, or worse, fly into my mouth, so I kept it tightly shut.

Slash, however, didn't seem bothered by the bugs or the potential for swallowing them. "I expected the insects to be worse than they are," he said to Vicente.

Vicente laughed. "It's early yet. Just wait until dusk. Then you'll get close with a thousand more bugs, all who'd like to make your acquaintance." The driver said something and Vicente turned around in his seat. "Oh, Jorge wants me to warn you of the enormous, poisonous Brazilian river spider that hangs on the bottom of leaves and drops on its prey. They're called three-steppers because once you've been bitten, you will take no more than three steps before you die. They've brought down everything from large cougars to monkeys and plenty of humans. So, keep an eye out for them."

Despite my fear of swallowing a bug, I opened my mouth to ask a question because I had to know. "A giant river spider? Are you *freaking* kidding me?"

Chapter Twenty

Lexi

"I'd never joke about the river spider," Vicente said solemnly, but the way he was grinning made me wonder.

Slash patted my knee, but said nothing. What was that pat supposed to mean? That I shouldn't worry? That Vicente was kidding? Or that I needed to be hyperaware of spiders so I didn't die? I really needed people to spell things out for me, otherwise I wasn't sure.

While I wanted to know more about the river spider—in case it involved my survival—I also didn't want to open my mouth any more for fear of swallowing insects. For two hours we barreled along on rutted, muddy roads mostly in silence until we reached a spot where the vehicles could no longer traverse. Although I wasn't looking forward to walking, at least we'd be out of the direct sun, so I was ready to face giant spiders and snakes as long as I could get out of the heat.

Once out I downed an entire bottle of water. I was dripping sweat as we collected the drinking water, coolers, equipment, and all the items we needed, doling them out between us to distribute the load as evenly as possible. Slash carried a backpack and the heaviest cooler.

I didn't envy him that. I had my laptop bag and equipment and backpack, but I also had to help carry water for the team. I hoped it wouldn't be a long trek, because it was heavy.

Once the supplies were distributed, we began to prepare to hike to the village along a footpath. I fell in beside Vicente.

"I noticed the drivers took the keys from the ignition and pocketed them," I said. "Who else would be out here to steal them?" I hadn't seen another human or animal in the entire two hours we'd been on the road.

"The rule of the river is to always be watchful, as danger lurks everywhere," Vicente replied cryptically. "And not just from the spiders."

The path became so narrow that we had to hike single file to the village. I was lost in drops of sweat and thinking about the last time I'd hiked through a jungle. At least this time I had Slash and no crazy Chinese assassins to worry about, so I counted that as a plus.

Once we'd reached the village, Salvador and our drivers/soldier guards remained on the fringes, so as to not frighten the natives. Slash might have also remained there, as well, but they needed him to haul the heavy cooler, so he was permitted to join us. We walked slowly toward the huts with Natelli and Vicente in the lead and Slash and I bringing up the rear.

We stopped a couple times to drink water. When we got close enough to the village, I could see several of the structures were made of wood with roofs of woven palms. There were no doors or windows, just open beams holding up the structure. Two men stood near a smoking fire watching us, one young and one old. Both men were naked except for loose shorts and elaborate necklaces and beaded armbands. The older one's necklace was bigger and heavier and his face was painted with red streaks around the top and bottom of his eyes. The younger one had red streaks of paint on his face, but below the eyes only. They did not smile as we approached.

We hung back as Vicente, our translator, approached first, issuing a greeting and presumably explaining our presence. After a moment, the older one spoke and there was a short back and forth before the younger man said something and villagers began to emerge from inside the huts. The children came first, followed by the women and elderly, all of whom eyed us curiously. I'm not sure if it was the entire village, but by my count, there were only about fifty people.

The people seemed welcoming enough and things seem to be progressing, with Vicente communicating with the villagers about the upcoming process. Martim strode forward and interrupted Vicente. Natelli joined them before Vicente relayed whatever Martim had just said. Unfortunately, the older villager became agitated and shook his head. The three of them returned to us and said we'd have to leave the village and return another day to do the vaccinations.

Ugh! That meant we'd have to carry all the equipment and water back again.

It didn't take much to see how furious Natelli was with Martim and whatever he'd insisted Vicente say to the villagers. Martim didn't seem to care and brushed past all of us with a superior air, presumably instructing the drivers to lead the way back to the jeeps. I exchanged a puzzled glance with Slash, who shrugged and picked up the cooler. We closed up the rear of the line.

Melinda, Gwen and Natelli were in front of us discussing not so quietly what Martim had done. Apparently, Martim had stirred up doubt about the vaccinations. Despite Natelli's objections and trying to set the record straight, the villagers had become uneasy and decided to reconvene again to discuss if the vaccination program was right for them.

"Why do you think he did that?" I said in a low voice to Slash.

He slowed a bit to give us more space behind the group. "I don't know. Maybe he thought he was doing his job. But he may have just killed a lot of children if they decide against getting the vaccination."

On the hike back, Slash's head swiveled constantly as he looked for threats. I wasn't sure if he was looking for people or giant spiders, but either way, it made me feel better to stay as close to him as possible. That was good because as we finally caught sight of the jeeps in the clearing, two guys jumped out from behind the trees, taking several years off my life. They started waving guns and yelling at us in Portuguese. Several of us, me included, hit the ground in case they started shooting.

Pirates!

The security guards reached for their weapons, but it was over before it started. One of the pirates grabbed Melinda and held a gun to her neck. After that, Martim took charge, insisting we should all surrender peacefully. The soldiers dropped their weapons and held up their hands.

"Everyone stay calm," Vicente translated for us as the pirates barked orders. "Just do what they say and they won't hurt us. They want us to line up by the vehicles and hand over any valuables we have."

Since I'd dropped to the grass, I dared sit up and look over my shoulder to see what Slash was doing. He'd vanished. Panicked, I scanned the rest of the group, but I still didn't see him.

"Lexi!" Vicente shouted. I blinked, realizing I still hadn't moved from my spot and one of the pirates was coming for me, waving a gun.

I scrambled to my feet, holding up my hands. "Whoa. Hey, it's cool. I'm coming."

The pirate reached out to grab my arm to hurry me along, but then stopped and gestured at my pants. On my right leg, just above my kneecap, a brown tarantula-looking spider the size of a small cat was crawling up my thigh.

Holy spidergeddon!

"AAAAAACK!" I screamed and started to jump around like a deranged person, trying to get it off my leg without actually touching it. Unfortunately, the spider wasn't having anything to do with that plan and clung to my pants like a long-lost lover.

I started to hyperventilate so badly, I was in fear of passing out. Holy crap, I was having a panic attack right in the middle of the rainforest. My brain had been hijacked by intense fear and was racing through a variety of horrifying scenarios that ended with my lifeless body being dragged into the rainforest for digestion. Little *eeps* were coming from mouth as I shook my leg harder and harder, but the spider wouldn't let go of me. I began to freak out so badly I completely forgot about the pirates, the guns, and the fact that Slash was nowhere to be found. Instead, my entire world had narrowed to this one moment in time where I was locked in a weird dance of survival with a giant spider.

Desperate, I ripped the laptop bag off my arm and swung it at my thigh, missing entirely. But the spider finally got the hint. He flew off my pants and scuttled away. Dripping with sweat, and gasping like I'd just run a marathon, I turned to face the guy with the gun.

Slash was standing in his place.

I almost had a heart attack right on the spot. I stepped back, clutching my chest. "What the—"

"Are you okay, *cara*?"

What had happened? I looked around in disbelief. The rest of the group were staring wide eyed at us. The two pirates were lying unconscious on the ground—one right next to me—both of them divested of their weapons. The guy near the jeep was being tied up by the soldiers and Slash had his boot on the back of the other.

"Where did you get that?" I pointed at the gun in his hand.

He jerked his head toward the guy on the ground. "He was reluctant to share, but I convinced him otherwise."

"What…happened?" I asked.

Slash put a hand on my shoulder. "Your timing was excellent, as always. As I was trying to figure out a distraction so I could take them down, you provided the perfect one."

"I did?"

"You did. Come on, *cara*, let's get going."

He took the arms of the pirate, dragging him back to the jeep and depositing him into the care of one of the guards. Gwen dashed over to me and gave me a big hug. "OMG! Are you all right, Lexi? That was so scary."

I had no idea if she was talking about the situation with the pirates or the spider. Honestly, I wasn't sure which one *had* been scarier for me. "I'm fine, Gwen. I'm glad it all turned out okay."

"You and Slash were amazing, working in perfect sync as always."

That was kind of a stretch, but I figured now wasn't the time to argue that point.

Gwen lowered her voice and dipped her head toward Melinda. "But not all of us are okay." The doctor was still shaking from her ordeal, and Salvador was talking with her, patting her on the back.

When the pirates were conscious again, Slash and the soldiers loaded them into the jeeps. Apparently, we were taking them back to camp with us. That meant it would be a super tight fit. We played a round of musical chairs in the jeeps until everyone was satisfied the pirates would be well monitored during the drive. Salvador drove one jeep and Vicente the other, and the soldiers sat next to the pirates. The rest of us had to squeeze in wherever we could. Comfortable, it was not.

Before she got in the jeep, Natelli touched my arm. "Good work, Lexi. You and Slash really do make a great team."

I'm not sure why she was including me in the accolades when Slash had done all the work. "Oh, thanks. I guess we do."

No one even mentioned the spider.

Chapter Twenty-One

Lexi

The ride back to the research camp seemed a lot longer than the drive to the village, but we were hot, upset, and even more cramped than before with the extra load. We finally arrived and turned the pirates over to the gruff security chief, Gabriel Costa, who was quickly briefed on events. We left it to Gabriel to get them turned over to the Brazilian authorities.

The rest of us—minus Martim, who apparently had to update some government officials on what had happened, and Natelli, who had to call Hayden and Lilith to explain the situation, offloaded the supplies and equipment and restocked them in the lab. Melinda stayed in the lab talking to the others about what had happened, so Gwen, Slash and I went to get something to eat in the dining area. We were eating when Natelli and Vicente returned to give us an update on the situation.

"Gabriel has taken the bandits into town," Natelli said, setting down a plate and bottle of water as she joined us at the table. "Apparently a quick check with the authorities in Coari has confirmed those two are known troublemakers and outlaws. They will be held in the jail until their trial. We're lucky no one got hurt."

"Absolutely." Vicente sat next to her, setting his food down in front of him. He glanced over at Slash. "That was impressive what you did out there. You took them both down quickly and efficiently. You've done that before."

It wasn't a question. Slash took a sip of his coffee and shrugged. "They're clearly hired muscle, not military, and I've had a bit of training."

"A bit? More like extensive training. You said you work in computers?"

"I do."

Vicente studied Slash for a moment longer, perhaps hoping he'd say something more. When he didn't, Vicente looked disappointed but didn't press. "Well, here's the interesting part. Gabriel said some of the authorities in Coari think these two guys may be associated with drug smugglers who have been setting up labs in remote area of this region."

"Drugs? What kind of drugs?" Gwen asked.

"Cocaine."

She furrowed her brow. "That's not likely. Cocaine doesn't grow at lower altitudes or in a rainforest environment."

Vicente set down his fork on his plate and picked up a napkin, wiping his mouth. "It does if it's being bioengineered to grow in this climate."

For a moment we all just stared at him.

"Bioengineered?" I repeated. "Is that even possible?"

"Apparently so. The Brazilian government has been trying to track them down to stop them before they get too much of a foothold, but not surprisingly, they don't have many antidrug resources in this part of the country. As a result, these troublemakers have been randomly causing problems up and down the Amazon for the last few months."

"So the men we caught were drug runners?" I asked.

"It's possible," Vicente said. "But if so, trust me, they'd never admit to it. They're more afraid of the drug lords than they are of the authorities."

I didn't doubt that was true. Still, to imagine that we'd run into possible drug runners was a scary thought. "So, what exactly happened today at the village? What did Martim say to the villagers to cause them to hesitate with the vaccines?"

Vicente exchanged a glance with Natelli, who sighed. "He basically undercut a lot of important work that had been done. We'd already spoken with the villagers, and they had their tribal sessions and made the decision to move forward with the vaccinations. Martim is a new addition to the team. Our long-time government representative, Paolo Ibáñez, was abruptly recalled to Brasilia just two days ago. We've briefed Martim on where we are with things, but he apparently likes to do things his own way."

"The wrong way," Gwen grumbled.

Natelli was being diplomatic, but it was easy to see how Martim could easily derail this entire process. It heightened my anxiety.

"So, what's the plan?" I asked. "Do we go back to that village again?"

She shook her head. "Not right away. We'll stick to the schedule, which means we go to a different village tomorrow. Lilith and Hayden are supposed to talk to Martim's boss to make sure he's clear that we've already done all the negotiating we need to do with the villagers. We can't afford a mistake of that caliber to happen again. As it stands now, we'll have to send a small team back out there again to see if they'll agree to do the vaccinations again."

"A wise move," Slash said.

"I just hope Martim gets the message. We don't have the luxury of egos at this point. All of which leads me to the following question. Who among you is willing to accompany us again? Melinda has decided to sit this one out, as she was quite shaken up today. I'd understand if none of you wish to go either."

"I'm totally going." Gwen lifted her chin. "I'm not going to let some drug thugs stop me."

Wow, Gwen kept surprising me. There was more to her than I'd expected—and that was a good thing.

"I'll go, too," I said, surprising myself. I hadn't really thought about it and had no idea why I said it except perhaps it was the principle of the matter. No way was I going to let drug runners interfere with helping children and infants get protected against malaria.

"I'm in, as well," Slash said. "I'll carry the needed coolers and equipment and be available to help security, if desired."

"Oh, yes, trust me, it's desired." Visible relief showed on Natelli's face. "Thank you so much. By the way, you all may feel more secure knowing Gabriel has assigned two extra men to our detail, one of which will be him. We had considered the lab to be the most vulnerable part of our operation, but we've changed our mind about that. It's us—the team. Gabriel wants to put more strict measures in place to protect us. He's bringing in some more guys to safeguard the lab and he's going to personally accompany us on all trips from here on out. He said he's grateful for your support today, Slash."

"It was my pleasure." The hard glitter in his eyes indicated to me that it probably was. Slash had little sympathy for people who ran drugs. Still, I wondered if Gabriel really welcomed Slash's help or resented it. It was hard to say when I hadn't seen them working together yet.

We talked for a bit more before heading back to the lab. Slash and I got to work on the computers—me reviewing Slash's enhancements and checking for anomalies, and him running additional diagnostic tests. We sat shoulder to shoulder working in a comfortable rhythm.

I was in the middle of writing a program when my email box dinged. I opened it and saw Mom had sent me an email. I weighed the pros and cons of opening it until, against my better judgment, I decided to open it.

Lexi, it's Mom. Can I be invited to the bachelorette party?

I must have gasped in horror, because Slash looked over at me. "What's wrong, *cara*?"

I quickly closed the email. "Nothing. Just my mother. Let's keep working. I found something. Take a look at this."

He leaned over to look at my screen, his elbow resting on the desk. He read through the data before pointing at a spot. "A penetration here."

"Yes," I confirmed. "It's a noncritical sector, but they broke through. The critical data is perfectly safe, but I notified Tim of the intrusion and to remind the staff not to post anything valuable on email, while keeping the normal traffic going."

Slash tapped a couple of keys on my keyboard. "Good. It looks like they're nowhere close to the hidden walls of the critical data."

"Not yet. We have to prepare for the contingency, though."

"*Si*, we do."

We kept working for a while longer until I stopped and turned in my chair to face him. "Something is bugging me, Slash. Why would drug runners ambush a vaccine expedition? If they were drug runners, it's a risky move. That kind of attack is bound to catch the eye of the government, bring their attention to the area, and that's just stupid, right?"

Slash kept watching the data scrolling across his screen. "Maybe they were just a couple of stupid, greedy guys who decided to do a quick grab and run with some valuables."

"Except you don't really believe that."

"No, I don't." He leaned back in his chair and rubbed the back of his neck. "But it should be on the table for consideration. The truth is, at this point, I also don't have enough data to postulate another theory."

"How did they find us? There's no way they just stumbled upon us in the rainforest. They either expected us, or followed us to the village. Do you think they were trying to disrupt the process? Scare us away from vaccinating the villagers? I suppose that would be an attack of another sort on the program."

"It would, but it would also mean they've got some reach high up in Brazilian government. If so, that's significant, a possible game changer. I checked the jeeps for tracking devices and didn't find anything. So, that means either someone told them we were going to be there or they tracked us some other way. I suppose a couple of drug runners could have been in the area, or we crossed some invisible zone that's being monitored by a drug lord, and they followed us, not knowing who we were. Then they decided we were easy targets and, *boom,* they attack. Didn't realize their mistake until it was too late. And if that turns out to be the truth, they're basically marked men. There won't be any protection for them in jail."

I had to agree it was a plausible scenario, but the bottom line was Slash was right. We didn't have enough hard data to know for sure. We were just throwing out suppositions, which wasn't terribly helpful. Unless those guys talked—which apparently they weren't going to do—we wouldn't have any clear answers.

I blew out a breath and started to get back to work, when Slash put a hand on my arm and lowered his voice so I could barely hear him. "We also can't discount the possibility that the hackers have someone on the inside, *cara.* Someone at this camp who might be disrupting the process, compromising the team, or be after the vaccine formula. We have to be vigilant for the insider threat."

I nodded. It had occurred to me, but seemed even more ominous and likely after the morning's events.

We couldn't trust anyone.

Chapter Twenty-Two

Lexi

There are a lot of uncomfortable aspects to camping, like cold showers, a variety of biting insects, lumpy beds and pillows, and strangers who snore. In my opinion, however, the worst part of camping is having to go to the bathroom in the middle of the night. You can't simply stumble out of bed and wander into the bathroom. No, when camping you have to put your clothes and shoes on and carry a flashlight to see where you're going. Don't even get me started on where to put that flashlight while taking care of business.

Unfortunately, as badly as I wanted to ignore it, nature was calling. Resigned, I rolled over and grabbed my clothes from the bottom of the bed. After I dressed and slipped my feet into the hiking boots, I checked the time on my watch. Three twenty-four a.m.

Ugh. Morning was going to come all too quickly.

I heard some light snoring as I slipped out of the building and headed to the outhouse. I passed a security guard, who gave me a curt nod and went on his way. He didn't even ask me where I was going, but I figured he knew. Where else would I go at three in the morning?

I arrived at the outhouse and quickly took care of business, my flashlight tucked awkwardly under my chin. On my way out, I caught a glimpse of a dark figure flitting past the dining building toward the lab. If I hadn't been looking in that exact direction, I would have missed it. The person hadn't been walking deliberately, but almost furtively. Instinctively, I pressed back against the side of outhouse, waiting until the figure passed in front of one of the hanging lanterns.

Vicente.

He hadn't come from the direction of the outhouse or the men's quarters, so I wondered where he'd been and what he was doing sneaking around the camp at three o'clock in the morning. I expected him to move toward the men's sleeping quarters, but instead he headed toward the lab, slipped around the building and disappeared into the darkness.

What the heck?

As far as I knew there wasn't anything behind the lab. Curious, I darted toward the lab and edged up to the corner, daring a quick peek around the corner. Vicente stood at the fence speaking quietly to a man through the barbed wire. The two men exchanged something and then the man outside of the fence melted into the darkness. I drew my head back and darted around the other side of the lab, pressing back against the building. I had to process what I'd just seen and I thought it might be better if he didn't know.

I heard Vicente's footsteps head toward the front of the lab. He rattled the doorknob twice and then stopped. Was he trying to get in or make sure it was locked?

I stood completely still, but my pulse jumped when I realized he was coming my direction. A quick calculation determined no matter how fast I ran, he'd see me. I'd have to face him. Taking a deep breath, I clicked on my flashlight and stepped around the corner.

We nearly collided.

Vicente jumped back in surprise and held up a hand to shield his eyes from my flashlight. "Lexi?"

"Vicente? Wow. You scared the crap out of me." I lowered my flashlight, pretending to be frightened, which wasn't much of a stretch because my heart was pounding like crazy.

"What are you doing out here at this hour?" he asked.

I jerked a thumb toward the outhouse. "Using the facilities. Too much coffee, I guess. Decaf, though. If I drink caffeine after three o'clock in the afternoon, I'd never sleep." I laughed a bit too manically, then snapped my mouth closed. I needed to shut up because I didn't want to raise his suspicions. I took a breath, tried to tone it down a bit. "What are you doing out here?"

He shrugged. "The same as you. Come, let me walk you back to your sleeping quarters."

"Sure. That would be nice of you. Thanks."

We walked in silence, not passing a guard once. Apparently they were more interested in keeping people out than monitoring the people who were already in.

When we arrived at the women's quarters, Vicente wished me a good night and walked toward the men's barracks. I slipped inside, sat on my bunk and tried to calm the rapid pounding of my heart. I had no idea what that'd been all about, but I couldn't wait to tell Slash in the morning.

Chapter Twenty-Three

Lexi

"So, what do you think he was doing out there?"

I kept my voice low and kept looking over my shoulder to make sure Vicente didn't somehow materialize and overhear our conversation. I hadn't been able to sleep for the rest of the night and had been up and waiting outside the women's quarters for at least an hour until Slash emerged, startled to see me waiting there. It might have been one of the first times in our entire relationship that I'd been up first. Thank God he was an earlier riser, because I might not have survived another hour sitting there in the sweltering humidity.

We moved to the shade near the lab while I quickly filled him in on the night's events. Slash took a minute to mull it over before he commented, "It's hard to say why he was out there. You're sure he exchanged something with someone on the outside of the fence?"

"I'm sure."

"Maybe he was talking to a guard who was patrolling the exterior, and he gave him a cigarette or something."

"At three o'clock in the morning?" I replied. "And why would he lie about it?"

"I don't know. Where exactly did this exchange take place?"

I took him around the back of lab to show him the spot. We didn't see anything unusual, including cigarette butts, but footsteps on the outside of the fence were visible.

"You're certain he didn't catch you watching him?" Slash asked.

"I don't think so. He seemed genuinely surprised to see me when we ran into each other."

"That was a risky move." He took me by the elbow, steering me toward the dining area. "If nothing else, from this point on, we keep a close eye on him. And no more late-night coffee for you, decaf or otherwise."

"No kidding."

We headed in for breakfast. No one was in there except for a couple of guards who looked like they were just getting off their shift. I tried to talk Slash into trying the *pingado*, warm milk with sweetened coffee served in a glass, but he declined. He didn't want anything in his coffee except coffee, and apparently he liked the strong taste of Brazilian beans. However, we both ate the *pão na chapa*, which were skillet-toasted French bread rolls smothered with real butter. They were delicious, so I ate four of them.

After a while we were joined by Natelli, Gwen, Sara, Melinda, Salvador and Doug, one of the lab technicians. Vicente was a no-show and Greta was apparently in the shower. Martim arrived, but didn't sit with us. Instead, he sat one table over, eating his food and ignoring us completely. He was turning out to be a real pompous jerk.

"So, what's the plan for today?" I asked Natelli.

She took a sip of her coffee and set it down, wrapping

her hands around the mug. "We're heading out in about a half hour. This time we'll take the jeeps to a spot on the river. From there, we'll have to take boats. This village is on the other side of the river."

Ugh! I liked riding in boats as much as I liked flying. But I've learned to suck it up when it's important, so I swallowed my misgivings and pretended I was cool with it. Slash knew better, however, so he patted my arm, giving me a sympathetic look. Still, his lack of genuine concern indicated he knew full well I could do it. I could. I just wasn't going to like it.

Salvador must have noticed my discomfort, because he leaned forward, eyes sympathetic. "Don't worry. It's a fairly quick boat ride and you'll enjoy the view so long as you don't trail your fingers in the water." I instinctively curled my fingers into fists, and he smiled. He was probably teasing me, but I couldn't be sure.

I wondered if I should mention that I sometimes got boat-sick, but decided against it. I just hoped I'd be so distracted by the fascinating flora and fauna that I'd forget to be sick. While unlikely, it wasn't outside the realm of possibility.

Slash and I left first to get our backpacks and spray each other with sunscreen and bug repellent. As a precaution, I took some motion-sickness medicine. Together we headed to the lab and grabbed the computer equipment. Natelli was overseeing the transfer of the coolers and accompanying them to the jeeps.

When all the equipment was loaded, we stood at the jeeps. Vicente had shown up a few minutes prior and helped carry the last of the boxes. I made eye contact and acted as normal as I could, which probably wasn't normal whatsoever. Still he didn't seem overly interested in me, so maybe that was a good thing.

Our group today included Natelli, Gwen, Slash, Salvador, Vicente, Martim, me, and four guards, including Gabriel. Eleven people. I hoped the boats were big enough for all of us because I had no intention of dying in piranha-infested waters as the boats sank from our weight. In fact, I really wished I knew everyone's weight, although I knew better than to ask, and the physical parameters of the boats so I could calculate the probability. Without it, I didn't have enough data to go on.

Gabriel and another of the guards carried a satellite phone on a rope around their necks. Gabriel had debriefed Slash after yesterday's events, but despite the fact that Slash had saved our butts, Gabriel hadn't offered to arm him. I thought it a big mistake, but since security wasn't my show, I didn't say anything and neither did Slash.

We piled into the jeeps and drove off. Thankfully, the drive was much shorter today. After about twenty minutes, we made it to the river and the boats. I'm not an expert on boats, but these seemed to be regular motorboats with a flat bottom, presumably to handle the shallow waters around the shore. Unfortunately, there was no cover or protection from the sun and the seating looked like uncomfortable planks. Two men, who I presumed were the owners of the boats, waited in the shade near a pickup truck, smoking cigarettes. They each lifted a hand in greeting when we arrived.

Salvador and Vicente went to talk to them while the rest of us got to work unloading the equipment and getting it on the boats. Eventually, there was a lot of discussion about who would go in which boat. Apparently,

of paramount importance were the coolers with the vaccines and the computer equipment, which Natelli insisted
we should split between the boats. After a heated discussion, Natelli, Gwen, Slash, Salvador and one guard were
assigned to the boat with the vaccine coolers. Vicente,
Martim, Gabriel, me and another guard were to go to
the boat with the laptop, water and additional medical
equipment. Slash asked to switch places with someone
in my boat, but Gabriel was insistent Slash stay with the
other boat. Privately, I think Gabriel wanted the two of
them in different boats so we'd be better protected. It was
a secret to no one that Slash was worth the other three
security guards put together, even if he wasn't armed.

I could tell Slash didn't like the arrangements at all,
and wanted to argue. But in the end, he acquiesced and
climbed on the boat with Gwen and Natelli. He gave me
a glance that clearly indicated I should stay out of trouble. Since I knew I'd be floating on a river filled with
piranha, the predatory black caiman—which tourists
often mistook as alligators—water snakes, and who the
heck knew what else, I had *no* intention of causing any
trouble whatsoever. I just hoped my little black cloud of
trouble stayed safely back in the States.

I swallowed my fear as I stepped into the motorboat.
It rocked precariously, so I sat down immediately in a
center seat, bracing myself the best I could against the
motion. The others climbed on and everyone took a seat.
Vicente sat next to me, which I wasn't thrilled about, but
what could I do? When Martim took the spot on the other
side of me even Slash also looked concerned about the
arrangement. But before I could try and move, the mo-
tors started and we pushed off. I was now officially on
the Amazon River.

Vicente told me it would take an hour by boat up the river and against the current to get to the path leading to the village. From there it would be another hour or so hike from the river's edge where we would leave the boats. Although I don't like boats or the water, the river was relatively calm, for which I was grateful.

"This isn't so bad," I said to no one in particular. "It seems peaceful."

Martim snorted. "It only appears calm because the river is so wide at this point. The narrower the river, the more treacherous it becomes. You'll see."

I considered decking him, but I restrained myself... for now.

We traveled for a while without any issues. At one point, we drove past a boat anchored in one of the side tributaries. The boat had two men in it. I thought it was a little strange as they weren't fishing or doing anything. Our driver said something in Portuguese, but Martim replied in a short curt voice, and moved over to sit closer to Gabriel who was watching the boat with interest.

"What was that all about?" I asked Vicente.

"Our driver claimed the boat holds bandits looking for easy prey. Martim said they were simply fishermen and we shouldn't worry."

Not long thereafter, I noticed a boat had started following us. It was hard to see clearly given the bright reflection from the sun on the water, but it appeared to be the boat we had passed. In fact, it seemed to be closing in on us. Gabriel had also noticed and was keeping a close eye on it. He had the satellite phone and used it to presumably contact Slash's boat. As soon as he hung up, our driver revved the engine, as did our other boat. Unfortunately, it became clear the boat had started to chase us. Gabriel fired a warning shot, but the boat kept coming, close enough to see there were two men in the boat with automatic weapons.

Holy pirate ship!

It took me about five seconds of calculations to realize we were facing a losing battle. Our boats had six people each and equipment, while the boat chasing us had only two men weighing it down. As far as I knew, we had more guns, but they were not automatic. The range and rate of fire difference would make it a losing battle if we tried to engage.

Gabriel must have realized that and had instructed our driver to head toward the shore. The rainforest would make the automatic weapons less valuable and our numbers a greater advantage. It was a smart move.

The guard in Slash's boat must have also fired a warning shot, but our pursuers did not slow in the slightest. Not a good sign.

Vicente told us to all hunch down in the boat to reduce our exposure and to help the boat go faster. We rounded a small bend in the river where a tributary entered the main channel from the left. Our driver steered the boat toward the bank past where the new tributary joined. As we neared the shore, the second boat, which had fallen slightly behind, suddenly veered off and headed up the tributary.

"Wait!" I shouted as the boat carrying Slash, Gwen and the others raced away. Even as I yelled, I realized that splitting up would allow one of the boats to call for help and arrange for rescue via the satellite phone. I was positive it was Slash's idea.

Behind us, the pursuing boat paused, trying to figure out which boat to follow. To my astonishment, Martim abruptly stood up in the boat, nearly tipping it over. He waved to the pirates, shouting something and pointing to the other boat racing away up the side stream. Whatever he said caused the pirates to leave us and chase after the other boat.

Gabriel angrily grabbed Martim by the arm, yanking him to the bench. A furious exchange ensued between the two men before Gabriel turned away, his face red with anger.

"What is going on?" I said in alarm. "Why are they chasing the other boat?"

Gabriel didn't answer because he'd picked up the satellite phone and had started speaking rapidly. But Vicente, who sat next to me, also glared at Martim and answered on his behalf.

"Martim was saving his own skin," he said in disgust. "He told them the other boat had more valuables."

I looked at Martim, astounded. "Are you freaking kidding me? What's wrong with you?"

Martim looked at me like I was nothing more than a piece of gum on the bottom of his shoe. "Why should I die on a futile mission?" He stroked his mustache, looking bored by the entire incident. "I warned everybody this project was a stupid idea. Stop complaining. I just saved your life, girl. You should be thanking me."

I'd never been madder in my life. I drew my fist back to punch him, but Vicente caught my arm, stopping me from landing a blow. "That won't help, Lexi. We need to get ashore while we can and figure out what to do next."

Get ashore? What in the world was he thinking? In fact, what was wrong with *all* these people?

"No!" I practically shouted. "What we need to do is go after that boat, right now."

Vicente tried to calm me. "Listen, Lexi. Salvador told us the tributary ends shortly. Both boats will end up on the shore, where they'll have a better chance against the pirates."

"We still have to help them," I insisted.

"We will."

Our driver finally maneuvered the boat onto a small beach that was mostly hidden from the main channel. Gabriel and the driver leapt from the boat, and everyone worked to pull it up on the beach and hide it.

"Okay, let's go." I headed down the shore in the direction where the other boat had disappeared. When I didn't hear anything I turned around and saw Martim and our boat driver heading in the opposite direction. Gabriel, Vicente and the other guard stood looking indecisively between us.

"What are you doing?" I asked.

"Martim ordered everyone to go this way," Vicente said, lifting his hands.

"But the boat went this way." I pointed down the shore.

"I know, but we have to listen to him. He outranks us. He's a government official and we have to do as he says."

"Well, I don't."

"You can't go after them alone, Lexi," Vicente argued. "Please. It's crazy."

"Fine. Call me crazy. I'm going after the other boat with or without you."

"That's not a good idea. In fact, it's a *really* bad idea."

I didn't care what he thought. I didn't care what *any* of them thought. I was furious and fed up. They could do what they wanted.

When it became clear I wasn't going to follow, Gabriel frowned and handed me the satellite phone. "I'm sorry, but Vicente is right. We must follow Martim. But if you will not go with us, at least take the phone. Call if you get into trouble."

I took the phone and slipped the cord around my neck.

Martim shouted over his shoulder at us, presumably insisting we follow. Vicente tried one last time to convince me to come with the others, but I turned away from him and plunged into the rainforest alone.

Chapter Twenty-Four

Lexi

Why did this stuff always happen to me? Two days into the trip and I was suddenly alone in the rainforest. That little black cloud had followed me to South America after all. Couldn't I ever get a break?

Even though I knew it was the right thing to do, being alone in the rainforest was not the best plan I'd ever had. I couldn't wander aimlessly—I would die for sure. I needed a solid plan of action.

Stopping by a tree, I reviewed everything I knew to this point. I was following the river from the cover of the jungle in case any more boats full of bandits sped by, but other than that, I had no idea what was next. First, I needed a better look at the phone. After I was sure no other boats were visible, I went to the shore and pulled the satellite phone off my neck. I studied it a minute and pulled out a small piece of paper in the little plastic pouch taped on the back and read the instructions, which were, thank God, in English.

I read the instructions carefully, pumping my fist when I saw the phone had a GPS feature. I examined the phone, turned it on, and walked around until I had a signal. I did a little jump of happiness when I saw the small icon indicating that location sharing was turned on.

"Yes," I breathed.

If I assumed the satellite phone was with the group, then I had a direct map leading me to them. Unfortunately, the phone location shared coordinates only, since there was no graphical mapping interface on the phone. Fortunately, comparing coordinates to determine a direction was merely a math problem, and I was really good at math problems. I quickly got to work, comparing my coordinates to theirs. When the calculations were done, I figured the group, or at least the phone, was no longer on the water, but on the shore, about a half mile to my south southeast.

It seemed simple, but I'd been turned around and needed to figure out which direction was north. To try and figure it out, I started moving in what I thought was the right direction, noting how the coordinates changed.

Just as I was calibrating my sense of directions, I heard a gunshot in the distance. It startled me so much, I almost dropped the phone. I froze and strained my ears listening for more noise, but heard nothing. It hadn't sounded like the pop of a pistol, but more the flat crack of a rifle. That alarmed me more than I wanted to admit.

My hands shaking, I checked my direction once more and realized I needed to head directly toward where I'd heard the sound. I moved as quickly as I could, given that a path did not exist and I had to plow through dense undergrowth. As much as I hated straying from a direct route, I figured I'd make better time following along the shoreline as much as possible.

When I came out from beneath the canopy of trees, I saw that I'd cut the corner on the upstream side of where

the tributary entered the Amazon and was now parallel-
ing the beach of the side stream. After a couple of anxious minutes and no more sounds, I came upon two boats
beached together on my side of the stream.

I found them!

I darted back into the trees and waited a precious five
minutes to see if anyone was guarding the boats. When
I didn't see anyone, I decided to risk it and check out
things. I crept out of the trees and approached the boats,
expecting any minute to be shot in the back. Thankfully,
nothing happened.

I peeked in the research team's boat first and saw
that everything was gone, including the cooler with vaccines. The pirates' boat was empty except for cigarette
butts and empty cans. Gross. I started to leave when I
had an idea and spent a minute more in each boat before departing.

Also while still on the beach, I took more precious
moments to compare the phone coordinates. I estimated I
was within a quarter mile of the other phone. I could see
a sandy trail leading away from the boats that everyone
must have run down. I headed down it as well, hoping I
didn't accidentally run into the bad guys.

After a few minutes, I stopped to check the coordinates. To my astonishment, I noticed the phone's coordinates had changed. I did a quick mental calculation
and determined the coordinates were moving...directly
toward me.

They were returning to the boats.

I had no idea if Slash, Gwen or Natelli were okay or
whether they were been captured or hurt. Regardless, if
I wanted to help them, I needed a plan. Looking around,
I spotted a tree that rose up over the path that had some

low-hanging branches. One thing was evident. I needed to get higher for a decent view, because on the ground, the dense foliage gave me no ability to see whatsoever. I strode toward the tree with confidence. Somehow, a delusional part of my brain had convinced me I could climb a tree to get a better look at the trail.

Taking a deep breath for courage, I quickly shinnied up the tree. Once up, I looked down and swallowed hard, thinking it was a lot farther down to the ground than I expected.

Holy geek in a tree.

I had no idea how I did it. Athleticism and me are not usually words used in the same sentence. In fact, I'm positive athleticism had *never* been used in reference to me. Not to mention, I'm scared of heights. What possessed me to climb a tree will likely remain a mystery for the entirety of my life, as long as it might last. I wasn't sure if my mother would be proud of my evolving skill set for surviving in the wild, but I knew Slash would appreciate it. If either of us ended up alive and could joke about it, of course.

I carefully maneuvered to a nook in the tree where I was hidden, and finally had a decent view of the path in the distance. My heart began to pound when I saw a trail of people approaching. I squinted to see if I could see Slash, but I couldn't. After a moment, one of the bad guys became visible in the front. He was carrying a rifle and the satellite phone hung around his neck. He had no idea it was on and I was tracking his location, so that gave me a small advantage that I'd have to figure out how to exploit.

Slowly the others came into view. I spotted Gwen's red hair, Natelli, Salvador and then, at the very back,

Slash, walking in front of the other bad guy, who was bringing up the rear. I closed my eyes, letting relief and emotion swamp me.

He's alive. They're all alive...so far.

They might not be alive for long if I didn't figure out a way to save them. My eyes snapped open. All of the people in the research group were walking with their hands folded on their heads except Slash, who was carrying the cooler of vaccines. That was good because his hands were not tied or restrained in any way. Still, I had precious little time to come up with a solution to take down two armed men without getting captured or putting the rest of the team at risk.

How can I do that? Think, Lexi, think.

At the first village, Slash had been looking for a distraction to make his move. So, if I were able to provide a distraction like before, it might allow him a chance to take out the men somehow. But what kind of distraction could I make? I was stuck in a tree without a weapon or anything to use. Maybe climbing the tree hadn't been the best idea I'd ever had.

My eyes scanned the terrain below without finding any solutions. I adjusted my position further out on a branch to get a better look at the terrain when I suddenly found myself next to a large python languishing on the same branch. I swallowed the scream that formed in my throat as I slowly backed down the branch, my heart racing.

Then, I had an idea. I could use the snake as a distraction. Its location was perfect—right over the path—but how could I use it? My mind started racing. If I could make the snake drop on one of the bad guys, that would certainly distract him. But how was I going to get the snake off the branch and on to the bad guy? There was no way I was going to touch it. Besides, using a snake had way too many variables that could go wrong.

But it was the only thing I had at my disposal and I was out of time.

I glanced at the group. They were getting closer. They'd be beneath me in three minutes or less. I had to figure out a way to get the lead guy to stop right beneath the tree. If I could do that, then perhaps I could get the snake to drop on him and cause pandemonium. I peered at the snake, and it still appeared to be sleeping and not paying me any attention. I glanced down by my foot and spotted a dead branch whose leaves had long fallen off. I wrapped my legs around the tree branch I was sitting on and yanked hard on the dead branch, ripping it free.

My breathing was coming too fast again, and I had to fight to slow it before I hyperventilated and fell out of the tree. I did some quick calculations—the lag time for a call based on the signal transmission time and the speed of the people walking—before turning on the satellite phone. I pinpointed a spot in the distance. When the lead bad guy was at the point in my vision, I dialed the phone. As the group got closer and the phone didn't ring, I cursed myself, thinking I'd miscalculated. Just as the guy stood under my branch, the satellite phone around his neck rang. He stopped where he was and looked at the phone, trying to figure out how to use it. I used the dead branch to poke the snake, but it didn't budge. It was a heck of a lot heavier than I imagined. I poked again, this time a lot harder. So hard, I almost fell off the branch. The snake hissed at me and lifted its head, staring balefully at me.

OMG! He was pissed.

Panicking about how long the guy would remain there trying to figure out the phone, I aggressively gave it another push, wrapping my legs around the branch for greater leverage. The snake, unhappy, flicked his tongue and narrowed those killer eyes as if it were contemplating eating me whole. It hissed furiously. For a second I thought it was going to strike at me, but I shook a fist at it as if commanding it to fall. To my shock, a miracle happened. The snake became unbalanced and fell.

The guy below screamed as the force of the snake's body knocked him to the ground. His gun skittered away beneath the foliage. Once on the ground, the angry snake reacted to the guy's movement by wrapping around his legs and slithering up his body. The guy kept screaming while everyone else started shouting, not knowing what to do. His buddy at the back hadn't seen the snake fall, but now pushed forward to see him partially constrained by a large snake. Waving his gun at everyone to shut them up, he cautiously approached his downed buddy, who was shrieking and holding the snake's head in his hands. The downed guy was screaming something over and over in Portuguese that I presumed to be "shoot it!" or something to that effect.

As the one pirate aimed to shoot the snake without hitting his partner, the scariest part of my plan was ready to be executed. I said a small prayer and gathered my legs beneath me. Just before I was about to jump, a movement caught the corner of my eye. I turned my head, and several trees away, I saw a dark-skinned native watching me. He was also in the treetops, and his face had multiple distinctive tattoos and markings. I blinked a couple of times to ensure I wasn't hallucinating, and when I looked again, he was gone.

Drawing my attention back to the scene below, I gauged my leap, closed my eyes and jumped. As I fell, I heard a gunshot, Slash yelling, and a hard thump before it all went black.

Chapter Twenty-Five

Lexi

When I came to, I found Slash staring into my face. He was holding me and we were both alive. I breathed in relief. Life was good. I didn't care about anything else, so I decided to go back to sleep.

Unfortunately, Slash patted my cheek insistently until I opened my eyes again. "*Cara*, are you okay?"

I wiggled my hands and feet, but I couldn't tell. "I'm not sure, Slash. I poked a snake, jumped out of a tree, and saw a native man watching me. I think I may be delusional."

"You probably have a concussion. You lost consciousness." Slash reached under his shirt and pulled out his cross, bringing it to his lips. Then he gently kissed my forehead. "Thank God, you're alive. That's all that matters."

After a moment, I was able to sit up and look around. The two pirates were down. Slash told me the one who was bruised from being squeezed by the python was also suffering from a gunshot wound to the shoulder inflicted by his partner, who'd had his aim adjusted due to unanticipated falling objects. The other one was unconscious due to a kick to the head by Slash's hiking boot.

I looked around worriedly. "Where's the snake?"

"He decided it was wise to make an exit after we pulled him off the guy, which wasn't easy, by the way."

I shuddered and rubbed the back of my head where I had a painful lump. "What about our group? Is anyone hurt?"

"We're fine, *cara*, thanks to you. Why are you alone? Where's everyone else?"

I gave him a quick rundown of what happened. Natelli, Gwen and the others crowded around to hear and were shocked when I told them what Martim had done.

"What's *wrong* with that guy?" Gwen exclaimed. "He was just going to leave us to die?"

"He won't see it that way," I said. "He'll probably claim credit for escaping and bringing the rescuers to you."

"Gabriel and Vicente went with him?" Natelli said. "They *left* you? That's unfathomable."

"Apparently Martim threatened to fire them," I said. "I almost decked Martim at one point, but Vicente stopped me."

Slash was angry, I could tell by the hard set of his jaw and the glitter in his eyes, but he said nothing. Instead he helped me stand with a gentle hand under my elbow. "Let's see if you can walk."

Once upright, I tested my legs. Miraculously nothing was broken. Apparently the bad guy I'd jumped on had broken my fall. I felt a bit guilty when I saw him lying there unconscious, but when I remembered how he'd waved a gun at Slash and the others, that guiltiness vanished.

After tying him up, Slash hoisted the unconscious guy on his back in a fireman's carry and headed toward the beach while Salvador and the boat driver lugged the vaccine cooler to the boats. The other security guard escorted the pirate who'd been shot, while Gwen, Natelli and I brought up the rear. Both women flanked me in case I stumbled.

"You're the most amazing woman I've ever met," Natelli said. "I can't believe what you just did."

"I got lucky," I said. "Really lucky. The satellite phone had a GPS and Slash had the foresight to turn it on. I was able to do the math in my head. Then the python just happened to be on a branch right where I needed it to be and somehow I managed to push it off. The universe lined things up for me."

Natelli shook her head. "Incredible. We are really lucky to have you."

When we got to the beach, I told Slash help was on the way.

"I know." He tapped the satellite phone. "While you were out, I called and gave them updated coordinates."

"You're so smart." I leaned into him, beyond thankful he was safe. He probably had no idea how scared I was when I saw the pirates chase after him.

He wrapped an arm around my shoulder and kissed the top of my head. "You were amazing, *cara*, dropping out of the tree like that. It surprised even me, given your fear of heights."

"Don't even ask me how I managed to climb a tree, because I'm not sure how I did it. I think I blacked out during the process."

"Hey, our driver can't get the boat started," Salvador

suddenly yelled at us. "The pirates must have disabled the boats."

I grinned sheepishly and reached into my pocket, pulling out a set of spark plugs for each boat. "Sorry. I didn't want them taking you away while I was trying to figure out what to do."

Salvador jogged over to get the spark plugs. "Good thinking, Lexi," he said, handing one set to the boat driver and pocketing the other. He wasn't going to give the pirates any chance to recover their boat.

Gwen put a hand on my other shoulder, shading her eyes with her hand. "Lexi, I can't believe you figured out how to take down two hardened drug runners with automatic rifles using nothing more than a python and the weight of your body. That's so freaking cool."

"Wait. Did you just say drug runners? How do you know they were drug runners?"

"Salvador told us that they were talking about getting a bonus for our capture. But we had to be alive," she explained. "They also knew all about the vaccines we were carrying, and they were to handle them carefully. They'd been warned that the foreigners were on the same boat and that they could be tough to handle. They were laughing at us, saying we hadn't been tough at all. They couldn't just be random pirates if they knew all that. The only other possibility I can think of is that they're drug runners with inside knowledge about our operation."

I exchanged a glance with Slash, but his eyes warned me to save any discussion for later. After a few minutes, the boat driver was able to get our boat working. We discussed going to Coari to turn the guys over to the police, but the boat driver suggested it would be best to wait, as there could be other drug boats out there looking for them. Before we had decided what to do, our rescue crew arrived in two boats.

Salvador told us that our rescuers included Coari's chief of police. Several other uniformed men carrying rifles quickly took charge of the prisoners. The one who got knocked out when I fell on him had regained consciousness, but seemed kind of woozy and in pain. He was saying something, clearly confused, when the police roared in laughter at him.

"What's going on over there?" I asked Salvador.

"They're telling him that an unarmed women took him and his friend out without getting a scratch. They find it quite humorous."

I didn't know what to say about that, so I sat down. Slash sat beside me, letting me lean my head on his shoulder. He linked hands with me and for a minute we sat there in companionable silence.

"I really don't want to get back on that boat again," I said.

"Would you like to spend the night here?" he suggested. "We could have a romantic evening under the stars listening to the chirp of birds, the slither of the python and his mate, and perhaps become friends with a couple of river spiders."

"Ha ha." I punched him in the arm. "Funny. Not."

When the police finally deemed it safe for us to board the boats, we did. The return trip seemed to go a lot faster. Our jeeps were where we left them. We climbed in and were escorted by the police, without incident, back to the research camp.

Vicente, Gabriel and others rushed out to greet us. Martim was nowhere to be found. Vicente reached me first and was about to say something when Slash stepped between us and crossed his arms. He didn't say anything, but the way he looked at Vicente, the message was clear.

Stay away from her.

Vicente took a surprised step back. I walked around them both and handed Gabriel the satellite phone. "Thanks, this really saved me."

"Lexi." Gabriel, clearly uncomfortable, looked like he wanted to say something, but after some internal struggling, he didn't. Instead he took the phone, and without another word, walked over to the authorities to speak with them.

I wanted nothing more than go to my bunk and collapse, but Slash steered me to Melinda and forced her to do a full examination. I didn't have any broken bones, just some scrapes, bruises, and a bump on the back of my head. She suspected a concussion and ordered me to bed as soon as I took a shower. While under the spray of the cold water, it occurred to me this was the second day in a row our attempt to deliver the vaccine to the indigenous populations had failed.

If Vaccitex's competitors were the ones behind this, they were succeeding beyond their wildest dreams, and they hadn't even needed to hack to do it.

Chapter Twenty-Six

Slash

The situation was fast becoming intolerable. Seeing Lexi drop out of the tree onto a guy with a gun had taken another ten years off his life. At this point, he was operating on negative years after only a year together with her. It was time to get a handle on what was going on. He was not going to be able to protect her—as well as the project—if he was only being reactive.

The question was where to start.

After making sure Lexi was thoroughly checked out by Melinda and ordered to rest, he showered, changed, and asked one of the security guards to take him to the police station in Coari. When the guard hesitated, he slipped him a hundred dollar bill. Once they arrived at the station and the driver agreed to wait, Slash went inside.

Unfortunately Portuguese was one of the few languages he didn't know, but he was fluent in Spanish, and luckily, one the officers also spoke it. That young man, who looked to be about fifteen, escorted him to the holding area where a group of guards were sitting around smoking. They quickly came to attention when he entered the room.

Slash introduced himself as a member of the research team interested in following up on the state of the prisoners. The young officer translated for him. To Slash's surprise, the other officers knew who he was and were quite interested in talking to him.

"How'd you do it?" one of the officers asked him. "Take out two bandits like that without a weapon? You ex-military?"

So, they'd heard about the escapade in the jungle after the first attack. He shouldn't have been surprised. Coari was a small town. The news about a bunch of scientists sending two sets of possible drug runners to jail in two days had probably been a record.

Slash shrugged. "Something like that."

"So, tell us what happened." The guys leaned forward, their eyes gleaming. They wanted details and a good story, and he wanted information. It seemed like a fair trade.

He told them what had happened, embellishing a lot of the story to make it sound like the battle was a lot tougher than it actually was. The young officer apparently translated sufficiently because the guys were transfixed. When it came time to ask his questions, they were happy to comply.

"So, you've got four new prisoners here," he said. "Know anything about them yet?"

The first officer leaned forward, lowering his voice. "Nothing yet on the two you deposited today, but we know a little about the two from yesterday. Both have criminal records and neither are local. They aren't even Brazilian. Their files indicate that they're originally from

Boa Vista, a small city up near the Venezuelan border. They deny any involvement with drug operations, but they both have a unique tattoo on their necks indicating that they're members of a gang headquartered in Venezuela that's heavily involved in cocaine trafficking."

Slash digested that information. They were drug runners after all. How did that play into concentrated attacks on the vaccine distribution process?

"Anyway we called a doctor for the guy who got shot, but he has not arrived yet," the officer continued. "He's pretty messed up and in a lot of pain, but he isn't getting any sympathy from us. We know what they are—parasites on the earth. His legs and lower abdomen are covered with bruises, thanks to the snake, and he was shot in the shoulder. Probably needs surgery or something, but he's not getting it in Coari, that's for sure. But we got a doctor on the way. They can't call us barbarians, despite the fact that they're worse than the scum on my feet."

Slash didn't feel even the slightest twinge of sympathy for the drug runners. "Did they say anything about the research project or the work we are doing? Or did they mention anything about orders to kidnap or demand ransom?"

"You know, that's exactly what Mr. FUNAI just asked. You guys working together or something?"

For a moment, Slash just looked at him. "Mr. FUNAI? A big guy with a mustache and attitude?"

They laughed, apparently finding his description funny. "Yeah, he was here about an hour ago. He interrogated the prisoners. Let me confirm the name." The officer pulled a card out of his pocket and flipped it toward Slash. He caught it between his fingers and read the name.

Martim Alves. Wasn't that interesting?

Slash handed the card back. "So, Mr. Alves has already interrogated them?"

"Yes, sir. He asked to do it alone, as he said he has experience with drug operators, and they wouldn't talk if a cop was present. He thought they might open up to him, since he's government and all. But I don't think he had much luck."

"Why do you say that?"

"He wanted us to let him know if we uncovered anything else about their motives or connections."

Slash let that sink in. "I see. Do you think you could notify me as well? I don't have a card, but I'm staying out at the research camp along with Mr. Alves. I'd appreciate it."

"Sure."

He shook hands with all the officers. After a bit of back slapping, he took his leave. The driver was waiting, so on the ride back to the camp, Slash reviewed the information at hand.

Unfortunately, none of it was adding up. Why would drug runners get involved with a research team trying to validate a vaccine for malaria? It was a stretch to think that a Vaccitex competitor would stoop to forming an alliance with a drug cartel, no matter how much money was at stake. And what was in it for the drug cartels? Why would they risk getting involved in a high-profile, international research effort? Making that kind of alliance would be a huge risk and stupid, despite the money.

Salvador had told them the two pirates had known they were carrying vaccines, had been instructed to take care with them, and had wanted the scientists alive. Why? To force them to reveal the ingredients and procedure? That seemed far-fetched even to his own mind. Why not just break down an actual sample of the vaccine?

It made more sense to follow the money trail. Who was paying them and to what end? That had to be the first question asked by interrogators. Who was funding their escapades to capture and detain the research scientists? And how did Martim Alves fit into this? Was he just a pompous jerk or did he have an ulterior motive? Maybe he'd just wanted to save his own skin when he sent the pirates away from his boat, and perhaps he legitimately came to interrogate the prisoners on behalf of the government. Still, that seemed an unusual responsibility for a paper-pushing bureaucrat who was supposedly looking out for the indigenous population. It just didn't fit.

Then there was Vicente Lopes. His gut was telling him there was something off about the guy, and he always trusted his gut. What had Vicente been doing the night before the trip, and what had he handed off to an unknown person outside of the camp?

He had a lot of questions, but unfortunately no answers when they finally pulled into the research camp.

Chapter Twenty-Seven

Lexi

I had a good night's sleep and awoke, after oversleeping, without a headache or any lasting effects of the day before, except for a few sore muscles and a couple of ugly bruises. I got dressed quickly, visited the facilities to wash my face and brush my teeth and headed into the dining area for coffee and food.

Natelli and Gwen were sitting together, drinking coffee and looking glum. I didn't see Slash anywhere.

I grabbed some coffee and joined them. "Good morning. Why all the glum faces?"

Gwen heaved a huge sigh. "Natelli thinks we should cancel the trials and go home. It's become too dangerous."

"*What?*" I glanced in shock at Natelli, but she wouldn't meet my gaze. "Natelli, you can't do that. It's exactly what they want you to do. They want to disrupt the project, and that's what will happen if we pack up and go home."

"We don't even know who *they* is," she answered heatedly. "People could have been killed yesterday, and the day before that. You could have died saving us, Lexi. I can't ask anyone else in good faith to put their lives on the line for this project."

I shook my head. "No. You don't get to do that."

She seemed taken aback by my firm voice. "Do what?"

"Make decisions about my life. Try to protect me. There are lives that need our protection. You've devoted your entire life to this vaccine, to helping people, most of them children. We *have* to do what we came to do, otherwise they win."

Before she could respond, Slash walked in with an elderly man who was dressed in black priest's robes with the white collar. I gasped in surprise, but other than a brief acknowledgment with his eyes, Slash led the priest to Natelli. We all rose from our chairs.

"Natelli, I'd like to introduce you to Father Rafa Quintela," Slash said. "He just arrived at the camp. We've been speaking in Spanish since my Portuguese leaves a lot to be desired. He doesn't speak English, but he's from Coari and he says he heard we have a problem with the people at the first village we visited. He heard that they're afraid to cooperate and is willing to help out as needed."

"How did he find out about that?" Natelli asked him curiously.

Slash translated the question and Father Quintela responded.

"He says news travels fast, and bad news even faster," Slash said. "His diocese received a call from the Vatican this morning, urging them to do what they could to help your effort. The father is here as a result of that phone call. He's happy to help us speak with the villagers, as he happens to know some of the tribesmen, and while they're not Christian, his church does have the respect of the village for their kindness and bartering."

I exchanged a glance with Slash, curious if he'd somehow brought the Vatican into this, and if so, why? But now wasn't the time to ask.

Natelli held out a hand to the priest and he shook it. "Thank you so much, Father. That's very kind of you to offer. But things are quite dangerous right now. We've had some...incidents."

After Slash told the priest what she said, he answered.

"He said he's not afraid," Slash said. "He quoted scripture, Joshua 1:9. *Have I not commanded you? Be strong and courageous. Do not be afraid; do not be discouraged, for the Lord, your God, will be with you wherever you go."*

I turned to Natelli. "Well, even the priest thinks we should move forward. So, does this mean we're back on for the vaccines?"

Slash looked between us, momentarily puzzled. "Were we off?"

"Natelli was thinking about cancelling the project," Gwen explained. "She was going to ask Lilith and Hayden if we could pull out for safety reasons. Just for the record, I didn't support that option."

"Me either," I said.

"I'm not letting a bunch of thugs stop me from helping people," Gwen added. "None of us should."

I had to give it to Gwen. While she occasionally irritated me with her nonstop cheery disposition and occasional fangirling, she was smart and stepped up when things counted. That made her okay in my book.

"I agree completely with Gwen," I said.

We all turned toward Natelli, and she threw up her

hands. "Well, what do you expect me to do? I'm scared for all of you. I don't want anyone to get hurt on my watch. But you're right, if we pull out, they win. We can't give up that easy." She started to pace. "It has to be voluntary for whomever wants to accompany us on the next trip. Gabriel must provide more security for those of us going out in the field. I'll not have a repeat of the past two attempts. Finally, no one but me will know in advance which village we are going to visit. I can't ignore that there may be someone within our camp who is trying to sabotage our efforts."

"Smart plan," Slash said.

Apparently having made up her mind, Natelli took a deep breath and faced the elderly priest. "Slash, please tell Father Quintela that we'll come for him when we're ready. And please have him thank the Vatican for their unwavering support. It's much appreciated."

"I will," Slash said. "Now what?"

A determined look crossed Natelli's face. "We get back to work."

Chapter Twenty-Eight

Lexi

I spent the rest of the day reviewing data and checking in with my team in New York. They were still under attack, but had created a good defense.

"Don't get cocky," I told Ken, my assistant who was overseeing the team in New York.

"We're not. They're good, whoever they are, and they're determined. If we don't find them soon, there's a fifty-fifty chance they'll break through. We have to keep one step ahead of them."

I reviewed the data and worked on some new encryption algorithms. My inbox indicated an email and I saw it was from my mom.

I added seventeen new dresses to the list for you to review. Look carefully at dress number eighty-one. This could be the one. Also what do you think about a color palette of light blue and white for your wedding colors to match the diamond in your engagement ring?

Seventeen new dresses? Jeez. I was only up to dress number twenty-three and that was only because Basia made me. Quickly, I closed the email, figuring I'd worry about it later.

I glanced around the lab. Gwen, Natelli, Sara, Melinda and Doug were busy checking the vaccine vials to ensure they were still preserved and untouched. I didn't have a chance to speak alone with Slash, until a bit later when we were working and no one else was around.

"So, what's with the priest showing up today?" I asked. "Does the Vatican knows you're here?"

"I don't think so. It could be a complete coincidence. The church often supports initiatives and research into vaccines, and this would be an important one. So definitely in the realm of possibility."

"But it's odd. You've never seen or heard of Father Quintela before?"

"Never. I just noticed a guard talking to him by the gate, and I went over to see if I could assist. He told me the same story he told you, so I took him to Natelli."

"Does he know of your connections to the Vatican?"

"No. As far as I know, no one does. I'd prefer to keep it that way until I'm sure of what we're dealing with here."

I didn't have a chance to respond because Gabriel showed up in the lab asking to speak to Slash. They spoke for a moment and Slash returned to his computer to shut it down.

"Gabriel wants to talk to me about security."

"Well, that's interesting considering he wouldn't even arm you."

"I'm sure he's bound by certain laws and regulations. I'm not holding that against him. I *am*, however, holding him responsible for abandoning you. We're about to discuss that in great detail."

I looked up in surprise. "Slash, don't do anything foolish. Just talk."

"We'll see." He disappeared out the door with Gabriel and I returned to my work, trying not to worry about what was happening between them.

Several hours passed and I went to dinner, hoping to see Slash, but he was nowhere to be found. There was an empty seat next to Salvador, so I sat down and we started talking.

"You've lived in this area all of your life?" I asked him, breaking a piece of bread in half.

"I have. I grew up in a small village just north of Coari, near the river."

"That's how you know this area so well."

"Yes. I'm quite familiar with this entire region, including the riverways. I've worked many jobs from fishing to hunting to mapping locations for the government. That's how I know where most of the indigenous tribes live, although there are some I've never actually seen."

"That's fascinating. How do you speak English so well?"

He laughed. "I listen to a lot of American and British music. Actually, I studied English in school and later at the university. I sometimes take tourists around, although tourists don't come here that much. Not yet, anyway."

"We're lucky to have you on the team."

He shook his head. "No, I'm lucky to be on the team. I volunteered."

"Volunteered?" I looked at him puzzled. "What do you mean?"

"When I heard about the vaccine trial, I wanted to help." He paused for a moment, staring down into his coffee cup before he cleared his throat. "I lost my daughter to malaria four years ago. She was three years old. I have a personal interest in this quest."

My heart dropped to my stomach. This was exactly why I never initiated conversation, because when I did, this kind of thing happened. Now, I had no idea what to say.

I decided to keep it simple and heartfelt. "I'm sorry, Salvador. I can't even imagine what that feels like. But you honor her memory by helping others to be safe."

A wisp of a smile crossed his lips. "Thank you, Lexi. Will you be accompanying us on our next visit to the village?"

"Someone has to protect the computer data, right?"

"And us." He lifted his mug to me and finished off his coffee. "Either way, I'll feel better knowing you're around."

I didn't see Slash until the next morning when we were all summoned for an early trip to the same village we'd been thwarted from reaching the day before yesterday. Natelli told us it would be the same team as before—minus Martim, who was apparently still recovering from his traumatic ordeal. Melinda was back and we had another boat filled with three new guards armed with automatic rifles.

Gwen, who was standing near us, leaned over and spoke in a hushed voice. "I heard Martim filed a complaint with the government that he was not sufficiently protected and that the entire operation was a farce."

"What a baby," I said. "At least it wasn't enough for the government to close down the operation…yet. They must have taken his complaints with a grain of salt. Why on earth did they send such an idiot to do this job?"

"Good question," Slash said. "However, I welcome the opportunity to spend the day without having to deal with his oversized personality, especially since I have my own hands full with my personal trouble magnet. By the way, we're traveling in the same boat today. That's a new, nonnegotiable item between Gabriel and me."

"What did you guys talk about all night?" I asked.

"Security. I gave him some advice and he took it. He also apologized for leaving you alone. He said it wouldn't happen again."

"I hope not. Did he give you a weapon?"

"Maybe. Maybe not. Or maybe I'm not allowed to talk about it."

I rolled my eyes. "Fine. Your secret. Did you know that Salvador lost his daughter to malaria when she was just three years old? He volunteered for the trials."

"I'm sorry to hear that. We're fortunate to have him on the team. He's a first-rate guide."

"He really is."

We piled into the jeeps, three jeeps this time, and headed to the boats. As promised, Slash was in a boat with Gwen, Natelli and me, which suited me just fine. Vicente wisely kept his distance from Slash, but the overall mood of the team was significantly lighter without Martim.

Regardless, I was anxious the entire boat ride, not only because I hate riding in boats, but also because I kept expecting pirates to zoom out of hidden tributaries and start shooting at us. However, the trip was blessedly uneventful, and Gwen even managed to get Slash and me to pose for a couple of photos.

After we landed and unloaded, we started our hike to the village carrying our supplies. I felt significantly more secure given the extra security and the knowledge that Slash was probably armed. However, I was sweating so badly within five minutes, I had to tie the bandana around my forehead to keep the sweat from dripping into my eyes.

At some point during the hike, Gwen sidled up to me. I shifted the water I was carrying to another hand so I could swat a mosquito that was buzzing around my neck.

"Lexi, please don't think I'm crazy, but I thought I saw something in the trees...actually, make that a *someone*. It was a guy's face, I think. He had tattoos on his cheeks, but when I squinted to get a better look, he was gone. So, I can't tell if I'm imagining things or I really saw something."

Her words reminded me of the impression of the native in the tree I'd had just before I jumped from the tree. In all the excitement, I'd completely forgotten about that.

"That's interesting, Gwen, because I thought I saw the same thing when we got separated and I was in the rainforest alone. But then the face was gone and I figured I'd just imagined it."

"That's really weird," she said, keeping her eyes glued to the trees.

"I wouldn't be worried. If there are natives out there, they're probably just curious about us."

"I hope so."

We finally reached the village and unloaded our equipment. Vicente and Natelli went over to talk to the village elder and the small group that ringed him. The villagers were dressed in a mix of clothes made from natural materials with a few brightly colored and well-worn T-shirts and an occasional pair of jeans. Children under five or six were naked. Everyone had bare feet and all the women were bare breasted. Most of the women wore loose skirts woven with some combination of leaves or grass. A few of the men wore loincloths. Interestingly, the man I suspected to be the village chief wore a pair of khaki shorts and a Nike Just Do It T-shirt.

A prolonged discussion between Vicente and the chief ensued. I suspected it was regarding our no-show yesterday. At some point, Vicente suddenly turned to me and pointed. Every villager in the place turned to look at me. Vicente wiggled his arm like a snake and mimicked jumping and falling over.

Oh, crap. They were talking about me and the rescue.

The villagers gasped, so Vicente hopped up and acted out the rest of the story in a dramatic retelling. The chief looked dubiously at me, but Salvador nodded vigorously, as if to provide verification.

To my surprise, the chief abruptly strode over to me. At five feet eleven, I was a good four inches taller, but I stood still as he examined my face and my hair, as if to uncover some hidden secret. Then he started firing off questions, which Vicente rapidly translated.

"I told him why we didn't come yesterday, and explained how you saved the group by throwing the snake at one of the pirates, then jumping out of the tree to take out the other one. So, the chief would like to know if you're a descendant of the *Amazonas*."

"Who are the *Amazonas*?" I asked.

"The *Amazonas* are a legendary tribe of women warriors who once lived and roamed the rainforest of South America," he explained. "The existence of this matriarchal group was confirmed by several Spanish and Portuguese explorers who wrote about the incredible strength and courage of the women warriors. Do you know where the Amazon River got its name?"

I shook my head. "I don't."

"The Amazon was named by Spanish soldier Francisco de Orellana, the first European to explore the Amazon, in 1541. He named the river after repeatedly fighting battles with tribes of ferocious female warriors whom he likened to the Amazons of Greek mythology. The local tribes all have legends of remote tribes of fierce warrior women. They were so skilled in battle and strategy that it was said that just one of these women was worth ten men. He himself has never seen one, but given what he was told about our adventures yesterday and your rescue of the team, he wonders if you're descended from them."

I had no earthly idea what to say to that. Should I acknowledge the legend, but say I'd just been thinking on my feet? I didn't want to say the wrong thing and then we'd all get sent home. Everyone was watching me, but I didn't have a clue. Panicked, I looked to Slash for help, and he did what he does best—gracefully rescued me from conversation.

"While Lexi is not an *Amazonas*," Slash said, "I have personally witnessed her perform remarkable and numerous feats of skill and bravery. She's a true woman warrior." He paused and then added, "However, you should be warned she's deathly afraid of spiders."

When Vicente translated, everyone laughed, even the children. Thankfully, the mood was now set, and the village was receptive and willing to receive the vaccine. I was glad, even if the laughter had been at my expense.

Natelli had Slash bring the vaccine cooler to a shaded area with a table, and she, Melinda and Gwen began to get the vaccines process set up. Vicente and Salvador

started organizing people for the vaccine, while I opened
my laptop and got ready to enter the data.

To track who received what level of dosage, a small,
durable anklet, like an identification bracelet in the hospital, would be put on each person after they received
their shot. The chief would receive the first shot, then
the warrior men, and then the mothers—all before the
children, so that they would be shown they had no need
to be afraid. It was a clever approach because it would
force the parents to put on a brave face to reduce crying or fear from the kids. I would record whatever data
Melinda, Natelli or Gwen would ask me to put into the
database so they could track the long-term effective-
ness and who was getting what dosage, based on their
weight and age.

The chief took the first dose from Melinda, looking at me while he got it. When he was finished, I gave
him a thumbs-up. As the process wound on, we got into
a good rhythm. I noticed out the corner of my eye that
Slash and the other security guards had set up a security checkpoint on the path leading up to the village to
prevent any interruptions.

At some point, Slash asked me to keep an eye on the
satellite phone, so I slipped it over my neck and made
sure it was off so we didn't run the battery down. The
entire process took about five hours and we didn't take
a break once, sneaking in gulps of water between pa-
tients so we didn't get dehydrated. When the last infant
was vaccinated and I had entered the last bit of data, I
encrypted it and shut down my laptop. I returned it to
the laptop bag and slipped it over my shoulder before
standing to stretch my back, neck and arms.

Gwen, Melinda and Natelli were talking among themselves, carefully collecting and counting all the vials and isolating the waste material, but essentially, I was finished. I looked around but didn't see Slash. Gabriel was standing down the village path, Salvador was talking to a villager, and Vicente was chatting to a mother with an infant. The other security guards were spread out around the perimeter, keeping watch and looking serious.

I had to go to the bathroom, but I didn't see anything that looked like an outhouse, and I didn't think anyone would understand if I asked, so I decide to investigate the village a bit to see if I could figure out where it was on my own. No one seemed to mind as I walked around a bit. There were several huts with grass roofs and raised wooden floors, which was smart because it helped keep the insides dry, given the continual Amazonian rain.

As I neared one hut, a little girl about six came running from the vaccine line to proudly show me where on her arm she'd got her shot. I knelt down so I was eye to eye with her and tried to show her that I was impressed. To my surprise, she took my hand and led me to a hut a little bit farther away. Apparently this was her home, because she showed me where she slept and a little carved wooden doll. Climbing up onto the hut floor, she waved her arms like a snake, then pretended to throw it to the ground and jump on it. She held her fists up with a fierce look on her face.

I couldn't help it, I clapped. "You go, girl. You're the real deal—a true blue *Amazonas*. Stay fierce."

Amused, I headed out of the hut, the girl bounding off in front of me. I'd taken three steps when I abruptly came face to face with a native man. I'd no idea where he'd come from. He'd just materialized out of nowhere. He wore nothing but a loincloth and a necklace made of twine and teeth. But his most remarkable features were the elaborate tattoos on his face.

The man I'd seen in the treetops!

Before I could react, he did the strangest thing. He held up the palm of his hand and, weirdly, blew me a kiss. At that exact moment, I was stung by an insect on my neck. I reached up and slapped at it, but felt the sting again. Fumbling, I swatted once more at my neck, pulling out a small wooden dart with a black feather. I stared at it, trying to make sense of what was happening, when the world started to spin.

Oh, no! I'm in trouble.

I took one step and opened my mouth to shout for Slash, but I wasn't sure if I actually did before the darkness rushed up and swallowed me whole.

Chapter Twenty-Nine

Lexi

I awoke to darkness and the smell of fire.

It took me a minute to get my bearings. My head was woozy and nausea bubbled in my throat. I reached out with my hands, realizing I was lying on packed dirt. I pushed myself to a sitting position, but as soon as I got upright, I threw up.

I vomited for at least a few minutes, successfully emptying whatever had been in my stomach for the past twenty-four hours. Wiping my mouth, I spent a moment remembering what happened. I'd been in the hut with the little girl. We were leaving to go back to the others when I spotted the tattooed native man. After that I remembered…not much.

I heard men's voices behind me laughing. I turned on my knees and saw a fire with about a dozen men sitting around it. The fire illuminated the face of the man closest to the fire. I recognized him immediately by his tattoos.

The man from the trees.

He called out to me, waving his hand as if to invite me to come over. I didn't move. He pointed to himself and said something. I didn't know if he was telling me his name, his title or that he was the one who kidnapped me.

Kidnapped!

I'd been kidnapped. But why? I looked down at my hands. I wasn't restrained in any manner, but if I ran, where would I go? I was stuck in the middle of the rainforest. I had no idea where I was. Reaching up, I touched a tender spot on my neck. I remembered the dart with a black feather. He must have drugged me and brought me here for…what?

I frantically searched the area for my laptop bag, but I didn't see it anywhere. I glanced back at the tattooed man and saw the satellite phone hanging around his neck. He must have seen me looking at it because he held it up proudly, although I was fairly sure he had no idea what it did.

I glanced at my watch to determine how long I'd been out. My heart sunk when I realized five hours had passed.

Slash. He'd be frantic that I'd gone missing. Again. Why did this always happen to me?

I wondered if the team had returned to the camp or were still at the village looking for me. Had anyone else been kidnapped? If not, why me? Was I a simple target of opportunity or had I been chosen for another reason?

I had endless questions and no answers. I could sit and speculate all night, or I could take stock of my situation and figure out what to do next.

First I had to take inventory. I was fully clothed, including my hiking boots, but after a quick check, I discovered my pockets were empty. My engagement ring was still on my finger, probably because my fingers had swollen so much in the heat and they couldn't get it off. They also left my watch on my wrist. Maybe they couldn't figure out how to get it off.

Suddenly one of the men approached me, holding out a small fruit and half-cooked fish. The fish hadn't been scaled, but its skin had been split from the heat. I could see the white, greasy meat in the firelight. My stomach revolted at the sight, so I refused the fish, but took the fruit. I ate it gingerly, and it made me realize how thirsty I was. After I finished the fruit, I motioned like I was drinking, and asked for water. A few minutes later, another man brought me a leather gourd that I hoped contained water. I knew that drinking the water was a bad idea for my digestive system, but I had little choice. I had to drink something or I'd die of dehydration.

The water was warm and brackish, but wet. I took small sips, trying to drink only the minimum. I was thirstier than I thought.

My neck was still throbbing from where I'd gotten hit by the dart. I decided it was time to find out what was in store for me.

I stood and walked over to the chief, lifting my hands in a questioning gesture, as if to ask why I was here. The chief and the other men simply stared at me without saying anything. I tried a variety of different pantomimes, but they either had no idea what I was trying to say or weren't inclined to answer.

I asked for the satellite phone, but the chief refused. Finally, he indicated it was time to sleep. While another guy banked the fire for the night, I was instructed to go back to the spot where I woke up.

I sat down in my spot, resting my chin on my knees. I contemplated trying to sneak off while everyone was asleep, but I had no idea where I was, and figured they would hear me as I stumbled around in the dark. Plus, darkness brought out scary predators I did not want to face on my own. As much as I didn't like it, the logical thing was to stay with the group and see what they had in mind in regards to my welfare. At least, for the time being, they didn't seem inclined to hurt me.

I scooted a little closer to the fire and curled up with my back to it. I didn't think I'd be able to sleep with all the strange jungle noises and the mosquitoes buzzing, but perhaps due to the heat and the residual effect of the drug from the dart, I quickly fell asleep.

Chapter Thirty

Lexi

I was roused by a foot.

I sat up and massaged my neck, which hurt from the dart and sleeping on the ground. The jungle was still dark, but a glimmer of dawn touched the sky. The men were packing up and preparing to leave, and it was clear I was going with them.

They gave me some more water before we left. Unfortunately, wherever we were going was mostly uphill. Since I wasn't accustomed to this steady uphill walking, and whatever drug they had given me sapped my energy, I asked them to stop frequently. Apparently, that disappointed them. Several of the men argued with the chief, probably over the value of keeping me. While I didn't want to be stuck with them, I certainly didn't want to be left alone in the jungle either. When the chief convinced them not abandon me, I breathed a sigh of relief.

As we climbed, the air and humidity became a little less oppressive. I didn't realize that the Amazon Basin had such drastic elevation changes, but I should have. We were on the far eastern slopes of the Andes, the mountains that funneled the water to the Amazon. So that made sense.

At one point, we diverted from the path and clambered up a steeper slope following a small stream. We stopped at a flat area with a crack in the rock where water was bubbling out. I guessed this was a spring that they used, and decided this was as good a water source as I was going to get. I drank as much as I could and got out of the way as the men filled their gourds from both the springhead and the stream that flowed from it. The water wasn't cold, but it was much cooler than the air temperature and it felt good in my mouth and throat.

Since I could, I washed some of the dirt off my face and hands. Some of the men sat down, so I assumed we were taking a break. I found a spot away from the men so I could watch them.

They sat around, animatedly talking about something, occasionally pointing at me. I had no idea what was going on.

Our break was shorter than I would have liked, but we returned to the trail and resumed the climb. Shortly after midday, the slope began to descend. Interestingly, the men who had been loose and chatty became increasingly wary and silent. One of them moved closer to me, keeping pace with me so that he was just a step away.

Clearly, there was some sort of danger here.

The trail was hard to traverse. I saw snakes everywhere, in the trees, on the path and lying on the rocks. Soon everything started to look like snakes. I tried not to freak out, even when I stumbled over uneven roots that looked like snakes. At some point, even the chief began to shadow me, catching me by the elbow to make sure I didn't land face-first. It seemed stealth was super important, which made me increasingly nervous. After two hours of this intense, silent traverse, the men started to relax. Whatever the danger was, we were apparently past it.

Looking down at my feet as I carefully stepped over the thousandth tree root of the day, I spied a large spider on my leg just below my knee.

Not again!

With a strangled cry, I jumped backward, right into the chief, knocking him down.

At that exact moment, the other guys suddenly whipped out their bows and darted off in the trees, leaving us alone.

"Hey!" I said, coming to my feet. "Where's everyone going?"

Maybe the chief thought I was going to follow them, or maybe he thought I'd make a run for it, so he grabbed me from behind, holding me tightly around the waist.

It was the first time any of them had gotten physical with me, and it scared me. "Hey!" I said, twisting in his grip. "Let go." When he didn't, I began kicking and thrashing.

I gave it everything I had, so the chief had a hard time holding me. My Krav Maga self-defense training started to come back to me, so I began to apply it, using my elbow to jab his throat and face. At one point, I kicked my legs out hard and connected with a tree. To my astonishment, a large snake fell out of a tree and landed on his left shoulder.

He grunted and his grip loosened on me. I took the opportunity to twist out of his grasp and made a run for it. I'd only run a few steps when one of the other guys materialized out of the trees and grabbed me by the arm.

When I whirled around, baring my teeth, he let go of me and stepped back, staring in surprise over my shoulder. Confused, I turned around and saw the chief holding the snake over his head, chanting something.

Everyone turned to look at me like I was poison or something.

Slowly, the men ringed me, effectively locking me in but not touching me. They started talking in a low voice and a couple of them kept looking upward worriedly as if somehow I would cause more snakes to fall from the trees.

Another of the men said something and motioned for everyone to come see. He pointed to an arrow in the tree right where the chief had been standing moments before I'd seen the spider on my leg and knocked him down. After watching them gesture, I determined that someone had shot at the chief. When I'd clumsily backed into him, knocking him down, whatever arrow that had been meant for him, missed.

Holy assassin! Had someone tried to shoot the chief? Was that why the men had all run off—to go looking for the shooter?

The chief tossed the snake in the bushes, looked at the arrow and then at me. Everyone followed his gaze until every eye was on me.

I held up my hands, hopefully indicating my innocence. "We're cool, right?"

The chief and his men started another fast and furious conversation. I'm not sure what was going on, but from all the gesturing, I think *they* thought I'd saved the chief's life by knocking him down. Suddenly, everyone was treating me with a new respect. I wondered if that would be enough to keep me alive—not that I had any idea what was going on.

I guess I'd find out soon enough.

Chapter Thirty-One

Lexi

We proceeded on our journey to wherever we were going. We'd been going uphill for the past few hours and I could barely walk anymore. I estimated we were approximately a few thousand feet higher than the river bottom, although that was impossible to tell since the heavy undergrowth limited my visibility in all directions. The ground felt rockier and there was an absence of lush growth under the canopy of trees. The trees, however, were looming giants, reaching several hundred feet in the air. They'd clearly been here for at least a thousand years or more.

The day dragged on. I was convinced I wouldn't be able to take another step when we suddenly broke into a clearing where a village was located. It backed up to a large rock face that rose nearly vertical over a hundred feet behind the village. A small stream flowed out of a crack in the base of the rock and pooled where it exited the rock as a small stream, providing fresh water to the villagers. If I hadn't been so exhausted, scared and starving, I might have fully appreciated the natural beauty of the location.

As we trudged closer, I counted more than twenty huts, some without sides or doors but all roofed with a woven combination of grass and fronds. Poles supported the wooden frames of the roofs. Unlike the huts I'd observed in the previous village, most of these huts did not have raised floors, but were made of dirt.

People ran out to greet us. The children were naked, and the women were topless and wearing loincloths or knee-length grass skirts. The men were clothed in loincloths similar to those of my captors. Several of the men had tattoos like the man I assumed was the chief, although none had any as extensive as his.

Unlike in the previous two villages, I saw no sign of outside influence on this village. As a result, I was an immediate sensation. Children stopped and stared at me as if I were an alien from another planet. That analogy probably wasn't far from the truth. I supposed they'd never seen anyone like me before.

Everyone began whispering, pointing and watching me intently. I was supremely uncomfortable with all the attention. One little girl darted close enough to examine my pants until a woman rushed forward to scoop her away in case I turned out to be a monster or something.

My stomach growled loudly. I hoped we would eat soon. I hadn't seen the men eat anything so far today, although I presume they'd eaten some of the fish they offered me last night. At this moment, I would have killed for a chocolate éclair and a huge glass of Diet Pepsi with a boatload of ice. I calculated that given my level of exertion, the hours of walking uphill, and my current caloric intake, which was none, I could eat at least six eclairs without gaining a pound. In fact, if I counted the high likelihood I'd be soon suffering from parasites or dysentery, I could up my éclair intake to ten.

Eventually people lost interest in me and headed toward the chief. Three women lined up to greet him, with each giving him some kind of offering. The chief accepted each gift and looked pleased. I wondered if they were his wives, mates or extended family.

After the women had finished presenting their offerings, the chief took the satellite phone off and placed it around the oldest woman's neck. She appeared deeply honored and turned around to show it off to the rest of the villagers.

Priority Number One. I had to get my hands on that phone.

Everyone gathered around her excitedly to examine it. After a few minutes, the chief made some kind of announcement and everyone sat down to listen to him. Bone weary from the hiking, I sat as well. No one stopped me, but no one sat next to me either. The only people who were not afraid to stare at me were the children, and they did so with big smiles, giggles and open curiosity.

As the chief droned on, a young woman shyly brought me a gourd and a small plate of fruit and berries. I thanked her and popped some of the berries in my mouth. They were tart and delicious. Baffled, I looked around, trying to figure out who these people were and what they wanted with me. If they had wanted to kill me, they could have done it a long time ago. From a first impression, they appeared to be an uncontacted village, so what had caused them to snatch me?

If I could just figure out where I was and how far it was to the village where I'd been abducted, I might consider making a run for it. But right now, I had no idea where I was or even in what direction to travel if I were to get free. I needed to bide my time and gather information. But most importantly, I needed to get my hands on the satellite phone.

Suddenly the chief said something in a dramatic tone of voice and pointed at me. I paused with a berry a millimeter from my mouth as the entire village turned to look at me. He continued talking, repeatedly using a word that sounded like "*a-muh-suh-ne.*" I didn't have a clue what it meant, but apparently it applied to me. I just hoped that whatever it meant, it didn't get me killed.

When the chief finally stopped talking, the members of the tribe stood. A few of the younger women approached me. I tried to back up, but they circled around, effectively trapping me. One of them, a young woman who looked to be about seventeen or eighteen with long, thick hair and brown eyes, took me by the hand. She was the tallest girl of the bunch, but I estimated her to be no more than five foot three inches. Not sure what would happen if I resisted, I reluctantly followed her to one of the huts, towering over everyone. For a minute, we crowded in the hut and stood, awkwardly staring at each other. I had no idea what came next and I wasn't sure they did either.

While we stood there, it occurred to me that these women looked a lot younger than me, and some appeared to be barely teenagers. Their skin was smooth and clear, missing the tattoos and markings of the older women. Also unlike the older women who wore longer grass skirts, these girls wore nothing more than tiny leather loincloths held up over the hips by a hide rope. The front of the loincloths were embroidered with a series of overlapping shells that appeared to come from some sort of snail.

It hit me suddenly. This was probably the hut for unmarried women. For some reason, I'd been assigned here. I wasn't sure if that was a good or bad development. I glanced down at my engagement ring and wondered what Slash would think of all this. I hoped he was still looking for me. Maybe he'd given me up for dead, although I didn't really believe that. As long as there was a chance I might still be alive, he'd be looking. Just thinking of him made me miss him terribly.

Since no one said anything, I decided to take the initiative. Using gestures, I asked for the location of the bathroom. They escorted me to a rocky area, pointing to some rocks. After studying the site, I was impressed. The rocky area funneled water from above and drained it down over some stone slabs and a small cliff into the valley below. I was certain, given the frequency of rain in the area, the toilet area was "flushed" every few days. More importantly, it flowed away from the spring that provided their drinking and cooking water, so there was little risk of cross contamination. It was an ingenious arrangement.

I quickly used the facilities, and thankfully, no one watched. On the way back, the girls pointed out a water pool and indicated this is where people should bathe. I only saw a couple of older women in the pool, splashing around. I had no idea if they had separate bathing areas for men and women. Until I figured that out, there was no way was I taking off my clothes.

When we got back to the hut, I decided to ask the young women a question. "What does *a-muh-suh-ne* mean?" I said the word a couple of times, emphasizing each syllable to make sure they understood what I was trying to communicate.

The girls stared at me transfixed before they burst out giggling. They pointed at me and continued giggling.

Confused, I pointed back. *"A-muh-suh-ne.* You're *a-muh-suh-ne*, too?"

They shook their heads and laughed again. Every finger in that room stayed pointed at me.

Whatever it meant, it only applied to me.

Chapter Thirty-Two

Slash

He wanted to kill someone.

Twenty-one hours and no trace of Lexi. She'd simply vanished in thin air, leaving behind her laptop bag with the laptop inside and untouched. How had this happened on his watch?

His mood had progressively gone from bad to foul. He tried to compartmentalize his thinking to avoid dwelling on whether she might be injured. He refused to let his mind go further than that. Gwen had broken down in tears, Natelli had been beside herself with guilt, and Vicente, Gabriel and Salvador had grimly helped him scour the entire area.

Slash had personally interrogated all the guards, including Gabriel, as well as everyone on the team, while they were still at the village, but no one had seen or heard anything. As much as he wanted to haul one of them in as a suspect, he was good enough at interrogation to know they were telling the truth. No one knew what had happened to Lexi.

So, where the hell did that leave him?

She'd disappeared without a trace. There were no

signs of a struggle, no blood, and no clues other than the laptop bag lying near a hut. He'd combed the entire area, exhausting every possibility. The last person who'd seen her was a little girl. After Vicente had gently interviewed her, the girl said Lexi had been in the hut with her. She'd shown Lexi her doll and then they'd left to go back to the others. The girl had skipped a little ahead, and when she turned around Lexi was gone. She hadn't heard a scream or any noise whatsoever. The only thing that had been proof that Lexi had been there was the laptop bag lying on the ground.

There were no scratches, no marks on the bag and nothing entered into the computer other than the vaccine data. Slash had scoured every inch of the area. No blood or signs of a scuffle, no screaming or shouting which would have certainly been present if a wild animal had attacked her. No drag marks either. The only explanation was that someone had knocked her unconscious without allowing her to make a sound, and then carried her—a five-foot-eleven woman—through the rainforest noiselessly even as the area was being heavily patrolled.

Who the hell could do that?

His only break was that the satellite phone was missing along with her. He'd searched the entire area and hadn't found it. He'd given it to her shortly before her disappearance because it had been low on battery. He prayed it was still around her neck and she would, at some point, turn it back on. But it had been twenty-one hours and nothing. No signal, no Lexi.

Where are you, cara?

He had to push aside emotion and think. Lexi was resourceful, smart and logical. If there was a way to get a message to him, she'd find it. He had to trust her to take care of herself, just as she trusted him to find her. That was the way it worked with them. Perfectly synced, perfectly matched.

He couldn't lose her.

In the meantime, the answers were in front of him, he just had to figure them out. He stood outside the lab, pacing back and forth, thinking. He had to move from *how* she'd been kidnapped to *why*. If she'd been taken by someone who wanted to disrupt the vaccine program, they had effectively done that. All trips to the villages had stopped. Resources were now being directed toward recovering Lexi. The CEO of Vaccitex, Lilith Burbridge, was on her way from New York, and they expected her to arrive at the camp within the hour. She had promised to make every resource available to them.

While he appreciated the gesture, that wouldn't help if he didn't know the motivations behind the kidnapping. He wasn't buying that drug runners had kidnapped her. That level of sophistication in kidnapping wasn't their style, and why leave the laptop behind? It made no sense. Besides, twenty-one hours later, there should have been threats issued or a ransom request.

He had nothing.

So, when you had nothing, where did you start? He considered his meager options. Maybe it was time to pay another visit to the captured drug dealers. According to Gabriel, they were still in the jail awaiting the Brazilian federal police to retrieve them. It wasn't the greatest plan he'd ever had, but it was something.

Gabriel drove him to the jail. When they arrived, the guards remembered him from the last visit, and were friendly and receptive.

Good.

Slash asked their permission to interview the prisoners while showing them a wad of cash. The guards accepted without hesitation and conveniently disappeared.

He and Gabriel decided to split up the interviews. Since all of them were from Venezuela, they both could speak to them in Spanish. The prisoners were being held in separate cells and, at first, refused to answer any initial questions, both combative and cocky. Slash didn't care, because his early questions had a simple purpose. He carefully observed their demeanor and behavior, looking for the weak link among them.

It didn't take him long to zero in on the guy who'd been shot in the shoulder by his buddy as Lexi had jumped on him from the tree. He'd apparently seen a doctor because he had a decent dressing, but it was obvious he was still in a lot of pain. Slash exchanged a glance with Gabriel, who walked over to the next cell, talking loudly to another prisoner.

Slash stood in front of the wounded guy's cell, making a big deal of opening his wallet and pulling out a small plastic bag with several white pills. He dangled them from his fingertips. "Painkillers. Nonprescription, but maximum strength. They're yours, if you answer a few questions."

"Are you kidding me?" The guy laughs hoarsely. "If I say anything, and I mean, *anything*, they'll kill me."

"Not if they don't know you said anything."

"They find out everything."

Slash looked around. "You see anyone else here? Just you and me. I guarantee your name never comes up. That's the price of the pills."

The guy tried not to be interested, but the desperation in his eyes made it too easy. "Who are you? Your accent...you're not even from Brazil."

"I'm not. But I'm in a good position to help you. And from the looks of things, you could use some help."

He wet his lips and stared at the bag. "Yes! I'm in a lot of pain. I need to see another doctor. The last one didn't give me enough medicine."

"That's because they don't care about you. They want you to rot in prison. You're lucky you saw a doctor at all. If you want relief, you've got me." He waved the plastic bag. "Talk a little and they're yours."

"How do I know I can trust you? I don't even know who you are. Your moves out there...they weren't like any scientist I've ever seen."

Slash shook his head, pretending he'd had enough. He started to slip the bag with the pills back into his pocket and the guy began to panic.

"Hey, hey, wait! You pulled that snake off of me. I guess I owe you for that. What kind of questions do you want to ask?"

"Who do you work for?"

"Oh, come on." He winced as if Slash had hit him. "Anything but that. Can't you ask me something else?"

Slash turned around to leave when the guy called him back. "Okay, okay. I've got a family to think about. They're innocent in this. You've got to keep my name out of it. I have your word?"

"You have my word. But if you play me, I'll hunt down your family myself."

The guy studied Slash for a minute, then blew out a breath and lowered his voice. "I work for *El Esqueleto*." He held out his left hand, displaying a small tattoo of a bony hand with fingers curling like a claw on his wrist.

Slash narrowed his eyes. "The Skeleton?" He'd heard of *El Esqueleto* before, and none of it good.

"*Si*. He's from Columbia, but I don't think he lives there anymore. He's a ghost, man. You can't ever find him or touch him. He has six countries looking for him, but he remains invisible. No one will *ever* find him."

"Why did *El Esqueleto* order you to attack us?"

"I don't know, man. That was just our directive. We were to capture a bunch of scientists and bring them, and their work, safely to a predetermined spot. We knew you were working on some kind of medicine, and we were to ensure it wasn't ruined or damaged. It was supposed to be an easy assignment."

Slash considered. They'd thought they were attacking a bunch of scientists who wouldn't have put up a big fight. An easy target, indeed. "Where was this predetermined spot you were supposed to take us?"

"I don't know. We were supposed to get instructions once we got back on the river. Someone was going to come to us by boat to make contact, but obviously that never happened. That crazy woman threw a snake on me and then jumped out of the tree, causing Paco to shoot me in the shoulder. Who the hell saw that coming?"

Slash remembered Lexi falling from the tree and his fists clenched. "Why would *El Esqueleto* want the medicine?"

"I have no idea, I swear. That's all I know. They don't tell me nothing. Please, just give me the pills and keep my name out of it."

After a moment, Slash tossed him the bag. He now had confirmation that the drug cartel *was* mixed up in this mess. He had no idea why, but at least he had a place to start.

Chapter Thirty-Three

Slash

It took twelve minutes of walking around Coari to find a decent signal before Slash could contact his coworker Charlie at the NSA with his cell.

"Hey, Slash," Charlie said once Slash was put through. "How's that vacation of yours going?"

He had no idea how long the signal would last, so he couldn't waste time on pleasantries. "I'm in Brazil, Lexi has been kidnapped, and I need everything you can give me on some guy named *El Esqueleto*. Unclassified sources only, as I don't have the equipment to handle anything else at this time."

"What?" Charlie gasped. "Are you kidding me?"

"I'm not. Send everything to this account." He rattled off the address and had Charlie read it back to him to make sure he had it right. "I can't stress how important expediency is right now."

"Understood, boss. Coming to you within the hour."

By the time he and Gabriel got back to the camp, and he returned to his computer in the lab, he had several links pointing him to open source information on *El Esqueleto,* whose real name was Lorenzo Molina.

After reviewing the links, he confirmed the prisoner had been right, there were multiple countries trying to run down the drug lord. Unfortunately, unlike the notorious Colombian drug lord, Pablo Escobar, who loved the limelight, *El Esqueleto* loved the shadows. His operation was global, but he rarely, if ever, traveled for fear of being spotted or captured. His followers had a tattoo with a bony hand with fingers curled like a claw—as confirmed by the prisoner. The last confirmed sighting of *El Esqueleto* had been in southern Venezuela three years prior when he was seen with a senior government official who had since been imprisoned.

Three years. Damn.

Exhausted, he pushed his hands through his hair and continued to read. *El Esqueleto's* operational style had him nurturing profitable relationships with government officials who in turn provided him with protection and information. Just like every other drug lord. There had to be *something* else about him that could be exploited.

For unknown reasons, *El Esqueleto* fell out of favor in Venezuela, and had been forced to move much of his operation elsewhere. Where, appeared to be unknown, although most sources suspected he was still in South America. It was possible *El Esqueleto* could have moved from southern Venezuela into Brazil. The police had minimal presence in northern Brazil, where there were large swaths of unpopulated rainforests, a small population, and much bigger problems with drugs and criminal gangs in the big cities and the south. All of which would make the region attractive to a drug lord who wanted to keep in the shadows.

The more he considered it, the more he liked that possible scenario. That might explain why *El Esqueleto* was using drug operators to keep strangers—especially ones with government backing—out of his new area. But that didn't answer the question of how he was staying in business. The region's ecology in this area wasn't suitable for growing the most profitable narcotics, although he'd heard some discussion of bioengineering cocaine. Even keeping that in mind, transportation to and from the area would be difficult with limited options for bulky drugs like cocaine and marijuana. In the end, none of this speculation provided him a single damn lead as to where Lexi might be.

He jerked when he felt a hand on his shoulder.

"I'm sorry to interrupt," a woman said softly. "We haven't been formally introduced. I'm Lilith Burbridge, CEO of Vaccitex. I'm sorry about Lexi. We're going to do everything we can to find her."

He glanced over the woman's shoulder and saw Gwen standing there as well. Her eyes were puffy and red from crying, her cheeks splotched with pink spots. She looked as miserable as he felt.

He rose and held out a hand to the woman, studying her for a long moment. Had he met her before? "Nice to meet you, Lilith. I'm sorry, I'm not much in a mood to talk."

"I understand. I just wanted to tell you the helicopter you chartered is parked at the airport, fully fueled and ready for a rapid response when you're ready. The pilot is at a hotel in Coari awaiting word from you."

"Thank you for helping me expedite that. I'm grateful." He glanced down beneath the table that held his laptop. A backpack that he'd packed and repacked several times sat ready to go. The contents held several packets of food, medical supplies, guns and ammunition, lights, and even night vision gear. In twelve hours, Gabriel had helped him secure everything he wanted. The helicopter he'd chartered could seat three, in addition to the pilot, but had a range of only about one hundred and fifty miles with a full load. If he took three people to help him, then there wouldn't be room for Lexi. But if he didn't take enough help, he might not be able to bring her back.

Tough decisions.

Who to take with him was the easy part. He hated to ask because his gut was still bugging him about Vicente, but he needed him. He had no idea who they might encounter and needed to be able to converse quickly and accurately in a variety of languages. He also needed Salvador because once they were on the ground, he needed the guide front and center in getting them to Lexi.

He'd spent time on the phone with the pilot going over the weight limits and the range tradeoff. The helicopter could carry more weight, but it would have a shorter range. In the end, he'd decided to take both Salvador and Vicente, and leave behind their gear if they needed to escape.

He'd just spent the best part of two days doing what he could. Now he needed a miracle. He reached under his shirt and pulled out the silver cross that had once been his father's. Pressing it to his lips, he prayed to God to give him a chance.

He had no idea if God would respond.

Chapter Thirty-Four

Arjun Singh

It was going to be a tough day when he needed to initiate damage control before he even had his first cup of coffee.

Arjun sat at his office desk reading a series of emails that were getting progressively worse. The first one was from his chief scientist reporting another failure of the process to replicate the malaria vaccine. Without it, they could not go into large-scale production, let alone have enough to run a trial.

He slammed a fist on his desk. This latest incompetent was the third chief scientist he'd had in the past two years.

Idiots, all of them.

He pushed away from his desk and walked across his office. Picking up a crystal decanter with whiskey, he popped it open and poured some into a glass. To hell with coffee. He needed a shot of something a lot stronger. The alcohol burned his throat, but he welcomed the sting. He needed to focus before the entire operation went to hell.

He took the glass and sat down in front of his computer again, taking another swallow before opening the next email. It was from one of his major investors asking him about his request for additional investment funding. The investor wondered why he wasn't reporting more progress on his key research projects, especially his potential blockbuster, the malaria vaccine.

You're already a year past your initial trial's date and there's no indication you have a working vaccine to test. We need some indication that you are close to fielding a vaccine before we invest any more.

Swearing, Arjun closed the email and opened the next one. Another one of his investors wrote he'd heard reports from a contact at the World Health Organization that a U.S. nonprofit called Vaccitex had already started the Phase 3 clinical trials of an anti-malaria vaccine in Brazil.

If they succeed—even if you get your product approved and to market—you will have a competitor well-positioned to beat your price and reduce the generous profit margins you have been promising. You're starting to look like a long shot, and under the current circumstances, it will be difficult for us to make another investment at this time.

Fighting the urge to throw the laptop across the room, Arjun picked up his phone and instructed his secretary to summon Vihaan and Krish to his office.

Both men arrived in under five minutes, which meant they were worried. Good, because if they weren't, he intended to put the fear of God in them. The current situation was unacceptable. Change had to happen *now*.

He didn't even waste time with greetings or inviting

them to sit down and instead, immediately confronted his brother from behind his desk. "Vihaan, as my Director of Security, I pray you have a favorable update for me on the situation in Brazil." He studied Vihaan as he made the request, looking for signs of anxiety or avoiding eye contact that might precede bad news. Thankfully, he saw none.

"I do." Vihaan spread his hands. "The vaccine trials have stopped for the moment."

Arjun absorbed the good news cautiously. "Why?"

"It wasn't part of the plan, but apparently one of the American staff has gone missing. Even better, no one knows why or what happened, not even our contact. The situation remains fluid, but for now the trials are completely shut down. We couldn't have asked for better luck."

"Interesting." He was both intrigued and worried. Was there something else going on he didn't know about? Still, a complete shutdown of the trials was exactly what he needed for the moment, so he permitted himself to relax a fraction. "How are you communicating with our contact?"

"Through an intermediary. We're still working on a permanent shutdown, but our contact requires more money. Apparently, keeping the appropriate government officials blind to the operation is not cheap."

He threw out his hands in disgust. "Is it no wonder that country is in shambles? Corrupt officials don't stay bought and now they demand pay raises? What mockery is that?"

Wisely, Vihaan remained silent. Arjun's tongue and actions were sharp when he was riled, and right now, he was looking for a fight.

He took deep breaths to calm himself. He needed his brother to keep their contact in Brazil happy and working. He looked for other options, but found none. At this critical juncture, he had no choice but to pay.

"Fine. One more payment, and the promise of a payout bonus, but only if the job has been done to our satisfaction," Arjun said. "They will not receive one cent more."

"Understood, brother."

"Good. Now, Krish, explain to me what's been happening on the cyber front."

The hairs on Krish's chin wobbled. Arjun had to resist the urge to pick the scissors off his desk and start cutting the damn things off.

"Yes, sir. Our computer intrusion has remained undetected. We continue to monitor all emails, but have received nothing of major importance other than generic planning and progress reports for the trials. To our knowledge, they have only managed to inoculate one village before the shutdown of the operation. We did lose access to the datasets that contained the research results for several days when they changed the passwords, but one of the IT admins foolishly included the new one in an email to a coworker, so we have access once again. None of the new data from Brazil is being added, as that's being collected and managed offsite by a subcontractor."

"What subcontractor?"

Krish pulled out his phone and flipped through some screens. "X-Corp Global Intelligence and Security. Located in Crystal City, Virginia."

Arjun had never heard of them. "I don't care about that right now. How close are we to obtaining the files on the vaccine and the vaccine replication process?"

"We're close."

He slammed his fist so hard on the desk, his laptop almost fell off. Both Vihaan and Krish jumped. "Close isn't good enough. Do you understand? I *must* have something soon or we'll be out of business."

Krish swallowed, his Adam's apple bobbing nervously. "I understand, sir, but I'm getting a little worried the longer this goes on. My intuition is they've detected our intrusion already, although there have been no indications to prove that."

"On what do you base that conclusion?"

Krish shifted uncomfortably on his feet. "While the communication traffic is normal, we aren't getting anything really useful."

"Why is that a problem?"

"Well, if I put myself in their shoes, I might do the same thing to see what we're after and determine who might be attacking them."

"Are they that knowledgeable?"

"Not if their computer security to date has been any indication. But something feels off. They've changed up some things and I worry they may have a plan of their own."

"I don't give a *damn* about their plans." He kept voice deadly calm, but he was barely keeping the lid on his frustration. "Can we, or can we not, get the vaccine and process details we need?"

"W-we can, sir," Krish stammered. "But if we attack their system using brute force, they'll know they've have been hacked."

"I don't care if they know, as long as they can't trace it back to us. We *need* that vaccine data right now. You have forty-eight hours to get it. I want a team of people working around the clock on it. Don't disappoint me. Have I made myself clear?" He let the threat hang in the air.

Krish nodded nervously. "Yes, sir."

"Good. Now both of you get out of my sight and get to work."

After they left, Arjun made a note to himself that once this crisis was over, Krish would shave the stubble on his chin or be fired.

Energized by the bit of good news regarding the vaccine trials, he returned to his desk to craft an email to his investors.

We are confident the nonprofit's trial will fail or be substantially delayed until we have our product on the market. As it stands now, the nonprofit has halted their vaccine distribution, perhaps permanently. Even if they were to claim their product was worthy, we have means to discredit their data and prevent them from selling or distributing their vaccine. More importantly, within mere days, we will be able to show you substantial proof of our progress. Once we have the vaccine ready to go, demand for it will be so high, we will be able to sell it to desperate governments and world health organizations for rates so high that it will make us billions of dollars in profits in less than a year. Gentlemen, we are on the eve of one of the most profitable ventures of our time.

He reread the email. Satisfied, even pleased, by his verbiage, he sent it. Standing, he retrieved his coffee mug and poured some coffee from the carafe. Grabbing the newspaper from one corner of his desk, he sat in one of his armchairs and began to read an article written by one of India's most popular journalists, Ajay Dewan.

He hated Dewan with a passion. At twenty-one years old, Dewan had become a self-righteous investigative reporter, determined to expose what he called the dark belly of India. It was laughable at first—a stupid young boy with a head filled with useless ideals and standards—until his first target had been the profiteering and corruption problem in the Indian pharmaceutical industry. Dewan had personally attacked Pharma Star and even Arjun himself over a manufacturing deal that had gone bad a few months prior. Arjun had never been so angry in his life after the article had been released. His public affairs department had issued a news release that had focused on how outraged and distraught Pharma Star executives were over the false accusations. He'd had to spend an ordinate amount of money to shut mouths and clean up the mess that had been part of that deal. He still hadn't forgiven Dewan for that.

Just thinking of it made him angry all over again. Setting aside the paper, he decided to send one more email, this one to his brother.

Remember Ajay Dewan, the stupid reporter who made our lives miserable a few months ago? Start looking at ways to make his life or his family's very, very uncomfortable unless he starts focusing his attention elsewhere. I don't need to deal with this when we are so close to announcing we have broken through with the vaccine.

After he sent it, he felt a lot better.

Chapter Thirty-Five

Lexi

Why did I ever agree to bathe?

At first, bathing had seemed like a good idea. It smelled like something had died in my armpits, and my hair was a snarl of dirt, sweat and tangles. I'd been watching the bathing area and I hadn't seen a man there, which was a big relief. So, I'd bravely gestured to the girls that I wanted to take a dip. They seemed excited about the idea, probably because I was stinking up the hut so badly.

A couple of the women went with me. As soon as we arrived, they gleefully stripped off their clothes without a shred of modesty and jumped into the water laughing. I got as close to the water as I could and sat down, trying to take off my clothes without showing the world everything I had. Folding my clothes, I placed them into a neat pile next to my hiking boots on the shore. Then, after checking that no one was watching, I used one hand to cover my nether area and the other to cover my breasts before plunging into the water.

Holy arctic!

It was so cold, it took my breath away. Gasping, I went

under and scrubbed my scalp and hair as hard as I could. When I came back up, the other women were swimming toward me. Even though my feet could touch the bottom and I was submerged to my neck in the water, I was self-conscious. I crossed my arms against my breasts, trying to act like I went skinny dipping in rainforest rivers all the time.

"Hey," I said when they arrived. "The water is really cold. Brrrr." I pretended to shiver and they laughed.

One of the girls reached out and pried my arm away from my breasts, clearly indicating I should follow her deeper into the water.

I shook my head vigorously. "No, no. I don't swim." I dramatically pretended to drown while they watched with wide eyes. I'm sure they had no idea what I was doing. They probably thought I was a complete nutcase. But no way was I going anywhere I couldn't touch the bottom.

Something brushed against my leg beneath the water. Instinctively, I reached down and grabbed something. When I yanked it out of the water, I realized it was a snake.

Holy swimming serpent!

"Eeek!" I cried, tossing it as far away as I could.

The girls all stared at me with open mouths, then immediately started swimming for shore.

"Hey, wait. Where's everyone going?" I followed awkwardly, splashing and jumping, heading for the spot on the shore where I'd left my clothes. Except when I got closer, I saw my clothes were no longer there. The only visible item of my clothing were my hiking boots.

"What the heck?" I ran to the shore, dripping like a

wet rat, shivering, and trying to cover my womanly parts with my hands. "Where are my clothes?"

The girls all threw me scared glances as they grabbed their loincloths and disappeared.

"Wait! Wait!" I cried. What the heck was happening? Why had they swum away from me? Who had taken my clothes?

I heard some rustling in the trees, so I darted behind a bush. "Who is it?" I called out.

There were some giggles and I saw a couple of children dart out from the trees holding my shirt and pants like a kite streaming out behind them.

"Stop," I called out, running after them. "Give those back. Those are mine."

They disappeared into the trees. There was no way I was going to chase them naked through the rainforest. Resigned, I returned to the shore and put on my socks and boots. I grabbed a couple of branches and tried my best to cover all essential areas as I walked back to the hut.

Unlike during my walk to the pool, every villager seemed to be out and about. Most stopped whatever they were doing to watch me. My cheeks burned, but I held my head high as I walked steadily to the hut. Unfortunately, while walking past one of the huts, one of my fronds caught on a protruding stick. In one second flat, the leaves covering my backside lay on the ground. I heard a collective gasp. It was embarrassingly obvious that these tribal men and women had never seen such a pasty white butt before.

Mortified, I ran the rest of the way to the hut. When I got there, hair dripping and out of breath, I tried to explain to the girls that the children had ran off with my clothes. While I was madly gesturing, one of the girls disappeared. When she returned, it wasn't with my clothes, but with a partially made loincloth and a collection of shells.

"Oh, no. I can't wear that," I said alarmed. "Please, bring me my clothes."

After some time of trying frustratedly to persuade them to retrieve my clothes, I sat down on the floor, dejected.

The tallest girl gently handed me the loincloth and started to arrange the snail shells on it, encouraging me to help. I really wanted my clothes back, but my choices at the moment were either a loincloth or nothing. I voted, reluctantly, for the loincloth.

While we were working, another girl shyly brought me a bowl of oil, indicating I should rub it over my body. I sniffed and it smelled like herbs. It occurred to me this was likely some kind of insect repellent, because the mosquitos weren't bugging any of them. Quickly, I rubbed the oil all over myself including the eyelids, behind the ears and even the soles of my feet.

While doing so, I tried to ask the girls why they'd swum away from me when we were in the water. After several minutes of gesturing, the girls finally understood what I was trying to ask.

The tall girl disappeared for a moment and came back with a stick. Carefully, she drew a stick figure holding a snake above its head. Then she pointed at me and said, *"A-muh-suh-ne."*

Chapter Thirty-Six

Lexi

The next day I discovered my stolen clothes had been distributed among the kids in the village. A girl who looked to be about eight years old had taken my bra and fashioned it into a hip-slung quiver for make-believe arrows. She walked around the village shooting at anything that moved, including me. Two boys were sharing my pants, wearing the legs as double hats on their heads. I tried a couple of times to creep up on them and get them back, but they were on to me. They darted away any time I tried. One of the older women was using my shirt as a sack. I was afraid to discover for what purpose they were using my underwear. It might have been humorous if I weren't walking around half naked because of it.

I'd finished the loincloth and the girls had helped me sew on the shells. When I put it on, it hung low on my hips and a good two inches beneath my belly button. The backside barely covered my butt. I would have to bend over very carefully. I supposed in some ways it was like wearing a bikini. But since I'd never worn a bikini in my life, I was completely self-conscious. When no one was looking, I stole a small fish net and wound it around my breasts. The girls looked at me completely mystified, but I felt one hundred percent better having all my private areas covered, so everyone was just going to have to live with it.

I felt like I'd made a connection with some of the girls, so I tried to figure out what was going on with my situation. I drew pictures in the dirt, tried gesturing, but we couldn't communicate. I still had no idea why I'd been kidnapped. Did it have anything to do with the vaccines or was it something else?

I'd also been looking to see if I could find the chief's wife—the one with the satellite phone—but I hadn't seen her. Frustration filled me. I was no closer to getting out of here than when I first arrived. I was surprised I hadn't been sick yet. I'd been drinking unfiltered water, which should have caused my intestines to cramp or hurt. But so far, I was okay on the stomach front. They'd been feeding me well. A wide variety of delicious fruits, unknown meats on a stick, different vegetables and fish. It was all quite tasty. But I was getting restless and worried. I'd been taken for some reason and until I knew what that was, I had to consider myself in danger.

It was late morning when I spotted one of the children running around with the satellite phone around his neck. I headed toward him, smiling and trying to look as unthreatening as possible. The second he saw me, he darted away. Blowing out a breath of frustration, I tried to come up with a strategy to attract him to me willingly.

It didn't take me long to come up with a plan. I found a flat spot in the village where the ground was mostly dirt, and not rock. Taking a stick, I drew a hopscotch pattern. Then I found a flat rock and began to play hopscotch. It took me less than five minutes to gain an audience. That audience included both adults and children, but it was obvious the children were the most interested and wanted to try, as well.

Perfect.

I began to show them how to play and had everyone line up. The girl holding my bra like a quiver was first. I indicated she had to put the bra down before she could play. She didn't want to, so I had the girl behind her go. After I taught her how to play, I noticed that the lure of playing the game had been too much to resist. The girl set the bra down and watched to see if I snatched it away.

I didn't.

Instead, I taught her to play and when we were done, I gestured for her to pick up the bra and get back in line. Delighted, she did just that. It went like this for about an hour until I noticed the little boy with the satellite phone on the periphery. When he finally got in line, my heart started beating faster. When it was his turn, I held out a hand for the phone. He slowly drew it over his head and handed it to me. While putting it on the ground, I switched it on, covering the screen with my hand until it went dark into battery mode. I prayed it still had enough battery life to get a signal to Slash.

When I finished teaching the boy how to play, I handed him back the phone. He happily darted away, the phone thumping against his chest. Thankfully, he didn't notice the light was still on.

I'd done what I could. It was in Slash's hands now.

Chapter Thirty-Seven

Slash

He was on his way to the laboratory from grabbing coffee to stay awake when the satellite phone in his pocket unexpectedly beeped. Not daring to breathe, he pulled it out carefully and brought the screen to life. After a couple of quick swipes, he stared at a set of coordinates. Not taking his eyes off the screen until he memorized them, he dug into his backpack to get a pen and paper to copy the coordinates down, not trusting his memory with something so important, and not knowing how long the signal would last.

After he jotted them down, he dashed into the lab. He needed a map and a large one of the rainforest was hanging the wall. Without saying a word, he burst into the lab and immediately started plotting out the coordinates' location. He'd been working for at least three minutes when he heard a voice.

"Slash, are you okay?"

Slash tore his gaze away from the map for a fraction of a second to see who was speaking. It was Lilith. But Lilith wasn't alone. Natelli, Gwen, Melinda, Martim, Gabriel and Vicente had all come into the lab, or maybe they were already there when he arrived. He hadn't paid any attention to who had been there, as his focus had been on the coordinates. Now they stood in a semicircle watching him scribble on the map. Good, because he'd only have to outline his plan once.

"I received a signal from the satellite phone. I don't know if it's Lexi or not, but I'm going to find out."

"Oh my God." Lilith gasped and covered her mouth. "Does this mean she's alive? Where's the signal coming from?"

Slash finished his calculation and then drew a circle on the map. "I don't know if it was Lexi who flipped the GPS on, but the signal came from here." He tapped on the circle. "It's a long way from the village where she went missing, and quite a distance from the river as well. It looks like the area is part of the *Parque Nacional Do Jau*. According to the map, there are no true navigable roads in the region."

"There aren't," Salvador confirmed. "It's an extremely isolated area. Much of that territory belongs to protected tribes, including several that have had little to no contact with the outside world."

"Which tribes?" Slash asked.

Slash stepped aside so Salvador could move forward and get a better look at the map. "Hard to say for certain, but that area is mostly Okampa territory. They have a number of villages in the area—no one really knows for sure how many—but they have a reputation for being extremely unfriendly to strangers."

"Then why is the satellite phone beaming from that location?"

Salvador shook his head, looking worried. "I don't know."

"Wait!" Gwen exclaimed. "I totally forgot, with everything that's happened, but when we were approaching the village where Lexi disappeared, I thought I saw a native person shadowing us in the trees. He had these strange tattoos on his face. When I tried to get a better look, he'd vanished, so I thought maybe it was my imagination. I mentioned it and the tattoos to Lexi, and she said the same thing had happened to her. She'd seen a tattooed face just like that when she was in the rainforest alone, right before she saved us."

Slash instantly stilled, trying to remember exactly what Lexi had said to him after she'd awakened from her concussion.

I poked a snake, jumped out of a tree, and saw a native man watching me. I think I may have been delusional.

"Gwen, what did the tattoos look like?" he asked, a note of urgency in his voice.

She closed her eyes, thinking. "They were black swirls and white slashes, but jagged ones like lightning. This man had them over every inch of his face. But I didn't see anyone like at the village."

He glanced at Salvador. "Does that mean anything to you?"

The guide lifted his hands. "Maybe. Most of the native tribes have tattoos of one sort or the other. However, the Okampa are known for their extensive facial tattoos. My guess is that if that man's entire face was covered, he'd be a very important member of the tribe."

Slash looked back at the map, considering, before he turned to Vicente. "Do you speak the language of the Okampa?"

"I don't even know what the language of the Okampa

is," Vicente replied. "No one knows. Outsiders who have tried to penetrate the area have always been turned back. There's so little known about them, that it's hard to say what we could expect."

"Is it possible they could have taken Lexi?"

"Anything is possible, but why?" Vicente looked as baffled as Slash felt.

"I don't know why." Frustrated, Slash reached for a plausible explanation because none were at hand. "Maybe for ransom or they kidnapped her on behalf of someone else, like a drug cartel."

"Why do you bring up drug cartels?" Vicente asked a bit sharply.

Slash studied him, wondering what had prompted the hard edge to his question. "Have you seen the tattoos on the wrists of the guys who tried to kidnap us? It's the mark of *El Esqueleto.*"

"Yes, I saw them. But what do *you* know of *El Esqueleto*?" Vicente asked.

Slash had clearly hit a nerve, but he wasn't sure why and didn't have time to deal with that now. Martim and Gabriel were also staring at him intently. Until he knew what was going on, it was better to play it safe and reveal nothing. "Enough to know he's a dangerous man."

Vicente studied Slash for a long moment, as if deciding to press him on it or let it go. "You think he took her?"

"Everything's on the table." He kept his tone light and noncommittal. "But I don't think so. We'd have received communication from someone in his organization by now. Ransom, hostage, some kind of deal or negotiation. We've heard nothing. Besides, the way she was kidnapped also doesn't fit the style of a cartel operation."

"You know a lot about cartels for a computer guy," Vicente said.

Slash shrugged. "I'm well read."

"I bet." Vicente said, but didn't push further.

"Well, if the cartels didn't take her, who did?" Salvador asked. "Then the only possibility left is a native abduction. And if natives took her, it would have to be for a totally different reason."

"What kind of reason?" Slash asked.

Salvador thought and then shook his head. "I don't know. I can't think of a single one that makes any sense."

A half dozen scenarios ran through Slash's head as to why a tribe would kidnap Lexi, and none of them ended well. He pushed those thoughts away to focus on what he *did* know. Turning back to the map, he ran calculations based on distance, weight and fuel capacity to determine if the helicopter would be able to get him close enough to the area.

"Are you sure you want to do this, Slash?" Natelli asked. "Think about the consequences."

He turned around slowly. "What consequences exactly do you want me to think about?"

"Well, how can we be sure Lexi is there?" Natelli said gently. "It could be a false signal or someone else has the phone. Going into that area is going to be extremely dangerous. You could get hurt or killed."

"She has a point," Lilith said. "I don't want to put you, or anyone else, in danger even if it means trying to save Lexi."

Slash kept his voice even. "You're not putting me in danger. This is my decision, not yours."

"I think Slash should go," Gwen piped up. "He can take care of himself, and we need to know if that's Lexi sending us a distress signal or not. If it's her, she needs us. If it's not, well, at least maybe we can find out where she is or what happened to her."

Slash glanced at Gwen, mildly surprised she was brave enough to stand up to those who seemed to be leaning toward an uncomfortable consensus against him. Although he didn't need her approval to go, he appreciated her vote of confidence.

His mind made up, he reached under his desk and pulled out his backpack. He slung it over his shoulder before yanking down the map and folding it. "Okay, here's what I know from a situational standpoint. According to my calculations, the area where the satellite phone pinged is within range of a helicopter, even if I take two more people with me. I don't want to ask anyone to risk their lives, but if Vicente and Salvador are willing to volunteer to accompany me, I'd appreciate it. I need both of your skills. That being said, it's likely to be dangerous and I understand if you'd prefer not to come."

To his surprise, Vicente immediately stepped forward. "I'm in. Let's find her and bring her back."

"I like Lexi. I'll go, too," Salvador said. "You'll definitely need me, although I must confess I've never been in this area before. But I'm generally familiar with the terrain and I'll do my best to get you there."

"Thank you."

For the first time, Martim exhaled heavily and moved forward until he stood face to face with Slash. "I'm afraid everyone is forgetting the most important part here. Danger is not your only problem. That's protected territory. You'd need approval from the Brazilian government in order to enter the area."

"Well, Martim, you're a government representative

who could authorize the rescue," Salvador said, a tinge of exasperation in his voice. "So, what's the problem?"

"The problem is, I forbid it." He put a hand on Slash's shoulder. "I will not have people running amok, trying to find a woman who got herself lost in the jungle, and endangering indigenous tribes that prefer to remain uncontacted."

In one quick movement, Slash pinned Martim against the wall, his forearm pressed against the minister's neck. His voice was hard. "Try to stop me."

It was telling that no one stepped in to protect the minister. Martim swallowed hard. "Of course. If that's what you feel you must do."

Slash dropped his forearm and Martim stumbled away, clutching his throat.

"We leave in thirty minutes," Slash said. "Grab your gear and meet me at one of the jeeps." Without another word, he strode from the lab.

No one stopped him.

Chapter Thirty-Eight

Martim Alves

He was going to make that American pay if it was the last thing he did.

That man had actually put his hands on him—an important government minister. He didn't know how they did things in America, but in Brazil, politicians were important people, deserving the utmost respect and deference.

Now things were going badly and fast. As soon as the American had stated his intention to travel to the area, Martim knew he had to get word to his contact.

He'd immediately ordered one of the guards at the research center to take him to Coari. Once he got there, he checked into the hotel room that had been reserved for him whenever he came into town. He opened his laptop and tried to log into his bank account. It took forever for the connection to come through, and after five minutes had passed and the little ball on his computer was still spinning, he cursed and hit his hand against the desk.

"What kind of backwater town is this?" He pushed away from the desk, disgusted. "It has the slowest Internet in the county."

He paced around the room for another five minutes before the connection was finally made. When he finally got into his bank account, he saw with satisfaction that the money had been deposited as promised.

"Those stupid Indians are so gullible," he muttered. "I can't believe they bought my story about needing additional money to keep officials pacified."

Apparently in India, you had to keep rebuying a politician or government official. That was not the way in Brazil. Once bought, you had to keep your promises, otherwise you were likely to find yourself out of business or, more likely, dead. After all, word tended to get around about people who kept their hands out for more. That one-time pricing certainly drove up the initial investment cost, but it reduced the uncertainty of what would have to be paid down the line. For those who wanted to grow their revenue, the key was offering to provide additional services.

He wasn't surprised they'd jumped on the bait when he offered to procure actual vials of the vaccine. It was so unfortunate that those low-level cartel enforcers were so incompetent. He'd set it up perfectly and did everything but heist the vaccines himself. And what had happened?

Taken down by an unarmed girl?

Idiots! It had been a perfect plan. The disappearance of the vaccine team would have shut down the project for some period of time, perhaps permanently. Then he would have been able to resell the vaccines to the Indians for a handsome bonus. Finally, it would have helped him honor his other commitment to use his official capacity to reduce traffic up the rivers and into the protected native areas. *El Esqueleto's* people were paying him good money to minimize government interference in the region, and make it unpopular for outsiders.

He was an important man who had a lot to offer his clients. He could restrict or approve any activity in the region that might threaten the native people's sovereignty. Therefore, as part of his arrangement with the cartel, he was able to contact hired cartel enforcers on the river to make it more dangerous to outsiders and alert them to potential traffic. It had been a stroke of brilliance to recognize the opportunity to use them to get paid for disrupting the vaccine project. Offering them a bonus for the vaccine recovery ensured they would follow his instructions.

He had been furious when the plan failed and the bandits were captured. Fortunately, no one knew he was the mastermind behind the plan. He was clever like that, and knew how to hide his tracks. He was, however, worried that *El Esqueleto* would be unhappy his effort had failed. He'd been planning how to explain that so it wouldn't reflect badly on him. After all, he could not be held responsible for the incompetence of others.

Unfortunately, that was the least of his problems at the moment. First, that despicable American rogue was headed right toward the area where *El Esqueleto* had set up his new operation. He had to be alerted and quickly. Even worse, the nosy American had seen the tattoo on one of the cartel men in the Coari jail and linked it to *El Esqueleto*. Things were beginning to get hot and he needed to cool things down or, at the very least, spin a web to protect himself.

Sitting down at his desk, he called up his email program and began to draft an email to his partner, one of the most powerful and dangerous men in South America.

Chapter Thirty-Nine

Lexi

The village was abuzz with excitement and I had no idea why. After playing hopscotch with the kids and turning on the satellite phone, I returned to the hut to find the girls in an excited state, all of them chattering constantly. Several were sitting on the floor, adding shells to their already intricately decorated loincloths. The tall girl was combing the hair of one of the younger girls and others were practically jumping around with excitement.

I tried to ask what was going on, and they tried to answer, but I still couldn't understand. The most I could determine was that everyone appeared to be getting ready for some event that was going to happen, probably this evening.

But what, I had no idea.

Not being able to follow what was going on in the hut, I wandered into the village where I discovered other preparations were going on. In an open area off to the side of the village, a large unlit fire was being prepared and the dirt area around it was being swept of leaves and debris. Felled logs surrounded three sides of the area, indicating this was a gathering area. The fire didn't look like one of their usual cooking fires as it was taller in design, with the wood stacked about three feet in height. Several of the younger men were doing the sweeping around the fire. They looked at me with an interest that made me want to find someplace else to go in a hurry.

As I continued walking around the village, I found several of the older women were preparing vegetables for cooking. Several dead, possum-size animals were lined up awaiting skinning for food or fur, though I didn't recall seeing fur in the village. As I wandered, I ran various probabilities in my head. If Slash had received my signal, how long would it take him to find and reach me? I figured I was at least a two-day hike from where I'd been captured. I trusted that Slash would be looking for the signal and coordinates from the phone, but after so many days, had he received the alert? I knew the phone battery had been working, at least for a short time, but I had no idea how long the battery had lasted after I turned it on. Had it been long enough to get a signal to Slash? That was an unknown variable.

I decide to take a short hike up to the highest point of the village to see if I could figure out where I was. I figured it was also possible I could find a way to signal for help, like starting a fire, but I didn't have a flint for the fire and I presumed any airborne observer would likely assume it was just a tribal fire. I started the hike up, and discovered after a few minutes that someone was following me at a discreet distance. They weren't boxing me in, but they weren't letting me roam around freely either.

I stopped when I got to a clearing with a rocky outcropping. I climbed up to the top of the rock pile and looked around. My breath caught in my throat. The view was one of the most beautiful I'd ever seen in my life.

Green in every direction with splashes of color and jutting gray rocks that stretched toward an azure sky. So stunning, in fact, that I had to give my brain time to acknowledge and appreciate all the aspects of such spectacular natural majesty.

As I stood there, I recalled some fascinating facts I'd learned about the rainforest. Forty to ninety percent of all life in the rainforest existed in the trees, *above* the ground. The canopy that covered the rainforest was made up of billions of leaves, most of them acting as solar panels, turning sunlight into energy. All of that meant the rainforest was critical for regulating and supporting global climate.

All of this beauty was vitally important to our world.

Unfortunately, I still had no clue where I was. The canopy stretched as far as I could see. No obvious landmarks or anything like that marred the perfect beauty of the landscape.

I heard a rustle in the bushes and the man who'd been following me stepped into view. He motioned at me that it was time to return. I took one last look at the view and climbed down off the rocks.

When we returned to the village, I checked my watch and saw it was four thirty in the afternoon. The girls seemed excited to see me and insisted I had to go with them to the pool to bathe. I wasn't crazy about the idea, especially after what had happened last time I bathed. I resisted, but they pulled me along, so I reluctantly followed. I sincerely hoped no one would steal my loincloth or fishnet bra. In the end, I left the loincloth on the shore, but kept the fishnet on, just in case.

Everyone seemed in such a good mood, I sincerely wondered what was going on. My anxiety spiked. I'm not necessarily suspicious by nature, but I do *not* like surprises, and all this excitement had me on high alert. Luckily my loincloth was waiting for me when we finished. After dressing, two of the girls linked arms with me as we headed back to the hut. I looked at both of them in surprise. How was it possible that while growing up, I'd never been included in any girl activities, but here, in the middle of the rainforest, I'd suddenly become one of the girls in such short order?

The universe had a strange sense of humor.

When we reassembled in the hut, we reapplied the oil to our bodies before the girls pointed to a spot they wanted me to sit. Puzzled, I obeyed. The tallest girl in the group, other than me, presented me with a new loincloth that had been elaborately decorated.

"Me?" I said. "That's for me?" I pointed to myself and all the girls nodded.

"Wow. That's amazing. Thank you." I accepted the loincloth, fairly sure all of them had participated in making it for me.

They motioned I should try it on. It felt weird getting dressed with everyone watching, but I didn't want to offend them, so I dropped the old loincloth and stepped into the new one. The tall girl fussed with the ropes on my hips and then, satisfied, stepped back. The other girls twittered in excitement.

The rest of the time the girls fixed each other's hair while I watched, baffled. I had no idea what was going on. It was after six o'clock when the chief's oldest wife appeared in the hut and all the chatter ceased immediately. She walked over to the tall girl and fussed with her hair. She spoke to the girl in a way that made me believe this was her mother, especially since she didn't fix anyone else's hair. That likely meant the girl was the chief's daughter, or at least one of them.

After the woman fixed the girl's hair to her satisfaction, she motioned for the rest of us to stand up. I scrambled to my feet, falling to the back of a line that had formed.

We walked out of the hut in a single-file line behind her, headed to the area where I'd seen the bonfire earlier. The fire had been lit and the flames leapt and crackled. We skirted the bonfire and headed to an area a short distance away near a large dirt circle ringed with stones.

We waited for several minutes until a procession arrived. The chief came first, wearing a short, colorful cape decorated with feathers. He stopped next to us and everyone fell silent. I had no idea what was going on, but I had started to get a bad feeling. A few minutes later, I heard a man's voice calling from the trees outside the village. It sounded like a wolf howl. He made the call exactly three times. After the third time, the chief made the same call back and then…nothing. We just continued to stand silently.

Several minutes later several men approached us. The one leading the group was an older, heavily tattooed man wearing a colorful, feathered headdress and a chest plate adorned with brightly colored bird feathers. He held a long staff that was as tall as he was. Behind him, another older man about the chief's age and several younger men who looked like they were in their late teens were following. When the group reached us, the feathered man with the staff made a complex gesture to the chief. The chief acknowledged him by beating his chest twice with his fist.

The man with the staff then moved to the center of

the area alone. My best guess was the guy with the staff was some sort of shaman or medicine man, because he had numerous vials and pouches around his neck. Everyone seemed afraid of him, and he seemed to be on an equal footing with the chief. He made a solemn and brief speech to those assembled, and then dramatically pointed at our group. I tried to shrink back into the shadows, but the men from the latter procession circled us until we were trapped inside.

The shaman finished his speech and immediately about half the young men stepped forward and started inspecting us. And by inspect, I meant looking at us like we were cattle or animals.

Oh, heck no. Absolutely not.

Everything became clear in that moment. I didn't have to understand the village language to figure out what was going on. These men were looking for wives or mates and I'd somehow been roped into a binding or wedding ceremony. But why me?

OMG! Slash, where are you?

I was at the very end of the line of women, but my brain began racing through scenario after scenario to provide me with the right time and opportunity to voice my objections, or, as a last resort, make a freaking run for it. Before I could come up with a good plan, one of the young men stood directly in front of me, his nose so close to my shoulder I could feel his breath. If he got any closer, I was going to deck him.

He stepped back and made some comment that caused the other men to snicker. The chief spoke curtly and they stopped snickering. One by one, the men continued to look us over.

Another of the young men coming down the line appeared to be particularly lecherous, and he kept touching the girls, unlike the other men. My anger bubbled furiously at his treatment of the girls. No way was he going to touch me like that.

Oddly, the tall girl, who'd moved to the back of the line and now stood next to me, wasn't watching the guy, but me. We exchanged a glance, and I saw the disgust in her eyes at his behavior. In that moment, we shared a moment of feminine unity that crossed all cultures. I clenched my fists by my sides, readying myself to deck him if he touched me.

I didn't have the chance.

When the guy stood in front of the chief's daughter and reached out to touch her, she took a swing at him. Her fist landed squarely against his jaw with a significant amount of force, especially since he was unprepared for it. He spun around once, his eyes rolled back in his head, and he collapsed to the ground.

For a second, it seemed that every noise in the rainforest silenced. I looked at her in surprise and then admiration.

You go, girl. What a freaking awesome hit.

The other girls looked at her with shocked expressions, while the rest of the young men stepped back in fear. The villagers were craning their necks to see what was going on. The tall girl turned to me and smiled, before giving the guys a fierce scowl. Crossing her arms against her chest, she said something to them sternly. I don't know exactly what she said, but they definitely got the message.

I looked over my shoulder, but neither the chief nor the shaman said or did anything to rebuke her. They just stood watching quietly. Maybe the girls decked the guys all the time. How would I know?

After another nervous minute, during which a couple of the young men dragged away the unconscious guy, the shaman barked another command. The next group of men stepped forward to complete a similar inspection of us.

This time the men were completely respectful. Not one girl got touched inappropriately, and not one of them came anywhere near me or the tall girl.

Good.

I needed to think. One part of me was panicking horribly, but the other part stayed calm and rational—analyzing and processing the situation. That was the part I needed. A quick count around the circle indicated there were eleven potential suitors and only seven women, including me. The mathematical part of me wondered how that would be resolved. By lots or a fight? I didn't see any weapons, which was a relief, but that didn't make sense as a long-term solution to managing a village's population anyway. My vote was for a fight of some kind, which would not be a bad thing because it could offer me cover to slip away.

The shaman spoke again. Whatever he said involved repeatedly pointing at us. When he finished his speech, he walked into the circle ringed by stones and started chanting. As soon as he was done, the rest of the villagers, who'd been quietly sitting on the logs, began to yell and bang sticks on the logs in a rhythmic thumping.

Oh, jeez. Things are about to get real. At least I'm not fodder for the bonfire, but that might actually be a better alternative to what's actually happening.

The shaman pointed at one of the girls in our group

and she came to stand at the top of the circle, just outside it. He then pointed to the group of young men. Without hesitation, one of them stepped forward into the ring. The shaman pointed to the other men, but after a brief wait, no one stepped forward. The chief took the young woman by the hand, brought her inside the stone circle and put her hand inside that of the young man. She seemed pleased and the young man had a broad smile. As the crowd cheered, the shaman turned to the young man, who reached into a small pouch hanging from his loincloth and pulled out what appeared to be a small rock. The shaman took the rock using a pair of wooden tongs and placed the object into the edge of the fire. After a couple of minutes during which the crowd had started a rhythmic chant, the rock was removed. The shaman presented the tongs to the young man. The girl, who looked extremely nervous, turned her face away from the tongs, as if she was afraid to look at them. The young man put his hand at the back of her head and pressed the hot stone into the cheek she provided for him.

Though it must have hurt horribly, the girl made no sound. After a second, he released her and dropped the rock and the tongs. The girl's eyes were watering from the pain, but she leaned forward and kissed her new mate.

What in the heck? Maybe this tradition was acceptable and okay for them, but it was *not* okay for me.

By all that is holy, if a man comes anywhere near my face with a hot stone, he'd better be prepared to fight for his life.

Still in shock, I watched the couple walk off and stand among a crowd of people who surrounded them, hugging them. Family, I presumed. Perversely, I wondered

what my mother would think of my snail shell loincloth,
fishnet bra, and hiking boots as wedding attire. I imagined her fainting.

Gah!

I snapped back to reality when the shaman summoned
a second woman from our group. She'd been led to the
top of the circle and the process was repeated. This time,
however, there were two suitors who expressed interest.
The shaman set them in the middle of the circle facing
each other and gave what I presumed were a few simple instructions. Then he stepped out of the ring and
thumped down his staff.

The men immediately charged at each other and
began wrestling. To my surprise, it wasn't what I expected. No one punched or boxed, it was more like a
pushing and wrestling match. Also, the villagers were
quietly watching, instead of cheering.

Suddenly one of the young men flipped the other to
the ground and tried to pull him toward the edge of the
ring. The man on the ground struggled, but was dragged
closer to the edge. When they were almost at the edge,
the man on the ground suddenly came alive. His weak-
ness had been a feint. He arched his back and thrust his
feet squarely into the chest of his opponent, pushing
him to the very edge of the circle. He teetered, trying
to avoid stepping over the line. Just as he appeared to
have regained his balance, his opponent bent forward
on his knees and gave him a final push out of the circle.

Now the villagers cheered. The apparent loser approached his opponent and made some kind of acknowledgment before bowing in front of the shaman, who
tapped him with the staff on his head. The loser returned
to the suitor group, while the chief then took the young

woman into the circle and presented her to the winner. She smiled widely, so perhaps it wasn't as traumatic for the women as I thought. How would I know?

The assembled crowd chanted again as the victor handed the shaman his rock. I turned my head away because I couldn't stand to watch the branding. Instead, I decided I would make my move the next time the attention was on the fighters.

At that moment, the tall girl slid beside me and slipped her hand into mine, squeezing it. I started at the physical contact, looking down at our linked hands. What did that mean? Was she trying to give me courage? Making me feel as if I weren't alone? Or could she tell I planned to bolt? How was I supposed to know? I couldn't interpret social signals in a society where I actually understood what people were saying, so how would I figure it out with people I couldn't even talk to?

She tapped her chest and said, "Amana."

Was she telling me her name? Just to make sure, I pointed at her and repeated in a questioning voice, "Amana?"

She nodded, so I pointed to myself and said, "Lexi."

My name must have sounded strange to her, because she tried to repeat it, but it came out more like "acky" instead of Lexi.

Despite the friendly gesture, her standing next to me presented a serious problem. I didn't know what she'd do if I ran for it. Would she alert the others? Would she let me slip away? It was probably suicide to plunge into the jungle in the middle of the night, but I was willing to risk it at this point.

To my surprise, she leaned closer to me, pointing at a young man with a jagged scar trailing down the length of his shoulder. I recalled he'd been watching her around the village, and she seemed to have reciprocated his attention. Then she pointed to the chief's older wife and shook her head sadly, motioning at a brute of a guy who stood at the edge of the suitor circle.

It took me a minute to figure out what she was trying to say. "Wait. You like scar guy, but the chief's wife, who is…your mother, I bet, likes muscle man over there?" I pointed at them one by one, until she nodded again, convinced I understood. She sighed unhappily.

Holy cow. I totally understood why she was upset. The shoulder scar guy was a *lot* smaller and was likely to get beat to a pulp by the muscled man. But Slash had taught me that being smaller than your opponent wasn't necessarily a bad thing. He always said that if you knew where to strike, and were committed to doing it, you could take down a larger opponent. I only hoped this held true for this guy.

Still, what was even *more* astonishing to me was that this girl was having mother issues on her wedding day. A girl who lived in the middle of a rainforest without running water or a computer, had a wedding issue with her mother just like I did a continent away. Except her mother was rooting for a different suitor and she didn't have the opportunity to make her own choice. But maybe this was a universal thing, and right now, my issue with my mother was a hundred times less troublesome than this one. Regardless, I felt even more connected to her, so I squeezed her hand in sympathy.

One by one the girls were called forward until Amana and I were the last two women standing. I exhaled in relief when the shaman pointed at her, motioning her forward. She gave me a reassuring look and released my hand.

As soon as she reached the spot outside the circle, the young man with the shoulder scar immediately stepped into the ring. The hulking guy took his time sauntering in, and then made a show of flexing his muscles. To his credit, the shoulder-scarred man didn't back down or look impressed. No doubt it would be a fierce fight. I glanced at Amana, noticing her attention stayed solely on the man of her choice. I hoped for her sake he was successful in his match.

As both of the men shook out their arms and legs waiting for the shaman to thump his staff, I noticed Amana's brow furrowed and her hands clenched nervously by her side.

Despite my intention to escape during this match, I couldn't help but watch a little. The match began differently than the previous one. The smaller man with the scar clearly realized his disadvantage in size and refused to engage the bigger man directly. Instead, he used his quickness to stay out of reach. The bigger man stalked him, trying to pin him against the side of the circle. But the smaller man was able to stay just out of reach. I wondered how this would end. Both men showed great patience, and the match continued tensely with each waiting for the other to make a mistake. It was great cover for me because the crowd was so mesmerized by the match I'd be able to slip away and no one would notice.

I peeked over my shoulder. There was no one behind me or between me and the trees.

Time to go.

I started backing up toward the safety of the trees. I

didn't really know what came next, except there was no way I would stay in the nuptial lineup. I was already engaged to the man I loved, and I wasn't trading him for anybody at this village.

I'd just reached the tree line, apparently unnoticed, when I heard the crowd roar. Glancing back at the circle, I saw two men lying on the ground, half in and half out of the circle. The young man with the scar was on top and had a huge smile on his face. Amana was jumping for joy.

Good for them.

Realizing this was my last chance, I ran for the trees. Unfortunately, I took about six steps before hooking my foot in the dark on a root and falling face-first on the ground. While I caught my breath and scrambled to my feet, I found myself being helped up by strong hands. When I got upright, I saw the chief looking at me with a worried expression on his face.

Oh, crap! Busted.

He looked me over to see if I were hurt. When he decided I wasn't, he took me firmly by the hand and led me toward the circle.

No, no, no! This isn't happening.

Amana had just received the mark on her face. She looked at me, beaming and holding on to the arm of her new mate. I was happy for her, but I was also seconds from throwing up. The rational part of my brain was calculating how many seconds it would take for me to grab a stick from the fire and brandish it at anyone who tried to approach me.

How could I stop this?

Oddly, the chief broke from the routine of the previous matches, and did something entirely different in regards to me. He launched into a long speech. I heard him say "a-muh-suh-ne" several times and motion toward me.

When the chief finished, the shaman came forward and stood inside the circle in front of me. For a long moment we waited, but none of the young men stepped forward. My spirits suddenly lifted.

No one wants me! What an amazing stroke of luck. How lucky am I?

Feeling incredibly relieved, I shrugged with mock disappointment and started to move away from the shaman. But before I could take a step, the village chief turned toward me with a huge smile and stepped into the circle.

Chapter Forty

Slash

He arrived at the airport approximately two hours after the satellite signal had gone off. It was two hours too long, but he had important things to arrange first.

After arriving, he spoke at great length with the pilot, both of them speaking in Spanish. He wanted the pilot to be absolutely clear they'd be flying into indigenous tribal territory and it would be dangerous. He offered to pay the pilot additional money to account for the danger, but he had no idea if the pilot would agree. To his enormous relief, he readily accepted.

One hurdle down.

After that, he and the pilot mapped out a flight plan to fit within the coordinates registered from the satellite phone.

"This will be a difficult flight," the pilot said. "It's a rugged terrain with high tree canopies. It will be hard to find a safe location to set the chopper down. I can't promise I'll find a place to set down, but I'll try."

"I appreciate that," he said. "Thank you."

He decided the pilot should stay with the copter in case they had to make a quick getaway. With the plan of action discussed and confirmed with the pilot, they began loading the gear on the helicopter.

Slash had just put a duffel on the plane when Vicente pulled him aside. "What's the plan for when we get there?"

Slash set his pack in the back of the helicopter. "I intend to minimize the impact on the native tribes as much as I can. But I'm not letting any of us get captured or hurt. And I intend to rescue Lexi, or at least find out where she is. If I have to shoot someone to do that, I'll do it."

Vicente nodded. "I figured that was the case. Then it will be my job to make sure you don't have to do that."

"Fair enough. In your opinion, what's the best way to approach the natives if they do have Lexi?"

"We're going to have to play it by ear. Let me handle it as much as I'm able. I think they're most suspicious when they don't understand the intentions of the strangers they meet, especially since there are routine conflicts between several of the indigenous tribes in the region. Just don't do anything threatening."

It was hardly a plan, but he'd settle for it. Less than ten minutes later they were airborne. After they'd flown for about fifty minutes, the pilot motioned them forward. He said something and Vicente translated.

"He says between that ridge of higher land between two rivers is where the coordinates appear to be," Vicente said. "If you look closely, you can see a faint trail of smoke rising from the canopy. See it?"

Slash saw it in the distance. "Yes. Can he find a place to set down that's not too far away?"

"He's looking. Stand by."

They circled around the ridge. On the far side, the

pilot found a place where a large tree had fallen, taking down a number of small trees and creating a small opening in the canopy.

The pilot shouted something.

"He's going to set down," Vicente said. "Brace yourselves."

As they lowered, the edges of the helicopter blades were close to the trees, but the lack of wind and the pilot's steady hand got them on the ground. Slash clapped the pilot's shoulder in a thankful gesture. They unloaded the gear and left a satellite phone that already had the return coordinates plugged in with the pilot.

The three of them set off into the rainforest, loaded with gear. Salvador took the lead, using his satellite phone to keep them going in the direction of the coordinates. Carrying their heavy packs, they soon began sweating profusely. In the absence of a trail, it was slow going and impossible to walk in a straight line. After another thirty minutes of gradual climbing, the thick vegetation thinned slightly as they rose from the river floor. They pressed onward steadily.

As they walked, Slash wondered about the motivations of the men with him. He understood why Salvador would volunteer to accompany him. He'd lost a loved one to malaria and was vested in resuming the distribution of the vaccine. But Vicente was a mystery. What was motivating him to come along? His behavior back at the research camp had been suspect. He didn't have any reason to trust Vicente, but he couldn't do without his language skills. If Vicente were trying to sabotage their efforts, he could have just been unwilling to support the rescue, yet here he was. He wasn't sure what it meant.

They were within a half mile when their path became

blocked by a near vertical escarpment of rock. There was no way they could climb it, so they looked in both directions and decided to go to the right to try to find a way up. After a hundred yards or so, they stumbled upon the first path they'd seen so far.

"This isn't an animal path," Salvador said quietly. "People have been here."

They glanced at each other and then moved on carefully. The path wound upwards until it flattened at the top. Salvador held up a hand, and they halted. A thumping noise could be heard in the distance. As they got closer, they heard a roar of voices, followed by some rhythmic chanting.

They'd found people. Now, what to do about it?

Slash motioned for Vicente and Salvador to wait while he slipped forward to investigate. He dropped his pack, and taking only a pistol and a pair of binoculars, he began a stealthy approach.

Although it was still daylight, dusk was probably less than an hour away. As it was, all the towering trees caused huge areas of shadows with occasional slices of light. He maneuvered so he stayed in the shadows until he found a perch where he could see into the clearing where all the noise was located.

Unfortunately, his view was partially obstructed by several tall tree trunks, so he could only see part of the event. He used the binoculars to scan the area. They'd definitely found a village, and it looked like most of the village had turned out for a wrestling match between two young men. It seemed like a lopsided match as one of the men was much larger than the other, but the smaller man was quicker and able to stay out of the bigger one's reach.

A tall man with a staff and a feathered outfit seemed to be officiating the match.

He did a scan for weapons, but didn't see any other than spears and bows. Didn't mean there weren't any there, but he was hopeful. Outside of the circle, villagers were sitting on logs or standing around, and children were playing in groups. He did another, more careful scan, looking explicitly for Lexi.

He didn't see anyone dressed in Western garb. Most of the men and women were dressed in loincloths and knee-length grassy skirts. Lexi should have stood out, but he didn't see her. His heart skipped a beat, but he calmed himself, adjusting his position for a better look at the entire area.

He had just moved when he heard a noise behind him. Turning quickly, he pointed the pistol, then lowered it when saw Vicente and Salvador had crept up behind him.

"What are you doing?" Slash said in a low voice. "I could have shot you."

"We're here to help," Vicente said, settling in on one side of him while Salvador took the other side. "So, let us help."

"Where's the gear?" he asked.

"Back where we dumped it," Vicente answered. "We didn't want to be encumbered if we needed to move quickly."

A huge roar sounded from the crowd. Slash turned his attention back to the stone circle. The two combatants lying on the ground with the smaller man on top. Apparently the fight was over.

As the smaller man stood up, a young woman in a decorative loincloth jumped up and down excitedly. The feathered man with the staff brought her to the apparent victor, who beamed proudly.

"Let me take a closer look," Vicente said, reaching for the binoculars. Slash reluctantly handed them over.

"It appears to be a marriage ritual." Vicente adjusted the view. "The men are fighting for the woman. In most of the indigenous tribes, this ritual happens once or twice a year. Men in the same tribe, but from other, smaller villages often come together to vie for eligible women who are of age, or who've lost their husbands. The guy with the staff is likely the shaman—a combination of the village elder and a medicine man."

"Who's the guy with the feathered cape?" Slash asked.

"My guess is the chief, simply by the number of tattoos on his face," Vicente said.

As they watched, the shaman knelt by the fire. Vicente swept the binoculars across the view. "Wait. The older woman behind the shaman is wearing a satellite phone."

For a moment, Slash couldn't breathe. He took the binoculars from Vicente and adjusted the binoculars. Sure enough, a satellite phone hung around her neck.

He closed his eyes for a moment, trying to figure out the meaning. Did it mean Lexi was dead? Had they stolen it from her? Found it? Before he figured it out, there was a commotion just out of his view. The man in the cape, the chief as Vicente called him, turned and ran to the left of him while everyone in the crowd stood to look in that direction.

After a moment, the villagers lost interest in whatever the chief was doing and sat down. The shaman held up tongs and returned to the victorious suitor.

"Watch this," Vicente said.

Slash shifted the binoculars to watch as the young man who won the match took the wooden tongs and pressed something to the side of the woman's face. She flinched, but did not scream.

"The marriage is now complete," Salvador said. "She has his mark. All who see her will know she's taken."

As the couple walked to the side of the clearing, the shaman beckoned to someone in the direction of where the chief had gone. The man with the cape stepped into view holding the arm of a woman in a loincloth. There was no mistaking who it was.

Lexi!

Relief, sharp and brutal, slammed into his gut, making it hard to breathe. Outwardly calm, he gave himself a few seconds before he adjusted the binoculars for a better look. He didn't like that the chief had his hands on her. Thankfully, she appeared unharmed, but was wearing the same type of decorated loincloth as the other women, except she'd bound her breasts with some kind of netting. She wasn't struggling to get away from the man, but he could tell she was equal parts furious and frightened by whatever was happening.

Thank God he'd been in time. Thank God she was still alive. They could figure out anything else together.

He slipped his father's cross from beneath his shirt and kissed it. Now he had to go get her.

He looked down, realizing he only had his semiautomatic pistol. It held ten rounds. It would probably be enough to reach Lexi, but he doubted he could protect her if they were subsequently attacked. The rest of the ammunition was in the pack he'd left a hundred yards back. He could run back and get it, but he didn't know if he had enough time to stop whatever was about to happen. Vicente and Salvador also had guns, thank God, but he wasn't anxious to start a shootout, especially with Lexi in the middle of it.

Before he could decide what to do, the man with the cape starting making a speech, his voice booming over the clearing, allowing them to hear.

Vicente cocked his head to better listen, then turned excitedly to Slash. "We're in luck. They're speaking a version of a local dialect I know. The chief is talking about Lexi. He says he believes she's a descendant of the *Amazonas*, the fierce tribe of women warriors from South America. Damn, we were just joking about that at the last village."

"I remember," Slash said. "Do you think one of these villagers overheard it and took it to heart?"

"It's possible," Vicente said. "Give me a minute to listen to what else he's saying."

Everyone fell silent, listening to the booming voice of the chief. After a bit, Vicente began translating softly.

"He says their village is in crisis. Their numbers are dwindling and they're under increasing attack from outside tribes and invaders. He believes Lexi's presence is a sign to the village."

"What kind of sign?"

Vicente shrugged. "I'm not sure. A sign of strength or good luck. Hard to say. Personally, I think the chief could be using her to strengthen his role in the eyes of the villagers and perhaps the surrounding tribes. I suspect that's why he or his warriors kidnapped her."

Slash's fists clenched in frustration. He wanted to run down there and drag her into his arms, but he had to proceed carefully if he wanted to get her out safely.

"The chief says he personally saw her defeat two men

and steal their prisoners using only a snake and her feet," Vicente said. "He also said she was able to sense when arrows were being fired from the enemy, and she protected him from the name of some tribe I don't recognize." He listened some more. "He said she personally saved his life."

Slash lowered the binoculars. "Do you think she has any idea what is going on?"

"Hard to say, but I doubt it."

Slash refocused the binoculars and trained them on Lexi. "What's happening now?" He pointed at the chief who was wrapping up his speech.

Vicente listened and then looked in alarm at Slash. "Uh-oh. We've got a problem. He just claimed her as his own."

"As his own *what*?" Slash said, his voice deadly calm.

"Mate, wife, whatever you want to call it. He's offered a challenge to anyone who wants to fight him for her."

He stood up. "Damn. Guess that's my cue."

"Whoa." Salvador grabbed his arm, trying to pull him back down. "Are you crazy? You can't just walk down there. They'll kill you."

"If I don't, *she'll* kill him. Look."

They all turned to look at Lexi who was standing on the balls of her feet, a thick branch in her hands, jabbing it toward the chief. She didn't intend to go down easy.

"Besides, he can't have her." Slash put a hand on Vicente's shoulder. "Look, I need you to come with me so you can tell him why I'm there. I'm going to fight for her one way or another. That being said, I understand the risk, so if you don't want to come along, I get it. I'll do it on my own. I only ask that you protect Lexi at all cost."

"Seriously?" Vicente asked. "You're going to do this?"

"I'm going to do this."

Vicente exhaled a deep breath. "Well, you leave me little choice. I'm not abandoning her like last time. I'll go with you."

"Are you sure?"

"No, I'm not sure. But if I get killed, I'm holding you personally responsible. Are you taking a gun?"

"No, I have to play by their rules. I'm going to fight for my woman fair and square, and the chief should understand that. But you should take one."

"I will, and I understand what you're doing. But you intend to take her away from the chief, and he isn't going to like that."

"I'll cross that bridge when I get to it. Salvador, go get our supplies, including the guns, but stay out of sight so we have a backup plan."

"What happens if you lose?" Salvador asked.

"I won't." He strode forward. "But be prepared. Remember, the primary goal is to get Lexi out safely. Come on, Vicente, let's go."

They began to walk down the slope, holding up their hands to appear nonthreatening. As they came into view of the villagers, a cry of alarm rose and men rushed to grab their bows.

Vicente stopped and called out loudly in their language. "Wait. We mean no harm, but the woman has another champion." He stepped aside so Slash could move forward. "He's here to challenge the chief and claim his woman."

Chapter Forty-One

Lexi

My life was over. I was destined to live the rest of my days in the rainforest without a computer or Slash. The universe had played the cruelest joke on me—shown me what I could have, and then taken it all away. Now I would suffer, realizing that for all the days of my life. The only bright side to any of this was I wouldn't have to pick out a wedding dress.

Oh, the irony.

Obviously, no one was going to challenge the chief. Who would be dumb enough to challenge the most accomplished man in the village. Was that why he'd kidnapped me? To make me one of his wives? It didn't make sense. Why me?

Still, I wasn't going down without a fight. No other man would challenge him, but I would…and I intended to win by any means I could. I dashed out of the circle and grabbed a large, thick branch, brandishing it in front of me as a weapon.

To my surprise and dismay, the chief didn't seem surprised or even worried by my action. He just calmly strode toward me.

"No," I said firmly, holding out the stick and making him stop. "I don't agree to this. Come closer and I'll hurt you."

I jabbed the stick at him to indicate I meant business, but then a commotion sounded from behind the chief. Some of the men dashed away and the chief abruptly turned away from me.

I heard some yelling, a silence, and two people stepped into view. I only had eyes for one.

Slash!

Our eyes met and my breath stopped. Without thinking, I ran toward him. The chief shot out a hand, grabbing me by the upper arm. Slash moved to confront him, when someone stopped him.

Vicente.

"You can't have her...yet," he said to Slash, loud enough so I could hear. "Don't make a move toward the chief or her until you've been granted the right to fight for her."

"What took you guys so long?" I whispered loudly.

"We couldn't find first-class accommodations to the area," Slash said in a low voice. "Are you okay, *cara*?"

"So far." I couldn't help it, my voice caught with emotion. "I'm so freaking glad you're here. I'm kind of in a bind right now."

"I know. Just sit tight. We'll get you out of here."

"Vicente, tell the chief I'm already engaged to Slash. This is some kind of marriage or mating ceremony. Once he knows I'm already spoken for, hopefully he'll let me go."

Vicente shook his head. "I don't think it's going to be that easy, Lexi. They think you're a descendant of the *Amazonas* tribe, a warrior woman here to assist the village. The chief is unlikely to simply surrender you."

"Oh, no! Not that again." I blew out a frustrated breath. "How exactly am I supposed to assist the village?"

"I have no idea. Stand by and let me see if I can figure things out." He began speaking with the chief.

I inhaled several deep breaths to try and calm my nerves, my eyes never leaving Slash's. His gaze was steady and assuring. No matter how dire our situation, he'd come for me. He'd *always* come for me. But how were we going to get out of this situation?

Vicente turned to us. "The chief says the village has fallen on difficult times. Apparently a few days ago, the shaman had a vision of a woman warrior holding a snake and believed it was some kind of message. Then the chief saw you, and how you commanded the snake to fall from the tree onto a man before you jumped down to save the others. From there, he apparently extrapolated that you were that woman in the shaman's vision. He said you could summon snakes at will, although I wasn't exactly clear on that part."

"Gah! I *knew* I saw someone right before I jumped," I said. "But I didn't have to summon anything. There are snakes everywhere. I pushed and prodded that snake with a stick until it fell out of the tree. The chief has everything all mixed up. I'm definitely not the warrior woman he thinks I am."

"Regardless, that's where we are." He turned to Slash. "The chief says he remembers you, too, from the raid where Lexi saved you and the prisoners. He watched you from the trees. He said you cared for her after she was hurt."

"Yes, because I love her."

My heart tripped. It took everything I had not to run to him and throw my arms around him.

Vicente relayed his words to the chief, and there was murmuring among the villagers. The chief looked at the shaman, while I exchanged a glance with Amana. Her expression was sympathetic. She understood what it meant to want to be with the one you loved. Lucky for her, she'd got her wish. Now it was my turn, I hoped.

The chief said something and several women stepped forward shyly. The chief motioned to Slash and then to the women.

"He's offering you a different woman," Vicente said. "Or multiple women. I'm not sure. Anyway, it's clearly your choice."

Slash bowed his head to the chief. "Tell him I am honored by his offer, but there's only one woman for me, and I'm not leaving here without her."

Slash pulled his shirt off over his head and dropped it to the ground. His father's crucifix gleamed against his bare chest in the firelight.

"Slash, what are you doing?" I asked, alarmed.

"Disrobing. I'm going to fight for you."

"What?"

"You're coming home with me one way or the other."

The chief and the shaman had started a deep discussion. Vicente was listening, but I had no idea what they were saying. My anxiety skyrocketed. How would this play out? Would they let me go even if Slash won? What if Slash didn't win? Would they let *him* go? Or would they kill him and Vicente on the spot?

Knowing Slash, he wouldn't go down easy, if at all. I assumed he had a backup plan. But that backup plan probably involved guns, and I didn't want any of the villagers to get hurt. While I wasn't happy I'd been kidnapped and had no desire to stay, these were good people.

I let out a breath, pressing a hand to my forehead where an anxiety headache had started. "Slash, if you fight the chief, you can't hurt him."

"Why not?"

"Because he has to lead these people. They need him."

By this time, Slash was down to his boxers and his physique was showing. He was taller and heavier than the chief and he held himself with a grace that signaled he was a man used to fighting. I almost felt sorry for the chief. Vicente returned, lowering his voice but speaking loud enough so I could hear it.

"The shaman told the chief he doesn't have to fight you. After all, it's the shaman's right to declare a victor even if a match is not fought. But the chief doesn't like that scenario. He says it's only proper that a warrior as powerful as Lexi have a mate who is also strong and willing to fight for her. He says Lexi must be very special if you followed her all the way from the river to reclaim her. How could he not challenge you for such a woman? And if he didn't, what would the Gods of the River think of him?"

I closed my eyes. That sealed it. The two men were going to fight. No matter what I said or demanded, it wouldn't be settled by me.

I didn't move, so the shaman took my arm, moving me out of the ring and into the spot where all the unmarried women had to watch their match.

The chief threw off his cape and stepped into the ring. Slash stepped in as well. It surprised me that Slash's sudden appearance and willingness to fight for me did not send the village into a panic. It seemed ridiculous that they thought I was any kind of warrior, and if I wasn't standing here in a loincloth about to watch a wrestling match for my hand, I might have laughed. I didn't want to be part of a rainforest legend, but it looked like I wasn't going to have any say in it.

Slash and the chief started slowly circling each other, trying to gauge each other's abilities.

"Are there any rules?" Slash asked me.

"From what I saw, you can't leave or step foot outside the stone circle. In earlier matches, it looked like they were wrestling to me. No punching or hitting, but be careful because I'm not entirely sure about that part. To win, you have to push your opponent out of the circle or make him step out. And remember, you can't hurt him."

"That's all?" Slash said. "Win, but don't win. Get him, but don't hurt him."

"You need to make it look like a heroic fight, Slash. I mean it. The chief needs to look like a hero in the villagers' eyes."

Just as I said that, the chief made the first move. He'd crouched down low and was making a wide swooping motion with his hand across the dirt. I wondered what the heck he was doing, as I hadn't seen that movement in any other fight. Suddenly, the chief put his hands behind his back and leaned forward. Without warning, he threw a handful of the dirt at Slash's face and lunged forward in an attempt to drive a blinded Slash from the circle.

Slash managed to get his arms in front of his face to avoid most of the dirt. Apparently he'd expected the subsequent rush, because he dropped to one knee, anchoring himself in the ground and lowering his center of gravity. When the chief lunged forward, he jammed his shoulder into the chief's stomach and used a modified judo throw to lay out the chief behind him.

Slash wiped the remaining dirt from his eyes as the chief rose to his feet and laughed. He said something and Vicente translated. "He says he's fighting a warrior worthy of having an *Amazonas* descendant. He says this will be a fight for the entire village to remember and pass down through the generations."

The two men circled each other twice more. I couldn't contain my nervousness or shut up. "Go get him, Slash. You've got this!"

I gave him a few more encouragements and then stopped, turning around. Everyone in the village, including the shaman, was staring at me. That's when I remembered the entire village had stayed quiet during the match.

Oops! Me and my big mouth.

Before I could say another thing, several women villagers abruptly pressed forward and started shouting at the men in the ring. Puzzled, I glanced over at Vicente. "What's going on? Why are they suddenly shouting?"

He listened and then laughed. "The villagers think you're giving your man instructions on how to fight. Not to be outdone, they're now offering suggestions to the chief."

Stunned, I looked around. What had previously been a silent battle among the competitors, was now a cacophony of calls and cheers, but from the women only. The men were staying quiet. Somehow I'd broken that taboo for the women.

I'd lost track of what was going on with the match, so I returned my attention to the ring. Twice the chief got close enough for Slash to grab him, spin him around and throw him to the ground. The second time, Slash did another martial arts movement, rolling the chief over his hip. For a second, my heart stopped when Slash lost his balance and teetered near the edge of the circle. The chief managed to slip away and lunged at Slash. Just as he was about to shove Slash out of the circle, Slash regained his balance and danced out of the way.

The villagers went wild, cheering and yelling, the men finally joining in. I pressed a hand to my chest where my heart was beating like crazy, until I saw the barely detectable smile on Slash's face. I blew out a breath, realizing he was adding drama to the fight.

The chief changed tactics and picked up the branch I'd dropped inside the ring. He whirled it around with impressive ability, then jabbed it at Slash. Slash feinted and then danced sideways, staying just out of reach of the stick. But the chief was highly experienced and wielded the stick with breathtaking speed. Twice he managed to club Slash hard on the side of the head, and I didn't think Slash had let him do it.

OMG! Slash couldn't lose.

Suddenly, there was a huge shift in the wind. Thick smoke from the bonfire started blowing into the circle, obscuring our view of the men.

Holy smoke!

Just as the smoke descended, the chief hit Slash in a brutal double tap. The first smash landed on Slash's right cheek, the second one went directly into his stomach. Slash stumbled backward as I gasped. The shaman quickly moved behind Slash to detect if he stepped out of the circle.

After that the chief began to rain blow after blow upon Slash. Concerned he was taking the acting too far,

I shouted at him, swinging my fists. "Come on, Slash, fight back. Get him, get him!"

But he didn't, and I began to seriously worry. It was hard to be sure, but it looked like his eyes were partially closed. Possibly to protect them from the smoke or had the chief's repeated hits to the head affected him? It was hard to tell.

I wished I could see his face better. The smoke had given him a shadowy, mysterious silhouette. It seemed like he was staggering. Apparently, the chief thought so, too. Ready to claim victory, the chief held the stick horizontally across his chest with both hands and bellowed, clearly intending to rush him. As he reared back to run at Slash, the smoke suddenly parted. In one giant leap, Slash leapt forward to confront the chief, grabbing on to the stick. For a moment, the two stood eye to eye, struggling to push it against the other. The crowd screamed in excitement, while my heart pounded so hard I could barely breathe.

Grunting, the two men fought for purchase in the soft dirt. Slash slowly began to make headway pushing the chief closer to the stones. When they were right at the edge, the chief stepped backward on a sharp rock and began a slow topple out of the circle. He windmilled his arms, defeat on his face. But before he landed, Slash shot out a hand, grabbed the chief's arm and yanked him back into the circle. Then he moved toward the center of the circle and motioned with his hand for the chief to continue the fight.

The village fell completely silent except for the occasional popping of the bonfire. The chief was frozen, the shaman's face was expressionless, and I covered my mouth with both hands because I wasn't sure if I should cheer or gasp.

I'd no idea if we'd won, if the match would continue, or if we were all about to die.

After what seemed like an eternity, the chief walked toward Slash and said something. Both Slash and I looked at Vicente for translation.

"The chief says you're a worthy warrior."

Slash dipped his head in acknowledgment of the compliment. "Tell him, he's a warrior worthy of leading this village."

Vicente translated. The chief then took a minute to survey all the villagers before he turned and stepped out of the circle.

The village went completely nuts. People were shouting, cheering and gathering around the chief. Apparently he had performed heroically, which made him successful in the villagers' eyes.

But I only had eyes for one man.

I ran to him, jumping into his arms, winding my arms around his neck and wrapping my legs around his waist. "You did it, Slash. You really did it." I rained kisses over his shoulders, neck and face. "Are you hurt? You got hit a lot of times."

He tightened his arms around me, pressing his face into the side of my cheek. "Right now, I'm good. In fact, the best I've ever been. You're alive and that's what matters."

Vicente joined us in celebrating, clapping Slash on the back and giving me a hug. After a couple of amazing kisses, Slash glanced over at Vicente, but kept his arm tight around me. "Okay, what's next?"

Vicente raised both hands. "Your guess is as good as mine. No idea."

Eventually the shaman approached us and stretched out a fisted hand to Slash. While we watched, he uncurled his fist. Nestled inside was a small stone.

Slash looked at Vicente, puzzled. "What's this for?"

Vicente translated the request to the shaman and after he heard the response, turned back to Slash. "He says Lexi must bear your mark."

I took a step back. "Oh, no. Tell him I do *not* want a mark."

Vicente translated, but the shaman shook his head. Again, he insisted that I must be marked.

I exchanged a worried glance with Slash and Vicente. "What are we going to do?"

Slash didn't respond. He was staring at his hand, turning the rock over and over in his palm, thinking.

Vicente tugged on my arm, trying to calm me down. "Lexi, listen to me. He has to mark you because if he doesn't, anyone could claim you again, including the chief. Slash would have to fight for you all over again. The younger, stronger warriors would also see it as a challenge, and they'd start lining up to take him on. If you want this to be official, you have to finish the ceremony."

"I'm *not* getting branded, and we aren't staying."

"I don't think they'll let you go if you don't finish the ceremony."

Slash finally spoke up. "I have an idea. Vicente, ask the shaman to give us a minute. *Cara*, can you give me your engagement ring?"

"I can't get it off my finger. My fingers have swollen from the heat."

"Can you try?"

I began to tug on the ring, twisting and pulling. It wouldn't budge. I twisted it some more, finally popping it over my knuckle after a serious stab of pain. "Ouch, that hurt like crazy." I handed it over to Slash. "What's your idea?"

"I'm not going to mark you. You're going to mark *me*—the small round mark of your engagement ring on the inside of my wrist."

"Wait. You're okay with that?"

"If it means I can take you home safely, yes."

I was not in favor of pain in any form, but I could see the possibility here. "Do you think it will work?"

"I have no idea, but if you have any other ideas, I'm open to suggestions."

I ran through a number of possible scenarios in my head, but couldn't come up with a better one. "Okay, we can try it."

Slash handed the shaman my engagement ring. The shaman took it and looked it over with great interest, murmuring something.

"He thinks it's magic," Vicente said. "I told him to put it in the fire."

The rest of the villagers began to chatter and murmur, pressing forward with great interest to see what would happen next. The shaman placed the ring between the tongs and thrust it into the fire. When the ring was glowing, he brought it to Slash. Slash carefully took the tongs and handed them to me.

The entire village gasped at the same time. Slash was right. They'd probably never seen a woman mark a man. This was going to be something the villagers would talk about for a long, long time.

Slash knelt in front of me and calmly held out his wrist. "Well, before I'm forever branded as yours, it seems like I should say something significant to mark our tribal wedding. So, will you, Lexi Carmichael, take me, Slash, aka Nicolo Cilento, aka Romeo Fortuna, as your…tribally wedded husband."

My hand was shaking so badly, I thought I might drop the ring. So many emotions and thoughts were pinging around inside of me. Had he just asked me to take him as my husband? If I said yes, did it mean we were getting married at exactly this moment in the middle of the rainforest? And how badly would this glowing hot ring hurt him?

I closed my eyes for a few seconds to calm down. One thing at a time. "Yes. Of course, I'll take all three of you. But I thought I'd be putting a ring on your finger, not burning it into your wrist."

"When getting married in the Brazilian rainforest, we do as they do. Press it to my skin firmly and count to three. Then lift it off. It's as easy as that."

"That doesn't sound easy, and just so you're clear, this is *not* how I thought our wedding vows would go either."

"Me neither. But oddly, it seems fitting for us, doesn't it?"

It did. As he knelt there, staring at me as if I were his whole world, happiness swept through me. It was a kind of happiness I'd never experienced before. This new happiness was a mixture of contentment, love and a surety that I was doing the right thing. Something far beyond an ordinary feeling of gladness. In fact, I'd never thought this kind of joy could happen to me. But somehow Slash had done it. Now here we were, the two of us standing half naked in the middle of the rainforest, professing our love for each other. Not only was it fitting, it felt exactly right.

"It does seem fitting, Slash. It *really* does." Before I lost my nerve, I pressed the glowing ring against the skin on his wrist, watching his expression. His eyes never wavered from mine. I counted to three and pulled the ring off. A small circular welt appeared.

"I'm *so* sorry," I said. "Are you okay?"

"I'm fine." He dropped his wrist and took the tongs from me. "I told you it was easy."

"Speak for yourself. That was *not* easy. Does it hurt?"

"A little, but it'll pass quickly."

I exhaled a deep breath and handed him the tongs. "Okay, my turn. Put the mark on my wrist, too, Slash. This will seal the deal for both of us."

Surprise flashed in his eyes. "Are you sure about this?"

I wasn't sure I'd ever be ready for pain, but if he could do it, so could I. "I presume this will hurt far less than a tattoo or a large brand on my face. Our scars will fade over time, leaving just a small circular mark on our wrists reminding us of this event. I think this will satisfy the tribal requirement and effectively bind us to each other. So, let's do it."

I lifted my wrist, holding it out to him. He studied my face, giving me time to back out if I changed my mind.

I didn't.

After a moment, he took my wrist in one hand, the other holding the ring just above my wrist. Slowly he raised his eyes to mine, waiting. I realized he paused to give me time to say something, much as he had. The problem was I hadn't rehearsed or prepared anything, so I'd have to speak from the heart, which was not my strong suit. My arm was shaking, but when I spoke my voice was calm.

"Will you, Slash, Nicolo, and Romeo, take me as your lawfully and tribally wedded warrior for now and forever and despite the little black cloud of trouble that endlessly follows me around?"

A smile touched his lips. "Absolutely."

I closed my eyes as he lowered the ring to my skin. It burned, but I remembered how the other girls hadn't screamed or flinched when getting branded on the face, so I managed to keep my composure. It was over faster than I expected.

He squeezed my hand. "Are you okay?"

I opened my eyes and looked at the burn. It hurt, but Slash was right, it would pass. "Actually, I'm fine. I think we just got married, Slash—me in a loincloth and you in your boxers. That was one clothing scenario I never imagined, and I imagined plenty."

Grinning, he reached out and cupped my face between his hands, looking deeply into my eyes. "As is my right, I'm going to give the bride a thorough kissing. And, as is your right, you're welcome to reciprocate or refuse."

Before he could say another word, I threw my arms around his neck and started kissing him. The entire village cheered.

When we pulled apart, Vicente held up a hand. "On behalf of the government of Brazil, I pronounce you lawfully bound in whatever way makes you happy. Congratulations."

Chapter Forty-Two

Lexi

"Vicente was just kidding about the lawfully bound part, right?"

I winced as Slash spread antibiotic ointment on my wrist. After all the congratulating had finished, Vicente asked the villagers if he could bring forth another friend who was waiting nearby. Salvador had appeared from the trees and joined us. Now, according to Slash, the rescue gang was all here.

Luckily, Salvador brought a first aid kit, so Slash and I were taking extra precautions to make sure our burns didn't get infected. We sat on one of the benches near the bonfire applying ointment to our burns while the villagers grouped around Vicente and Salvador, peppering them with questions. At some point, one of the men presented Slash with a loincloth, which he graciously accepted, stepping into it while keeping his boxers on underneath.

After he secured it to his hips, I gave him a thumbs-up. "You look sexy in that. Actually, you look sexy in everything, but this takes sexy to a new level for you."

"Thanks. I think."

The village was in full celebration mode with people eating, drinking, singing and dancing. "Do you think we can leave now?"

"Not yet." He shook his head and picked up a roll of gauze. "According to Vicente, we must participate in the ritual ceremony for newly bound couples. I'm not sure when that takes place. Additionally, I have to prove that I can survive being bound to an *Amazonas*. And I mean that in the carnal sense."

"Are you serious?"

"Completely." He wound a piece of gauze around my wrist, securing it. "Did I mention they also want to see you handle the snakes while naked?"

Surely, he had to be joking, although I didn't find it funny in the slightest. I glared at him, my eyes narrowing. "You made that up, right?"

His lips twitched. "You're going to have to conquer your fear of them someday, *cara*. You're an amazing warrior, an wizard wielder of snakes, a master of saving lives, and apparently divine in bed. The latter I can confirm, by the way."

"Ha ha. How long do you think this ceremony will take?"

"I have no idea, but I suspect all night. Salvador said he radioed the helicopter pilot using the satellite phone. The pilot will return home and await our instructions for his return. He also called Lilith to let her and the rest of the camp know we found you and would be bringing you home soon. They were elated to hear you're alive."

"Great. Will they resume the vaccine trials?"

"I don't know, but I hope so."

"We'll have to convince them if they're wavering.

But I suspect this delay means I have to spend another night on the ground."

He slipped a finger under my chin and nudged it up. "Don't complain. It's our wedding night, after all."

"Hey, if you're here, I'm *not* complaining. Trust me on that." I slid my hand to the back of his neck and kissed him again, not caring who was watching.

A young girl holding a bowl approached us shyly. Inside the bowl was a sweet-smelling oil. I glanced over at the other bound couples and saw they were spreading the oil on each other.

"Well, this is going to be awkward," I said, accepting the bowl from her.

Slash watched the girl go, a puzzled look on his face. "Is that your bra?"

"Not anymore. Now, it's a quiver that holds invisible arrows. Don't ask me where my underwear is."

He chuckled, and we spent the next little while smoothing oil on to each other, which made us super slippery. Even though I hadn't let Slash put any on my bottom or private areas, just sitting was dangerous because I felt like I could slide off any moment. At some point, another young girl brought us jewelry. Slash had a feathered necklace placed around his neck, and I got a beaded crown.

Vicente and Salvador joined us. They looked like they were having a great time.

"I have to thank you, Lexi," Vicente said. "This has been one of the most fascinating cultural experiences of my life. I guess I shouldn't be surprised that their language is so close to the others in the area. But it's been an incredible experience to confirm that and for me to learn more about the Okampa tribe."

"I agree," Salvador said. "It's a once-in-a-lifetime experience. Although, I'm not sure they would have been so welcoming if we weren't friends of a descendant of a legendary race of women warriors."

"Not that I had anything to do with this, but you're welcome, I guess."

The chief returned to the stone circle and made an announcement. The other newly bound couples rose, and Vicente instructed us to do the same.

"You're now going to complete the ritual," he told us. "Hold hands and, along with the other couples, you're to go seven times clockwise around the sacred bonfire."

"Well, this doesn't seem so bad," I said as Slash and I fell in line and starting walking.

The villagers joined us on the seventh round. When we were done, the shaman poured water on each of our open palms before he waved a smoking stick over each of us to cleanse and heal us. Then we were led to the bathing pool where each couple cast one stone together into the pool.

"The stone creates ripples when you throw it in," Vicente explained. "The ripples are life. The solid stone represents your love and how you will stay together for all of eternity while life ebbs and flows around you."

"That's incredibly meaningful," I said softly.

Slash pressed a kiss against my hair. "It really is."

After that, the men started doing a dance, which Vicente explained was some kind of fighting dance. One of the men motioned for Slash to join in.

"You're going to do it?" I asked when he stood up.

"I'm going to try."

He joined the other warriors and began imitating their motions and steps. Given his long dark hair and Mediterranean complexion he might have blended in perfectly if it hadn't been for his boxer shorts. He missed some steps and started laughing. Astonished, I realized he was having a good time…and in some strange way, so was I.

While we were watching the men, the women started bringing out the food. Plates heavy with fruits, vegetables, meats and fish were passed around. Slash returned to my side and plucked a piece of fish from my tray.

"I didn't know you could dance like that," I said, eating a piece of the fish.

"Like what?"

"You know, following the steps and all. You did great."

"I was passable. Barely." Slash finished his piece of fish and took another. "This fish is really good."

"I was thinking the same thing." As I said that, he got up from my left side and went to sit on my right.

"Why do you keep doing that?" I asked.

"Doing what?"

"Making sure you're always on my right side."

"I love how observant you are. I stay on your right side for a practical reason. I'm right handed, and I want to keep my right hand free in case I have to fight off any more warriors who want to challenge me for you."

I thought he was kidding, but after studying his face, I wasn't sure. Before I could ask, the shaman approached me and offered me a pipe.

"Oh, no, thank you," I said, declining. "I don't smoke."

Slash took the pipe and bowed to the shaman. "You'll smoke tonight. One puff is all it should take." He took one before handing it to me. "It's part of the ceremony. He's offered it to all the other couples."

I tried not to be grossed out, thinking of their mouths on it. "I don't think that's very sanitary. What's in it?"

"My best guess is a mild hallucinogen."

"Are you out of your mind?" I looked at him, stunned he even considered such a thing. "I'm not smoking drugs."

"To refuse would be disrespectful and could possibly invalidate our union," he replied calmly. "You'll be fine. Just don't breathe too deeply."

Reluctantly, I took the pipe and inhaled as shallow a puff as I could manage. I handed the pipe back to the shaman who look satisfied and moved on. As soon as he left I started coughing. "Yuck. Whatever that was, it was strong."

"We'll survive."

After the pipe, people largely left us alone except to bring us more food and a gourd filled with a warm spicy liquid.

"All of this food and drink is really delicious." I lifted the gourd and took another large swallow. "I wonder what this drink is? It's wonderful."

He tasted it, considered. "It's sweet. I suspect it contains sugar cane and water, along with some herbs and spices added for taste and relaxation purposes."

I stopped with the gourd inches from my lips. "Define relaxation purposes. You mean more drugs?"

"Possibly."

I immediately put the gourd down. Between the drink, the pipe, and the heat, I was already feeling way too relaxed. I didn't want to fall face-first into the fire.

Someone started playing on the drums and the beat began to thump in time with my heart. My eyes began to droop from all the excitement and emotion I'd been through during the day.

"You know, I'm feeling reeeally good," I said to Slash. My words slurred. I squeezed one eye shut to see if it would help me focus. It didn't. "And definitely uninhibited. No more pipes and gourds for me."

"Rest here." He put an arm around me and I laid my head on his shoulder. The flames had started to look like fiery figures, dancing around the blaze, waving their arms around wildly.

Finally one of the older women motioned to Slash and me to follow her. She led us to one of the huts where some furs had been laid out on the dirt floor. Compared to what I'd been sleeping on, which was nothing but dirt with my arm as a pillow, this was pure luxury.

"I presume this is the bridal suite," he said.

I took a step and stumbled. Slash caught me before I fell.

"Wow, everything is spinning in here," I said, pointing upward. "Is that a disco ball up there?"

Slash gently laid me down on the furs and joined me. He took my left hand and somehow put my engagement ring back on. It may have taken him a long time to get it over my knuckle…or maybe not. Time had somehow become quite fluid.

"The ring is no worse for the wear," he said. "It needs a thorough cleaning, but it came through just fine. Nonna will love this story."

"Did I tell you how much I love Nonna?" I closed my eyes to keep the ceiling from jumping around. "She doesn't take crap from anyone. Plus, the way she cooks is mystical. Seriously, she is a cooking shaman. Ha, ha. Did you see how I tied that in to our current situation?"

"Oh, aren't you the clever one? So, what would your mother have thought of that ceremony?"

I laughed, perhaps a bit too loudly because there was a weird ringing in my ears. "She would have passed out as soon as she saw me in the loincloth and fishnet bra. Trust me, that wasn't one of the options for a wedding gown she emailed me." I started giggling. "What about your mother, Juliette? What would she think of us?"

"I think she would have loved it. She'll definitely enjoy hearing the story." I felt his hand on my arm, inspecting the bandage that hid the mark of the ring. "How's your wrist feel?"

"Strangely, it doesn't hurt at all. Not one little teeny tiny bit. In fact, I can't even feel my arms. They're still attached to my body, right?"

"Right."

"Thank goodness. What about my feet?"

I heard him chuckle. "Yes, arms and legs are all attached. I just took off your boots, though." He slipped his arms around me, pulling me in tight against him. It felt good to be snuggled up against the hard length of his body. I put the hand with my bandaged wrist on his chest, feeling his heart beat.

"I missed you, Slash. A lot. I never expected this level of loneliness without you. Did you know you have an amazing body? All strong and manly. But you also smell good. Even when you're in the jungle and have oil of unknown origin smeared all over you."

"Do I now?"

"Yes, you do. But in case you were wondering, I married you for your mind. I really did. You're one smart cookie. Did I ever mention how amazingly attractive that is?"

"I'm glad you mentioned that, because for a minute there, I was starting to feel really cheap."

"Happy Wedding Day," I yawned. "I don't even know what day it is."

"Me neither. Does it matter?"

"Not really as long as you're with me. I love you, Slash. Especially because you love me. I'm not sure a lot of men would have come after me like you did."

"I'll *always* come for you. I'll *always* love you, too."

Safe in his arms, I felt as if I were drifting through the night sky with a hundred brilliant stars twinkling and shining, blinding me with their warmth and brightness. I let myself float upward, buoyed by a happiness I'd never experienced before.

That's when I heard him whisper.

"My beloved *cara*, I vow to always protect you from harm. To not only listen, but to hear what you say and respect it, whether I agree or not. To always be honest and to trust you. To trust *us*. But most of all, I'll allow myself to be loved by you. You're in my heart forever."

It was the most beautiful thing I'd ever heard. I wanted to say that, to tell him how much I loved him for trusting me with his heart—a man who had gone through so much pain and disappointment in his life. Did he realize how much he'd changed me and bettered my life by bringing me out of my shell? How much he'd become my real-life hero?

But no matter how hard I tried, I couldn't speak. A sparkling star drifted by, so I reached out to catch it. The star was hot, but I held on and flew into a dazzling bright light, hoping I'd brought him with me.

Chapter Forty-Three

Lexi

I wished the construction guys would stop all the hammering and banging that was going on outside. It was really annoying.

I felt Slash sit up beside me, so I opened my eyes. It took me a minute to process the light, the hut, and the fact that we weren't at home in Silver Spring, Maryland, but in the middle of the rainforest in Brazil. I sat up, but the pounding in my head turned into a jackhammer and I had to squeeze my eyes shut and press a hand to my forehead until it passed. When I finally managed to open my eyes, I saw Vicente standing in the doorway.

"Good morning," he said. "I'm afraid we have a problem."

"What kind of problem?" Slash asked, coming to his feet.

I glanced up, shading my eyes with my hand. Even in the covered hut, the sun was too bright. Slash looked like he'd just slept at a five-star resort, his eyes bright and hair tousled to perfection. Even his stubbled chin looked sexy. It was unfair that he could be instantly awake the moment he opened his eyes when I needed a gigantic cup of coffee and a freaking hour to feel human. Neither of which I was going to get this morning.

"I don't know. But they're asking for Lexi." Vicente squinted, looking at me closer. "You feeling okay, Lexi?"

Okay was a gross overstatement, but I'd live. I hoped. "I'm fine, Vicente. Can you give us a minute, please?"

"Sure." He disappeared out the doorway.

Slash, still in his boxers and loincloth and stretched out a hand to help me up. It was weird how easily we'd adapted to being in a constant state of near nakedness. I'd never worn a bikini in my entire life, and now I was living in a teeny tiny one.

When I got upright, I tested my balance which seemed fairly normal, thank goodness. My head still hurt, though.

He brushed a strand of hair from my throat. "You're feeling okay this morning?"

"Other than the hammer in my head, I'm fine. I'm embarrassed to say I passed out on our wedding night. But don't worry, I'll tell the villagers stories about your legendary prowess in bed."

"Thank you for protecting my reputation. Even hung over, you're beautiful," he murmured, kissing my neck.

Thirst parched my throat, so I picked up a gourd that had been left near the bed. I took a cautious sip. Water. Relieved, I took several large glugs. Feeling marginally better, I handed it over to Slash. My stomach was still a bit shaky and I couldn't even run my fingers through my tangled hair, but the pounding in my head lessened, which meant I'd been dehydrated.

He took a drink, then unwrapped the bandage on my wrist, inspected the small welt, and bound it back up.

"No redness or evidence of infection and it looks good. You ready to face whatever issue is happening outside?"

"Not really, but do we have a choice?"

"Not much, I'm afraid." He looked around. "Other than my boots, I don't know where my clothes are."

"Might as well kiss them goodbye. I'm sure they have a new purpose."

He shrugged and slid his feet into his boots. I did the same, pulling my hair into a bun at the back of my neck, using a stick from the ground to hold it in place. That was as good as it was going to get.

We didn't have to get dressed, obviously, so we exited the hut. There was a group of villagers huddled around, looking worried and speaking in a low voice. We hurried over. When we got closer, I saw Vicente speaking with the chief and Salvador on one knee next to a villager who was lying on the ground, writhing in pain. The shaman arrived at the same time as us and knelt on the other side of the man.

"What happened?" I asked Salvador.

"Apparently two scouts went out early this morning and came upon a strange new village on the edge of their territory," he responded. "He's been shot. They arrived just a few minutes ago."

Slash knelt down and gently pulled the man's bloody hand from the wound near his shoulder. Slash raised his eyes to mine. I returned the look, stricken. He'd lost a lot of blood.

"Salvador, get me the first aid kit, please," Slash said calmly.

Salvador dashed off to get it, just as the shaman also barked something at one of the villagers.

Vicente left the chief and knelt next to Slash who

was pressing his hand on the wound to stop the blood. "They'll want to treat it in their own way," he said to Slash.

"Understood. But that doesn't mean we can't offer our assistance. Luckily it looks like the bullet passed through cleanly."

"Technically we should exit now and leave them to handle this on their own," Vicente said. "The chief wants to retaliate."

I shot an alarmed glance at Slash, who furrowed his brow. "Who do you think shot him? Loggers? Poachers? Drug runners?"

Vicente rubbed his unshaven chin, thinking. "They said they saw a strange new village. It's got to be something that's been built there recently."

"A building?" Slash considered. "That sounds like drugs to me. Meth lab? Cocaine?"

"We'll find out soon enough. The chief is preparing the village for war. Someone has encamped on their tribal ground. They intend to go fight to protect it."

"If those people have guns, especially automatic weapons, the villagers could be massacred," I said, worried.

At that moment, Salvador returned with the first aid kit and handed it to Slash. He took it, but didn't open it. "Vicente, ask them if they'll accept our help in treating this man."

Vicente turned to the shaman, speaking to him softly. After a moment, he turned around. "The shaman said you may assist. But let him do what needs to be done first."

"Understood," Slash said.

The shaman already held a cup of liquid with what

looked like crushed herbs. He motioned to one of his men, who lifted the injured man into a sitting position. The cup was lifted to his lips and he drank deeply, coughing a bit before lying back down. The shaman then took a smoking stick and waved it several times over the man while chanting. The injured man writhed and moaned in pain, but a bit of color had returned to his cheeks.

After several minutes of this, the shaman motioned to Vicente.

"We're on," he said to Slash.

Slash opened the backpack, handing me some alcohol pads. "If you do the first aid, it might be better received."

Was he kidding? I knew next to nothing about nursing. "Me? I don't know how to treat a gunshot wound."

"I'll walk you through it. Hurry. He's lost a lot of blood."

"Let me wash my hands first." I dashed over to the pool and scrubbed them as clean as I could before returning.

Slash had arranged all the supplies on the ground and motioned for me to get started. He walked me through preparing a shot of morphine for the pain and then directed me how to administer it. When I cleaned the wound with alcohol, the man cried out in pain. After adding antibiotic ointment, I wrapped the wound tightly with a bandage per Slash's instructions, and had Vicente tell him to rest and not move his arm for several days to avoid opening up the wound. I then asked for the man's mate to come forward. I demonstrated how to remove and rewrap the bandages using Slash's hands as an example. I told her she should do it every other day and gave her a large roll of sterile wrap.

While we'd been tending to the injured man, the chief had assembled almost every man in the village. From what I could tell only the wounded man, the shaman, a few elderly men and some young boys under ten were not preparing for war.

"What are we going to do?" I asked Slash. "We have to help them."

Vicente surprised me by picking up one of the backpacks and pulling it on. "It's against my better judgment as we shouldn't be getting involved, but I'll ask permission to go with them and check it out. At the very least, I can warn them about the guns."

"You'd do that?" I asked.

"Yes. If those guys turn out to be armed drug runners or bandits, you're right, it's not a fair fight. Having said that, it's up to the chief whether he'll permit me to accompany them."

"I'd like to go, too," Salvador said. "At the very least, I want to know where this strange village is located, so I can report to the government if it's not legitimate."

Slash exchanged a glance with me and without speaking we both knew what we wanted. "Add us to the group," I said. "If they're willing to permit all of us to go."

Vicente walked over to the chief and began an animated discussion. After a few minutes, he returned. "We're in luck. He's permitted all of us to accompany them."

I breathed a sigh of relief. I'm not sure what good we would be, but at least we could prepare them to face weapons, or at least I hoped we could.

Slash insisted I keep one of the satellite phones, so I slipped it around my neck while he kept one and left a third at the village with one of the packs. He took the backpack with weapons, slinging it over his shoulder. I filled up our water bottles and we set off—Slash in his loincloth, boxers and hiking boots, and me in my loincloth, fishnet bra and boots.

My mother would be appalled. I wondered why I wasn't.

I took one last look at the village over my shoulder as we headed into the trees. Amana had been staring at her new husband, but now she lifted a hand at me in farewell. I raised my hand back, trying to appear confident and strong, just as an *Amazonas* warrior would be.

Good thing she didn't know I was scared to death.

Chapter Forty-Four

Lexi

We traveled silently and single file. The villagers had realized early on we, the outsiders, were a huge liability in terms of moving in stealth, so we were relegated to the back. The chief took the front, guided by the warrior who had accompanied the man who'd got shot. I was thankful we were following the higher ground because the vegetation was thinner and made for easier footing.

Eventually, we descended until the chief gave us a signal to stop, indicating the village was ahead. We crept forward to look out over the so-called new village.

Three buildings were visible, but constructed beneath the tree canopy and painted green and brown so they could not be easily spotted from above. I didn't see any people, but I could hear what sounded like a gasoline engine running somewhere. Possibly a generator. Just beyond the buildings, tall trees had been cleared and waist-high bushes planted on the rocky, cleared hillside where the ground sloped away.

The warrior who'd been with the man who got shot pointed to a spot near the right end of the buildings, apparently indicating that was the spot they'd been attacked. I smelled a fire and spotted a lazy trail of smoke coming from the smallest of the buildings on the left.

Salvador leaned over next to Slash and me. "Those look like young coca trees," he murmured. "I didn't think you could grow coca trees at this low an elevation."

"You can't," I said. "I bet they're trying to bioengineer them, just like you said, Vicente."

"Someone went to a lot of extra trouble to put these buildings under the trees to keep them hidden," Slash replied. He reached into his backpack and pulled out a pistol. "In my opinion, this all adds up to a drug plantation, right on Okampa territory and well within a protected national park."

While we were discussing this, the chief sent a reconnaissance group out to stealthily approach the buildings. I glanced down at my watch. It was morning, coming up on nine thirty. The sun was bright and hot, the humidity oppressive, as always. Sweat trickled down my temples and back, causing further anxiety. Much to my relief, the scouting group made it undetected to the first building. I held my breath as they entered. After a moment, they came out unscathed, indicating no one had been inside. They did that for all the buildings and determined there was no one presently at the area.

I sighed in relief. The villagers fanned out, while the chief permitted Slash and I to follow a small group into the compound.

"It looks like whoever was here is not here at the moment," Slash said in a low voice. "But they'll be back. They left the generator running. Come on, the large building with the generator is the one I want to get a better look at."

Slash slipped inside, indicating that I should wait,

then after a moment, cautiously gestured for me to enter. As soon as I was inside, I understood why Slash wanted me. Two laptops were sitting open and running. Slash sat down at the first one, his fingers flying across the keyboard. He didn't need to tell me what to do. I took the other one and started investigating.

It took me a total of five seconds to log on. "What a joke," I commented. "There's no log-in or security." Astonished, I zoomed around the computer without a single constraint. "Either these guys are complete idiots or they figured they were completely safe because no one would ever come out here."

"Exactly. Not only can I access the files, but they've left their network woefully unprotected."

"Yep. Seven seconds and I'm already in," I said. "The network file servers had some basic security, but it was so minimal, I could have hacked this in the first grade."

"Good for us." Slash reached for his pistol when Vicente slipped inside. Relaxing, he set it back down on the desk.

"What did you find?" Vicente asked.

Slash returned his attention to the monitor as he flipped through some documents. "Drugs, drugs, and more drugs. I presume this data will be exceptionally interesting to Brazilian law enforcement, as well as the international intelligence community."

"Any connection to *El Esqueleto*?" he asked, looking over Slash's shoulder.

"Not yet. But I've only scratched the surface so far."

"Who's *El Esqueleto?*" I asked.

"He's one of the most successful and least known international drugs kingpins, presiding over a multibillion-dollar worldwide enterprise," Vicente answered. "Governments and police all over the world are looking for him."

"Sounds like a stand-up guy...not."

"*Not* is right. I'd like you to let me know if you see something that names him explicitly," Vicente said. "As it is, we need to get this information to the authorities. Is there any way to do that?"

"There are." Slash looked over at me. "You got any ideas on the best way to do this, *cara*?"

I appreciated that he asked, so I considered, trying to decide what would be the fastest and most secure method. "I think we should proceed carefully. We need to minimize the possibility they might detect and shut us down while we're transferring this information out through their network portals. I'll send everything I've got to your laptop, Slash, which apparently has no monitoring, and we'll relay using the satellite link."

"Good idea. I've got a secure drop I've established for just such circumstances. We can move it to the authorities from there."

"Sounds good to me," Vicente said. "But whatever you do, we've got to hurry. How long do you think it will take?"

"Hard to say," I answered. "But not too long, I hope. I don't want to stick around here another moment than necessary."

"I'm with you on that." He headed for the door. "I'll let Salvador and the chief know what you're doing."

After he left, we quickly put our plan into motion, working silently and efficiently. We must have been working intently for about ten or fifteen minutes when Slash spoke. "I've just informed the NSA of this location and how to access the files when they're finally uploaded. I'll let them figure out who to send them to in the Brazilian government."

"Smart thinking," I said. "But we've got a heck of a lot of files and the satellite connection is slow. My optimistic estimation is that it'll take several hours to download and retransmit the files."

"Agreed. Our job is to get this information transferred and let the Brazilian government take care of the compound. While you've been funneling me the information, I've set up a download and transfer program to run automatically and unattended. When it's done, it will delete all trace of the program's existence and shut down. That way, we can get out of here before anyone returns to the compound and the information will continue to transfer."

"Excellent," I said. "But we'll have to hide the fact that the computers are on."

"Good point."

We turned off the monitors and found some black electrician's tape and started covering up the power switch. "I'll finish here, *cara*. See if you can get Vicente to convince the chief to round up his men. It's time to get out of here. Somehow he needs to convince the chief to pull back the warriors until we can get the authorities here."

"Will do." I exited the building, quickly bringing Salvador and Vicente up to speed on the situation.

The three of us agreed it would be faster if we split up. Salvador went to try and gather the warriors, while Vicente and I headed over to talk to the chief. It wasn't easy convincing him to leave without waiting for the enemy, but eventually he agreed, whistling softly. Almost immediately, the warriors begin gathering back at the edge of the compound. Looking around, I noticed a movement off to the side of one of the buildings in the trees. Thinking it was a native straggler, I headed in that direction. I had to hustle a bit, as the shadowy figure was moving away from me. When I got closer, I realized it wasn't a villager, but a man wearing clothes and carrying an AK-47. He moved into the shadows of several large trees where several other similarly armed men melted out of the darkness to talk in hushed voices.

My heart pounding, I slid back into the shadow of a tree and pressed my back to the bark.

Holy drug runners! They were here and heavily armed.

I was about to dart back to the chief to raise the alarm when a hand suddenly clamped over my mouth, cutting off a scream. I was so frightened, it took me several seconds to realize who'd attacked me.

Vicente.

Chapter Forty-Five

Lexi

I shook in terror, blinking rapidly at Vicente. My brain and body were in shock. What was he doing? Did he know the drug runners were just few feet away?

I struggled to move, but he pressed his hand harder against my mouth, his head shaking in warning. Seconds later, the drug men passed just steps away without seeing us. He waited another minute or so before he lifted his hand from my mouth.

"Sorry I scared you," he murmured.

"I almost had a freaking heart attack," I whispered. "I didn't know if you were with them or against them. We have to warn them."

"We're too late." He pointed down at the compound where the gunmen had already engaged the natives. A cry arose as the warriors began to load their bows and move forward. They appeared concerned, but not frightened, since they easily outnumbered the men. One of the more confident villagers stepped forward to warn off the gunmen and was subsequently shot in the leg. He went down screaming while the chief and the rest of the villagers froze in shock.

I quickly grabbed the satellite phone from around my neck, dialing Slash's phone. It took what felt like forever to connect, but Slash answered right away.

"They're here," I whispered, telling him what he certainly already knew by this point.

"I know, *cara*. I'm going to hide the phone and leave it on so you can hear what's going on. Mute the phone now so you can listen, but not give away its location. Go get help as soon as you can. We'll surrender and wait for you to bring back the authorities. Be careful and...*ti amo*."

There were so many things I wanted to say and no time to say them. I heard the door to the building in which Slash was located crash open and then people yelling. Alarmed, I muted the phone and looked at Vicente, who was listening intently. I could hear Salvador in the background shouting something, but I had no idea what until Vicente translated for me.

"They're speaking in Spanish," he said. "Definitely Venezuelan. Salvador is telling everyone to put down their weapons and surrender peacefully. He told the drug runners he's a scientist living and studying the native population and they came upon the compound by accident."

"What about Slash?" I whispered, my heart constricting in my chest. I couldn't hear his voice among the cacophony of shouting voices. "Is he okay?"

"I think so. It's possible they think he's just another native. After all, he's dressed like one of them and sort of looks like them, too."

I considered the possibility. Vicente could be right. Slash was wearing a loincloth and his Mediterranean complexion and dark hair helped him to blend in, even though he wore hiking boots. He was a master of disguise, so it was possible he could pull it off. It was too hard to say which way that would go at this point.

"They've rounded up everyone and are putting them into the same building where you were with the computers," Vicente said.

That was good news because that meant we could monitor what was happening via satellite phone. It was also bad news, because with all the people in there, the fact the computer was on and uploading the drug runners' records could be discovered at any moment.

Panicked, I watched as armed men moved through the area collecting the weapons the villagers had surrendered. Once they finished, they gathered by the open door of the computer building to talk. Wherever Slash had hid the phone, it was close enough to pick up on the conversation.

"What are they saying?" I asked Vicente in a hushed voice.

"They're discussing what to do with the natives. One of the men says they should kill them as a warning to any of the other tribes to stay away from them. Obviously the warning shot they gave yesterday didn't get that meaning across."

I didn't want to ask, but I needed to know. My imagination raced through a dizzying array of scary scenarios. "What else?"

"One of the drug runners is worried about Salvador. He isn't buying the scientist angle, especially since they found the backpack with the guns. They wonder if Salvador is working for another drug cartel. They think he might be trying to steal their research for growing coca plants in lower elevations."

I closed my eyes. "Oh, no. Are they going to kill him?"

"Not yet. They're afraid if they kill them before the boss has a chance to question him, the boss might not be very happy."

"Where's the boss? And what about the villagers? Are they going to hurt them?" It was hard to think through the panic. My brain screamed at me to run and get help before the drug runners hurt anyone else. But I couldn't get through the rainforest without Vicente, and we needed information, so I had to force myself to stay cool.

"The guy said if they kill the natives, it might make the others more reluctant to talk since they think they'll have nothing to lose." Vicente paused, his eyes suddenly narrowing. "Wait. He says the boss might be bringing *El Esqueleto* here tonight." He pumped a fist in the air. "I knew it."

"Knew what?"

"That *El Esqueleto* is involved in this. This is our chance to get him."

"How?"

"I've got to contact the authorities. But first, it's time you knew something about me, Lexi. I need you to keep it confidential, but I'm with the Brazilian *policía federal*, or the federal police. I've been working undercover narcotics for eleven months trying to find *El Esqueleto*."

I stared at him in disbelief and shock. "You're a federal agent and you never said anything? I thought you were a translator."

"I *am* a translator, or I was until I was recruited three years ago by the police for their undercover narcotics unit."

This was a lot for me to process at a time when my

brain was holding everything together by a thread. "Explain to me why, if you're a federal agent, you're working for Vaccitex as a translator?"

"It's a complicated situation, but basically, I'm part of a larger operation. The government genuinely wants to help the native populations with the malaria vaccine, but when we received intelligence indicating that *El Esqueleto* had set up a lab in this area, we decided to combine efforts and put an agent on the project in order to keep track of a suspect who'd also been assigned to the vaccine project and was under suspicion for being on *El Esqueleto's* payroll. Due to my language skills, it was a simple decision for them to assign me to the operation."

It took me a few seconds to get there. "Wait. That suspect is Martim Alves, isn't it?"

When Vicente nodded, I clenched my fists. "Are you kidding me? That jerk is working for a drug lord?"

"Possibly. We don't have proof of that…yet. It's why Gabriel and I had to follow him instead of you in the rainforest the other day. We had intelligence that indicated a drug operation might be taking place in this remote area. Our suspicions were raised when Martim angled hard to get the oversight position on the Vaccitex project to supposedly help the government protect the native populations in this region. We believed he wanted the position to be able to give *El Esqueleto's* men advance warning if, for some reason, the vaccine participants strayed too close to the new operation. We saw it as an opportunity to get a line on *El Esqueleto*, so as I said earlier, the government immediately dispatched me as the translator for the project. It took them a bit longer to recall the man who'd already been assigned to protect the natives and replace him with Martim. I felt bad for the natives because Martim is such an idiot."

"So, that's why he was a last-minute addition to the project," I said.

"Yes. But everything went to hell the minute you were kidnapped. We'd no idea what was going on, whether it was *El Esqueleto* or someone else. But when no ransom note appeared, we had to think it was something else. But in no way did I want the villagers, Slash and Salvador to be captured and in their hands. These men will not be merciful, so we must hurry."

I handed him the satellite phone. "Okay. Call for backup. Now."

"We can't." He carefully took the phone, but didn't disconnect. "Slash told you to keep the line open because he's providing us an operational advantage. And don't try to convince me he's just a computer guy, because I know specialized training when I see it. Why he's here with you, I don't know, but we can sort that out later. Right now, we can't break that connection, not even to call for help. It's our only advantage to getting everyone out alive. We need to know what they're doing and planning. We also need to know if and when *El Esqueleto* arrives. We must get back to the village quickly and retrieve the other satellite phone to call for backup. If we jog, it should take us under two hours."

A lot could happen in two hours. But Vicente and I couldn't save them with one pistol between us. No one seemed in imminent danger of execution, although that could change instantly. It looked like we had no other choice. The thought of me jogging through the jungle was hilarious, except this situation wasn't even remotely funny.

"What's in your backpack?" I asked.

"Ammunition and water."

"No guns?"

He shook his head. "Only this one."

There had to be a quicker, better solution, but I didn't see it. "Do you know how to get back to the village?"

"I think so, but we're going to have to move fast. I need you to keep up with me. Can you do it, Lexi?"

If it meant saving Slash and the villagers, then I could. I absolutely could. Narrowing my eyes with determination, I nodded. "Let's get out of here."

Chapter Forty-Six

Lexi

It was the hardest thing I'd ever done, to turn my back on Slash and the others and begin jogging back to the village. I was stressed to the max, straining to hear the sounds coming from the phone that Vicente now wore around his neck. So far it was just random talking, no gunshots...yet.

Despite the extreme humidity and the sweat pouring off me, adrenaline and determination gave me strength to keep a steady pace with Vicente. I only tripped a few times, but nothing that actually brought me down. During the jog I made a sincere promise to myself that I was going to take exercise more seriously. We stopped every now and again to hydrate and catch our breath, but I was eager to push on and so was Vicente. We could still hear random talking through the phone, so we presumed all was well for the time being.

My hopes rose when I spotted a faint trail that looked vaguely familiar. "I think we're going the right way," I said, panting.

We crossed a rocky patch and started walking along the vegetation line on the other side looking for where the trail continued, but the path seemed to have disappeared. For a moment, we stood there looking around, completely unsure which way to go next.

Vicente was softly cursing in Portuguese, I think, which wasn't a good sign.

"Which way?" I asked.

"I don't know," he said, bending over to catch his breath. "Damn, I'm not sure which way from here."

I closed my eyes, fighting back the frustration and anxiety in my emotional half, because my intellectual half was telling me to stay calm and think. Focus and compartmentalize, as Slash told me a million times.

How did ancient navigators find their way? I peered up into the midday sun. Nope, that only worked when you had some idea where you were in the first place. I'd been turned around so often, I didn't know which direction I was facing. I searched for evidence of people, a path, trampled leaves or brush, but came up with exactly nothing.

"We've got to pick a way," I said. "We're wasting time."

Vicente's face was beet red and he was sweating as much as I was. We agreed on a direction and headed uphill when a young native girl stepped out of the trees.

I was so startled, I nearly fell backwards on my butt. It was the one who wore my bra as an empty quiver. Quiver Girl, as I'd started to call her in my head.

"A-muh-suh-ne," she said and looked behind me if looking for the others.

Vicente immediately spoke to her and I assumed he was asking her if she could lead us back to the village. She darted off into the vegetation, leaving us behind.

"Hey, wait," I called out as we ran to catch up with her. "Vicente, did you tell her it was urgent to get us back fast?"

"I did. Let's try to keep up."

We'd been closer to the village than we thought. I began to recognize more and more landmarks. As we neared the village, the young girl raced ahead of us, alerting all of the remaining villagers. By the time Vicente and I dashed into the village, they were waiting for us, all of them looking alarmed. He gave them a quick explanation what had happened while I found the third satellite phone. Vicente took the phone, handed me the phone around his neck, and walked away to make his call. I pressed the phone to my ear, listening for Slash's voice. I heard nothing except for shuffling and the murmur of voices. When I looked up, I saw the entire village watching me. I glanced over at Vicente, who was speaking rapidly on the phone, pacing back and forth. Finally, he hung up and came over to me.

"Help is coming, but there's no way the agents can assemble the team, their gear, the helicopters, and the agents until morning. Even with special training, it would be too dangerous to land the helicopters in the dark. There's also going to have to be multiple helicopter landings in order to bring as many agents as we'd need to take on the drug runners. They're going to try and send one group before sunset, so I'm going to leave shortly to wait for them at the same place where we landed the helicopter before. All of us will camp there for the night and wait for the others to arrive. When we have the entire team in place, I'll lead them to the compound. If *El Esqueleto* comes tonight, the odds are high he'll stay the night."

"But what if those men change their minds and start shooting?" I asked, panicked. "What then?"

"We have to pray that doesn't happen. I've got to head out now. I don't want to be trekking in the jungle in the dark. Let's switch phones."

I considered and shook my head. "No. I want to keep this phone. If I hear that *El Esqueleto* has arrived or if they're planning to start killing the prisoners, I'll hang up and let you know right away. Either way, I'll hang up the phone by six in the morning, so you can call me and we can discuss where you're at with the rescue."

He thought about it. "Okay. Fair enough."

He gave the villagers a quick rundown of what had happened, and what he intended to do. Then with a sympathetic glance at them and me, he set off for the helicopter landing spot.

After he left, the village fell completely silent. I counted thirty-seven men, women and children all staring at me. There were three men—two other elderly men and the one guy who'd been shot in the arm—and nine children all under ten, including an infant. That left twenty-five—no, twenty-six—women including me. I'd never felt so helpless and useless.

Suddenly, Amana stepped forward and took my hand. She smiled with calmness and confidence.

"A-muh-suh-ne," she said, pointing at me.

To my astonishment, the women came forward one by one to stand in front of me…warriors ready for battle.

It was a moment of epiphany.

The women were upset, but they weren't paralyzed

like me. They were ready to fight for their men and the future of their village. They were the true *Amazonas*.

I was just the scared woman who was going to help them.

Chapter Forty-Seven

Lexi

Once it became clear the women weren't going to wait for the worst to happen, the planning began. I sincerely hoped the federal agents would arrive in the morning and handle everything before anyone got hurt, but in case they couldn't, we'd be there to step in to save the men as needed.

There was nothing new happening on the phone, including gunshots or screams, which was just fine with me. That meant, for the time being, everyone was relatively safe. It gave us time to work together and focus on the plan.

Given our small numbers and lack of guns, it was clear our advantage would be the element of surprise. No one would expect us to come and everyone, other than me, could move with incredible stealth. Another advantage would be knowing and understanding the rainforest. The women could use its resources in ways I couldn't even fathom.

Amana made it clear we should leave as soon as possible, and the man who'd been wounded in the arm seemed confident he'd be able to lead us back to the compound.

Moving through the rainforest at night concerned me, but the women weren't afraid and it would provide us the cover of darkness. Plus, it was likely some of the drug runners at the compound would be asleep, leaving fewer of them to deal with, at least initially. We certainly had to expect roving guards and men watching the prisoners both inside and outside, however.

But how would we take on men with guns and automatic weapons?

While I was musing this over, Amana walked over to me. She placed five blowguns—four short-range and one long-range—one bow, two quivers filled with arrows, two spears, four stone knives and a basket with just a few blow darts on the ground.

It wasn't the arsenal I'd hoped for, but we'd make it work.

It took some time, but after gesturing for a while, I managed to ask whether they could make more blowguns. Amana looked over at one of the elderly men and asked him something. He shook his head sadly. Apparently, those took more time than we had. But when I pointed to the darts, he immediately gathered some of the other women, hopefully to make more.

I gingerly picked up one of the blowguns and handed it to the woman next to me, wondering if she could use it. She shook her head, looking over at Amana. The tall girl confidently took the long-range blowgun from me while four other women retrieved the short-ranged ones. Okay, that was settled.

I held up the only bow and, to my surprise, Quiver Girl stepped forward and claimed it. Surprised, I looked around, but no one interfered. I sincerely hoped she could shoot more than pretend arrows. Somewhat reluctantly, I handed the bow over. A child archer. I tried not to be discouraged, because she looked so sure of herself. Hopefully her aim was as true as her confidence.

I found an open area in the dirt and began sketching out the arrangement of the buildings in the compound. Everyone peered over my shoulder to see. Other than the building with the laptops where everyone was now gathered, I hadn't gone near the other buildings. I presumed the one with the smoke was the kitchen/eating area. I had no idea if anyone would be there at night, but figured probably not. There was a large building in the middle, which I thought was the lab, and a smaller building next to it, which was likely the sleeping quarters.

Our focus needed to be the computer building because that was where the prisoners were being held. I put an X in front of the building to indicate that there would be a guard there, and put a couple inside. Because I couldn't be sure, I put a bunch of X's around the area where I suspected the guards might be located. It was hardly scientific, but it was an educated guess and the best I had to go with for the time being.

I sat back on my heels thinking, when three small children approached me holding out gifts. A gourd filled with water, a large green leaf holding the white pulp of a sweet, juicy fruit, and a handful of berries. I realized I was ravenous. I sniffed the air, smelling the scent of meat. Thank goodness, because we'd need a good meal to fortify us for the trek.

At some point, I checked on the elderly man making the darts. He and his helpers already had an array of three dozen darts in two groupings, with another thirty or so in various stages of production. The women work-

ing with him were quick and adept at following his instructions.

As I stood there, a small group of women returned
and showed me a small basket of brightly colored frogs
and a small basket of leaves. The elderly man pointed to
a pot of boiling water where the leaves were dumped and
stirred. Then I watched as he took one of the frogs and
killed it. He dipped the tips of several of the darts into
the carcass and set them aside to dry, point up.

Holy crap, poison darts. They weren't kidding around.
I almost felt sorry for the drug runners.

I listened on and off to the phone for noises or shots,
but it had been mostly quiet. At one point, I'd heard
Slash's voice, which confirmed they were still housed in
the room with the laptops and also served to strengthen
my determination to rescue him…*all* of them. I checked
the phone and saw it had about thirty percent battery life
left. I knew I couldn't keep it on much longer. I needed
to speak with Vicente in the morning, and I had to have
juice to do that.

I stared at the phone in my hand. I'd only been married—well, sort of married—for less than twenty-four
hours, and I already found it hard to do the logical thing.
However, if I didn't want to be a widow after a day and a
half, I was going to have to make some tough decisions.
With great reluctance, I pushed the button and ended the
call, before shutting the phone off completely.

Everyone began packing up our gear while we ate
a quick meal of meat, vegetables and water. Soon the
women from dart production arrived carrying several
baskets, followed by the elderly dart maker. Quiver Girl
stepped forward ready with the bow and quivers of arrows, one of them being my bra. There would be no more

pretending. She was going to have to shoot the real things tonight, if we went in.

Amana stepped forward, indicating it was time to go. The older man apparently gave last-minute instructions regarding the darts, presumably reminding everyone to be careful about handling them, especially the ones in the dark-skinned bag.

The villagers watched Amana, waiting for her signal. She exchanged a glance with me, then lifted a hand. After a moment, she turned and disappeared into the rainforest.

We followed her.

Chapter Forty-Eight

Lexi

We set out single file as dusk arrived with Amana and the man who'd been wounded in the arm leading the way. We moved quietly, quickly and with purpose. I stayed in the back, close to one of the women who looked out for me, pointing out places where the footing was treacherous or lending me a steadying hand when I needed it. I was the weak link in this operation, and I didn't want my clumsiness to jeopardize anyone.

While we walked I ran the mission sequence in my mind over and over, looking for gaps or things we might have overlooked. I was so lost in the planning that it surprised me when I discovered we were already close to the compound.

Twenty minutes later, we'd carefully and quietly crept into a position where we could see all the buildings through the trees. The shadows were getting long and the only light we had was the rising moon. Occasionally, we could see a man walking between the buildings, but there was little other movement. I could hear the thrum of the generator that was powering the lights inside the workshop.

Now we waited. A few of the women disappeared behind a row of bushes and when they returned, I noticed they'd darkened their skin with a coating of mud. Smart. One by one, everyone disappeared to camouflage themselves. At some point it was my turn, and Quiver Girl seemed to enjoy putting a double-thick paste on me.

Night had finally claimed the rainforest and we settled in. I started feeling optimistic that nothing would happen and the agents would be able to successfully rescue the men in the morning. But we had to stay vigilant.

One of the woman scouts who had been sent out to count the number of people in the compound found Amana and held up nine fingers. She pointed to the building with the prisoners and held up two fingers. She then pretended to be sleeping and held up six fingers. One guard was apparently walking around. Nine guards total. Those weren't bad odds, so long as she hadn't missed anyone and we were able to disable them one at a time. But for now, we had nothing to do except wait and watch the movement at the compound.

The combination of nervous energy and the need to be still made the hours go by glacially. It was painful knowing Slash was so close and yet dangerously out of reach. The good news was that it appeared there was only one outside guard sitting outside the compound, and from the intelligence we'd gathered, only one more guard awake inside.

The outside guard spent most of his time in a chair, leaning back against the side of the building. He was clearly visible from the light inside the room which spilled out of the window. I thought he might be dozing, but periodically he'd get up from his chair, stretch and take a slow saunter around the building before returning to the chair. Just as my scout had indicated, there was only one guard roving around the grounds. He apparently wasn't confident enough to penetrate the rainforest in the dark, so I felt we were relatively safe.

While lying on my stomach and watching the movement in the compound, I felt something crawling up my leg. Holding my breath so I didn't scream, I motioned frantically to Quiver Girl who was lying next to me. Puzzled, the girl followed my finger to where it was pointing. When she saw the spider, she calmly whacked it with the back of her hand before picking it up off my leg and popping it into her mouth. She grinned broadly at me, as if thanking me for the tasty morsel.

Holy crawly snack!

Shortly after midnight, according to my watch, I detected movement by the bunkhouse. I tapped the wounded guy on the shoulder, making sure he was watching. A man approached the workshop, said something to the guard outside, and disappeared inside. A few minutes later, he came out holding another man by the arm. A prisoner. That man turned his head toward the moonlight, and I got a clear view.

Salvador.

His hands were tied behind his back, his face looked swollen. The guard had ominously removed his gun and held it in his other hand. Salvador was staggering, barely able to walk. Alarmed, I tapped Amana on the shoulder, and she quietly alerted everyone in case we had to put our plan into action. For now, we would get in position and wait.

Within a minute, we were all in our positions. The landscape was black except for the pool of light surrounding the workshop building and the moonlight.

Thankfully, the sounds of the night creatures and the generator were enough to mask our movement. Quietly we crept forward, stopping near the edge of a pool of light by the building. The guard was dragging Salvador toward the bigger building, and Salvador didn't want to go. The panic and fear in his voice worried me. I exchanged glances with Amana, who'd already removed the long-range blowgun. Quiver Girl quietly nocked an arrow.

At that moment, Salvador broke free from the man's hold and started to run toward the rainforest. The guy who'd been dragging him angrily raised his gun to shoot before he abruptly gave a single yelp, then crumpled to the ground without discharging his weapon. Amazed, I looked over at Amana, who held up a finger. In the space of mere seconds, Amana had hit him with a dart, and he'd gone down just like that. Impressed, I gave her a look of admiration and a thumbs-up sign.

Salvador was still running toward the trees, so I ran parallel to intercept him. "Salvador," I hissed when I caught up with him. "Stop. It's me, Lexi."

He froze, then dropped to his knees. "Lexi?"

"Shhh," I warned. "Keep your voice down. What's happening?"

"They were about to kill me. Oh my God."

"Who are they?"

"I don't know exactly. Drug runners from Venezuela. Their boss arrived tonight. They questioned me once, beat me up some, but they weren't sure what was going on. I sincerely didn't know enough about anything to convince them I was more than what I told them I was, and that the guns they found in the backpack were for protection only. Luckily, we weren't carrying much and none of them were automatic. I think they were partially convinced I was just a scientist, because one of the guys told me I was nothing more than an inconvenience. He said the boss had no further use for us and they were going to kill us and dump our bodies in the river."

My anxiety skyrocketed. "Where's Slash?"

"Still in the workshop. He's okay as far as I know. I'm surprised they didn't beat him up because he kept trying to draw attention to himself and away from the natives. But not by speaking, mind you. If they discovered he spoke Spanish, they would have definitely suspected a setup. But just between you and me, I think the drug runners mostly left him alone because they were afraid of him."

As they well should have been. However, if the so-called big boss was still awake and ordering executions, we couldn't afford to wait any longer. We had to save the men.

"Go that way along the tree line," I whispered to him. "Quietly. The other villagers are lying in wait there."

He looked at me in astonishment. "What other villagers?"

"The women," I said. "They've come to save you."

Chapter Forty-Nine

Lexi

Now that one guard was down and Salvador had escaped, it was clear the full plan had to go into action. It was only a matter of time before they were discovered missing.

I quickly returned to where Amana and Quiver Girl were waiting. Their position gave me an excellent view of the door, windows and guard. The guard sat oblivious to what had just happened fifty yards away, but our risk of detection increased as every minute passed. Patting her bag of heavily sedative, nonlethal darts, Amana moved into position. Right on cue, the guard got up from his chair and began walking around the building. I heard the soft *pffft* of the dart gun—*once, twice*—and the guard went down. Two more women stepped out of the trees, pulling the man noiselessly into the rainforest. They made it look effortless.

Two down and seven to go, including the big boss man.

Silently, we headed toward the bunkhouse. One of the women had already opened the door, so we began a cautious and silent entry. I could hear snoring and loud breathing. Within two minutes, there were one or two women alongside each of the five men sleeping in their hammocks. One of the women motioned to a separate room, apparently occupied by the boss man. Two of us decided to take him together. I opened the door quietly and we slipped inside, readying ourselves. As soon as we heard the quiet whistle that served as our signal, we plunged the darts into their neck, where the toxins could most quickly reach the brain and heart and render them unconscious. After inserting the darts, we threw our bodies across the men to hold them down while the neurotoxins took effect. Their cries of alarm were few and brief because the neurotoxins were so fast acting. I surprised myself by how coolheaded and steady-handed I felt.

We were down to one guard.

Now came the trickiest part of the plan. We exited the bunkhouse and everyone except me melted into the shadows. I crept toward the front door of the lit up building. Some of the coolheaded feeling evaporated. Slash was inside that building, and one wrong move by me could lead to his becoming injured or worse. I tried to calm my pounding heart by reciting Fermat's Theorem, but it wasn't helping. If I messed this up, the guard might start shooting everyone on sight, starting with me.

When I reached the front door, I knocked twice, then darted around the side of the building, pressing back against the wall. After a moment, the guard inside yelled something. When there was no response, he opened the door, but didn't come out. He called for his partner, who didn't answer.

Deciding to investigate, he cradled his automatic weapon and carefully surveyed the outside. He stepped out of the door cautiously and started to move towards the chair where the outside guard had sat. I heard the first dart thud into his chest, followed by another and another. He must have been a big man, because he fired several random shots into the darkness and still didn't go down. I prayed no one was in the line of fire.

Finally he toppled to the ground. I got to him first, kicking his gun away and checking to see if he was out.

He was and an arrow was lodged in his gun hand. Quiver Girl's aim had been impeccable.

Amana emerged first and, after a moment, gave me a thumbs-up. The other women silently joined us. Carefully we approached the building where the men were being held with Amana in the lead. She motioned to me, so I slowly opened the door while the other women waited with blowguns and bow ready. After a moment, Amana stepped into the building with the blowgun to her mouth. She disappeared inside while I held my breath. A few seconds later she emerged, motioning for us to enter. We piled into the building where the men greeted us with happy shouts. I wound my way among the men to Slash and knelt down beside him, sliding my arms around his neck and kissing him repeatedly.

"Slash, thank God you're okay."

"Took you long enough," he said.

"Jeez. You're welcome." I noticed that something was missing, so I tapped his bare chest. "Where's your father's cross?"

"I took it off before they captured us. Didn't figure there was a good way to explain that. It's in my pocket."

"Good thinking."

He angled forward so I could free his hands from the ropes. "How in the world did you pull this off?"

"I didn't pull off anything. It was Amana, the chief's

daughter, and the other village women. They're the real *Amazonas*. I was mostly a supportive bystander."

I worked on unraveling his knots while filling him in on what happened. He stopped me when I got to the part about Vicente being a federal narcotics agent.

"Federal narcotics?" Slash repeated.

"I know, right? I didn't expect to hear that. Anyway, he left me at the village and went to meet the agents at the same spot where we landed the helicopter. The intent was to come here on foot. But since we've already taken out everyone, there shouldn't be any reason why they can't land right here. Vicente is going to be surprised when he hears what we did."

"I'm sure he is. I need to catch you up on everything that's happened while you were gone. There hasn't been time."

"No kidding," I said. "You and Vicente need to talk, as well. Looks like you both ended up on the same page regarding this creepy *El Esqueleto* guy. And to think Martim Alves may be involved. I knew there was another reason I didn't like that guy, in addition to his arrogant, sexist and self-inflated impression of himself."

"You and me both. But we need to keep that information about Martim under wraps for now, especially if it's still an active investigation."

"Fine. I hope I never see him again." I finished off the last knot and pulled his hands free of the rope. "My biggest regret is not punching him when I had the chance."

Slash quickly flexed his wrists and fingers, getting the blood back into them. "Do you know if *El Esqueleto* is here?"

"I have no idea. Some big boss guy was here. He was sleeping in a separate room. But it was dark and I don't know what *El Esquleto* looks like or when he was supposed to arrive. I do know, however, that whoever was in that room will be unconscious for several hours. I helped take him down by sticking a dart into his neck."

He leaned forward and kissed me. "You've turned into quite the agent. I'm beyond impressed."

"Trust me, I was the weak link. The village women did all the hard work. They were amazing, Slash. Brilliant, actually."

"I'm sure they were." He pulled me into a one-armed hug and kissed the top of my head. "We need to quickly get those drug runners tied up and ready for the agents when they arrive. The villagers also have to get out of here before the agents arrives. Some of us will have to be here to keep an eye on things until they arrive."

"Some of us, meaning you and me?"

"And Salvador. But right now, I need you on those laptops. We had a bit of luck and no one noticed them running. Can you check to see if the files have been uploaded?"

"Of course. But what are we going to do about Vicente? If he's really an undercover narcotics agent, will he still work to help get the vaccines get distributed? Or was that just part of a larger operation for the government? If he abandons the project, will the entire project fold?"

"I can't answer those questions, so, we'll have to cross that bridge when the time comes. There are a lot of moving pieces. Right now, we have to take one operational aspect at a time. Since we don't know when the federal police will arrive, whether *El Esqueleto* will show up with a new entourage, and how long the neurotoxins will remain effective, I think we should move the drugged men into the forest, away from the compound, so if they do awaken, they can't alert anyone to our presence."

"Fair enough. I'll call Vicente as soon I finish up here."

"Get an estimated time of arrival from him, okay?" He found the satellite phone he'd hidden in the building and checked it, plugging it in to give it some more juice. "Three percent battery left. Do you still have power on your satellite phone?"

"Not a lot, but more than three percent. I turned it off before we headed here to rescue you. Quiver Girl is keeping it safe for the time being."

"Quiver Girl?"

"The girl using my bra as a quiver. Lucky for us, it turns out she doesn't just shoot pretend arrows."

"Impressive and good to know. The bow had to be as big as she is."

"Didn't hinder her accuracy one bit."

While I brought Slash up to speed, the women and Salvador freed the rest of the men. Slash and several of the men left to survey the situation and tie up the guys we'd incapacitated, while a few women stayed in the building with me. I glanced at my watch. It was still another hour or so until daylight, but I could tell the villagers were ready to move on, and I agreed we didn't want to stay in the compound especially if more of them were scheduled to arrive.

I quickly sat down in front of the laptops to confirm the data had been sent safely to Slash's secret repository.

It had.

It shocked me that no one had even checked on the laptops once the entire evening. I presumed drug runners weren't expected to have mad skills at the keyboard, but a cursory check *should* have been a given. Plus, they'd had no online security, no password protection, no nothing. Just a bunch of arrogant, stupid idiots. Somehow they thought their data would be safe because they were in the middle of nowhere. The problem was, it didn't matter where you were. If you were online and connected, you were vulnerable.

I was still at the keyboard, with several natives curiously looking over my shoulder, when Slash returned.

"It wasn't *El Esqueleto,*" he said. I could tell he was disappointed.

"Are you sure?"

"I am." He put both hands on my shoulders and started massaging. It felt wonderful as the tension slowly drained from my knotted muscles. "But I'm pretty sure this is his operation. Did the files all upload?"

"They did. No one even bothered to check the laptops."

He didn't seem surprised to hear it. "I suspect the computer is used primarily by the biologist and for communications. I saw some scientific references to coca trees when I was flipping through the documents." He slid into the chair in front of the other laptop and started typing. One glance confirmed he was looking through their email system. While he was doing that, the villagers lost interest and left Slash and me alone in the building.

"What are you doing?" I asked.

"Using a tried and true strategy of trying to find the top boss. I'm looking for someone asking for approval to do something. I'll go up the chain from there."

"That's a good idea. I'm done here, so I'm going to get the phone and give Vicente a call."

"Good idea. Whoa." He suddenly tapped something on the screen. "Well, hello there."

"What did you find?" I walked back, peering over his shoulder. The text was in Spanish, so it meant nothing to me.

"A gem—a big one. Stand by." His fingers flew across the keyboard. Then, with a dramatic flair, he hit the return button. "Well, that should generate a little unplanned excitement."

Before he could tell me what was going on, Salvador rushed into the building. "The villager who got shot in the leg is taking a turn for worse. The shaman is asking if we could assist him."

"Do we have the first aid kit?" I asked Slash.

"Probably, but they took our backpacks," Slash said. "We can try to look for them, but I suggest looking in the bathroom or kitchen first. I suspect the compound will also have medical supplies available."

We split up, Slash and I going to the bunkhouse and Salvador to the kitchen. I found a basic first aid kit and ran back to where the villagers had gathered. Salvador found our backpacks and Slash came back with some more gauze and towels.

The shaman was quietly chanting over the man, who was writhing on the ground in pain. One of the women had cradled his head in her lap. With permission from the shaman, I cleaned the wound, wrapped his leg and gave him antibiotics and a painkiller.

"You're becoming quite the nurse," Slash observed.

"Practice helps," I said. "Although I'd rather not have to do this again. I think they want to get him back to the village as soon as possible. But there's a catch. They want me to go with them."

Slash lifted his head sharply. "What? Why?"

"I don't know. But the chief indicated either I go with them or they all stay."

He thought it over and then shook his head. "You're not going back to that village without me."

"I agree, but someone has to stay here and keep an eye on the drug runners until Vicente and the other agents arrive. No one else has the experience that you do."

Slash pushed his fingers through his hair, thinking. All of us were going on twenty-four hours with no sleep, little if any food, and emotional exhaustion. It was amazing our brains were even functioning. "Before any decisions are made, call Vicente and get an estimated time of arrival."

"Okay."

I found Quiver Girl and she handed over the phone. I dialed Vicente's number right where I stood. He picked up almost immediately.

"Hello?" I could hear the rotors of a helicopter whirring in the background, presumably more agents arriving.

"Vicente, it's Lexi."

"Lexi?" He raised his voice, presumably to make sure I heard him over the rotors. "Where are you?"

"I'm at the drug compound. The area is clear and all prisoners are safe. You'll be able to speed your arrival by having the pilot land right at the compound."

"What did you say?"

I raised my voice hoping he could hear me better. "I said the prisoners are free and the drug runners are all tied up. You can fly right here to the compound."

"Tied up? Who did that?"

"The villagers. The women villagers, to be exact. They kicked ass."

For at least fifteen seconds all I could hear was the *whoop, whoop* of the helicopter blades. Then he spoke.

"Did you just say the village women took down an entire compound of drug runners...with no guns?"

"That's exactly what I said. How far out are you?"

I heard him talking to someone for a minute and then came back on the line. "About an hour. Is *El Esqueleto* there?"

"Slash says no. Or not yet, anyway. There's a chance he might be arriving today."

"We're counting on that. Where will you be and where are the prisoners?"

"We've moved the prisoners away from the compound so they won't immediately alert anyone that something has gone awry. Slash and Salvador will stay with the prisoners until you arrive, but we want to get the villagers out of here before you show up."

Our line was breaking up, probably due to helicopter interference with the satellite line.

"Good idea," he said. "Be careful."

"I will. I'm going to turn off this phone to save the battery."

"Understood. Over and out."

He hung up, and I did the same, turning off the phone and hanging it around my neck. I walked back to the building where Slash had just finished up.

"One hour," I said as soon as I crossed the threshold. "The agents are on their way."

Chapter Fifty

Lexi

No matter how hard Slash, Salvador or I tried, the chief wouldn't budge about me. Either the entire village stayed at the compound, including the wounded man, or I went with them back to the village.

"Why aren't they listening to reason?" Slash said, frustrated, scratching at his chin where a beard was growing in. "They should have left twenty minutes ago. It's not safe, and I don't want them here when the agents arrive."

"I don't have a clue why the chief is being so stubborn. I tried to explain, but it's really hard to communicate without Vicente. Obviously, I can't justify their reasoning if I don't understand it." I checked the battery on the satellite phone to see how fast it was charging and set it back down. "Look, Slash, we know the villagers aren't going to hurt me. Let me go back with them to the village. When Vicente arrives, take his phone and call me at two o'clock sharp on the satellite phone. If all is quiet at the compound, you can return to the village to retrieve me, tell me to wait, or I'll ask one of the villagers to escort me back here so we can catch a helicopter out. Would that work?"

He shook his head. "I don't like it. We'll be separated again, there are too many variables, and I don't know what the chief is thinking."

I touched his cheek. "He knows I belong to you. I don't like being separated any better than you, but it's the best plan we've got. It's the *only* plan if we want to get the villagers out of here now."

He pulled me into his arms, resting his chin on top of my head. "This goes against my better judgment, but if you're sure about this, I'll support you. But be careful, *cara*. Don't make me come after you again."

"Believe me, that's *not* part of the plan…not that I actually have a plan. But somehow it's important to the chief that I return with them, and I don't want them here when the agents and helicopter arrives. Plus, I think the sooner they get the injured man home, the better."

"Agreed." He wound a strand of my hair around his finger. "Just take care of my wife, okay?"

"I promise." I kissed him for a long time before I went to tell the chief I was ready to leave.

We made good time walking to the village. Either I was in better shape or I'd somehow become adept at walking among the roots and branches. I was also getting better at spotting snakes, making sure to give them a wide berth, my supposed mystical skill with them notwithstanding. The other villagers who'd stayed behind greeted us with great excitement when we burst into the village. There were lots of hugs, cheers and happy chattering as the group reunited.

I wasn't sure what I was supposed to do or where to

go, so I took a seat on a log near the fire, while the chief gave a dramatic speech, apparently updating everyone on the events of the past twenty-four hours. Several times he pointed at me, but I had no idea what he was saying.

While he was doing that, the eldest of the chief's wives directed several women and girls to gather firewood for a separate fire. She stacked the wood carefully, as if she were building something. A few minutes later, one of the young girls arrived with a burning stick and added it to the timber. The girls quickly got on their hands and knees and began blowing and adding more tinder.

I was unsure what purpose an additional fire served, but I didn't interfere. After a few minutes, the fire roared and the women pulled grape-size objects from the small pouches on their belts and began placing them at the edge of the fire. I moved a little closer so I could see what they were.

Little black stones.

I studied them, wondering what was going on. The men were talking among themselves until finally the chief's eldest wife stepped forward, getting everyone's attention and making the tribe fall silent. After a moment, the chief stepped forward to face his eldest wife. For a moment, they stared into each other's eyes before the chief held out his arm to her, wrist up. Using a leaf she had double or triple folded, she picked up the hot stone from the edge of the fire and pressed it firmly against the inside of his wrist.

Holy cow!

The women were marking their men as equals. And why shouldn't they? They were amazing women and fierce warriors. The chief murmured something to his wife and she pulled the stone off, throwing her arms around his neck and kissing him soundly. I wondered how the chief felt about all this female empowerment, but when he glanced my way, his eyes twinkled with pride.

Well, *that* was a big relief.

The ritual was repeated by woman after woman with her mate until all the taken men had been marked. The *Amazonas* legend had become a reality in this village. Maybe that's why they had invited me back—they wanted me to see it firsthand.

Soon afterward, a feast was prepared. We ate, drank and celebrated the victory over the drug runners. I received a few small gifts—necklaces, bracelets, belts, tiny purses, and even my underwear back. I was used to going without undies at this point, so I insisted the little girl who had taken them, keep them. It seemed clear the village was wishing me a farewell.

Eventually, I lay down to take a quick nap. I set an alarm on my watch for one fifty-five, hoping all was well with Slash and the others back at the compound.

I fell asleep holding the satellite phone and dreaming of helicopters.

Chapter Fifty-One

Lexi

"A-muh-suh-ne?"

I blinked a couple of times and quickly sat up. Quiver Girl knelt next to me pointing at my watch. It beeped incessantly. Gah! Somehow, I'd slept through the alarm for ten freaking minutes.

Crap!

I turned on the phone, furious at myself. I might have missed their call and had no plan for a callback. I wanted to call to check on things, but if they were in the middle of an operation, a ringing phone would not be something they'd want to hear. That meant I had to wait for them to call me.

I left the phone on and rubbed my eyes. I was pretty sure I could have slept for another sixteen hours. I found the gourd of water sitting next to me and took a big gulp. It helped invigorate me slightly. When the phone rang, it caused me to startle. I spilled a bit of the water before I quickly set the gourd aside and answered the phone.

"Vicente?"

"Cara, is that you?"

"Slash?" A rush of relief swept through me. "Are you okay?"

"I'm fine. We're all fine. It's over for now and no one else got hurt. Are you safe?"

"I'm safe and, wow, that's great news." I closed my eyes, thankful nothing bad had happened to anyone else. "So the agents arrived on time? Did *El Esqueleto* ever show?"

"Let me answer your questions in order. Yes, Vicente and the narcotics agents arrived not long after you left. Unfortunately, we didn't get *El Esqueleto*—he was a no-show. But the nine men you rounded up—including the biologist and close personal friend of *El Esqueleto*, Jasiel Galíndez—were a real coup for the narcotics team. They're one step closer to getting *El Esqueleto*, and are quite thankful for your work."

"Our work," I corrected him. "What about the files we uploaded?"

"Found and retrieved by the NSA. They'll be distributing them via appropriate channels to the Brazilian government shortly. We've had no one else show so far, but the agents will wait until nightfall. But even without nabbing *El Esqueleto*, this is a crushing blow to his cartel."

"I'm really glad to hear that." I paused, weighing the impact of this statement. "Does the involvement of the NSA mean General Maxwell will find out?"

He sighed. "He already knows. I'll worry about that later."

I wondered if we'd be summoned to the White House again, and whether we'd be lauded for helping the Brazilian government put a huge dent into a drug lord's empire, or whether they'd now force Slash to take a vacation until Christmas.

"So, what about the drug compound? Are they going to leave it empty and let the trees grow as is?"

"I don't know what they intend to do with the buildings, it's more likely they will turn them into a park station. That's up to the Brazilian government. But it's a big no on letting those bioengineered trees grow. At this very moment, there are several agents poisoning the trees. They didn't want to do a burn, as it would scar the land even worse than the clearing. Apparently the chemical they're using will eliminate the coca trees and allow local vegetation to return. This should keep the Okampa as isolated as possible, given the recent events."

"Please tell me all of this means we can return to Coari and the research station now."

He paused. "You sure you feel up for that?"

"I most certainly do." Now that I personally knew the villagers, their health and safety was even more important to me. "What about you?"

"Absolutely."

"Good. So, what's next?"

"That's up to you and the chief. Any idea why he wanted you back at the village?"

I watched Amana and her new husband walk by, holding hands, both of them looking at his new mark on his wrist. Then she looked at me over her shoulder and smiled.

"Yeah, I think they wanted to say goodbye. I can go now. I'll explain it all later. Let me see if I can get someone to lead me back to the compound—to you. Will you be waiting?"

"Always." I could hear the tenderness in his voice. "I'll always wait for you, *cara*."

Chapter Fifty-Two

Slash

The research station seemed like a five-star hotel after being in the rainforest for so many days. A real bed. Hot water for shaving. Even wearing clothes again took some adjustment. It amused him that his pants were chafing his legs.

He'd insisted that Lexi get a full checkup at the hospital in Coari, even though she didn't want one. They'd both been able to take showers and were given antibiotics and antiparasitic medicine as a precaution given their time spent in the rainforest. But even then, Lexi hadn't wanted to spend a night in a hotel. She wanted to get back to the research camp as soon as possible, to check in with her cyber team and get caught up on what she'd missed.

His wife. She was by far the most amazing woman he'd ever known.

During the helicopter ride to Coari, Vicente told them the information on the drug cartel had to stay secret for the time being, which would allow the federal police to handle the release of the story and spin it in a way that would work for them. Slash was fine with that. As far as he was concerned, his phase in that part of the operation was done.

When they'd arrived back at the research station, they were swarmed with everyone greeting them and asking questions about what had happened. Gwen hugged him so hard, he was impressed. In fact, he was hugged enthusiastically by everyone, even those he didn't know well. He wasn't sure if it was because they were safe or because they'd returned to the research camp.

Guess it didn't matter either way.

Martim was holed up in a Coari hotel, which was good because it would have been hard not to pound the guy to a pulp the second he set eyes on him. He was glad Salvador had beat them back to the camp by a couple of hours, so he'd already filled everyone in on some of the events of the past few days. Apparently, he'd also been sworn to secrecy regarding the narcotics operation, so for the time being, the story was his injuries had come about when he fell down a hill in the rainforest. He didn't think Melinda, the medical doctor, bought it, but at least she didn't press him on it.

"So, you and Lexi really got married?" Gwen asked him. "Salvador said you fought the chief for her and you had to brand each other with a tattoo on your wrists to mark your commitment to each other."

"It's not a tattoo," Lexi answered, holding up the mark on her wrist. "It's just a small mark from my engagement ring."

"That's really cool. Did it hurt?"

"A little." Lexi glanced at him and he held up his wrist to show his mark, too.

"So, you had a ceremony and everything?" Natelli asked.

"Yes," Lexi answered. "But it was really done just to ensure I wasn't married off to someone else."

"Wow," Gwen said. "That sounds so romantic, dangerous, and...kind of weird."

"No, it wasn't weird at all." She looked down at her hands and he knew she was struggling to put into words the same thing he was thinking. "It was actually quite nice. We walked around a fire seven times, threw stones in the water, there was this excellent feast, and Slash even danced."

When all eyes turned to him in surprise, he deadpanned, "And Lexi passed out from smoking the ceremonial pipe."

Everyone burst into laughter, and Lexi threw him a look that was equal parts adorable and annoyed.

"So, you aren't really married, then," Natelli said.

"We're married in the eyes of the tribe," he clarified. "And, I suppose, in the eyes of each other."

The smile that blossomed across Lexi's face warmed his heart.

"But not legally," Natelli persisted.

Before he could reply, Lilith broke in. "Let me get this straight, the natives really thought Lexi was one of the descendants of a legendary race of warrior women?"

"They really did," he answered. "That's why they abducted her."

"A tribal kidnapping by a previously uncontacted tribe," she said, studying Lexi. "That's the first I've ever heard of anything like this. It's beyond fascinating. Maybe we could talk about it at greater length someday."

"Sure," Lexi said. "Someday. But now, we have to talk about reviving the vaccine trials. That's our most important focus at the moment. We're all on board again, and we want to get things up to speed."

"Are you sure?" Lilith said. "You've all been through a traumatic experience. It doesn't feel right asking you to stay."

"I'm staying." Lexi looked over at him to confirm. "Slash and I are *both* staying. After experiencing tribal life, we really want to continue this important project for them."

He nodded. "We're both committed to seeing this through, Lilith."

"Me, too," Salvador said.

Lilith's expression indicated genuine appreciation. "I don't know how to thank you. But what about Vicente? We can't proceed without him."

"He told me he'll be here sometime tomorrow." Slash moved closer to Lexi and slipped his arm around her. She looked ready to fall asleep on her feet. "The show will go on. But for now, we need some sleep, so we can get caught up on everything we missed while we were gone."

"Of course," Lilith said. "I'm sorry we're bombarding you with a million questions."

"No problem. It's completely understandable," he answered.

"I'll need to check in with my team in New York first thing in the morning to see what's been going on while I've been gone," Lexi said. "Does anyone know if a break-in has happened?"

"Tim hasn't said anything," Lilith said. "But you should check with him yourself in the morning. Please, get some rest. It can wait. I cannot express how grateful we are that you're back safe and sound."

"We're grateful, too," Slash said.

He steered Lexi out the door and toward the women's barracks. "To bed with you, woman. You look like you're about to collapse."

"At least I took a little nap," Lexi said. "What about you? You've got to be dead on your feet."

"Pretty close to that. I'm headed to bed, as well. Unfortunately, it's a bed other than yours."

These past few days had reminded him how much he hated sleeping without her. He missed how she always kissed his forehead before setting her head on his chest and falling asleep, her hair spread across him and the pillowcase. Sometimes he'd stroke her hair while they talked themselves to sleep. She was the best sounding board he'd ever had. When she wasn't there, the quiet was a cold and silent reminder that she was missing from him. Even though she hogged the blankets, put her cold feet on his legs and slept like the dead, he wouldn't have it any other way. He loved her so fiercely that sometimes it defied even his own logical thinking.

She slid her hand into his and they bumped shoulders as they walked. "That really stinks, but hopefully it isn't for too much longer."

"It better not be, because I really don't like being away from my wife." He marveled at how easy the words fell from his lips.

She squeezed his hand and gave him a smile that lit up even the darkest parts of his heart. God, how he loved her. "Me, neither, Slash. Hopefully, it's only for a few more days."

"It'll still be a few days too many. Good night, *cara*. *Ti amo*."

"*Ti amo*, Slash." She pressed a soft kiss against his mouth and disappeared into the women's barracks.

Instead of heading for the men's quarters, he walked to an area behind the building that was relatively private and pulled out the satellite phone. He punched in a number and waited until someone picked up.

"*Alo.*"

"Vicente? It's Slash."

There was a pause, as if the man was moving somewhere he couldn't be overheard. "Are you back at the camp?"

"I am. Martim Alves isn't here. He's still in Coari at a hotel."

"How do you know that?" He could hear the surprise in Vicente's voice.

"Money talks. Can you put a tail on him? He's deeply connected to what is going on here at the camp and what just happened at the compound. No time to explain how I know. You're going to have to trust me on that."

There was silence as if Vicente wanted more details, but didn't want to discuss on an unsecure phone either.

"I do trust you," he finally said. "Give me the details on Alves's location and I'll see what I can arrange."

Slash gave him the name of the hotel. "I've got some threads of my own to pull. We'll talk soon."

Vicente paused. "Just for your operational awareness, Gabriel knows what is going on and is in the loop in regards to the operation, so you can trust him if you need anything. I'm in Manaus now with the prisoners, but I'll keep close to the phone. I intend to be back in Coari soon, and hopefully I'll have some news for you then."

"Looking forward to it."

Slash hung up the phone and headed to his bunk for some much needed sleep.

Chapter Fifty-Three

Lexi

I felt good when I awoke—my head was clear, my body rested. I attributed it to sleeping in a real bed with a mattress, sheets and a pillow. Holy cow, I would never, ever, *ever*, take a bed for granted again.

After visiting the bathroom and brushing my teeth, I swung by the dining area for breakfast and coffee. There was no one in the dining area except for a couple of security guards, so I scarfed down some food, took my medicine with an excellent glass of guava juice and took my beloved coffee to the lab with me.

Natelli and Lilith were deep in conversation when I arrived, and Melinda, Gwen and Sara were checking samples under a microscope. No sign of Slash.

"Good morning, Lexi," Lilith said, waving me over. "How'd you sleep?"

"Like the dead," I said. "A real bed felt wonderful, but I'm ready to get started this morning."

"I'm happy to hear that. I have a call with Hayden in about thirty minutes, so I'm anxious to hear what you find out from your team. I updated him briefly yesterday on your and Slash's desire to continue with the project, so based on that, we'll decide how to proceed. The Brazilian government has assured us they will increase their presence and patrols in our area, and Gabriel has already hired more guards for us. We aren't going to do this unless we do it right. Every person on this team will have a personal bodyguard. And I intend to go out in the field, as well."

I looked at her with new appreciation. A CEO who was willing to get her hands dirty was someone I could learn to like. "Sounds like a good plan to me."

After she left, I quickly checked my emails, getting caught up with what had happened in my absence. It took me several long explanations to all of my team members and an extra-long email to Finn, but finally everyone was convinced I was fine, unharmed and ready to continue the vaccine project. Thankfully, Finn had not contacted my parents about my kidnapping, so they were none the wiser. I had thirteen wedding-related emails from Mom, which I delegated to a later viewing.

I wanted to know what had happened on the cyber front while I'd been at the village. Thankfully, my team and Tim had done an excellent job of noting every penetration attempt and their countermeasures to stop it. I began carefully reviewing the activity logs of all the attempts to crack into the internal firewall at Vaccitex. The attempts had become bolder and more inventive, but I wasn't worried. When I was in New York the first time around, I'd moved all the critical files to an even more deeply buried and masked part of Vaccitex's system, leaving little behind the firewall. After strengthening the firewall a little to make it look like we were making counter-defensive movements, I embedded a code that allowed me to better track their hacking activi-

ties. I could see that while they were routinely harvest-
ing internal Vaccitex emails, most of their efforts were
targeted at breaking through the firewall and trying to
cover their tracks. It didn't take long for me to see a pattern emerge. Within the past few days while Vaccitex's
operation had been shut down, their level of attacks and
sophistication had increased significantly. Their attempts
were setting off internal alarms on a daily basis, but I'd
rerouted those alarms to a hidden folder so the hackers
would think they remained undetected.

The more I studied their behavior, the more I thought
the level of activity was unbelievably reckless. Did they
really think they were remaining undetected? Something
here smacked of desperation...or maybe something else.
I couldn't believe any decent hacker—and the hacking
I'd seen was fairly sophisticated—would behave in this
manner, which led to me believe the hackers weren't
calling the shots. A good hacker would always prioritize
stealth over speed, because once they were detected, the
opportunity was gone. That was good news for me because that lack of caution would play right into my hands.

It was time to turn the tables from defense to offense.

I located the honeypot folders, a bunch of fake documents filled with harmless information that had been
created for me. My team, in coordination with some of
Vaccitex's scientists, had carefully doctored the real and
sensitive vaccine files so the information in them was
seemingly real, but actually fake. I also discreetly added
a few tools of my own that would implant themselves
into the hacker's system once they were downloaded and
opened. The files would create a backdoor, notify me of
how to break in and then erase all signs of their presence.

My exploits, once downloaded and launched, would give me significant access to their network.

I made sure that the file names containing my exploit codes would be impossible to resist for someone desperate to get their hands on Vaccitex's technology, processes and recipe. If my opponent was careful, he'd be checking for such a common maneuver. But I was counting on the fact that my opponent was under a lot of pressure to produce the information, and would likely open them or be ordered to open them.

Now was the time to lure the hackers to the honeypot in a way that wouldn't make them suspicious. I created a fake email exchange between Tim and a researcher at the company who'd supposedly just returned from vacation. The researcher couldn't access the project data and was asking for the latest firewall password. The IT admin's response included a password reference that indicated the new one was a derivation of a previous password that I knew the attackers had already compromised. Once I'd completed my trap, I created a few alerts to notify me when the hackers had broken in and were downloading the data.

I looked up realizing several hours had passed while I'd been in the zone, and I hadn't seen Slash yet. Gwen was working with Natelli and they were checking something in a test tube. I headed over her way to chat.

"Hey, Gwen. Have you seen Slash this morning?" I asked.

She set the test tube down in a tray and took off her safety goggles, leaving them around her neck. "Yeah, I saw him getting some coffee this morning. I think he headed into town with Gabriel."

"Oh." I wondered why he'd gone back into town and

hadn't told me. I rolled my stiff neck a couple of times, suddenly ravenous. "You want to catch some lunch?"

"Sure." She took off her gloves, coat and goggles, leaving them on a chair. Natelli asked if she could join us, so the three of us headed for the dining area. We were served a delicious meal of beans, rice, fish and vegetables, accompanied by a strong shot of espresso. I ate two servings and might have had a third, but opted for the dessert instead, an incredibly tasty flan.

"I'm totally interested in this tribal mating ceremony you experienced," Natelli said. "You say the men fought a wrestling match for the women?"

"Yes, something like that."

"And Slash actually fought for you against a native?"

"Yes. Against the chief." I still wasn't sure how much of it had been real and how much had been an act. "Then we had a bonding ceremony." I looked down at my wrist where the redness of burn was almost gone. "We told you guys all this last night."

"But it made you married in the eyes of the villagers?" she persisted.

"Bonded, mated, married, whatever you want to call it." I'd started to feel a little uncomfortable with her continued probing questions. Part of me wanted to keep the details of our ceremony private, because it had been such an intimate and special moment between the two of us.

Natelli asked a couple more questions about the ceremony that I managed to evade when, to my surprise, Gwen came to my rescue.

"What I really want to know, Lexi, is how you liked being unplugged for those few days?" Gwen asked. "No laptop, no cell phone, no running water or bathroom. How did you manage to do it?"

"It wasn't that hard. There were so many interesting things to learn." Grateful for the change of subject, I told them how the Okampa had created a bathing and bathroom area away from the water source they drew for cooking. I threw in some information about the way they cooked and socialized. They were both fascinated.

"Anyway, I didn't miss the computer that much because I was too busy trying to survive. In a way, it was an eye-opening experience for me. That being said, I'm not sorry to be back in front of my computer, using a shower, and sleeping in a real bed again."

We chatted for a bit more and then headed back to the lab, ready to get to work. When we were walking out of the dining building, Gwen realized she'd left her coffee mug on the table, and went back for it. Natelli and I walked on to the lab.

"Your adventure sounded frightening, interesting and incredibly exhausting," she said. "I bet after the project is finished, you'll be glad to get back to life as usual at X-Corp, and Slash at the NSA."

I immediately stopped walking and turned toward her. "What did you say?"

She seemed confused by my question. "I just asked if you and Slash would be glad to be going back to work in a more civilized location."

I stared at her, my gaze broken only when Gwen caught up with us. "Hey, guys, thanks for waiting for me."

Without responding, I turned and headed for the lab. I had a lot of work to do, and suddenly, not all of it had to do with hacking.

Chapter Fifty-Four

Martim Alves

Even though he had the air-conditioning blowing full blast, it was insufferably hot sitting in a parked car outside the small building at the airport. He checked his watch. Fifteen minutes until the rendezvous.

He'd become increasingly nervous. For the fourteenth time, he unfolded and read the email that led him to this location. Things had not been going as planned for the past week. Last night, that damn American had returned from the jungle with his woman and was reporting that the government would be beefing up security in the area.

What a disaster.

The American's woman and the intolerable lead scientist—he couldn't remember either of their names—were already saying the vaccine project could be ramped back up to full operation in twenty-four hours. His government sources also reported that the federal police had become very active in the area, although no one seemed able to confirm why.

What the hell were they doing?

The situation had become even worse because *El Esqueleto*, or one of his representatives, had somehow received word of the problems at their new compound, and they were trying to pin the blame on him. It was shocking and despicable. How could he possibly have known in advance one of the natives would kidnap a random woman? He was good at predicting things, but they couldn't possibly believe he would foresee that.

Thankfully, they'd finally responded to the email he'd sent them days ago protesting his innocence. Somewhat ominously, they'd requested a personal meeting. He'd never personally met anyone from *El Esqueleto's* entourage, and frankly, he never wanted to. But one didn't say no to the drug lord, so here he sat in the car, sweating from more than just the heat and waiting for his meeting to begin.

He reread the note in his hand.

We've received some disappointing reports of additional government involvement in your area. Our understanding was that you'd prevent such activity. We'd like to reaffirm your commitment to preventing such activity in the future, per our agreement. If mistakes have been made, we want to know how they will be corrected so they will not happen again. A person of authority will meet with you at five in the afternoon on Tuesday at the old Odebrecht hangar. Do not be late.

El Esqueleto had a reputation for not tolerating mistakes, or at least repeat mistakes. He racked his brain trying to identify any failures on his part that would be of concern to the cartel. He couldn't think of any. His single biggest problem at the moment was how to slow or prevent the resumption of the vaccine project, but that was for a different client. He was comfortable that the cartel didn't know he'd used their men to disrupt and steal from the project. Even if they did, he could point out it was in their interest to stop the outsiders who were straying into the new cartel region of operations.

He calmed himself by noting that the cartel's representatives were good businessmen. Besides, he was an important man in an important position, one they could utilize in many ways, including business expansion. So, he hoped that meant this meeting was less about mistakes on his part, and more about figuring out how to use him more effectively.

Still, he wasn't foolish. Negotiating with the cartel was like negotiating with a scorpion. They could suddenly decide he was a threat and with one jab of the stinger, he'd be dead. He'd definitely have to tread carefully. It would be important to take careful measure of whomever they'd sent to talk with him.

He glanced at his phone and saw it was two minutes before five. Time to go. He hadn't seen anyone approach the building since he had arrived a half hour ago. But there were entrances on the back that faced the runway. They might have come in that way.

Inhaling a deep breath, he grabbed the handle of his briefcase that contained his Ruger automatic gun that he'd placed there fully loaded last night. He was sure they would search him for weapons and microphones before they let him in. *El Esqueleto's* cartel didn't survive by being careless. But he wasn't going in unarmed, and he could say he had the gun to protect himself from the lawlessness of the area. Putting the weapon in his briefcase rather than on himself was hopefully a good compromise.

As he walked toward the building, he angled his approach so he could see behind it. He expected to see a car, but instead he saw an empty airplane parked on the concrete apron close to the building. Whoever he was meeting with had come from out of town. It looked like the plane could seat three people besides the pilot, so undoubtedly he'd brought some muscle along with his contact.

As he approached the door, it swung open, startling him. A large man with black hair and a well-trimmed moustache that angled sharply down at the edges of his mouth waved him inside. Striding forward assuredly, Martim stepped into a small entryway. The man asked him for the briefcase, set it aside without opening it, and then asked him to spread his arms and legs. He'd never experienced a pat down before, but the actions went beyond thorough, in fact, stopping just short of oral surgery.

His briefcase was similarly inspected. The man removed and carefully inspected his gun, the spare magazine he carried, as well as the other contents. Then without a word, he put everything back in the briefcase, including the loaded gun, and gave it to him. Noting his surprised look, the big man replied in accented Portuguese, "If you make the slightest attempt to retrieve this gun, I'll have already emptied an entire clip into your body and reloaded before you even popped the case opened."

Martim gulped, having absolutely no reason to doubt him.

He was ushered through another door and into a larger room that was dimly lit by the light streaming in from two dirty windows at the far end. An unusually thin man in an open-collar suit sat at a small card table with two chairs. His face was in shadowy contrast to the back-lit windows.

Martim resisted the urge to tug at his tie to loosen it. The heat in the building was suffocating. As he got closer to the man, he was struck by his unusual hair. It was white, not like an albino, but brighter than the silver gray that men get when they age. The eyes on his face were sunken deep into his sockets, their color impossible to determine in the dim light. The man stretched out a hand, and Martim realized the man was not just thin, but gaunt, almost skeletal.

Martim realized with a surge of adrenaline that he was facing the cartel chief himself, *El Esqueleto*.

"Do you know who I am?" the man asked him in Spanish.

Martim didn't dare say anything, so he just nodded.

"Good, we use no names here. Sit down and let's talk. Please tell me what has been happening here and what you've been doing. I've been doing my research and have my sources, so I urge you not to leave anything out."

One sentence into his explanation, Martim found himself babbling as he began explaining everything he'd done, from bribing a "friend" to have the representative from the Ministry of Health removed and replaced by himself to better oversee operations in the region, to keeping the Americans and their vaccine research disrupted and out of the cartel's new operation area as much as possible.

El Esqueleto didn't interrupt or ask any questions, just listened intently while his hired thug watched every move Martim made.

After a few minutes, he felt like he'd regained control

of his confidence. By the time he got to the point where *El Esqueleto's* men had been captured after the boat debacle, he was back in full control, and able to express his sincere disappointment in their failure for not kidnapping the researchers and stealing part of their valuable supply of vaccines. Regardless, a stroke of luck with a native kidnapping one of the scientists had shut down the vaccine operation for several days, so his work had been indirectly successful.

When he finished, he paused and waited for a response from *El Esqueleto.* The man didn't say anything for what seemed like a very long time. When he finally spoke, he asked a question that caught Martim completely off guard.

"What about the recent federal police raids into the tribal regions that targeted my property? Why didn't you warn me they were coming? I lost some valuable men, an entire research facility, and my lead biologist. Those raids have set me back several years. I was counting on you to prevent that from occurring."

Martim stared at the man in shock. He didn't know anything about the raids or the fact that *El Esqueleto* had lost men. He'd heard some helicopter traffic over the past few days, but he thought they'd been out looking for the American. How was he to know?

Sweat started sliding down his temples. This was catastrophic. *El Esqueleto* wouldn't just walk away from this kind of mistake, and he wouldn't be here in person either if it weren't a very serious situation.

Martim realized his next words were going to determine if he lived or died.

"I promise you, sir, I knew nothing about the police raids. This is the first I've heard of them. My sources failed me horribly, but I promise you, I'll rectify their errors. They're paid far too well to have failed so miserably."

He considered begging for a second chance, but knew it would make him look weak. No, he had to use his full powers of persuasion to explain how he could fix this. "I can't recover your men or bring your biologist back, but no one is better positioned in this area to help you succeed in the long run than I am." He hoped his voice carried the right amount of indignation and earnestness. "I have important contacts and well-positioned men who understand how a proper business relationship works and who can turn this whole region over to you by the next election. If you start fresh with someone else in the government, you'll run the risk of even more interference in your operations. I *will* find out who failed me regarding the raids, and it will *never* happen again."

El Esqueleto's silence stretched on for what seemed like an eternity. Martim's shoulder blades were uncontrollably tightening, as if that would help stop a bullet from behind him.

At last, *El Esqueleto* spoke. "Tell me about your contacts within the federal police. It's important to me to make an example of who failed me, if it was not you. If I'm satisfied your resources within the police remain sufficient for our current business arrangement, then you'll explain exactly how your other contacts will help me gain full control of this region in order to dominate the next election."

Relief swept through Martim. He was saved. "Of course, of course. Everything you want to know. It's important that you trust me."

"Good. In turn, I'll be honest with you. I came here

fully expecting to terminate our relationship. It's been a disappointment so far. But you're correct that it would take me longer to recover my operations here in this region if I have continued interference from the federal police. I'm very interested in making this region more stable for my business pursuits. So, before I change my mind and move forward with finding a new partner, I'd like to confirm you have the relationships and abilities that you claim. So, prove to me why we should continue together."

Martim didn't hold back. He spent the next hour demonstrating his unwavering loyalty to *El Esqueleto* by naming the important and high-ranking government, political and law enforcement connections who could deliver. *El Esqueleto* only interrupted him a few times to ask how he was convinced that these men wouldn't turn on him. Thankfully, Martim was able to provide him with specific examples of how they'd helped him in the past, described in detail the debts they owed him and the crimes they'd committed. When he said that he had just talked to one of them yesterday, *El Esqueleto* made him open his mobile phone and prove it.

The more he spoke, the more relieved he felt. He knew he'd convinced the man when his questions changed from the details about the people he'd mentioned toward what else Martim might be able to do to advance their collective business interests. He was just winding up when he heard a thump from behind him.

Startled, he shifted in his seat, stunned to see Slash—the American who'd attacked him—stroll into the room, pointing a gun at them.

What in the world was going on?

"Well, well, why am I not surprised to see you here?"

Slash said to him. "Discussing your criminal enterprise, I presume. You keep unusual and dangerous company for a representative of the Brazilian government. I recommend you both surrender, as the police will be here shortly. And don't count on any help from your friend back there." Slash pointed over his shoulder where Martim could no longer see the hired muscle. "He's taking a very long nap."

Shocked, Martim turned to look at *El Esqueleto*. The man was frozen, his position unchanged since Slash entered. Martim was certain it meant the man had additional resources coming. It was unfathomable to imagine he had only one man protecting him. They just needed to stall the American until the others could get into place.

Martim clutched his briefcase across his chest. He'd all but forgotten about it as he spun his story to *El Esqueleto*. Now he remembered he had a gun inside. He slid his hand inside the partially open briefcase waiting for the right moment to withdraw it. When Slash moved closer, his focus on *El Esqueleto*, Martim yanked out the gun.

"Drop your gun!" Martim yelled at the American, his palms sweaty. His heart was racing, but more with excitement than fear. This would be the final test of his loyalty to *El Esqueleto*.

The American looked at him in surprise. "The guard let you keep a gun?"

"I said, drop it," Martim said with more authority. "I'll blow your head off."

After a moment, Slash dropped the gun.

"Good. Now, kick it away from you." The American did what he said, and then to Martim's amusement, tried to bargain his way out of the situation.

"You're making a big mistake," he said. "None of your actions to date have been associated with murder. But if you pull that trigger, you'll have added significantly to your list of crimes. You can drop the gun or use it to help us arrest one of the most wanted criminals in Brazil. Prove where your loyalties lie and receive leniency. Otherwise, you'll rot in prison."

Nervously, Martim stole a glance at *El Esqueleto*. The man had nerves of steel. He still hadn't moved, as if he were testing Martim's loyalty, too. Martim considered turning him in for just a fraction of a second, knowing that if he betrayed the cartel, he'd die a horrible and gruesome death. So, in the end, he really had no choice.

He looked at the American and pulled the trigger.

Chapter Fifty-Five

Lexi

I should have been reviewing the files from my team in New York, but instead, I'd spent the past hour doing research on Natelli Sherwood. What I'd found out had been interesting.

She'd been born in Boston. Her mother was a professor of genetics at Harvard and her father owned an advertising agency. She'd attended Johns Hopkins University in Maryland, earning an undergraduate degree in biology with a minor in chemistry. She'd gone to MIT for a master's degree, and then a PhD in microbiology, just as she'd told us when we first arrived. She'd never married nor had any children. She'd been involved with Vaccitex at its inception eleven years prior, and was personal friends with founders Hayden Pogue and Lilith Burbridge. When she was a junior at Johns Hopkins, Natelli had gone on a yearlong study at Sapienza University in Rome, just as she'd mentioned to Slash and me. When I compared the dates to her life, her timing in Italy coincided with exactly the time that Slash had been born and subsequently abandoned at a church led by Father Emilio Armando.

Slash's past was filled with mystery. He'd been left at Father Armando's church when he was just three days old and eventually turned over to the Italian social services. Shortly thereafter, a foster family had taken him in and subsequently disappeared with him for seven years. Father Armando had never stopped looking for the baby. Eventually Slash had turned up at a hospital in Sperlonga, identified by his fingerprints. Just a few months ago, he'd discovered the identity of his biological father, and learned his biological mother was still alive. Slash had elected not to seek her out, but the memory of what we'd learned was fresh in my head. I'm curious by nature and felt obligated to check it out.

Regardless, the fact that Natelli had been in Italy at the same time Slash was left at the church proved exactly nothing, but that wasn't the compelling evidence for me. That evidence had been found in her PhD dissertation titled *Investigations into Malaria Pathogenesis*. Not the topic nor the findings—which had been interesting and had certainly played a role in her current occupation— but the short message of acknowledgment. Natelli had thanked her parents, her thesis advisor, the Italian microbiologist who had mentored her as an undergraduate biology student, and her close friend and confidant, Father Emilio Armando. That was the connection I'd been looking for—a direct link to Slash. Father Emilio Armando, the man who was like a father to him.

Could Natelli Sherwood be Slash's biological mother?

I knew it was a reach, but it wasn't inconceivable that she'd somehow learned of our discovery regarding Slash's father and found a way to insert herself into our lives just to get a better look at us without revealing herself.

Or had I lost my mind?

Ever since we'd got to Brazil I felt like she'd been overly interested in Slash. I caught her looking at him several times, a wistful look on her face. While lots of people looked at Slash because of his uncommonly good looks, her expression was different, more thoughtful. But more importantly, how did she know Slash worked at the NSA? No one knew that. Finn and I hadn't told Hayden or Lilith because his occupation was not for personal consumption. As far as they were concerned, he was the CEO of Frisson International and that was it. I thought maybe Gwen had spilled the beans, but when I pulled her over after lunch, she swore she hadn't mentioned it to Natelli or to anyone. She understood security concerns, so I believed her.

Then how had Natelli known Slash worked at the NSA?

A ping indicating I'd received an email interrupted my train of thought. It was from Slash. He'd sent it about an hour prior, but with the slow connection, it had taken that long to show up in my box.

I opened it and started reading. It was one sentence. He told me to read the attachment and take whatever actions I saw necessary. I opened the attachment and quickly flipped through the material. It was a compendium of emails in English between an executive of the Indian pharmaceutical company, Pharma Star, and Martim Alves.

Martim Alves? What the heck?

I had no idea where or how Slash had found these documents, but they were a freaking gold mine. I didn't know if they were the reason why he'd unexpectedly gone into town or if he had another reason, but it didn't really matter at this point.

What I *did* know was that Pharma Star was one of the primary competitors to Vaccitex and had been one of the competitors under suspicion for the hacking. The most recent email was from someone named Vihaan Singh, the Director of Security at Pharma Star, to Martim. It confirmed his latest payment for work directly related to the successful delay and disruption of the Vaccitex project. Additionally, it offered him a bonus if he could send them samples of the vaccine being tested, as they wanted to compare it with their research.

That pompous jerkwad was working for a drug cartel *and* a company trying to steal the vaccine from Vaccitex? Could he be any more smarmy?

Anger swept through me. Pharma Star was about to go down and so was that total slimeball, Martim Alves. I started to read through more of Slash's email trove when I received an alert letting me know that someone had accessed the honeypot and begun downloading the false data.

Score! They'd taken the bait!

I considered logging in to monitor their progress, but ultimately decided I didn't want to risk them discovering me hovering. Instead, I forced myself to be patient and wait for them to open my loaded files. Soon enough, my bots would phone home and I'd be in.

I pushed away from the computer so I wasn't tempted to log in. I walked over to Natelli who was sitting at a desk, comparing data on two spreadsheets side by side.

"Hey, what are you doing?" I asked, looking over her shoulder.

"Making sure we've enough supplies for the antici-pated trips we are going to take. What are you doing?"

"Taking a break. I needed to clear my head."

Natelli took off her reading glasses and leaned back in her chair, stretching her arms over her head. "I can't tell you how glad I am that we're restarting the distribu-tion. I'm glad you're okay, Lexi, and that all turned out well. I know Slash must be really relieved."

"He is. I've been thinking how cool it is that you both attended Sapienza University in Italy, although at dif-ferent times. It must have been fun to study abroad."

"Oh, it was. Italy was magical and I was so young. It was a really exciting, heady time for me."

"Did you have a lot of friends when you were there?" I asked.

"I did. The Italians, they're so friendly, and the men, oh so handsome, as you well know." A faraway expres-sion crossed her face.

"So, how did you meet Father Armando?"

She blinked and then frowned. "Excuse me?"

"How did you meet Father Emilio Armando? You're friends with him, right? You thanked him in your dis-sertation."

She stared at me for a long moment. "You read my dissertation?"

"Not entirely, but I happened to notice the part where you thanked him for his friendship in the acknowledg-ments."

"Yes, he's a friend…" Her voice trailed off and a wary light appeared in her eyes. "Why are you asking me all these questions?"

"I just wondered if you knew that Father Armando

is like a surrogate father to Slash? What a coincidence that you both know him so well."

Guilt, nervousness and something else streaked across her face. She was definitely hiding something. "I... I may have heard something like that."

Emboldened, I pressed on. "Why did you ask me so many questions about Slash, Natelli? Why do you have such an interest in him?"

Tension and silence stretched between us before she finally answered. "Of course I'm interested in him. He's on my team, and I always like to know my team members well."

"So that's why you asked me when he'd be returning to the NSA?"

She seemed bewildered by my question. "Why does that matter? I just assumed he'd return to work when this project was over."

"How did you know he worked there? No one said anything about him working for the NSA. So, how did you know? I'm just curious."

At this point, alarm flashed in her eyes. She was clearly flustered, which only made me think I was on to something.

"How did I know that? I... I must have heard it somewhere. Yes, that's it."

"She knew because I told her." A voice came from behind me. "It's okay, Natelli. I should have expected this. Emilio warned us she's smart."

I turned around and saw Lilith standing there. "Come, Lexi. Let's go for a walk."

I stood for a moment, trying to piece it all together, but I was still missing something. She motioned to me again, so I followed her. Once outside, we didn't say anything for a full minute until finally she spoke.

"I'm sorry, Lexi. I didn't mean for this to happen."

"For what to happen?"

"For everything. Slash coming with you, you being kidnapped, me having to come to the rainforest to see you and Slash, and for you finding out about me this way. I didn't want any of this to happen."

Holy freaking cow. I'd been right…and wrong. Lilith Burbridge was Slash's biological mother.

"You're his biological mother." It sounded funny falling from my lips.

"Yes."

Her simple response took my breath away. My emotions were dangerously uneven at the moment. Anger, relief, curiosity and anxiety all jumbled through me at the same time.

"So, why didn't you tell us up front?" I asked, indignation in my voice. "Is that why you came to X-Corp to hire me? You wanted to insert yourself in my life, and by extension into Slash's, too? If you wanted to meet him or reveal who you are to him, there are a lot easier and better ways to have done this."

"I know." Sadness swept across her face. "Let me assure you, this situation did *not* come about because I wanted to put myself into your life or his. It came about because I truly needed you and your skills. I had no idea you'd bring Slash with you nor that I would ever be here with you both. I've been working on this vaccine with Natelli for most of my life and when the hackers started getting close, I needed the best person on the planet to protect it. All fingers pointed to you. Call it the universe at work, God amusing himself with me, random coincidence, or Slash's father orchestrating everything from heaven, but that person turned out to be you, Lexi. It's really as simple as that, although I'm sure you don't see it that way."

"I'm not sure I do." I wasn't sure of anything at this point. Emotions are not easy for me to process and this situation was pulling out all the big ones in me. But I'm also the kind of person who tends to give a person the benefit of the doubt, so I dug a little deeper. "You really didn't want Slash to find you?"

"What I want and what I intended are two different things. This isn't an easy situation for any of us."

"No it isn't, and I'm not feeling exceptionally charitable toward you at the moment." I had no idea why I just said that. Somehow my emotions had answered instead of my brain. Why was I so angry at this woman when I didn't even know her or her circumstances?

She winced as I said the words. "What I meant to say, Lexi, is that I had no intention of disrupting either of your lives by stepping into them. The truth is I didn't think you'd find out about me. Emilio warned me you were smart and exceptionally resourceful—both of you—but I never figured you'd connect the dots so quickly...or even consider that I was connected to you or him. How did you figure it out?"

"Natelli asked me if Slash was going to return to the NSA."

She gave me an incredulous look. "From that you extrapolated that Natelli was Slash's mother?"

"It raised a red flag, as we hadn't told anyone where he worked. Only Gwen knew, and she swore she didn't tell anyone. Natelli was in Italy at the time he would have been conceived, born, and eventually left at Father Armando's church. I also saw her watching him sometimes, and she seemed sad or perhaps wistful. She'd even attended Sapienza University, like he had years later. But that wasn't it, really. Her overt curiosity about him—but not me—raised my suspicions. Then when Father Quintela appeared, I figured we had someone in the group who had a connection to the Vatican, after Slash said it wasn't him. Then, when I discovered Natelli had thanked Father Armando personally in her dissertation, I had a direct connection. It didn't seem that hard to connect the dots at that point, except I didn't get it quite right."

Lilith closed her eyes. "A dissertation acknowledgment? Really?"

"Really."

She let out a deep sigh. "Natelli is my best friend. We met in Italy. She knew Slash's father, and she was there when we fell in love. She also stood by me when he left me for the church and I discovered I was pregnant. It was the most difficult decision of my life to give up my baby for adoption. Regardless, there was no question about leaving him with the one person I trusted the most—Father Armando. Natelli held the baby on the day he was born, and I think she fell a little bit in love with him then, too."

I swallowed hard. I wanted to sympathize, but I was also angry at her for abandoning the man I loved, even while understanding it wasn't my place to judge her or her actions. My emotions were all over the freaking place. "Why did you give him up?"

"Because I couldn't keep him. My parents had no idea I was pregnant, and I was afraid they'd disown me if they found out. It was a different time back then. My baby's father had left me for the church, and I had no husband, job or ability to support us. And, the truth is, I wasn't sure I could withstand the memory of losing his father every time I looked at him. I was young and made the best decision I could at the time. Regardless, a day doesn't go by that I don't regret that decision. Trust me, I'm living my purgatory."

I rubbed my eyes to push away the headache that was brewing there. A part of me wanted to feed on anger and hate her for abandoning and hurting him as she had. That was the easy way. But as much as I wanted to, I couldn't.

"You never told Slash's father you were pregnant," I said.

"No, I didn't. What would have been the point? He was in love with the church, not me. He would have left the church for me and the baby, if I'd asked. But I loved him too much to do that. He never would have been truly happy, and as much as I hated the truth of that, I accepted it."

"You're the reason Slash has American citizenship."

"I am. I hoped someday he might feel a pull toward America, and by extension, me, so I made sure he had a birth certificate, which essentially gave him that choice. I've been closely following his career and life. I don't expect you to understand, but even though he's *apart* from me, he's still *a part* of me."

I didn't want to acknowledge it, but I *did* understand, although a piece of me still nursed anger at how it had all turned out and how it had hurt him in ways I couldn't even comprehend. But just like all of us, Slash had become who he was in part due to the choices made by others.

"He reminds me so much of his father," Lilith said softly. "I didn't expect it to hit me this hard. Being in such close proximity to him is both exhilarating and exhausting. Every time he talks or gestures, I see his father. I am beyond proud of the man he's become, and his single-minded dedication and loyalty to those he loves, including you. I'm proud of the small part I played in bringing him into this world."

I had a million more questions, but one seemed more important than the others. "You never contacted him, never tried to reach him once in thirty-four years. Why?"

I studied her, curious what her answer would be. I expected her to look away or avoid eye contact entirely, but her light blue eyes met mine without flinching. For a startling moment, her expression reminded me of Slash.

Her voice shook a little as she spoke. "I didn't contact him because I wasn't sure I could take it if he hated me, which he has every right to do. This way, I could watch from afar and love him without him ever knowing." She paused. "Are you going to tell him about me?"

I didn't have to think it over because I already knew the answer. "Yes. I'm sorry, Lilith, but we don't keep secrets from each other anymore."

Her expression crumbled for a brief moment, a deep sadness and vulnerability in her eyes. Then the strong, capable CEO of Vaccitex emerged and her expression toughened, hiding what was surely pain and regret. "I understand."

"However, if you want to tell him first, I'll give you the opportunity to do that." I'm not sure why I extended that branch, but I had. I didn't know if Slash would thank me or be angry at me for doing it, but I'd deal with that later.

She seemed surprised I offered. "Thank you, Lexi. I appreciate you letting me do this on my own terms."

"Good luck." I couldn't think of anything else to say except the obvious.

She nodded, closing her eyes for a moment before speaking again. "May I ask one more thing of you? Will you take care of him?"

"That's a given," I promised.

"Good. You know, I used to imagine the girl he'd marry, and although I never could see her clearly, I knew she'd be smart, strong and capable. You're all of that and much more. He's met his match in you and I couldn't be more delighted."

I looked down at the little circle on my wrist and my engagement ring. A circle had been a symbol of love for centuries—no beginning, no end, just unbreakable eternity. Now I had two circles, both with a hole in the center that to me represented a portal to a future that held events both known and unknown.

Life is the sum of all your choices and the choices others made on your behalf. There was no way to predict that Lilith's choices and my choices would one day intersect, but here we were, standing in the crossroads, brought together by our love for one man.

There really wasn't any more I could say to her. I'd made my choice to stand beside Slash, and long ago, she'd made her choice to leave him. Now it was *his* choice to decide how he wanted to deal with that.

Chapter Fifty-Six

Martim Alves

There was a click, but no shot.

Panicked, he pulled the trigger again and again with the same results. He stared at the gun in disbelief, and when he finally looked up, Slash stood right in front of him, holding a small piece of metal between his fingers.

"Won't fire without a firing pin," he said in Spanish. "But since you didn't know that when you pulled the trigger, it's still attempted murder under the Brazilian criminal code."

Martim glanced behind Slash and saw the man who had given him the pat down emerge from the entryway behind Slash and approach him quietly. A smile crept on Martim's face.

Thank God. About time the backup arrived.

But instead of taking down or shooting Slash, the man stopped beside him. Bewildered, Martim looked between them.

"Let me introduce you to Police Sergeant Alberto Santos," Slash said. "He made sure the firing pin I removed was still missing from the gun when he inspected it earlier."

What was happening? Had he been set up? A million thoughts ran through his head. What exactly had he said? What had he confessed to? Could he claim it was all made up and that he was just saying that because he was in fear of his life from *El Esqueleto*?

Before he could say anything in his own defense, Slash motioned to the door. "Let me introduce another police officer you already know."

Vicente Lopes walked in the door, a deep scowl on his face. Martim felt as if he'd been punched in the gut. This was going from bad to worse.

Vicente approached Martim with a pair of handcuffs dangling from his fingers. Panic gripped in his throat.

"You may have thought I was nothing more than a lowly translator helping out on the vaccine trial," Vicente said. "I am, and I'm proud to be associated with the group because it's going to save lives and help preserve an important cultural and social piece of Brazil's history. However, I'm also a federal narcotics agent specifically assigned to watch you, Martim Alves. We suspected you of being involved in government corruption and taking bribes from the drug cartels. We knew you were abusing your position and figured you wanted to be assigned here to protect the drug cartel's expansion in this area, but we really had no idea to what extent. Thank you for not only implicating yourself, but for so graciously listing all the other government and police officials on your payroll. We really appreciate that. And, in some perverse way, I'm impressed. After what I heard and saw you do today, you've brought the word *corruption* to a new level in Brazil."

Martim couldn't breathe. Vicente Lopes was a federal narcotics agent? He'd been under investigation? There had to be some way to fix this. His mind scrambled to think of something until he had a sudden moment of an inspiration. He just had to be confident enough to pull it off.

"What are you talking about, Vicente? Don't be an idiot. This was all planned. You have no idea who this man is." He dramatically pointed at *El Esqueleto*. "I've been trying to lure him here for some time so we could capture him. His name is *El Esqueleto* and he's wanted in a dozen countries. His capture is a coup for all of us. This wouldn't have happened without me and I'll prove that in court. It will be your word against mine."

"Is that so?" Vicente raised an eyebrow. "*You* arranged this? You happened to have *El Esqueleto's* number on speed dial and didn't share that?"

"Of course not. I had an intermediary contact him on my behalf. An intermediary I planned on turning over to the police as soon as this operation was over. I intended to meet *El Esqueleto* and get information that would lead to his capture. I was going to call the police as soon as I left to arrange for his capture."

Vicente clapped three times. "Wow, your bravery knows no bounds. Standing up to *El Esqueleto* and bringing him down. Unfortunately, that isn't at all what you both were talking about in your conversation, which we recorded, by the way."

"I was just soliciting information," he protested.

"By listing all your contacts in the government and police force? How odd."

The American pulled a piece of paper out of his pocket and began to read. "Is this the message you received from the cartel? *A person of authority will meet with you at five o'clock in the afternoon on Tuesday at the old Odebrecht hangar. They will be waiting. Don't be late.*"

He passed over a copy of the email and Martim took it, sweat sliding down his temple. He wanted to wipe it away, but didn't want to draw attention to his anxiety.

"Yes, yes," he confirmed. "I requested the meeting and agreed to it so he would meet me here and I could eventually lead the police to him."

The American laughed. "Nice try, Martim. You didn't arrange this meeting, because I did. I sent you that email from a laptop and email account the federal police confiscated at *El Esqueleto's* drug compound. And this man sitting across from you, well, he isn't *El Esqueleto*. He's Police Sergeant Jose Silva in a wig and some makeup."

The man Martim thought was *El Esqueleto* stood up and made a mock bow. Martim's eyes widened. "This is a trap."

"No trap," Vicente said. "Just good old-fashioned police work, and you helping us with your blustering, arrogant behavior. The real *El Esqueleto* was captured this morning in a federal police raid on a new coca farm in a protected area for which you just happen to be responsible. By the way, *El Esqueleto* is a short, portly bald man. He looks nothing like what you might expect from the nickname, The Skeleton. Anyway, along with a complete electronic record of your communications with the cartel, and interestingly enough, an Indian pharmaceutical company with whom you're plotting to ruin the vaccine project, your days as a free man are numbered. I might add that *El Esqueleto*, whose real name is Joaquin Rojas, has been speaking quite highly of you, and how you've helped him so much." He shook his head as if disappointed. "My, my, you've been quite the busy man, Mr. Alves."

"This is extortion," Martim yelled. He was losing his cool, but they were closing in on him from all sides, and he had to put a stop to it. "I have no idea what you're talking about. As soon as I get out of here, I'm going to make sure you never work another day in your life."

Vicente put both hands down on the table and leaned forward. "You aren't getting out of this, Martim. You've been under suspicion for months, and today is the day you're going down. Your laptop, email communications and bank statements—all handily accessed with the assistance of this amazingly talented computer man, Slash—have put you away for good."

Furious, he jabbed a finger at the American. "He's lying to you. He has nothing on me. He made it all up. Besides, it's impossible. My laptop is encrypted, and it's kept in my locked briefcase. I rarely let it out of my sight."

The American crossed his arms and gave him an amused look. It infuriated him more than he could say. "You left your hotel room from one thirty-two this afternoon until eight minutes after three. Do you recall if you had your briefcase at that time?"

The dribble of sweat had turned into rivers and his heart pounded furiously with a mixture of fear and anger. He had left for that time and hadn't taken his briefcase. "This is a setup. No one will believe you."

Vicente slapped a hand down on the table so hard, Martim jumped. "We executed a warrant, entering your hotel room with full legal authority. By the way, Martim, the information on your laptop, your phone and bank records, as well as the little show you just put on—which was recorded both by police audio and camera—should prove quite helpful at the trial you're so anxious to attend."

"That's impossible. All of this is a farce."

The American chuckled, causing Martim's face to heat with anger. "Think again. The police have been monitoring your actions for some time. You left your briefcase in the room, and we accessed it while executing the warrant. I broke into your laptop in exactly seven minutes and forty-two seconds under the careful eye and with full permission from the Brazilian police and government. Your gun, which, by the way, is unlicensed and illegally possessed, had its firing pin removed by another agent, so if you were so inclined to shoot someone—and you were—the gun wouldn't fire."

"No, no, no," Martim said. "You didn't do that."

"You don't believe me?" The American spread his hands, looking so confident, Martim wanted to punch him. "Your briefcase lock combination was 4045, which was just one combination click from what you left it set at. In America, we call that the Lazy Man's Approach. But it's not really lazy, it's just plain stupid. Additionally, your briefcase helpfully contained a small booklet with all your passwords, which was quite helpful and expedient to the police while reviewing all of your financial and online holdings."

How in the hell can this be happening? I am an important man, and just need an opportunity to reach my contacts who could extract me from this mess.

"Not coincidentally, your comments to the man you thought was *El Esqueleto* confirm the same names and relationships in the government and the police that you had in your booklet," Vicente added. "So, thank you for that."

"You have no idea what you're doing," Martim bluffed. "You will be fired within the hour. Do you know who I am?"

"A man with no power or contacts." Vicente leaned forward so his face was mere inches away "We could have convicted you for thirty years with just the corruption and bribery charges. But during the raid earlier today on *El Esqueleto* I lost one of my best officers. He was killed and two others were injured. I hold you personally responsible for that. He was as good a man as you're filth. So, it was my sincere pleasure to watch you attempt to shoot Slash in cold blood. Now, you will rot in prison until you die, and I couldn't be any happier about it."

"No!" Martim jumped to his feet, his heart exploding with panic. "You can't do this. I've been framed."

"Only by yourself." Vicente roughly yanked his hands behind his back, forcing him to bend over the table as he snapped on the handcuffs. "Martim Alves, it's my duty to inform you, you're officially under arrest."

Chapter Fifty-Seven

Arjun Singh

"You'd better have a good report for me or you're all fired." He'd had enough of the stalling, the excuses, and the technical mumbo jumbo. How hard could it be to hack through one firewall?

"We do," Vihaan said, exchanging a glance with Krish, his IT guru. "A really good report, brother."

The band of tension around his neck loosened slightly. He had been encouraged by the fact the vaccine trials had come to a complete halt, but it didn't do them any good if they couldn't get the vaccine recipe. "Then what is it?"

"We've broken through the firewall and obtained access to the files you wanted. We've downloaded them all."

"Do they contain the information on the vaccine recipe?"

Krish hesitated uncertainly. "Sir, I don't know. I don't think it's prudent to open the files quite yet. They might contain a malware or viruses. My suggestion is to create a virtual server that's offline from their current systems, transfer the files to the virtual server, and then carefully open and screen each file in that isolated environment."

Arjun felt his blood pressure rise. "How long would that take?"

"Only a couple of days, but it would ensure that no one could plant hostile code into our systems."

Arjun bolted up from his chair. "A couple of days? We don't have time for that. Besides, think about it. They're a nonprofit organization. They don't have the money and aren't sophisticated enough to do something like that. Open the damn files and get them to our scientists, so that they can tell me what we have. *Now!*"

"Sir, I must protest—" Krish started when Arjun cut him off.

"Do your job or I'll find someone else who can."

Krish immediately rose. "Yes, sir."

"Now get to it. This is your number one priority. Do *not* fail me. Vihaan, stay a moment, please."

After Krish had left, Arjun turned to his brother. He stuck a finger in Vihaan's chest. "It's your job to make sure he does what's he's supposed to. He doesn't leave this building until it's done. Are we clear?"

"Yes, brother."

"Good, and once those files are open, get the information to the scientists at once."

"Understood."

As Vihaan headed out the door, Arjun picked up the phone to contact all of his investors about their recent breakthrough. It was about damn time. They'd finally struck gold, and now he needed to make sure everything was lined up perfectly for the grand finale.

Lexi

I still felt shaken by the conversation with Natelli and Lilith, but I had work to do. I pushed aside my emotions and focused.

While waiting for the alert from my computer regarding the files, I started doing more in-depth research on Pharma Star. I couldn't find them listed on the National Stock Exchange of India, or any other exchange I could find, so I determined they must be privately held. A minute later I was able to find their corporate website in English. It didn't provide much more than some marketing information. It did mention that they, nonspecifically, were working on solving some of "the world's biggest problems" and they were on the threshold of commercializing an amazing discovery. The picture of the CEO was plastered on almost every page on the site. Arjun Singh.

I did a cursory security check of the site. It was adequate, but given how little content there was on the site, I suspected there wasn't much behind the scenes. Besides, I wasn't going to waste time there when I had another way to get deeper within their system and a lot faster.

I widened my search involving the company and came across several investigative reports written by a reporter from a newspaper in Mumbai. The author, Ajay Dewan, was a young journalist who had somehow stumbled upon some dirty tricks that Pharma Star had done in terms of providing faulty medical devices to Indian hospitals that largely served the poorer population. Subsequent articles by Dewan indicated Pharma Star had been suspiciously absolved of any wrongdoing by a leading Indian politician who had later been arrested in a huge political corruption scandal. It looked like the company hadn't changed their ways much.

I'd just started reading another article when I received an alert ping from my laptop. I leaned forward, watching the data scroll across my screen.

Score.

The thieves had downloaded the files and my software was now worming its way deep into their system. When my bots were finished, I'd have an invisible backdoor. If the hackers came from Pharma Star, as I expected, I was going to take special pleasure in bringing them down.

Chapter Fifty-Eight

Slash

He returned to the research camp in a good mood. Martim was headed for prison. *El Esqueleto* had been captured, and his entire drug empire was about to tumble down. He'd sent Lexi some material he'd gathered from Martim's laptop regarding his connection to the Vaccitex hackers in India, and now it was just a matter of time before they brought them down, too. To top it off, he'd had an intimate, unplanned, and private wedding to the woman he loved with no one in attendance he really knew, and it'd been the best night of his life.

Things were damn good.

He hopped out of the jeep with Gabriel and headed toward the lab when Lilith intercepted him. "Excuse me, Slash. May I have a word with you?"

He was itching to see where Lexi had gone with the material he'd sent regarding the Indian hackers, but he couldn't see a way to get out of speaking to her. "Of course. What's up?"

"Would you mind walking with me for a moment?"

The research camp, with its barrack-like structures, roving guards and barbed wire fence, was hardly the place for a stroll, but he accommodated her. They strolled along for a minute before she spoke.

"This is going to be terribly awkward, but I'd like to speak with you about something personal."

"Okay."

It took two revolutions around the camp before she spoke again. "The decisions we make when we are young can have a lifetime effect on ourselves and others—others who are innocent, and don't have a choice in the matter. I made a decision that directly impacted *your* life's trajectory, Slash. I want to start this conversation by saying I'm sorry, and every day I wish I could change the past."

He stopped, turning to look at directly her. "Hello, Mother."

The look on her face was one he'd never forget for as long as he lived. Shock, disbelief, anguish, and shame chased across her face. She pressed a hand to her breast, gasping as if he'd hit her in the stomach. "You knew?"

He'd wondered if she'd ever acknowledge his existence, and in return, he considered what he'd say to her if they were to ever discuss his birth. In fact, this scene had played out in his head dozens of times, in a variety of different ways. But now that the moment had arrived, he had no idea how the conversation would go. But he would start, because he was entitled to that.

"Lilith Imogen Burbridge, born in Baltimore, Maryland, on the twentieth of October to Addison Burbridge, a physician, and his wife, Isabella, a fascinating scientist and inventor in her own right. You attended Johns Hopkins University, graduating with a degree in biochemistry. You spent a year in Rome, studying biochemistry at Sapienza University with your lifelong friend Natelli

Sherwood. Eventually, you received an MBA, and later a PhD in cellular biology, both of those at Johns Hopkins as well. You accomplished all of this by the age of twenty-six, which is quite impressive. You worked for several years at the Food and Drug Administration, reviewing and making recommendations regarding clinical trials, and assessing the safety and efficacy of vaccines. At thirty-five, you began working for a nonprofit start-up World Vaccines, developing vaccines for impoverished countries. You became a superstar at the company, engineering several revolutionary biochemical concepts that would eventually pave the way for a much-needed malaria vaccine that could save millions of lives, most of them children. You eventually founded your own company, Vaccitex, with your childhood friend and multimillionaire businessman Hayden Pogue, with whom you lived for some time, but never married. You've spent your life's work focused on saving children. I read in one article about you, that you considered saving children an obsession. Which is interesting, given you have no *known* children of your own."

He left it at that, annoyed at himself for letting the hurt creep into his voice. When he'd said it in his head, his voice had been cool and dispassionate. He hadn't expected this conversation to affect him this deeply. He'd told himself a thousand times it didn't matter if she ever acknowledged him or not, and he'd believed it, but here he was suddenly fighting to keep his emotions under wrap.

Lilith managed to collect herself and began to walk again. He matched her stride, remaining silent, waiting to hear what came next.

"How did you know?" she finally asked.

"I saw you coming out of Father Armando's office several months ago when I was in Italy. Then, when you arrived here at the camp a few days ago and I saw you in person for the first time, I remembered your face...and your eyes. You were crying that day. I wondered how the CEO of Vaccitex knew Father Armando. At first, it never crossed my mind that you might be my biological mother. I was simply curious at the connection, thinking the Vatican supported your admirable effort. However, the more I learned about you, and the unusual way your life seemed to intertwine with mine, the easier it was for me to piece things together. Especially since I'd recently discovered the identity of my father and knew my mother was still alive."

"Why didn't you say anything to me before?" She spoke so softly he could hardly hear her.

"Because I was more concerned about finding and rescuing the woman I loved than making contact with a woman who perhaps never intended to tell me she was my biological mother. If you hadn't come to me, I wouldn't have come to you, Lilith. We could have maintained a professional relationship all of our lives, and that would have been fine with me. Apparently, that's the way you wanted it, so I would have respected that."

His words hurt her, he could tell. He wasn't handling this as well as he would have liked, but every word she said to him was like a knife in the heart. He hadn't expected this level of grief and pain.

She lifted a trembling hand to her hair, pushing it away from her face. "Actually, I've wanted to tell you all of my life. But I didn't feel as if I deserved that opportunity, and even if I did, how could I tell you? How do I face the child, who's now a man, and explain that even though I gave you up for adoption, I've never forgotten you? How do I explain the depths of my love for someone I only knew for nine months and three days? The truth is, I love you today as much as I loved you the day you were born and nestled at my breast. Here we stand—two people who once shared the most intimate connections of life through an umbilical cord—and yet we're strangers. Would you believe you're in my thoughts and prayers every single night?"

A hard twist yanked at his heart, but he worked to keep his face impassive, his emotions under control. He said nothing.

"You probably wonder why I gave you up for adoption if I loved you so much, but the truth is, the day I handed you over to Father Armando was the saddest day of my life. Father Armando told me he explained to you how your father and I loved each other deeply, but he could not balance that love for me and his love for the church. He made his choice, and it was not me. I was young, a student in a foreign country, and had parents who would not have approved of my pregnancy nor permitted me to keep a baby. But I want you to know you were conceived in love. *So* much love." Emotion caught in her throat and she paused for a moment to compose herself.

"A storm was coming when I sat in the back of a taxi that drove me to the church in San Mauro Cilento. The sky thundered ominously and raindrops had started to patter against the car window. I covered your head with the blanket when I left the taxi to make sure you didn't get wet. When I approached the church, I stopped when I saw a single white lily growing near the doorway, stretching up to the sky and lifting its petals as if to welcome the rain. I believed the lily was a sign, just for me, Lilith, to share a last moment of beauty with my newborn son. I lifted the blanket as the rain fell gently and showed it to you. Your eyes opened wide and they looked at the flower and then at me. Moments later, I walked through the door of the church and handed you over to Father Armando. To this day, I cannot see a white lily without thinking of that moment."

He closed his eyes, picturing the two of them on the steps of the church, and his breath caught in his throat.

"I'm so sorry for giving you up," she said softly. "I've wanted to reach out to you since the day I handed you over. But I felt I had no right, that I didn't deserve to be in your life. I've followed your studies and careers as much as I've been able to over the years. Father Armando helped me with that, thank God."

"Then you know I almost joined the priesthood."

"I knew, and it was somewhat shocking seeing as how you'd never even known your father. I'm certain he's been watching over you, filling you with his love."

He had so many questions and wanted to ask them all…and none. But one was important to him. "Was it you who got me the job at the NSA?"

"Absolutely not. You're a brilliant man. You've earned every single thing you've received. That being said, I admit to putting in a good word for you with the Deputy Director, who was at the time a close friend of mine. I also provided him with your birth certificate and encouraged him to review your résumé. In spite of that, I don't think it was my recommendation that swayed him. He was quite impressed by your own credentials and certainly the personal intervention of the pope on your behalf."

Conflicted feelings continued to sweep through him,

emotions he didn't want to unpack and examine while his birth mother stood in front of him. What he wanted, *needed*, was the one woman he considered his rock—his wife. He wished she were here with him now.

He forced back the emotions and swept out a hand to encompass the research center. "So, what about this project and Vaccitex? Did you bring Lexi on board because you wanted to check her out? Did you know I'd come along?"

She shook her head vigorously. "I brought Lexi on because we needed the best, and all my sources told me that X-Corp, but specifically she, was the best. I had no idea you'd be coming along. When I discovered you wanted to be a part of the project, I was equal parts terrified and elated. I admit to being curious about Lexi, and I welcomed the opportunity to meet her face to face with no expectations and no judgment. She's a remarkable woman, Slash, although you already know that. She's also fiercely loyal to you, and you should know she confronted me about being your mother. She initially thought it was Natelli, but I came clean to her."

He didn't think he could be more astonished by this conversation, but he was. "Lexi knew, too?"

"Only as of a couple of hours ago. Natelli let it slip that she knew you worked at the NSA and Lexi confronted her about it. I overheard them talking and told Lexi it was me. She was going to tell you, but she gave me the chance to speak to you first. I'm indebted to her for that."

He was still trying to wrap his head around the fact that Lexi had figured it out when Lilith came to a sudden stop behind the men's barracks. "I know we can't turn back time, as much as I wish we could. But I hope someday you'll be able to forgive me and figure out a way to let me be a small part of your future. I do *not* intend in any way to interfere with your relationship with Lexi, Father Armando or your wonderful adoptive family. I do *not* want to interrupt or insert myself into yours or Lexi's life. But I'd be lying if I didn't say I'd like a second chance to know you, just as friends or acquaintances, if that's more comfortable for you. If that isn't something you'd like, you can walk away from me, no questions asked. Regardless of your response, know I'll always wish the best for you. I want you to know I've never, *ever* forgotten you and never will."

He stood motionless, swamped with emotions he hadn't expected and feeling like a bandage had been ripped off of an open wound. He needed time to process, to think over what he knew, what she'd revealed, and how he felt about it. None of it would be resolved in the next few minutes, if ever, and now he had other matters to attend to.

He gave her a brief nod and said the only thing he could. "I'll think about it and get back to you."

Chapter Fifty-Nine

Lexi

Slash and Vicente walked into the lab at the same time.

As soon as I saw Slash, I rose from my chair. To my surprise, he came directly for me, pulling me into his arms and giving me a hug and burying his face in my neck.

"How are you, *cara*?" he murmured.

"I'm fine. Where have you been? There's so much to tell you."

"I know."

Before he could say more, Vicente spoke. "Lexi, I just wanted to let you know Martim Alves has been taken to Manaus kicking and screaming for his lawyer all the way. Doesn't matter how much he complains, he's going to get put away for a long time."

Vicente gave me a brief rundown of what had happened at a hangar near the airport, detailing his crimes, which were extensive. Even given that, I barely heard anything after the part where Martim had tried to shoot Slash.

I looked at him with a mixture of disbelief and exasperation. "Seriously? You let him point a loaded gun at you?"

"A loaded gun without a firing pin," Slash responded with a shrug. "It was completely safe."

"Completely safe is no gun at all. Jeez." I thought about belaboring the point, but realized there was no sense in that. It was over now, and all had ended well, thank goodness. Still I needed a bit more reassurance. "When you say Martim will be put away for a long time, what exactly does that mean in terms of years?"

"Thirty to forty years, maybe more when we add in the bribe taking. I should also mention Brazilian prisons aren't nearly as nice as American prisons. He'll be quite uncomfortable, especially having lived most of his life in an elite status. I promise to keep you updated on the sentencing." He held out a hand to Slash, giving him more of a slap than a handshake. "I couldn't have done it without you, man."

"Anytime. I owe you. Thank you for coming with me to get Lexi."

"Are you kidding me? That was the adventure of a lifetime." He laughed and pulled out a cell phone from his pocket. "By the way, I snapped a couple of photos at your wedding. You want to see them?"

We crowded around him to see the photos. The first one was of Slash on his knee in front of me just as I was about to brand him with my engagement ring. The second one was of the two of us standing at the edge of the water ready to throw in our stone together. Slash had his arm around me while I rested my head on his shoulder. Two simple photos, two absolutely precious moments captured in time.

Slash raised his eyes to look at me. "Can you shoot those photos to me?" he asked.

"Of course," Vicente responded. Slash gave him a number, so he sent them and put his phone away. "Next time we get back to civilization, they're yours. So what's next for you two newlyweds?"

"A real wedding, I guess," I answered. "It's time to make it legal."

Vicente laughed, holding up his hands. "No need to do that. It's already legal. According to Brazilian law, you are technically man and wife. Since international law recognizes Brazilian marriages, that means you're officially hitched."

"What?" Slash and I said at exactly the same time.

"Brazil has special provisions for the indigenous tribes because they technically do not fall under the administration of the Brazilian government," he explained. "We needed a way to legitimize the marriages for those people who left the indigenous tribal regions to live in the cities, for example. So, a law was passed that made marriages between indigenous peoples legal under the Brazilian legal code."

"Neither one of us is an indigenous person," I pointed out.

"True, but there's a special provision that accounts for marriages performed by an indigenous tribe member between a tribal member and an outsider. Those marriages are considered legal if a government representative is present."

"You're still not making sense," I said. "Neither of us fits the indigenous criteria, and we just happened to forget to invite a government representative to our wedding."

He looked positively giddy when he answered. "Wrong on both counts. The law also addresses marriage ceremonies *performed* by indigenous people regardless if those getting married are native or not. Your unusual circumstance met exactly this criteria, and there *was* an government representative present...me. So, let me be the first to officially congratulate you on your marriage. Your marriage certificate should arrive in the mail in a couple of months—I'll see to that personally. So, congratulations to you both."

Slash and I looked at each other and started laughing. Gwen, Natelli, and some of the other researchers in the lab who were eavesdropping on our conversation, cheered and started congratulating us.

After that died down, I asked Vicente if he intended to remain a part of the vaccine trials.

"I wouldn't miss it for the world. I have special permission from the government to do exactly that. Now with most, if not all, the obstacles out of our way, we can finally do what we came to do."

I couldn't have agreed more.

Chapter Sixty

Arjun Singh

"The data makes absolutely no sense!"

Arjun paced back and forth in front of his computer guy, Krish Anand, madder than he could ever remember being. "Our scientists can't make heads or tails of it. They believe it's all bogus. Either you grabbed the wrong stuff or they played you for a fool. You're a useless idiot and deserve to be fired for incompetence."

As he finished his rant, his brother and Director of Security, Vihaan, entered the office, not even issuing a greeting before speaking. "Brother, I have some bad news. Our contact in Brazil is no longer communicating with us. In fact, his email appears to have been shut down. I can't reach him."

Arjun closed his eyes, feeling his blood pressure going through the roof. "I promised our investors a big breakthrough surprise this week, and we have *nothing*. We're facing a significant crisis. Start setting some resources aside while we still have some in case we have to shut down quickly and start over again somewhere else."

He heard a knock on the door that was ajar and saw his secretary standing there. "Excuse me, sir. This just arrived for you." She brought him a sealed envelope with nothing but his name on the front.

Arjun held the envelope gingerly in his hand as if it were a bomb. "What's this? It can't possibly be more bad news, because it can't get any worse than it already is."

Vihaan snatched it out of his hand. "As your Director of Security, let me read it first." He tore open the envelope and pulled out two sheets of paper, scanning the contents on the first page. Slowly he raised his gaze to meet his brother's.

"It's from Ajay Dewan, that punk journalist. He's telling us that he'll be doing an interview about the company at eleven o'clock on the local news, and invites us to watch." Vihaan glanced at his watch. "That's in ten minutes. He also says it's been quite an enlightening experience going through all of our company and personal emails that were provided to him anonymously."

"What?" Arjun whirled on Krish. "He can't have our emails, can he?"

"I warned you that downloading the information from Vaccitex without isolating it was dangerous," Krish retorted. "But you were willing to accept the risk because it was urgent."

"That's ridiculous. You were supposed to prevent this from happening. That's what I pay you for. This is a disaster."

"Of your own making," Krish shot back with such venom, it caught him totally off guard. "You don't have to fire me because I quit! Good luck finding someone else who will put up with your underhanded and shady dealings. You're a disgrace to your country."

Krish stormed out of the office, leaving him and Vihaan with mouths wide open. Arjun ran a hand through his hair, wondering if he should have insisted on getting all the passwords to everything before he'd left. "Can we salvage anything from this?"

Vihaan shook his head. "I doubt it." He handed his brother the second sheet. "He has our investor pitch."

"No. How is that possible? That's proprietary information."

"Someone has access to all our files apparently. Dewan says he intends to broadcast copies of the documents to prove that once we developed the vaccine, we intended to charge India and some of the poorest countries in the world over five hundred times the cost of a dose of vaccine. We could do it because we were going to have a monopoly. But that isn't all, they have access to everything. That means all of the deals, the bribes and cover-ups. It could all be exposed."

Panic filled him. "We need to make plans to cut our losses and run." He dashed to his computer and pulled up his banking information. "No! They've frozen our accounts." He banged his fist on the keyboard. "They can't do this."

His secretary stepped into his office again. "Excuse me, sir. The news is coming on the television now, and I've been informed the company is going to be featured on it. Would you like to watch it?"

The woman had no clue. He glanced in despair at his brother. "What do we do, Vihaan?"

His brother closed his eyes, a pained look on his face. "We surrender."

Chapter Sixty-One

Lexi

"So, she told you?"

Slash and I sat under a tree near the dining building. A week ago I wouldn't have been able to stand being outside for more than a few minutes, but those few days living in the rainforest had changed me. I'd almost become used to the humidity and heat.

"She did," he said. "She told me you figured it out, as well."

"There were a lot of flags. It wasn't as complicated as I expected. I was going to tell you if she didn't."

"Thank you, I appreciate that, but I already knew. I saw her coming out of Father Armando's office when I was in Italy. When she arrived here at the camp, I remembered her face, so I did a little digging. It took me under an hour to piece it together. It's interesting you and I came at it from completely different angles, and yet we came to the same conclusion."

"Great minds and all that," I said with a smile.

"I would have told you sooner, but there wasn't a right time or place." He reached over and tugged on my ponytail until I brought my mouth closer to his, where he planted a kiss. "Anyway, she intercepted me on the way back from nabbing Martim and told me."

"Do you want to talk about it?"

I couldn't see his eyes because they were hidden behind sunglasses, but I could tell by the tone of his voice that the meeting had affected him deeply. "Yes, and no. It was an unusual experience. She had an emotional attachment to me that I couldn't reciprocate."

"That's understandable. You don't know her, while she's had her whole life to know you."

He considered that. "I called her Mother, because biologically, she is, but I didn't have the same feelings for her as I do for my actual mother. Even thinking of her as my mother felt somehow disloyal."

I laid my head against his shoulder. "That's not an unusual reaction. Your mom, stepfather and Father Armando *are* your parents in all the ways it counts. You've bonded with them over the years, and you love and care for them deeply, as you should. They're a part of your life story."

"*Si*, yet there's a part of me that wonders about her... Lilith."

"Whether you like it or not, she's a part of your life story, too."

He bent his knees and clasped his hands in front of him. "Yes, she is. Ever since I learned about my father, I'm conflicted. Part of me never wanted to meet her, while another part wants to know more about my heritage and history. Is that wrong? Do you think getting to know her would hurt my family in any way?"

I put a gentle hand on his biceps. "No, I don't. You've got a lot of things to process, Slash, but guilt isn't one of them. I haven't met your mother or stepfather in person yet, but I have a feeling they'd support you whether you decide to pursue a relationship with her or not. As will I. And why would it be wrong to want to know more about from where you come? We're human, which means we have a desire to learn more about ourselves and how we fit into this world."

He slipped an arm around me, pulling me closer. "Thank you. And you're right. I need time to sort it out. I hope at some point, my decision will become clear. At this point, I don't know where, or if, I want her story with me to end. But I do know I'd never get through it if you weren't part of that process."

"At least *that's* not a problem." I held up my wrist displaying the small circle. "You're bound to me now. I'm in for the long haul."

"Lucky me." He leaned over, pressing a kiss against the mark.

"So, what do we do about our other wedding, Slash?" I asked. "Now that we're already married, I'm a lot more relaxed about the whole thing."

"Funny you say that, because I feel the same way. It's certainly important to me that Father Armando blesses our union in the church, and it's also important to your mother and our family and friends that we recite our vows in front of the family in a gown and tux."

"Then let's do it. We've already had an intimate wedding that, for all practical purposes, was ours and ours alone. Other than Vicente and Salvador, no one else even understood what we were saying to each other. It was truly perfect."

"It was both the scariest and happiest day of my life," he said. "I thought I'd lost you, and then I found you, and in response, I promptly married you. In my opinion, anything that comes after that will be significantly anticlimactic."

I laughed, bumping my shoulder against his. He had this way of making me feel like I was the only girl in the world, despite there being millions. "What a crazy, wonderful, marvelous wedding we had. What do you think, Slash? Do I let my mother and Basia run amok with the planning for the other one?"

"That's your call. I'll be happy with whatever you or your mother decide."

"That's a pretty diplomatic call." I leaned back against him, the most relaxed I'd been in weeks. "Okay. Well, I guess I'd better give my mom a call to sort it out."

He twirled a strand of my hair around his finger. "Not a bad idea, but let me use the satellite phone first. There's someone I want to talk to right away."

Chapter Sixty-Two

Slash

The phone rang four times before it she finally picked it up. "Hello?"

"*Ciao*, Mama."

"Romeo?" He'd caught her by surprise—he could tell by the background noise and the fluster in her voice. He heard her moving to a quieter place, and once she was there, the flustered tone turned to warmth and love. "Is that really you?" she asked, speaking to him in Italian, their preferred language of conversation.

"It is. I hope I'm not disturbing you."

"Of course, you aren't. It's so wonderful to hear your voice. How are you?"

"I'm good. I wanted you to be the first to know. Lexi and I got married while we were on assignment in Brazil. It's a long story as to how it happened, and it was completely unplanned and unexpected, but we're legally married. I think you'll greatly enjoy hearing the story, but I want to tell you all the details in person and with Lexi by my side."

"Brazil? It sounds terribly exciting."

"That it was. Regardless, we still intend to have a

church wedding in the U.S. and we'd like to have a nice reception with family and friends to celebrate. Do you think you and Papa can make it?"

"What a silly question. We wouldn't miss it for the world. As soon as you give me the details, I'll be sure to clear my shift well in advance at the hospital. I'm so happy for you, Romeo. You deserve every moment of happiness you receive."

"Thank you. We don't have details on the wedding yet, but I believe they'll be coming shortly. I can't wait for you to meet Lexi. She's extraordinary."

"I'm sure of that. I'm looking forward to meeting the woman who's stolen my little boy's heart. You're bringing her to Giorgio's wedding, right?"

"I am." It made him happy to imagine how fun it would be when Lexi was finally surrounded by his entire family. "Also, if you have another minute, there's something else I'd like to talk to you about. Something I should have said a long time ago."

"I have as much time as you need." She must have heard something in his voice because she added, "Is everything okay?"

She was his adoptive mother, and she knew him better than anyone except for Lexi. "It's more than okay. The truth is, I'm the best I've ever been in my life. Everything seems to have fallen into place for me. I couldn't possibly ask for any more. I'm an incredibly lucky man."

"That makes my heart so happy to hear."

"You're a big part of that." There had never been a time when he doubted her support for his pursuits in life and he loved her for it. "I'm not sure I ever told you how grateful I am that you took in a child you didn't know, a child that wasn't your own. Your patience and love saved me—a broken child. How can I put into words what that means me?"

He heard the soft intake of her breath. "Oh, Romeo. You don't have to say a thing." Her voice caught with emotion. "You've brought incredible joy into my life— into all of our lives. I'm proud of the man you've become and all you've accomplished. You're truly a special and brilliant soul. It's my honor to be your mother."

"Being your son made me the man I am today." He closed his eyes, taking a moment to compose himself, because her love for him was about to undo him. "While I've always appreciated what you've done for me, I'm not sure I ever fully understood the sacrifices you made for me until recently. Your love and acceptance gave me the courage to find my own way and eventually my own love."

She didn't speak right away, and he wondered if she was collecting herself much as he had just done. "That's a beautiful thing to say. Thank you. Although I haven't met Lexi yet, I already love her as if she were my own. She's captured your heart so completely, Romeo, and that's not an insignificant achievement."

She, of all people, would understand that. "I know. Sometimes when I look at her, I can't believe how fortunate I am to have found her. It's been hard for me to trust people."

"That's completely understandable."

"Perhaps, but you were the first person to whom I gave my trust, and you kept it safe. Now I've extended that trust to my wife. Thank you for that."

"My heart is bursting with happiness for you. I can't wait to see you."

"I can't wait to see you either. I love you, Mama."

"I love you, too, *cucciolo*. And remember no matter what happens in your life, if you have your family beside you, you'll be rich. *Amor vence tudo*."

For the first time in his life, his head was clear, his heart was full. "*Si*, Mama, love conquers all."

Chapter Sixty-Three

Lexi

"Hi, Mom, it's me, Lexi."

"Lexi, where are you? You haven't been answering my emails." Her voice held a mixture of annoyance and worry, so I knew I had to reassure her everything was fine. She had no idea about my kidnapping or the particulars of my assignment, and I intended to keep it that way, at least for the time being.

"I'm sorry about that. I'm in South America on assignment, remember? We're using satellite connectivity here and it's not overly reliable. Plus, we're really busy."

"What kind of computer people go to South America on assignment? Why can't you do it virtually?"

"That's a great question, Mom, and most of the time, I can do it virtually. But since the connection is spotty here in Brazil, I needed to be here in person to oversee everything."

She let out an exasperated huff. "Well, how are we supposed to be making progress on the wedding front if you go to places where I can't reach you?"

"I figured you had it covered."

There was a pause. "Is Slash there with you, too? He's not responding to his emails either."

Oh, crap. We were both busted. "We've been really busy on this project. I'm sorry we didn't get back to you sooner."

"Are you still in South America?"

"We are. We're hoping to be home in about a week or so. But I wanted to give you a call to talk to you about the wedding."

"Really?" I could hear genuine surprise in her voice.

"Really. But first, I want to tell you that Slash and I had a civil wedding ceremony in Brazil. It's a long and complicated story as to how it happened and why, but I promise you all the details when we get back. That being said, it wasn't a church wedding, which is what we want, followed by a nice reception that involves all of our family and friends. So, actually, nothing has really changed except for the legal part."

A long minute of silence stretched on until she finally spoke. "You eloped…in Brazil?"

"It wasn't a planned elopement and there were special circumstances that required it." I looked down at the circle on my wrist. I'd always consider the village wedding our special, intimate ceremony, no matter what wedding came after. "But I'll explain all that later, as it's a long story. What's important is that during the ceremony, I learned something about myself and my perceptions regarding a wedding. I realize now that a wedding is a celebration of love no matter where you live, what language you speak, or what you do in a ceremony to show that love. Everybody wants something different, and that's okay. Slash and I also realized it's important to us that everyone we love has a chance to share in our celebration. I got so overwhelmed by the details, I forgot to look at the big picture—family. But now I understand sharing our love with others is the true purpose of a wedding, so I'm ready to stop dragging my feet and help you plan it. We can even ask Amanda McCormick to help us, if she's available and wants in on it."

My mother remained silent, so to fill the awkward pause, I decided to plunge ahead. A small part of my brain might have been telling me this was the longest speech I'd ever made. "Anyway, all of that is a long-winded way to say I get why the wedding, my wedding, is so important to you, Mom, and to the rest of the family. I'm sorry I didn't understand that before. Will you forgive me?"

She *still* didn't say anything. Panicked, a hundred thoughts raced through my head. Was she disowning me? Hurt? Angry? Thrilled she could do whatever she wanted?

How would I know, if she decided to never speak to me again?

I almost died with relief when she finally spoke. "Well, Lexi, I'm certainly curious to hear why you had to legally tie the knot in Brazil. It doesn't have to do with babies, does it?"

I choked on a breath. "Gah! No, Mom, no. No babies." Jeez. Leave it to my mother to think I was pregnant.

She sighed. "I'm sorry, too. I know I may have been coming on a bit too strong about the wedding planning, but you're my only daughter, and I want everything to be perfect for you."

"I know, and I really appreciate it. I just didn't get why it was so important to everyone but me until now. You should know I'm slow coming to those kinds of realizations. I love you, Mom. You, Dad, Grandma and Grandpa and even Beau and Rock…you guys are the best."

"We love you, too, Lexi. However, I do have one important request regarding the planning."

"Which is?"

"You and Slash had better start answering my texts, phone calls and emails about the wedding…or else I'm going to televise the ceremony."

Holy crap. She'd do it, too. "Threat acknowledged, Mom. I hereby promise from this moment on, I'll be better about responding to wedding-related emails and calls. Slash, too."

"Don't make me get it in writing from your lawyer friend."

"I won't. I promise." I laughed, feeling a huge weight lift from my shoulders. "Oh, and before I hang up, I found a wedding dress I like. I want to get your opinion on it."

"Really?" Her voice couldn't contain her excitement. "Is it one of the ones we looked at?"

"It is. It's dress number forty-two."

"Forty-two? Let me look it up on my phone." There was a long pause and then a sharp intake of breath. "Oh, that's a gorgeous dress, Lexi. I love the way it's gathered at the waist, drapes over one shoulder, and is completely open in the back. I even like that delicate gold band that rests on the top of your head. The whole look is so unusually beautiful, but perfectly suited to someone as tall and slender as you. You're going to look just like the goddess Athena in that dress."

I touched the circle on my wrist, smiling. "Yep, that's the idea. And, Mom, you're welcome to add the president to the guest list if you want. I have no idea if he'll come, but if he does, Slash and I would be honored to introduce you to him. An invitation can't hurt, right?"

She squealed in excitement. "Oh, that would be such a coup. This wedding is going to be so incredibly memorable."

For a moment, I let my mind drift back to the bonfire when I stood next to Slash in my loincloth and fishnet bra. Happiness swept through me. Whatever came next in my life would only be the proverbial icing on the wedding cake. Right now, I had it all—a great family, the best friends a girl could ever need, and a wonderful husband.

"The wedding will be great, Mom. I know it truly will be."

* * * * *

Reviews are an invaluable tool when it comes to spreading the word about great reads.
Please consider leaving an honest review for this, or any of Carina Press's other titles that you've read, on your favorite retailer or review site.

For more books by Julie Moffett, visit her website at www.juliemoffett.com

Acknowledgments

Writing late at night, which is typically when I sit down at the keyboard and become immersed in the world of Lexi Carmichael and her nerd herd, can be both exhilarating and lonely. It's often hard, especially after a long day of work at the day job and an evening filled with homework, sports and family time. I'm not sure I could do it time and time again without the unflagging love and support of my family—Mom, Dad, Brad, Beth, Sandy, Scott, Lucas, Alexander, Katy and the rest of my extended circle of close friends. You know who you are. I appreciate and love you all so much. I'm especially close to my brother, Brad, who has always been a mentor and teacher to me in all things writing. He has a quiet brilliance that I admire and a gentle way of giving advice that always makes me better. Thank you for being the best big brother in the world!

I also want to give a special shout-out to all the amazing and wonderful fans in my Facebook fan club. I can't tell you how much your jokes, comments and posts keep me laughing every day. Thanks for becoming another family to me. I also want to acknowledge superfan Deanna Sherwood, who won one of my newsletter contests last year, earning the right to name a character, and chose her granddaughter, Natelli. Congratulations, Deanna and Natelli!

Lastly, I want to thank my never ordinary, but always extraordinary editor, Alissa Davis. She's the best editor I've ever had. Not only does she guide me, but she makes me a better writer with each book. I'm so grateful to have her on this journey with me.

About the Author

Julie Moffett is the bestselling author of the long-running Lexi Carmichael Mystery Series and the young adult White Knights spin-off series featuring really cool geek girls. She's been publishing books for 25 years, but writing for a lot longer. She writes in the genres of mystery, young adult, historical romance and paranormal romance. She has won numerous awards, including the Mystery & Mayhem Award for Best YA/New Adult Mystery, the HOLT Award for Best Novel with Romantic Elements, a HOLT Merit Award for Best Novel by a Virginia Author (twice!), the Award of Excellence, a PRISM Award for Best Romantic Time-Travel AND Best of the Best Paranormal Books, and an EPIC Award for Best Action/Adventure Novel. She has also garnered additional nominations for the Booksellers' Best Award, Daphne du Maurier Award, the Dante Rossetti Award for Best Young Adult Novel, the YARWA Award for Best Young Adult Novel, and the Gayle Wilson Award of Excellence.

Julie is a military brat (Air Force) and has traveled extensively. Her more exciting exploits include attending high school in Okinawa, Japan; backpacking around Europe and Scandinavia for several months; a yearlong college graduate study in Warsaw, Poland; and a wonderful trip to Scotland and Ireland where she fell in love with castles, kilts and brogues.

Julie has a B.A. in Political Science and Russian Language from Colorado College, an M.A. in International Affairs from The George Washington University in Washington, D.C. and an M.Ed from Liberty University. She has worked as a proposal writer, journalist, teacher, librarian and researcher. Julie speaks Russian and Polish and has two awesome sons.

Visit Julie's website at www.juliemoffett.com.

Follow Julie on Social Media:

Facebook Fan Group (official):
https://www.facebook.com/groups/vanessa88/

Facebook:
https://www.facebook.com/JulieMoffettAuthor

Twitter: https://twitter.com/JMoffettAuthor

Instagram: https://www.instagram.com/julie_moffett/

Lexi Carmichael book trailer:
https://www.youtube.com/watch?v=memhgojYeXM